P9-DDV-725

MIND DUELS

Imma Argiro
&
Pat Argiro

Over the centuries, many men have defended themselves valiantly in bloody battles using the sword as an end to a means. While others sought justice by logic and reason, thereby using the mind as a means to an end. Some would argue that ideas smeared on canvas prove deadlier than the sharpest edge; while others stoutly defend that the sword is the mightiest. This ongoing saga of which is mightier the pen or the sword may still present much debate for many years to come.

To Jennifer,

Hope you enjoy Book 1 of this my skry trilogy.

Patrick Argon

Jennifer,
I hope you enjoy many of the twists and turns! Best wishes! Imma Argon

Copyright © 2005 by Imma & Patrick Argiro
All rights reserved
Published in Canada
Printed in Canada

All rights are reserved to the authors. No part of this
publication may be reproduced, stored, or transmitted in
any form or by any means (electronically, mechanical,
photocopying, recording, or otherwise) without the prior
written permission of the copyright owners.

This is a work of fiction. All names, characters, incidents,
and places are either the product of the author's
imagination or are used fictitiously and any resemblance
to actual persons, living or dead, events, business
enterprises, or locales is entirely coincidental.

For everyone who believes in the free world, and especially to those who have laid down their lives to preserve our great nation.

MIND DUELS

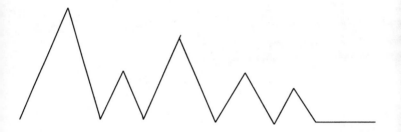

BOOK ONE

Chapter 1

A sadistic grin crossed his face as strokes from the fountain pen continued to smear the white canvas.

Dear Chief:
Voices in my head that want her dead,
All her troubles have come to an end.
With the light of God her sins will expire,
A knife through her heart will end her desires…

His brow furrowed as he remained pensive, slowly replaying the images in his mind one frame at a time. A sinister look crossed his face, and he felt a deep inner gratification. Satisfied, he then slowly rose from his seat ready to surrender to a good nights rest.

Tic …Toc…Tic…Toc…Tic…Toc…

Exuding a cool persona, shielded behind his shades, Jack sprinted out of the front door slamming its solidness firmly shut. Still gripping the door's handle, a strong resonance streamed throughout his entire body. This unwelcome sensation lasted only a split second, before Jack locked the front door and deposited the key into his left pocket.

Unexpectedly, a chilly fall crept onto the citizens of Somerset, New Jersey. As Jack stepped into the open, he noticed the sun's rays had already cast shadows, but welcomed its radiating heat beaming down on the back of his neck. He took several deep breaths filling his lungs with the morning's crisp air. It was a picture perfect day for his morning jog, and

Jack had just missed the hustle and bustle of commuters driving to work and children waiting for school buses.

A black ominous shadow was nearly covered by Jack's next footstep. Harboring an irreverent presence, its sudden loud mournful cries cranked Jack's neck high into the sky. It emerged without any warning, something evil, which would prey on the unsuspecting.

A raven perched itself high on a tree branch leaving him temporarily immobilized by its contemptuous piercing glare. Jack was left gazing helplessly into the bright blue sky trying hopelessly to come to terms with his past. Caught in a daze, he quickly rebuked himself.

Jack Trempton continued with his light stretching, pausing briefly to absorb the morning's beauty before beginning with his lengthy jog. He took immense pride in his physique much like his hey-days in college; Jack's motto had always been a healthy heart equals a healthy mind.

Much time had elapsed from his glory days and at thirty-eight, he still maintained a youthful appearance. Just eclipsing the six foot mark, Jack stood tall with a muscular build and a well chiseled chest. Jack often broke free from his hectic schedule and set sail during the summer months giving him a healthy tan. Although he often remained unaware, many young women were mesmerized by his good looks and charming personality.

He felt beads of perspiration forming as he brushed back a mass of black wavy hair which cascaded slightly over his forehead, softening his sharp angular features. Jack's agility and speed allowed him to speedily capture several streets before reaching the park's entrance. It was his preferred route, although a couple of other accesses to the park existed. Except for a few of the park's small inhabitants, the park remained virtually sound asleep.

His senses deepened, allured by the beauty of the transitional seasons. The leaves instead of being uniform and unvaried were dressed in beautiful variegated russets and gold tones. Scattered indiscriminately, they covered the park's surface like a picturesque hand-woven blanket. It was a splendid time of the year to experience such a stunning masterpiece of nature, unequalled in richness by any other season. Jack's nimble strides propelled him briskly across the terrain. He got a rush hearing the crisp crunching sounds of the lifeless leaves underfoot. Justice didn't serve well as nature's twisted irony baffled Jack's sense of logic and sound reasoning. Leaves had always fascinated him by their ability to transform into more vibrant and colorful tones, whereas roses simply continue to shrivel withering into obscurity.

Pausing briefly to catch his breath, Jack supported himself against a tree trunk. Tilting his head slightly, a bright smile lit Jack's face. The squirrels were dancing gracefully from branch to branch without missing a beat. They lived in harmonious cohabitation with a wide variety of bird species whose melodies filled the air with beautiful songs. Although, Jack's favorite was observing the ducks swimming rhythmically downstream, while at the same time being enchanted by the sounds of rushing water.

Jack picked up a little bit of speed before reaching an incline. His heart rate accelerated from this exertion, and he breathed a sigh of relief having reached peak, although this was short lived. *Oh no,* thought Jack. Renewed anxiety set in upon spotting Sandy approaching like a speeding bullet. A quick flashback of the previous week caused Jack to quickly brace himself, just as Sandy's paws came thundering up against his chest. Her tail wagged exultantly from side to side.

"Hey girl, you're looking bright and cheerful this morning," exclaimed Jack trying to be a good sport, while continuing to stroke her gingerly behind the ears. Sandy was a friendly tri-colored German Shepherd with a lot of spunk and great zeal for life.

Brad finally caught up to his dog. "Sorry Jack, I hope she hasn't soiled your shirt. Sandy just becomes terribly excited every time she sees you," apologized Brad somewhat flushed.

"Ha -- you mean this old rag," teased Jack with a light chuckle.

"I guess with the nice weather, you'll continue to jog for the next little while," commented Brad while Sandy sniffed the ground near him.

"You bet, there's no better way to begin my day," conceded Jack.

"In a few months, it'll be much more difficult tracking through the park, especially with snow knee-deep." Brad turned his gaze towards the bottom of the valley.

"Yeah, but I'm sure Sandy will be up for the challenge," reassured Jack.

Out of the corner of his eye he watched his dog's attention drawn to a dainty brown squirrel, which darted up an elm tree. She stretched her front legs up the tree desperately trying to reach it, while barking non-stop. Jack and Brad laughed bemused by her vain efforts. Brad whistled loudly a few times, but grew increasingly frustrated by her disobedience.

"Sandy come!" Disappointed, Brad decided to take a firmer stance. He jogged over and tugged at Sandy's brown leather collar. "Go fetch girl," Brad tossed the frisbee high into the sky.

Sandy's attention reverted back to the flying object spinning dizzily out of control. Particles of dust and grass flew up in the air as Sandy sped off to intercept her target. Her body became air-borne leaving Jack to admire her brilliance in co-ordination. Her launch had been deadly accurate; the swirling frisbee came to an abrupt halt clenched between Sandy's jaws. She sped back to her master anticipating another toss.

"Good girl," Brad acknowledged petting Sandy's head. He waved the frisbee high above his head and watched her excitedly bounce up and down, before tossing it to Jack.

"Wow, she's impressive. Have you ever considered entering her in a dog show?"

Jack unleashed all his power into the frisbee sending it soaring towards the clouds. In this instance, out of sight didn't mean out of mind, Sandy continued in hot pursuit. She sprung forward, reaching full speed after only a few strides.

"Actually, I entered her in a local show two months ago and she finished first," Brad beamed radiantly. Brad was a much smaller man in both height and stature. In his mid forties, he sported a moustache and a thinning hair line.

The bright frisbee lay stark on the pale sand, just shy of the meandering river. It lay immediately in front of Sandy just begging to be sent soaring back into flight. Oddly enough, Sandy acted indifferently, apparently distracted by some unknown force. She repeatedly circled around it, but dared not touch it.

Jack glanced at his Swiss watch, and was surprised by his tardiness, "Well, I should be heading home."

"Take care, I'll see you tomorrow," Brad admired Jack's speed.

Jack be swift; Jack be quick, thought Jack as he tracked back.

Brad looked around, but oddly enough his dog had vanished much like the flying frisbee. His heart sank. "Sandy, Sandy!" shouted Brad at the top of his lungs. He immediately rushed towards the hill, instinctively fearing something was amiss.

Sandy remained in a fixed stance behaving rather uneasy; her back legs trembled uncontrollably. She sniffed the air aggressively while continuously twitching her nose. Brad held a confused look. Oddly, Sandy remained motionless adjacent to the river bed. Without any warning, she became riled and began barking aggressively, leaving Brad totally perplexed. "Let's go!" he commanded sternly wondering what the hell she was barking at. But before he could even flinch, Sandy began to dig furiously. Brad immediately took cover and stepped backwards as a sand storm ensued. "Hey, cut that out!" It was very disturbing, not to mention disheartening observing his dog's erratic behavior. Within seconds she managed to unearth a mound of dirt. Brad made the mistake of trying to pull her away.

"Errr…" A flash of a full set of teeth jolted him back.

"Easy girl," Brad shielded himself wondering if his dog had gone completely mad. He cautiously backtracked towards the river feeling quite anxious. Inadvertently, he strode too close to the river bed and suddenly felt his feet sinking into the wet sand. "Whoa," Brad quickly steadied himself nearly taking a plunge.

The softness of the ground made it much trickier to regain control, and during early spring this feat would have been unimaginable, not to mention treacherous. The river-bank swelled into a raging torrent and one could easily be swept underneath the powerful current.

Jack reached for the water dispenser to pour himself a tall glass of ice-cold water. He chugged it down quickly. "Ahhh," sighed Jack. It felt refreshing flowing down his overheated body and he then waved the glass across his forehead appreciating its coldness. Satisfied, he placed the glass on the Venetian granite countertop.

He rewound his answering machine and was surprised to see there were no new messages. Jack wondered if John was still planning to join him for dinner.

It was evident that Jack took pride in decorating his home. The theme of gold and brown tones carried into the living room. The room was bright and lively as the morning sunshine flooded through a large bay window. He turned on the high definition TV while enjoying his morning fix. It was hooked up to the state of the art surround sound system creating a dynamic 3-dimensional effect. The total impact was so inspiring that it cast Jack into a fantasy dream-like state. Many mornings, he found himself dozed off on his favorite buttery soft brown leather recliner. After listening to the morning news, Jack sprung from his seat and stepped into the kitchen to prepare breakfast.

Even though Jack had a hectic schedule, he still managed to find some downtime. He recalled one day in particular. A large crowd was poised in front of the pet store, and Jack's curiosity lured him in that direction. Now in the thick of the crowd, he observed her attracting a lot of attention. She constantly repeated 'good mornin'' to all the passer-bys, immediately captivating Jack's heart. Being a bachelor, he was determined on gaining a friend. He received a crash course on her diet, and gladly left with a new friend. The six foot enclosure was placed next to the bay window giving his friend a panoramic view. Feeling a touch guilty seeing her enclosed in a steel cage, Jack relieved his conscience by letting her fly freely while at home.

Clothed in a dazzling display of beautiful bright colors, Tara was predominantly green, with a sunshine yellow head, and had a dab of red splashed on both wings. After only a couple of months, she became really fond of Jack. She unmistakably recognized the sounds of Jack's footsteps upon his arrival. They were unique, much like a set of fingerprints.

Perched smartly on the Manzanite wood next to her latch, Tara anticipated liberation. Upon seeing him, she would shrill Jack swift; Jack quick. Jack's laughter echoed emphatically upon hearing his darling little friend. She thrived on their friendship and all the affection thrown her way, and became increasingly jealous during the presence of visitors. Cautiously, Tara would smartly perch herself on his shoulder keeping everyone at bay, but while alone she felt less threatened and would settle herself on the top of a chair opposite him.

Jack finished his breakfast and headed upstairs. Although a little shocking at first, a cold shower felt really invigorating, giving him a much needed boost for the day.

As he stepped outside, Jack didn't notice its ominous shadow. Overhead, it silently kept watch. He slid into the driver's seat of his sporty 2006 BMW convertible, and cruised along Maple Avenue. Driving mostly on local streets, he rarely experienced the thrill of greater speeds possible only on highways. It was a short pleasant drive to work with surrounding areas still remaining untouched. The area was marked by gently rolling hills covered in thick luscious grass. Rock gardens and flower beds provided interesting highlight points, while spruce and maple trees accentuated the landscape. Jack never grew tired of this route, since it was not only the shortest but also the most breath-taking. The morning traffic was congested more than usual. Jack continued to travel east on Bramgate Drive, then steered smoothly, handling a sharp right turn on Mount Pleasant Lane, leading him into Fernheight's Security Depot.

"Good mornin' sir -- may I please see your security pass?" asked the spectacled patrol officer in a heavy southern drawl. "Thank you Mr. Trempton and would you please place your hand up to ---" Jack's hand was already against the digital scanner confirming his identity. "Thank you sir," responded David embarrassed.

Jack drove through the open gate and parked in his reserved space.

Brad was still gasping for air as he stared at Sandy in disbelief. "What the hell has gotten into you?" he cursed.

Trembling, covered in wet sand, Sandy slowly crawled back and let forth a succession of yowls. Suddenly, Brad turned around with a look of dismay, "Jesus Christ! What ..." Slowly, but surely, everything was beginning to make sense. It still remained indiscernible, obscured by much sand. He tried to take a closer look, but the stench was unbearable. Brad nearly gagged. Hurriedly, he backed away. Glancing over to his left, Sandy looked very apprehensive. She whimpered while remaining crouched over in a low stance. "It's okay girl, it's okay," he petted her gently trying to calm her down.

Brad frantically reached into his pocket barely controlling his trembling hand as he dialed 911. "Damn static, just my bloody luck." Unable to connect, he once again fumbled with the keypad. "Come on, come on. Unbelievable -- why is this happening?" He desperately raced uphill to reach higher ground.

"He-hello," Brad's nervousness was clearly evident. The words stuttered from his nerve rattled jaws.

"Hello -- sir, please calm down. What's wrong?" the voice at the other end keenly sensed his distress.

"There's something ... there seems to be ... well I just happened ...," his incoherent rambling continued unabated until a firm voice interrupted him at the other end.

"Is someone in trouble?" the dispatcher awaited a reply, but was just left hanging in suspended animation. "Is someone in trouble?" she repeated hoping to prompt a timely response. She was beginning to lose her patience. Finally after a lengthy wait, Brad's voice eclipsed the line's static.

"No, my dog started acting crazy. Then she went totally berserk," muttered Brad.

"Did she attack someone?" her voice sounded shaky.

"No, Sandy would never hurt anyone," the inflection in his voice emphasized this point.

"Please sir, take a moment and relax," she suggested.

Brad remained jittery, and barely managed to whisper. "There's a corpse at Stetson Highland Park by the riverbed."

"I'm dispatching the police immediately. In the meantime, please try to remain calm. I'll remain on the line with you," she reassured. The conversation was mostly one-sided, since Brad was too distressed to say much of anything, and instead paced about nervously.

Shortly afterwards, and much to his relief he could hear the wailing sirens approaching closer and closer. Brad saw four uniformed officers standing on the hill-top. They soon spotted him. Two of the officers quickly descended the hill encircling the partially unearthed figure. But they were careful not to approach too closely, fearing they could destroy vital evidence. Brad finished his phone conversation as the other two officers headed towards him.

"Are you Brad?" a burly officer asked in a husky tone while pulling out a pad of paper from his back pocket.

"Yes," responded Brad rather timidly, already feeling drained.

"Can I see some ID?" The younger officer wearing shades seemed rather anxious to unravel the mystery cut in, "Please tell us what happened?"

"We were tossing the frisbee."

The older officer scouted the area, "Sorry, but is there someone else?"

"I usually bump into Jack while exercising my dog. She's quite fond of him, and was enjoying retrieving the frisbee. But he left before she began acting strangely," explained Brad.

"Do you come to the park often?" the older officer continued to probe.

"Yes, it gives my dog a chance to keep fit," Brad was overwhelmed by the whole situation.

"Well, she has certainly gotten her exercise today. Have you noticed anything unusual lately?" The officer detected a strained look on Brad's face.

"No. I usually come early morning around eight, while the park is still fairly quiet," explained Brad.

"Do you usually come alone?" there seemed to be no end to his voracious appetite for answers.

An eerie feeling that he was a potential suspect was setting in. "Not always. Sometimes, my wife joins me for a morning stroll. We live just a couple of blocks from here," indicated Brad. The officer continued to ask Brad numerous questions, before handing back his ID.

"You are free to go now, but we may need to contact you later."

"No problem," Brad made off quickly still overwhelmed by the whole situation.

The other officers were to section off the area with yellow tape. Brad heard one of them stating that the park would be closed pending an investigation. Just a few feet away another officer was busy calling the coroner's office. A special team would be assigned to the murder investigation.

"For the last time stand back," an exasperated officer pleaded with onlookers. The crowd was eventually ordered to leave the park.

Jack walked through Fernheights's corridor, his clean shaven reflection shot back at him from the granite floor. The lobby was spacious with light streaming through the domed glass ceiling. He admired the cascading motion from the twin waterfalls.

He pushed the button and rode the elevator to the third floor. The delightful aroma of fresh coffee saturated the air as Jack stepped into his suite.

"Good morning Samantha," greeted Jack.

"Good morning Jack, I've just prepared some fresh coffee." She gazed into his dazzling emerald eyes.

"Thanks." Samantha was a real beauty; she had the ability to make men's hearts beat just a little quicker. Jack's mind was often distracted by her presence. He really wanted to get to know her better, but thought it best not to mix business with pleasure.

Samantha had been the receptionist at Fernheights for over three years landing her job not only for her talents, but also for her warm personality. She was looking forward to dancing at her favorite local night-club, La Cabana, later that evening.

"Good morning, Samantha," acknowledged Yvonne.

"Good morning," responded Samantha.

"Did you retrieve the files I requested?" Yvonne asked while walking towards her desk.

"Yes, they're on your desk," Samantha snubbed her nose as Yvonne walked away. *There goes Miss Prissy, never even bothered to ask how my weekend was or how I was doing,* thought Samantha. Samantha was bored from the same routine. Lately, she had other career aspirations in mind, and the title of Office Manager had a much nicer ring. *Soon I plan to stand in your shoes,* Samantha smiled slyly. As Office Manager, Yvonne Wright hadn't a clue her job was being coveted, nor was she aware of Samantha's true feelings.

Jack settled back in his leather recliner enjoying the soft music playing in the background. He flicked on his computer and a high pitched voice prompted him which files needed to be retrieved. His computer was connected to a giant wall-size screen impressing clients with visual presentations. As Marketing Director, conferences were often conducted in his office.

As Jack's eyes remained glued to the flat screen, Scott Matheson, the Executive Director at Fernheights, walked into his office. In his late fifties, tall, rugged looking, and topped off with a husky build, Scott could be quite intimidating.

"Good morning Jack, how was your weekend?" asked Scott, startling Jack.

"Good morning, my weekend was blasé," Jack confessed. "Luckily, it gave me the opportunity to nearly wrap up Tormac's file."

"Well, I've just reviewed it and your ideas are exceptional. Would you be able to finalize everything today and drop it by my office later?" there was a trace of urgency in his voice.

"Sure, I just need to make some minor revisions." responded Jack confidently.

Over the last couple of months, Jack poured his heart and soul into the project. Drawing his ideas on paper was not within Jack's realm. He counted on Henri Levine, a graphic artist to capture his ideas on paper. Over the years, they had become good friends. Jack had introduced Yvonne to Henri, and they had hit it off from day one.

Scott was about to make a call when Jack knocked on his door. "Please come in," invited Scott.

"Here you go," Jack handed him the file.

The mall was being transformed from a mid range to a high end market. "The skylights will certainly brighten things considerably," noted Scott.

"New prominent retailers have already jumped on board," Jack stated enthusiastically.

Scott's euphoria was in full display. "Very well done, well done indeed," commended his boss.

A police officer kept watch at the top of the hill. He escorted the forensic team to the body, which now lay partially exposed at the bottom of the valley near the river.

Tim pulled out his Nikon and snapped some shots of the crime scene. Careful not to destroy any vital evidence, each of Tim's steps were carefully calculated. He noted the dog's imprints all over the sand.

"Too bad they're not human prints, or we might have a good lead to go on," Tim said mordantly.

Anne shot him back a quick glance. "I don't think it's going to be that easy," she scoffed.

Tim was a seasoned veteran who left nothing to chance, but analyzed everything in minute detail. He couldn't help but wonder if the dog had destroyed any clues, while at the same time realizing that if it wasn't for Sandy the body would still be buried deep beneath the sand. Time was an important factor, and with each passing moment crucial evidence would be lost forever.

Tim paused momentarily noting the unusual positioning of the head; the victim's head lay perpendicular to the running water. He frowned while pondering this for a brief moment. "Did you guys notice something odd?" he quizzed.

"Like what?" Anne looked puzzled.

"Look how the body has been positioned." Anne and Mike stared dumbfounded.

"I'm not sure I follow," Mike cut in.

"Perhaps, the water spilling over the head is symbolic to that of a religious ceremony," Tim conjectured.

"Oh," Anne paused. "I never even thought about that, but you might be onto something," she reasoned.

Tim continued shooting photographs while Anne and Mike hauled a dozen different tools and set them down on the sand. They fervently swiped their nets over the corpse to collect insects. Different insect colonization and larvae would provide the team with vital clues. It would help determine whether the body had been transported after death, and how long she'd been dead.

Mike raised the glass and examined the contents; he was quite knowledgeable about insects and confidently identified them as skuttle flies. With careful strides, they closed in from different angles trying to determine how to unearth the corpse without disturbing it. Experience told them they would remain at the crime scene for at least several hours. It was now just shortly after 1:00.

Anne held the trowel-like tool trying to unearth some of the sand away from the face. She placed a sample into a tube to be brought for testing. The body had been wrapped in a cloth, which was quickly deteriorating. Dropping the trowel back into a pail, she reached for a soft nylon brush and gently brushed the sand away from the forehead. Clusters of hair covered the face, although the sand made it difficult to decipher the victim's hair color. Anne noted the bloated greenish color of the victim's face indicative that the victim had been buried recently.

Right next to her, Mike quietly toiled with knees already buried in sand. "I think I've found something," he announced excitedly. Anne stopped in her tracks.

"Yeah, she's holding something, but it's hard to tell with all this dirt." Tim squinted unable to make out the object.

"Here use this brush, we don't want anything destroyed," offered Anne. With steady hands, Mike diligently brushed for what seemed like eternity.

Three sets of eyes stared with equal intensity. "Gees, that almost looks like some sort of twig," Anne surmised.

After several more careful strokes, it stood in plain view. What once had been a bright lively red rose was now shriveled into a brownish–wine color.

Momentarily, they all remained pensive, before a bewildered expression took hold of them. Mike was simply revolted, "One thing is for damn sure; whoever we're dealing with is one deranged whacko." He couldn't understand how someone could take another person's life and then have the audacity to leave a love object behind. Anne could not help but notice Mike's exasperated expression.

"I can't put aside this nagging feeling that this is just the beginning. If he's psychotic, there'll be more brutal slayings," forewarned Tim. "We'll need to handle it carefully," he advised.

"Use these tweezers," suggested Anne. Carefully, Mike lifted the rose and placed it into a cardboard box.

"Jesus Christ!" yelled Tim clearly frustrated, he bolted up and flung his arms in the air. A grimaced expression enhanced his weathered face revealing his apparent disgust.

Anne and Mike studied the opening. With the opposite end of the tweezers, Mike gently lifted the seared blouse. The incision measured over two inches.

"Is the killer trying to make a point, or was he simply enraged?" Tim looked puzzled.

"Maybe both," Mike's mind drifted weighing different scenarios.

The skies seemed to shift; overcast replaced the blue horizon.

"The forecast is calling for rain later this afternoon. We need to move quickly," Mike interjected.

In unison, they moved back to the corpse. Miraculously, the body remained in a relatively preserved state. Judging by the fact the body was still quite discernible, it must have been buried fairly recently. The decomposition process had been significantly reduced by the very dry summer, leaving the body fairly intact.

Her hands were clasped together. Anne took over Tim's previous position. She gently feathered away traces of debris around the fingers. An odd mystified feeling swept throughout her. She could not explain it, but somehow instinctively knew they would uncover something. Her hands were in full display, and they waited until Tim snapped more close-up photos. Anne carefully lifted the victim's left hand. An ivory rosary dangled from the corpse's clutched fingers. Her intuition proved correct. *Weird*, thought Anne, *how the hell did I pick that up?*

All three of them were baffled by this latest discovery and hadn't even noticed the officer descending the steep hill. The maggots had been thriving on her flesh nearly reducing her hands to mere bones. As grains of sand fell off, sparkles of bright colors beamed from her diamond ring. It was impossible to miss the nails; they had grown long, curly, and pointed. They were intertwined around the rosary clutching it tightly. As Anne fumbled to unravel the rosary it accidentally caught onto one of the victim's finger nails. Anne cringed. "Damn unbelievable!" Feeling guilty, she cursed loudly. "Crap -- the entire nail has just snapped off."

"Umm, place it in here and we'll place the ring in this other plastic bag," Mike held open a plastic bag.

"It looks like you guys could sure use a break," stated the officer. "I'm going for coffee. What can I get you guys?"

Mike and Tim turned to Anne. "A coffee with cream, please."

"Cream, double sugar for me," answered Mike.

"Black coffee for me and a chocolate donut," Tim said half laughing. "Well if anyone cares for the perfect recipe for a pot belly, it's the following: one pot belly equals two too many donuts," Tim joked, lightening the mood.

"I'll be back in a few minutes," the officer stated.

A few drops of rain fell and they tried to unearth the remaining dirt as quickly as possible. The face could still be discerned, although it had decomposed slightly leaving darkened sockets. The body was clothed in full length sleeves and ankle length pants concealing any other markings or disfigurements. Mike wondered if she was fully intact. Two feet of sand had already been removed around the perimeter of the body, exposing considerable moisture close to the earth's base. This was natural due to the close proximity to the river.

With all their combined experience none of them had seen anything quite like this before. The murderer not only made a point of marking his victim, but sure went through a lot of trouble burying her. *Why not just dump her body? Perhaps, it was some sort of sacred ritual? It* was still early in the investigation, and for now there were far too many questions and no answers.

The officer returned with their coffees, and one donut.

They removed their gloves and masks. Anne felt the strain in her legs; it was strenuous tucking her six foot frame for so long. "Damn, I think I have a kink in my leg," she complained momentarily losing her balance.

"This donut is mouth watering," hints of chocolate glaze were smeared around Tim's mouth. A smirk flashed across his partners' faces.

Thunder erupted from the ominous skies. Moments later, a lightning bolt shot perilously close to them.

"It's going to start pouring any minute," Mike frantically stated the obvious.

"There's not enough time to retrieve the body," Anne panicked.

"Damn! We have no choice, but to cover her up again," just the thought disturbed Tim.

"We better hurry up," Anne added. They partially refilled the shallow grave; the rain intensified. Pressed for time, they laid a tarp over the burial area. It began pouring.

They made a quick break for the hill. Rain pelted down against their fatigued bodies. It was difficult for them to breathe against the heavy rainfall, suffocating the air supply from within them. An officer tried offering them umbrellas, but the gale winds created havoc with them. The incline was slick and treacherous causing them to slide, but some force guided them safely to the hill's peak. Another greater peril was now in their midst, and ultimately fate would play out its hand. Their lives were in real jeopardy and the enemy literally unstoppable. They could only run as there was nowhere to hide. Haphazardly, they navigated their way blindly relying mostly on instinct. The sky became brightly illuminated by a multitude of lightning flashes, followed by deafening bolts of thunder. Fearing the worst, they quickened their pace hoping to avert a possible tragedy. They had lost sight of one another, but no one dared to look back. A dark eerie silence followed.

Chapter 2

Jack flicked on the TV while coating the ribs. *"I've got sunshine on a rainy day,"* he hummed. Unlike many men he knew, cooking was a real joy for him. Jack froze in his tracks. The brush remained suspended in mid-air as he listened attentively.

"A middle-aged man was found dead earlier today. His remains were found underneath an old maple tree. Apparently, the man appears to be the tragic victim of a wicked lightning storm. He was found curled up, as though desperately trying to seek refuge from the storm, but the exact cause of death will be determined following an autopsy report. His identity won't be released until his next of kin have been notified. This unfortunate occurrence reminds us we should never take Mother Nature too lightly," the reporter continued sheltered by an umbrella just as the police prepared to place the corpse into a body bag.

Jack was repulsed and clicked the TV off. He placed the ribs in the oven along with the baked potatoes, and then sliced the whole wheat bread. Everything would be ready before John's arrival.

"Tara, you rascal! What's our guest going to think if he sees only a crust of bread," Jack scolded his feathery friend.

Tara swooped down in a second valiant attempt to snatch another morsel of bread.

"Now you stop that and behave yourself!"

"Beehve self, beehve self," Tara mimicked.

Jack was amused. Tara's imitation acted like a domino effect, each day, increasing his adoration for her. He was about to double check on the ribs, when he thought he heard the front door bell ringing. John must have arrived, thought Jack.

Tic…Toc…Tic…Toc…Tic…Toc…

"Hey, just in time, please come in," welcomed Jack. Jack was about to slide the closet door open to hang John's jacket, but oddly, only the staggering movements of a well-built figure was reflected in the eight foot length closet mirror. "Excuse me for a minute while I grab the newspaper; I see it on the other side of the driveway." Make yourself comfortable -- I'll be back in a minute," stated Jack as he headed out.

"Daddy's home," Tara stated perched on a chair post.

"Say hi to John," pleaded Jack. Tara remained silent staring seemingly into space, oblivious to his presence. This troubled Jack and he looked momentarily confused, but he dismissed it as an isolated incident.

The tantalizing aroma fueled John's already voracious appetite. "Well something sure smells awfully good, I hope you didn't go through too much trouble," remarked John. A half bottle of whiskey sat on the countertop with a partially filled glass next to it.

Jack chortled, "No trouble at all. Spare ribs and potatoes are tonight's specialty. If Tara doesn't eat the entire loaf, we may have some bread with our meal." Jack became aware that Tara wasn't perched on his shoulder like she normally did during the presence of other guests. He pondered this for a brief moment watching her nibble on a snatched morsel, perched directly across from him.

"Ha-ha..." now it was John's turn to laugh. He found Tara quite adorable and occasionally would sway her gently on her little swing. Ironically, besides Jack, he was the only one that Tara seemed to like and this flattered John.

"Well it's been awhile since I saw you last," reminisced Jack.

John sighed and nodded in agreement. "Sure has been. I've been busy trying to keep up. I was assigned a major file and have been working around the clock for the last few months," explained John.

"Ditto for me. It's going to be awhile before dinner is ready. We could relax and watch some television in the meantime." Jack gestured for John to make himself comfortable on the sofa. "I'll get us a couple of cold ones in the fridge." He came back with two beers and turned on the TV. Jack twisted off his beer cap and cheered John. Indeed, Jack thought it was a well deserved toast to their hard earned success, bringing with it much respect and admiration. The beer was ice cold just the way Jack liked it.

"Early this morning, a body was found buried at Stetson Highland Park." A bright and cheerful atmosphere was eclipsed by a dark and somber mood.

Oh shit more bad news, thought Jack.

"It was discovered inadvertently by a man playing frisbee with his dog." Jack's eyes bulged. "The victim's identity and cause of death are still a mystery. Hopefully, an autopsy will shed some light once her body is recovered. Police detectives have been sweeping the park, and the grounds will remain closed pending a thorough investigation," the reporter was a young man in his early thirties who sounded a little nervous.

Jack continued to stare in utter disbelief. He fidgeted in his seat, "I...I was just at the park this morning, playing frisbee with Brad's dog." He was so shocked with this discovery that it left him rather shaken and totally unsettled. Years ago, Jack learnt to disassociate himself, whenever confronted with an uncomfortable or painful situation.

John was taken aback. "Good God -- what happened?" John questioned.

Jack looked downward pensively while rubbing his chin. He reflected on the news, but still remained quite puzzled. "To be quite honest, I'm not exactly sure. I went out for my usual morning jog and bumped into Brad and his dog, Sandy, at the park. It was getting late, but before leaving I tossed the frisbee to Sandy. They must have found the body afterwards." Jack looked baffled and tried to visualize how this bizarre situation had unfolded. "I just can't believe it; I go to that park almost every day. It's such a beautiful and relaxing place. This is totally unbelievable, not in a million years would I have imagined something so horrid."

John nodded in agreement. "Yeah, that's just awful," John was still nursing fresh wounds, which might leave him permanently scarred.

The aroma stirred Jack's senses as he entered the kitchen to check-up on dinner. He cut a portion of the spare ribs to see if they were ready. Satisfied, he removed them as well as the potatoes from the oven and they seated themselves at the kitchen table ready to feast.

"How are the ribs?" Jack asked in between mouthfuls.

"Mmmm, they're delicious. So where have you acquired your culinary skills?" John inquired thoroughly enjoying his food.

"More practice than anythin' else," Jack had no magic formula except for the fact that he loved to cook. A side dish of Caesar's salad seemed to magically disappear. "Would you like some coffee?"

"Sure," John always welcomed a fresh cup of coffee after dinner.

In a true sense, Jack and John's life were a mirror image of one another, they both shared similar career paths, hobbies, interests, and astonishingly looked like the spitting image of each other. John like Jack was also enslaved to his career. As a financial analyst, he was a master at number crunching and would scour meticulously through a company's books, successfully boosting a company's profits by at least twenty percent. John's vast business knowledge made it easy discussing different aspects of the business world. They spent hours discussing mergers and acquisitions, corporate restructuring, and of course the stock market.

John's parents emigrated from London, England, in the late seventies. His father, Daniel, was asked by his employer to immigrate overseas. The company was in expansion mode and required candidates with his expertise in America. Both of his parents were respectable hard working middle-class citizens. Daniel had worked mostly in sales promoting fine china to various retail chains. Extensive travel throughout the USA was a must, although his family unequivocally remained his first priority. Barbara cherished spending time with her only son and it wasn't until he turned five that Barbara resumed her career as a social worker for the government.

Jack poured John's coffee into a tall mug.

"Thanks," John sipped it while it was still steaming hot.

John had always excelled academically and during high school the business world captivated his heart. Afterwards, he pursued his master's degree in business and graduated with honors in 1992, the same year as Jack.

John's vast scholastic achievements were proudly displayed within a glass enclosure in his study. The first three shelves were lined with countless trophies from having excelled at different studies, as well as his natural athletic ability, in particular his love for track and field. John's athleticism had vastly increased his popularity with peers. Interestingly, it had been something more than just talent which attracted people to John. He possessed something rare; perhaps it was his general love for humanity. John always took time to listen to his peers' concerns, bringing him much admiration. These attributes spilled over into his career life, and both his colleagues and his superiors were drawn to his charismatic character.

But, absolute tragedy tore his world apart four years ago, suppressing John's passion for life. Like a mirror's image, Jack could see the sorrow lingering behind his eyes, haunting him and tentatively holding him hostage.

John painfully remembered the events of that bone chilling winter morning. A light dusting of snow created a magical scene often captured only on film. He enjoyed the luxury of his new black Mercedes E320, equipped with all the bells and whistles. The car symbolized prestige and power instilling a quiet confidence in John.

The calamity occurred early one morning in late December. He arrived at work shocked to learn that a huge pane of glass had crashed down into one of the office suites. Oddly enough, the glass had fallen without any apparent reason. Fragments of shattered glass were scattered everywhere including three long jagged pieces, which pierced deeply into the boardroom table, much like flying daggers. John felt quite unsettled and equated the broken glass as a bad omen. One of his co-workers was rushed by paramedics to a nearby hospital for multiple lacerations to her arm. Later, he learnt that Sharon was lucky to have escaped with only deep cuts to her right arm, barely escaping death. Inches closer, and the glass would have sliced her.

"Is everything okay?" Jack noticed John's morbid reflection as he glanced into his shadowed eyes.

"Sorry, everything is fine; I was just thinking," John politely feigned a smile, trying to re-shift his focus from the past to the present.

John continued to remain distant as Jack prepared dessert. Tonight's specialty was home-made apple pie with vanilla ice-cream, topped off with delectable caramel sauce. It was his grandmother's secret recipe passed down only to close family members.

John's mind drifted helplessly back to one particular Christmas. His daughter, Alicia, was the eldest of his two children and in two months she would have officially become a teenager. Alicia's easy going personality made her quite popular with classmates. After school, Alicia would attend ballet classes three times a week. Both children were enrolled in private school.

Timothy, Alicia's younger brother, was just shy of his seventh birthday before catastrophe struck. In contrast to his sister's light hair, his was ebony black. He lounged endlessly in front of the TV playing the latest video games. John's eyes watered as he recalled the news of the tragic accident; it happened just days before Christmas. John had been working when he received a disturbing call from the hospital. The caller's voice sounded frantic. He was told there had been an accident at his home, but refused to give John any details over the phone. John pressed him for information, but to no avail. *Sir, please just come quickly,* were the last words he remembered. His mind raced crazily as he drove to the hospital. John just hoped and prayed to God that everything would be fine. Ignoring all the parking prohibitions, he parked his car near the front entrance. Instinctively, he rushed to the hospital's emergency ward.

He could still remember the doctor leading him down a long corridor to a private room. The doctor had explained that a natural gas explosion had occurred at his home; the explosion caused extensive damage tearing the entire structure apart. Unfortunately, the children were inside at the time. John gasped. His eyes were fully glazed and he stared intently ahead, a man clearly in shock. Unfortunately, his only distraction from this travesty was his heart pounding heavily against his chest causing him even more discomfort. He tried lessening the pain by reassuring him that his children hadn't suffered any pain, but had died instantly. John learned that his wife had been walking towards the house with groceries in hand at the moment of impact. She suffered numerous injuries, but was still breathing upon arrival to the hospital. They did everything humanly possible to save her, but unfortunately she succumbed to numerous internal injuries. The doctor offered his condolences and expressed his deepest sympathies. John remained speechless, almost frozen in time. He had just spoken with his wife a couple of hours earlier and her last words to him had been, 'I love you.' These words kept echoing in his head so clearly that his mind refused to believe it, thinking it was a terrible nightmare from which he would awaken. The horror did not register until he saw his wife's body. He stared at her in despair. The body was badly burnt; John had been sick to his stomach. Luckily, her face was still recognizable and remained mostly intact helping him to preserve his sanity. He gently caressed her skin feeling its softness, just as he always had. Part of him wanted to scream at the top of his lungs, but instead he repeatedly stroked her silky hair, whispering her name in an agonizingly painful tone.

John's heart raced. His watery eyes shed an endless flow of tears, and he sobbed incessantly. Those were his last moments with his wife. Ironically, her hands still remained remarkably warm. This memory remained firmly implanted in John's mind, and occasional flashbacks renewed his sorrow. The doctor advised him against seeing the children's bodies or little that was left of them. Already emotionally drained and exhausted, he heeded the doctor's advice.

John never fully recovered from his shock; his sorrow was simply unbearable and darkness cloaked his heart slipping him into a major depression. Most of his days had been spent in an eclipsed setting with curtains drawn; even sunlight caused him great discomfort. He lacked the energy or desire to do anything, and simply stared blankly ahead oblivious to his surroundings.

Luckily, his family stood close by him and helped him through his crises. His parents took over the household chores including all of his personal finances. John refused to seek counseling, but was on anti-depressants having even lost the will to live. His mourning continued seemingly endlessly. Even though his parents were somewhat discouraged, they never lost hope and stood by him until he finally summoned enough courage to move on.

The richness of the rose fragrance dazzled her senses, making her feel very feminine and uninhibited. Yvonne lay in the whirlpool, lying perfectly still, letting the water's warmth relax every inch of her body. She felt herself slip into a dreamy state with magical steam clouds rising higher and higher.

Reluctantly she stepped out of her fantasy, wrapping the towel around her shoulders and let it glide it freely down her silky-smooth streamlined body.

Despite her long days at work, she still found herself with a bountiful amount of energy. She was hopelessly in love and would constantly toss and turn just thinking of him. But despite her restless nights, Yvonne still felt refreshed in the morning. With the towel still wrapped around her, she rummaged through her walk-in-closet, "No -- not this one, definitely not this one," she let out a low laugh. Tonight, she wanted to look dazzling. She pulled out an above knee length skirt, which would certainly accentuate her long lean legs. She then flipped through dozens of shirts and blouses which were stacked in the upper rack of her closet. She had expensive taste and constantly shopped for the latest fashions. She reached for the scoop-necked ivory cashmere sweater.

Yvonne took a quick glance into the mirror for approval and smiled confidently. Running late, she quickly brushed her shoulder length golden brown hair, which had been recently highlighted with complimentary blonde streaks. She hesitated, before reaching into her make-up bag for her light coral blush. Yvonne dabbed it on lightly giving herself a livelier complexion. She then applied her hot pink lip liner further accentuating her full lips.

Even though she had only been dating Henri for awhile, she still felt a touch nervous. The first time they met her heart had thumped wildly against her sweater, her stomach had been in knots. Yvonne reached over and splashed her favorite floral fragrance on each wrist. The light scent was invigorating helping to calm her shaky nerves.

Henri sipped his white wine quite satisfied with his selection. He glanced at his watch and smiled realizing he never grew impatient waiting for Yvonne; nonetheless, she was twenty minutes late -- it was now 7:20. Henri eased back in his chair extending his long legs beneath the table while admiring the restaurant's elegant appearance. The chandeliers lit the room well, but still maintained a romantic ambiance. The room was painted in a gold color cultivating a sophisticated style.

"Hello Henri," Yvonne greeted happily. She looked radiant. He rose and gently brushed her cheek with a kiss. Henri's dark eyes shone brilliantly, simply enchanted by her beauty.

"Ou-la-la. You look beautiful as always," the lingering scent of her perfume stirred his senses.

"Thank you, sorry that I'm running a little bit late," Yvonne blushed.

"But you're consistently late," chuckled Henri. He lavished her with another kiss, but this time on the lips before returning to his seat. Yvonne's color deepened.

"What would you like to drink?" he offered. "Perhaps you would like to try some of my white wine?"

"Mmmm, it's actually quite good," Yvonne enjoyed its light-bodied taste.

With a wave of his hand, Henri gestured to the waiter. His French accent was quite appealing, "The lady would like a glass of this white wine, please."

"Certainly, are you ready to place your order?" Henri noticed the uncertainty on Yvonne's face and asked the waiter to give them five minutes.

Yvonne loved Henri's mannerism; especially his sexy appeal. Women constantly flirted with him, since he was tall, dark, and extremely handsome. She looked longingly into his warm eyes. He reciprocated, loving to gaze into her sparkling blue eyes. He gently pulled her to him and kissed her tenderly on the lips. "You look marvelous as always," he complimented once again with a huge grin.

Yvonne sat speechless, overwhelmed with emotion. She couldn't remember a time when she felt happier. Presently, everything in her life was just perfect. She was successful, had a loving family, and now had a wonderful man to share her life with. Henri was everything she'd ever dreamed of.

"The sole dipped in the wine sauce sounds delicious," suggested Henri. Yvonne read the menu and agreed it was well worth trying.

"So how was your day?" Henri asked.

"Swamped, I can't remember such a long and hectic day." Yvonne sighed deeply. "I spent well over an hour looking for a client's file. Surprisingly, it wasn't on the corner of my desk where I usually leave it, before stepping into the washroom. Anyways, Jack had to reprint fifty pages, while we had important clients waiting well over half an hour. The boss wasn't impressed to say the least," Yvonne's voice cracked, apparently stressed over the whole fiasco.

"That's odd -- I know how extremely organized you are," Henri observed. "Perhaps, it was accidentally misplaced," he suggested gently. He deeply cared for Yvonne and hated to see her troubled. But privately, he couldn't dismiss the possibility of foul play.

Henri had emigrated from France at the young age of thirteen. His father moved his family to continue his career as a civil engineer. Henri had been elated; after all, some of his favorite actors lived in the glamorous USA. Up to now, his life had been generally easy-going, without too many bumps. But not until meeting Yvonne had he felt truly fulfilled.

"I've been thinking about you all day," Henri reached for Yvonne's hand. "I've enjoyed our time together and have grown very fond of you. I hope I'm not being too presumptuous, but I feel we have a strong chemistry; I guess what I'm trying to say is I would like to take our relationship to the next level." Yvonne's eyes lit up. Henri was open with his feelings, and generally expressed himself diplomatically, letting people know exactly where they stood with him. He didn't put up a pretentious front.

Yvonne loved this facet, and despite the fact they had only dated for a few months, she felt as though she had been in love with him forever.

"How's everything?" inquired the waiter.

"Dinner was delicious," complimented Henri.

"Are you ready for dessert?"

"Do you have any suggestions?"

"The chocolate pecan cream pie is an all time favorite."

Henri glanced at Yvonne for approval. "Okay, we're sold." Henri winked at her. "While we wait for dessert would you care to dance?" Yvonne embraced Henri's extended arm as he led her to the dance floor.

Henri and Yvonne nestled against each other lost in their own world. They were the last couple on the dance floor, not to mention the only ones left in the restaurant. It wasn't until the lights dimmed that they realized the restaurant would soon be closing.

Jack cleared the table, stacking the dishes in the sink. John's visit left him feeling rather on edge and quite uneasy. It was troubling seeing his friend in a distraught frame of mind, dwelling in a past he could not change, and a future he was barely facing. It would be refreshing to see his friend move on with his life and enjoy a new start. He slowly climbed the staircase nearly stumbling on the last step. "How clumsy," he stated trying to steady himself. Shadows were cast from the full lit moon, which was suspended directly above his bedroom. As he lay in bed, he became increasingly restless. He could barely keep his eyes closed let alone trying to fall asleep. Tossing his blankets aside, Jack stepped onto the hardwood floor.

The basement was chillier than the upper two levels, but Jack looked forward to a good workout. It was completely renovated including: a small bar, bathroom, entertainment room, and Jack's own training room. His exercise room included a wide variety of exercise equipment including a treadmill, a stationary bicycle, weights, a punching bag, and workout mats.

Jack steadily increased his speed enjoying the workout. After ten minutes of running, he was beginning to feel beads of sweat trickling down the length of his backbone. He took a short break; he could feel his heart beat return back to a more normal pace. In the meantime he prepared the bar bells. In his prime, it would have been an easy feat to bench press over four hundred pounds. Wisely, he recognized the importance of gradually easing to that level. Along with bench presses, Jack performed curls, and dead lifts. He liked the firm tone of his muscular biceps. Jack could hear the echoing sound from his mean punch, leaving several indentations. During his teen years, he had learnt some boxing techniques coupled with martial arts moves. His mean uppercut earned him quite the reputation.

These disciplines came in handy one day while walking home from school. Pressed for time, Jack took a shortcut through a narrow alley. It was littered with filth and rubbish, and the walls were spray painted with graffiti and profanity. Red and yellow spray paints marked their favorite rock groups and their impression of authority figures. The bright colors jumped out from the dull brown bricks. His headset had been turned on full blast to Van Halen, so he relied on his other senses. The alley was fairly dark and the nauseating stench was revolting, Jack almost did a one eighty. But, it was too little too late. Jack was on the ground gasping for air, after taking a solid boot to the stomach. In agonizing pain and winded, he couldn't muster enough strength to even groan.

'Jack be swift, Jack be quick.'

His life was in jeopardy, and he needed to focus damn quickly.

Years of training allowed him to steady his breathing and override the intense pain. Out of the corner of his eye, he could see the three adolescents closing in on him. Quickly, Jack rolled away from the thugs. He needed to buy some time. Then with a clever acrobatic move he flipped back onto his feet.

"Hand me your money!" demanded one of the burly punks in a curt tone. Jack was poised in a defensive stance oblivious to any pain or emotions.

"Go to hell, you bunch of freaks!" dared Jack waving his fists.

A rush of adrenaline engulfed him, he was ready to battle. He sidestepped away from a wielding knife fearing a life-threatening gash. The skinhead continued to swipe at Jack, but he was easily able to outmaneuver his opponent's moves. A few quick moves allowed Jack to drop-kick the knife out of the youth's hand sending it airborne into a pile of litter. This nifty move startled the hoodlums who sought safety in numbers and they tried encircling Jack. Anticipating this move, he immediately repositioned himself to offset their efforts. With a flurry of wicked kicks and punches the three young adolescents were sprawled on the ground in agony.

The memories of the event infuriated Jack, as he repeatedly nailed the punching bag. He then lowered himself onto the mat, clearly exhausted.

He desperately needed to re-hydrate. The bottle of ice cold spring water felt so good in his hands; he halved its content in just one gulp relieving the dryness in his throat. "Whew, that was good," Jack spoke out loud as he finished his drink. He could hear Tara flying about in her cage. "It's okay Tara," he spoke softly. "Don't worry, it's just me and everything is fine when daddy's home," he encouraged. Tara settled on her favorite branch. It disturbed Jack seeing her all ruffled up.

Jack totally exhausted, quickly showered, and went to bed.

"I could hold you here with me forever." Henri showered her mouth with soft gentle kisses before engaging in a long passionate one. Yvonne suddenly felt light-headed, seemingly the room seemed to be swirling. She wanted the moment to last forever.

Their eyes met, and they both knew exactly how the other felt. "We should leave before they get tired of us and kick us out," Henri suggested. Yvonne purposely hesitated, simply wanting to cherish the moment forever. She was rudely awakened by the cold wind as they stepped outside; it woke her from her dreamy state.

"Has anyone ever told you just how beautiful you are?" Yvonne felt herself quickly warming up, despite the bitter cold. A radiant glow brightened her face as Henri embraced her, drawing her closer to him. Yvonne's heart skipped a few beats as a deep passion fervently swept throughout her body, rendering her limbs limp, but she felt secure with his strong powerful arms wrapped around her.

Henri realized he could never let this woman go; she had become a part of him. In all his twenty-eight years, he never felt as passionate about anyone. He felt her shivering lightly. It was so tempting to take her home with him, but Henri felt it still might be premature and didn't want to take advantage of her. Little did he realize that Yvonne felt the same way. "It's getting late and tomorrow is another working day," acknowledged Henri half-heartedly. "Any plans for Saturday night?" he asked.

"Yes, I'm going to a movie with an old school friend," she stated casually.

A worried expression spread across Henri's face.

"I'm just kidding," teased Yvonne placing a reassuring hand on his shoulder.

"Fine, I'll pick you up around seven," he stated with renewed confidence.

"I'll see you then. Have a good night," she quickly slipped into her car.

Henri felt a multitude of emotions rush through him; he found it extremely difficult to part from her. The temperature gradually dropped, but Henri didn't feel its biting sting. His passion not to mention his hormones were keeping him plenty warm.

Anne, Mike, and Tim carefully descended the steep hill.

"I would hate to roll down this hill," Mike stated.

Anne silently agreed as she continued to take slow steps, and sighed having reached flat terrain. Large pools of water covered the tarp. "We're going to have to remove some of these spikes to let the water drain out," instructed Mike. Once he yanked the last spike, they lifted the tarp and watched the water slowly trickle back into the river.

They silently encircled the corpse. Anne noticed the sand was heavier, despite the tarp some rain still managed to trickle down from the hill.

It was some time before Anne saw the corpse's shape beginning to form. She switched from the hand held shovel to using a soft bristle brush to uncover the victim. Anne's muscles were cramped from her crouched position, despite her knee-pads she felt a terrible strain building.

"Unearthing a body, but twice -- Jesus," Mike blurted shaking his wrists to remove some of his own kinks. Each of them felt stressed. It was frustrating, not to mention unnerving, being extra careful not to mar the body. But, it was the least they could do for someone whose life had been viciously taken.

Tim just stared at the decomposing body, which stood in plain view. A foul smell lingered in the air; its caustic odor made it difficult to work. In his initial year as an officer Tim had preconceived images of what a person would look like after being dead for a lengthy period of time. Now, even after so many viewings, he had to admit it was still nerve-racking.

Tim wondered if the body had been immediately buried at the river bank or had been transported to its current resting place. The body would certainly be examined for any lividity markings during the autopsy as well as for different types of insect colonization. Slowly, Tim stood up feeling his cramped muscles.

"It's a good thing we don't have to do this everyday; I don't know about you guys, but my body aches all over," Tim broke the silence.

"Let's take a break; it's nearly 11:00, and sure as hell not going to rain today. Let's send out for some coffee," suggested Mike.

It was the first time Anne had unearthed a corpse. The discovery weighed heavily on her, even more so than the fetid smell. Anne needed a diversion and decided to take a stroll along the river bank. It was very relaxing and peaceful at this time of year, and as Anne continued to watch the ripples flow downstream, she felt some of her inner tension slowly being released.

"Is everything okay?" Tim caught up to her.

"Yeah, I'll feel much better once she receives a proper burial."

"It'll be especially devastating for her family."

"Imaginably so," Anne acknowledged. "I would hate to be the one breaking the news." Anne felt a rush of sympathy for the victim's loved ones, imagining how the family had coped with her disappearance. The loss must have brought a lot of grief and turmoil in their lives. Now any hope of a miracle would be quashed forever. Anne thought back, trying to recall any recent women's report, but none came to mind. Although some closure would be brought to their lives, the mystery still remained unsolved. *Would the killer ever be brought to justice? Why was her burial conducted in such a bizarre fashion? And of course the million dollar question, would the killer strike again?* She felt troubled as a myriad of questions continued to flash through her mind.

Steam rose from the coffee cups; it was still quite hot. "Well, our work is nearly done. I'll ask the officer to send us a stretcher along with additional manpower. It's too heavy for the three of us and I don't know about you guys, but I'm exhausted," Mike stated wearily gazing to the hill-top. No one disagreed.

Anne was going to support the victim's head while the others would lift her onto the stretcher.

"Okay, are you ready?" Mike led the group. Anne's hand dug underneath the earth. Her fingers dug away at the soil to find the centre of the skull. It was imperative she had a firm grip, but her fingers slipped and Anne inadvertently gripped her upper neck.

"Ahhh, God no!" she screamed out in horror shocking the rest of the team. Everyone simply watched baffled. Were Anne's fingers caught on something, thought Mike? Her loud cries carried to the hill-top. "Oh my God!" she frantically yanked her hands out. Color drained completely from Anne's face leaving her with a ghastly complexion. Sheer terror struck within her, from the realization that her fingers had plunged through what once had been layers of skin. Her hands were now dripping with skin, clumps of nerve tissue, and gunky stuff. This was so revolting and appalling it made her cringe; she flung her arms away from herself in disgust. The slimy material continued to slither to the ground. Mike steadied her from behind, fearful she might faint. Other officers rushed to the river filling pails with water, and then scurried over to help her clean-up. Tim tried comforting Anne with reassuring words observing her erratic breathing. One of the officers offered her some water, but she gestured no as she was still in shock and gasping for air. No one had anticipated how quickly the body was decomposing. The moisture from underneath the body was causing it to deteriorate much more quickly. Minutes later,

Anne's complexion was beginning to show some color, and slowly she regained her composure, determined to finish the task at hand.

"Perhaps you should rest awhile longer," Mike gently persuaded.

Her skyward gaze shifted from the heavens back to him. "I'll be okay, I need to do this." Anne's pride and perhaps stubbornness were even bigger than her large stature.

"Let's try and slide these boards underneath. If that doesn't work, then we'll attempt to roll the body over." Tim lifted one pant leg while Mike suspended the other into mid-air. The officer's working space was considerably limited making it difficult for him to maintain the hefty board at the same level, causing the board to repeatedly dig into the sand. "Shit," the officer cursed becoming increasingly frustrated from his failed attempts. After several more tries, he finally managed to drive the board through the mounds of sand. Now, somehow, they would have to raise the upper torso to support the entire body.

"Perhaps, we should lift her from her sleeves. As we lift her body, we can support the head and try sliding the board underneath," Mike contemplated his idea.

"It's at least worth a try," Tim stated in agreement.

They gently raised the sleeves into mid-air. Anne positioned a smaller board from the side of the body to support the back of the head. Mike felt the stitching starting to tear. "Crap," he quickly tried to lower the arm, but despite his lightning reflexes it ripped before he could set it down. "Dammit! It ripped so darn fast," Mike swore in disgust. The arm lay limp in an awkward position. He was visibly upset, and his complexion deepened to a deep red.

"Let's use the tarp instead," Tim was repulsed and could not handle seeing anymore of the body dismantled. The removal of the body was beginning to become some sort of freak show as parts of her were becoming dismembered. "Her underneath is obviously decomposed, so let's try to roll it over like paramedics do with unconscious victims," Tim suggested.

They bent the right knee outward on a forty-five degree angle. Anne was going to support the head. Mike positioned his arm behind the right shoulder blade while the other two officers supported other areas of the body. "On the count of three we will roll over the body: one, two, and three," Tim stated. They rolled her over onto the stretched tarp.

The horrid smell of the decomposing body hung in the air making it unbearable to breathe even with their masks on.

"Damn," Mike failed to grab the long slimy worm, which measured at least eight inches long, as it repeatedly slipped from his grip. The worm slithered away and burrowed itself in the middle of her back. Mike held on tightly and with one quick pull yanked the wiggly coil out. The crew looked on in disgust, but reserved their opinions. The victim's sunken pockets were clearly visible underneath the torn clothes. Each of them silently cursed the bastard who killed her. The four officers grabbed each corner and hauled her onto the stretcher. The last feat would be to safely reach the top of the hill.

Tim felt it difficult to breathe against the cold wind. His mood turned somber lacking any desire to crack any more jokes. One could clearly see deep stress lines weathered across his face.

"I think we should set her down," Mike suggested. They carefully lowered the stretcher, giving Mike a minute to stretch.

Momentarily, everyone stared as they watched in a trance.

"Hurry up -- it's rolling down the hill!" Anne yelled as she watched it increasingly gain speed. Tim frantically chased after it managing to run in front, stopping it from rolling any further, just in the nick of time.

Tim's patience had expired. "Damn, the wheel must have come unlocked," he explained in between breaths, while securing the wheel in a locked position. They carefully continued their steep climb.

"Whew, that was one hell of an ordeal," sighed an exasperated Mike.

It had been sheer hell removing the body. It seemed that an invisible force thwarted their every step. Perhaps, the victim wished to be left undisturbed to rest eternally.

Despite the cold weather, trickles of perspiration coated their foreheads. "I hope we don't have to repeat this feat again," lamented Anne.

Anne quickly shot a glance back to the uncovered burial site. "Did you hear that?" she sounded spooked, but no one had heard anything. She listened acutely, but now the only distinguished sounds were of birds chirping. Desperately, Anne tried pushing aside disturbing thoughts of potentially more bodies decomposing throughout the park. Tomorrow the forensic team would return to the park to search for more hidden bodies, or at least probe for any clues. But today, they had a corpse to deliver to the morgue.

Chapter 3

Tic…Toc…Tic…Toc…Tic…Toc…

Even though John generally dreaded being late, he didn't regret reflecting on his past. Yesterday's reminiscing had sprung open a flood gate of memories, which left him feeling uneasy. And today John looked forward to chatting with Edward, appreciating his natural ability to shed light on the most challenging situations.

John buckled up and sped off, cornering smoothly around several bends before reaching his destination. Edward's home was situated on a quiet crescent backing onto a small lake. Mostly old money lived in this area, thus it was not surprising that only a dozen estate homes sat on this crescent. Only the elite could afford the magnificent architectural splendor encompassing these mansions.

John drove through the open wrought iron gate while observing the interlocking stone work; it had multiple designs and in-laid borders, ranging in color from forest green to rustic orange. These colors nicely complemented the homes' variegated stone work. After climbing seven steps, he reached the front door. John held the metal knocker with his left hand admiring the lady's figure stylishly dressed in the old Spanish tradition. A loud rap followed. Within seconds, he was greeted by Harold, the butler.

"Come in, Edward is expecting you," he welcomed. His voice echoed throughout the foyer due to an extended ceiling, which spanned at least sixteen feet. "Please make yourself comfortable," gestured the gracious host pointing to a recliner. Everything in the room certainly reflected a Spanish ambience. Mexican tiles spread throughout the foyer and a large painting of an actual bull run nearly covered the entire length of a wall.

It depicted pools of dust in uprising clouds from a bull's hoofs. Different size Mexican hats hung throughout the room in an array of poignant colors.

"Buenos Dias -- good to see you my friend. I was beginning to worry that something had happened," confessed Edward with a warm smile and a firm handshake.

John didn't like to make it a habit of lying, but was caught off guard. "My alarm didn't go off this morning." He tried to maintain a poker face hoping his friend wouldn't catch onto the façade.

Edward escorted him through a wide hallway leading to his study. John was bewildered by the vast amount of artifacts displayed on the walls and book shelves. Pausing briefly, he admired the double-edged swords which shone brilliantly. The hilt had been cast in iron as had the rest of the double-edge blade. They were mounted in a cross position symbolizing the onset of an upcoming duel.

It had been years after his heroic feats, and Edward was now in his late sixties. He still maintained his stocky athletic stature standing six feet tall with just a slight slouch, but had put on a few pounds since his battle days. He had served in Nam and his feats became somewhat legendary earning him several medals. During one battle, he came perilously close to losing his life as a mortar round exploded in front of his battalion wounding several of his compatriots. Edward single-handedly warded off the enemy, thus saving his men. After many years in service, he gained recognition as one of the best in the Marine Corps. He remained undefeated in battle, both on the field and in the ring. There was never any hesitation for him to enter a boxing match; his success in the arena earned him a formidable reputation. To put it bluntly Edward was as tough as nails.

"Would you like some coffee?" offered Edward.

"Don't mind if I do." He poured himself a cup with just a hint of cream. John quickly noticed the remarkable difference in taste. The roasted blends percolated a stronger full-bodied flavor that he had ever tasted. Obviously money was no object. Edward could certainly afford to spend his money extravagantly and acquire the best of everything. An avid collector of rare paintings and antiques, he indulged in the finest things life offered including fine cars and yachts. He traveled extensively, not only to enrich his knowledge of different parts of the world, but also to appreciate the best in life.

"Make yourself comfortable," motioned Edward. He leaned back in his brown leather chair gently swaying back and forth. "It's a bright beautiful day today, although I'm a bit surprised to see you this early," remarked Edward. Sometimes, it was rather difficult comprehending Edward. Being the eternal optimist, he was always able to put a positive spin on everything. On a hot scorching day, he would comment that the weather was lovely; during a miserable dreary rainstorm, he would comment it was nature's way of keeping the grass nice and green. Despite all the hardships and sorrow life had dealt him, Edward still remained upbeat. He had watched his wife courageously endure a lengthy battle with cancer, before succumbing to her illness. In another tragic episode he lost his eldest son. Their family owned aircraft nose-dived into a field after the engine stalled. Apparently, a routine inspection of the small plane a day prior failed to detect any deficiencies. Yet despite these heart-aches, Edward still managed to maintain a positive outlook on life.

"I've been thinking about my family a lot," confessed John.

"It must bring back a lot of memories -- is there something specifically that's bothering you?" John stared blankly at the ceiling. Surprisingly, John felt a warm radiant heat sweep throughout him. Edward caught a sudden whimsical expression surface on his face.

John thought back to his family's adventurous outing at Sea World. "We had a splendid view, seated in the front row, watching the killer whales and their acrobatic routine. One of the most applauded acts was the killer whale reaching high into the sky touching the suspended balloon, twenty feet overhead. The jump was a marvelous feat, regardless of the fact that its landing created quite a splash soaking everyone in the front row," John chuckled. "Our amusement came to a sharp halt with Timothy's unceasingly loud cries. We couldn't understand what brought on the crying; and despite our best efforts to comfort him, he kept wailing." John struggled to continue as he fought back tears. "We were forced to leave, and I treated everyone to ice-cream. After less than a minute of savoring it, Timothy's face was covered with chocolate and it dripped down smudging his Mickey Mouse shirt."

'Ice-cweam,' he spluttered and everyone broke out laughing. John shared his memory.

Edward was ecstatic to see the profound effect this memory had on John, it was nice seeing him smile. John often felt like Dr. Jekyll and Mr. Hyde. His inner emotions often dragged him from a state of euphoria to one of doom and gloom. After John's loss, it was almost like a second religion to visit Edward. The somber feeling in John's heart seemed to be lifted by his friend's passion for life and uplifting dialogue. John glanced at his watch, and was surprised to see an hour had elapsed. He genuinely expressed his appreciation, particularly Edward's allowance on such short notice.

"Well I'm looking forward to seeing you soon," Edward expressed his heartfelt warmth. "Remember keep your spirits up." He accompanied John to the entertainment room. Once again, it was easy to see Edward's love for the Spanish culture in his memorabilia. John's gaze turned towards a large hand-crafted sailboat situated on top of the fireplace mantle. It was unlike any he had ever seen, and the sails were cleverly carved and arched just as they actually would while sailing at sea.

Edward noted the gleam in John's eyes. "It's part of my antique collection and dates back over two hundred years. I purchased it at an auction; apparently it has a legend attached to it," Edward explained. He placed a Spanish colonial hat on and patch over his right eye for added emphasis then faced John, "Err Johnny -- have you ever sailed the high seas?" Edward had a natural flair for the theatrics and could successfully play the role of an evil pirate.

"A Spanish King had acquired a scepter with the intention of giving it to his Queen. It was a magnificent treasure gleaming in solid gold, and it glittered with splendid gemstones embedded throughout its entire length. The top was the crowning glory with a stunning emerald. Its rare beauty and size definitely made it one of a kind, and the King anticipated it would melt his wife's heart. He was well pleased with the scepter's intricate design, but dismissed tales of it possessing magical powers. The pirates thought otherwise; they believed it would give great power and dominating authority to whoever possessed it and were ready to die for it. During the late 1700's, a famous pirate known for his heroic feats was determined to swindle it from the King. Accompanied by his comrades, he managed to intercept the Royal ship's route. Guided by telescope, they maintained a safe distance. They managed to remain out of sight for a period of days. Early one morning an over-bearing fog presented them with the perfect opportunity. The pirates quickly boarded the King's ship and quickly subdued the few men on deck. Surprisingly, they knew the exact location of the scepter; it was well hidden in a small wooden chest enclosed in a secret compartment. With the prize in hand, they made off quickly before the remaining crew awakened. They boarded their own vessel and set sail to South America. Minutes later, the sailors became aware of what had transpired. Immediately, they set chase. The distance between the two ships was too great to open fire. Besides, they damn well knew if they sunk the vessel the scepter would never be recovered. Their pursuit continued for hours and the King's men were closing in on the thieves. It was now only a matter of time. Great fear gripped the pirates as they kept vigilance through their telescope. If caught a slow torturous death was a certainty. Unfortunately there was no recourse, since they didn't have the firepower or skills of a well trained army. One of the pirates thought of making a deal. They would tie the scepter over the edge with a rope. Unfortunately there was no recourse, the calm sea started to become turbulent. The waves intensified, the clouds darkened, and a strong wind threatened their sails. Stubbornly, the pirates were determined to maintain their course and continued sailing through the rough waters. Smartly, the pursuing ship did a one-eighty, apparently valuing their lives more than the treasure. The storm worsened; huge two story waves tossed the small vessel about. Eventually, the mighty seas proved too overpowering and capsized the pirate ship. Before their deaths one of the pirates cursed, 'Damn these waters.' To this day some believe that is how the curse of the Bermuda Triangle came to be," Edward retold enthusiastically.

"That's quite some story," John wondered just how much of the tale was true. Nonetheless, his visit with Edward left him with a renewed sense of hope and in a more optimistic frame of mind.

Back at the park, the officer's footing cut deep into the earth's surface. The ground was like quagmire making it difficult to maintain his balance. He swept the metal detector along the length of the tree trunk, but before completing his swipe, he lost his balance and toppled backwards landing on top of a thicket. Large beeping sounds engulfed the air. "Shit!" the officer managed to pull himself upright. Supported by the thick under-brush, the officer thought it was impossible for the metal detector to have broken, since it still bounced on top of the branches. The only other possibility was that something lay underneath. His spirits soared realizing this could be their big break. Hurriedly, he spoke into his walkie-talkie to dispatch other fellow officers.

"Let's photograph the tree, the under-brush, and everything within a ten meter radius," Mike excitedly instructed the team. The Nikon telephoto zoomed in. Its powerful lens was capable of capturing the minutest detail without disturbing any potential evidence.

"Have them circle the entire area," Officer Neally commanded. They circled, sniffed, but the canine unit came up empty.

BEEEEP-BEEEEP-BEEEEP... One by one, Mike connected all the points forming a letter X. It measured eight inches both in width and length. He circumscribed a circle about sixteen inches from the center of the X.

"I don't know about you guys, but this endeavor is becoming like a game of bad back-gammon."

Mike and Anne could always count on Tim's humor.

"We better switch to these plastic hand-held trowels," Mike retrieved one from a plastic container.

Slowly, bit by bit, they began unearthing. Samples of soil were dumped into a box to be tested for traces of blood or other contaminants. Tim's trowel cut through the earth's soft crust when his body stiffened feeling a razor sharp pain firing down his back. The shovel suddenly flew from his hand. Tim winced as he tried to stand upright while supporting his lower back with his right hand, "God the pain is excruciating!"

"Would you like some aspirin?" offered Mike worriedly noting his hunched position.

"I'll be okay, if anything get me some oil. I need to lubricate my hinges."

Mike smirked.

"Bingo! We've found something," Anne distinctively heard a metal clinking sound.

Final grains of sand were brushed aside exposing a rusted metal tin box. Anne gently hoisted it from the ground. It was relatively light in weight. "I can hear something rattling inside. Spread open the tarp so we don't lose anything."

Excitedly, Mike envisioned a breakthrough, "Anybody care to wager what's inside?"

"Hopefully the killer has tripped up," Tim added.

Several screeching and creaking sounds had the crew biting their nails. Anne continued and carefully pried the lid open. "It needs to be oiled worse than I do," Tim just couldn't help himself. His humor eased Anne's anxiety as she envisioned a blood-drenched knife.

The lid popped open. They stared in disbelief; it was moments before anyone uttered a single word. Disappointment engulfed them, since it definitely wasn't what they were expecting to find.

"Bloody unbelievable!" Anne cursed with a sunken look.

Beer bottle caps lined the bottom of the metal box. "Probably a group of teenagers buried them afraid of being caught drinking," Mike reasoned.

"Excuse me," hollered the officer to the individual.

Half startled, Barry turned around and approached the officer, "Yes officer."

"What the hell's the matter with you -- can't you read? The park is off limits pending a murder investigation," the officer yelled while pointing to the sign, obviously upset at his apparent disrespect and disregard for the law.

"My name is Barry -- I'm the Park Manager," he justified.

The officer cleared his throat and toned down a notch, "Oh I see, we'll contact you as soon as we finish our work here. If you could jot down your address and phone number, I'll give you a call." The officer handed him a pen along with a note pad and then added, "We'll also need to ask you some questions, it's just procedure." Barry could have sworn he heard his name being called from a distance. He then caught a glimpse of a figure scampering away.

"Hey you -- hold it right there!" warned the officer in a sharp tone. But instead, the man darted towards the safe haven of the trees. A quick glance back confirmed two officers chasing in hot pursuit. It was difficult maintaining his velocity up the steep slope allowing the officers to gain on him.

"Stop -- stop!" he heard them yelling repeatedly.

Their voices were approaching closer and closer by the second; fear ripped through him. The deck was stacked against him and perhaps his only ace in the hole was his familiarity with the park's grounds. He cut in between trees and inadvertently plunged through a pointy branch cutting open his right shoulder. *The pain was excruciating, but he dared not scream.* Determined not to be caught, he frantically swerved in and out of the thick under-brush simultaneously feeling a series of pokes and scrapes pricking his entire body. Blood drizzled down his arm smearing his brand new white cotton shirt. Momentarily, they lost sight of him. He remained steadfast and cut through a bunch of thick trees while trudging down a steep hill, allowing him to pick up speed without exerting too much effort.

He ran for his life.

"Over there -- he's running down the hill," pointed one of the officers.

"I'll cut to the left. Cut around those trees -- in case he changes direction," the other officer ordered.

The figure looked back. He saw them closing in on him; he couldn't allow himself to be caught. The threat was real and his life was in jeopardy.

"Stop or I'll shoot!" demanded the officer. But puzzling enough, the man sped towards a group of civilians.

"Bery, Bery," the group heard the desperate cries of someone shouting followed by a deafening gunshot fire. Barry turned around and was paralyzed with fear. One of the police officers had his gun drawn.

A bullet must have grazed Tommy, Barry saw Tommy's right sleeve drenched in blood, the blood continued to ooze from the wound spilling all over his right side. They were ready to bring down their mark. One officer took a firm stance while taking aim at his target. An ear-piercing sound ensued followed by billowing gun-smoke from the barrel of a 9mm cannon obscuring the officer's identity. The target had been viciously assaulted, and Tommy sprawled forward helplessly to the ground. In an instant, a man's life had become a blur; Tommy's body lay motionless facing the ground. His plain white shirt was smeared in a sea of blood, a testimonial of how merciless bullets viciously tear through bodily flesh. Barry stared blankly ahead, mouth gaped wide open.

Reality flashed back like lightning as Barry snapped out of his trance upon hearing the frantic cries of his distressed friend.

"Don't shoot, don't shoot," Barry yelled repeatedly while he flung his arms in the air trying to avert a tragedy. Barry raced towards Tommy for dear life with his arms still high in the sky. Tommy threw himself at Barry. He was breathing quite erratically. A surge of relief spread through Barry, grateful that his friend wasn't seriously hurt. Everyone's worst nightmare had been narrowly averted. "It's okay, they won't hurt you. They're here to help; they're investigating a murder," Barry gently explained while Tommy just clasped tightly onto him.

As the officers approached them, everything became quite clear, Tommy was slightly handicapped. Terror swept through the officers realizing their near fatal error. "We sincerely apologize. We had no idea -- he was far off in the distance. Will he be okay?" the officer asked genuinely concerned.

"Give him a few minutes to calm down. He'll be okay. I need to go back to the office and grab the first-aid kit." Tommy's arm was still bleeding quite badly and blood oozed out from his gash.

"Good morning, may I help you," Samantha answered.

"Hi Samantha."

"How are you Jack?"

"Could be better. I'll be working from home today, but I may have forgotten one of my files on the filing cabinet. The page I need has a rough sketch."

Samantha's heart skipped a beat; she was attracted to Jack and found herself frequently fantasizing about him. "Okay I'll go check -- just give me a minute," Samantha strolled down the hall briskly. She found it exactly where he stated. "Yes, you left it on the cabinet."

"Can you e-mail it to me? It's the first or second page in the file."

"No problem, I'll send it right away."

"Thanks Samantha, I appreciate it."

"I can't believe I forgot it; I must be getting absent-minded," Jack spoke out loud.

"Abzent-mend, abzent-mend," shrilled Tara.

"You cut that out," Jack said half laughingly.

Tara perched herself on the computer monitor, chirping now and again, as she continued to watch him work. He checked his inbox and opened the appropriate file. Jack studied it extensively. The mall needed major changes; it presently looked outdated and run down, since it had not been renovated since 1989. He reviewed the strategic revisions, which would involve some major alterations to the mall's architectural structure. His software program cast everything in 3-D bringing everything to life. He jumped at the sound of the cuckoo clocks ringing. Seven birds poked their heads out every hour on the hour. Tara enjoyed their synchronized sounds.

"Cu, Cook," Tara tried to repeat its sound.

Jack laughed, "Let's take a break." He turned on the CD player and watched Tara enjoy the classical music. She perched herself on the swing knowing full well that her master would gently send it swinging back and forth. "Are you having fun?"

"Fun, fun," she repeated.

That's exactly why Jack adored his feathered friend. She was a joy to be with and she never angered him or caused him any headaches. "I'll take that to mean that you're enjoying yourself."

The telephone rang. Jack tried to concentrate on what Samantha Palms was telling him, but was distracted by a racket in the kitchen. "I'll have to call you back." Tara was stirring up a fuss. Her water bowl had flipped over creating a puddle. "I'm sorry my little feathered friend; I'll refill it for you," Jack apologized.

"Sowy, sowy," repeated Tara.

"Okay you don't have to rub it in too much," joked Jack stroking her gently.

Jack had to be cautious of his vocabulary for fear of embarrassment. Imagine Tara repeatedly swearing in the presence of guests, or even more embarrassing would be having her repeat something very personal.

The weary officer entered Larry William's office, grudgingly chosen to be the bearer of bad news. "We have identified the murder victim. The dental work allowed us to make a positive identification. It'll still be a couple of more days before the autopsy report is completed," the officer continued.

Suspense was written all over the Chief's face. "Well are you going to just stand there and keep me hanging? Come on, who's the victim?" The Chief was growing more and more impatient by the second.

"With all due respect sir, I think you should be seated," the apprehensive officer suggested politely. The officer was forewarned that the news would be upsetting and tried using the outmost discretion.

This was a first. It wasn't customary for anyone in the force to give orders to the Big Boss. The Chief appeared more puzzled than shocked, but noted the officer's reluctance to confer the victim's name. "Alright," the Chief drudgingly sat down. Little did he realize how shocking the news would be. He anxiously waited, nervously clenching the armrests of his chair.

The somewhat dreary officer cleared his throat, preparing to speak. Pausing for a second, he then slowly divulged the victim's identity. "The body we found at the park is that of Dianne Summers."

The Chief's face reddened; shock filled him.

"We'll have a thorough report completed within a couple of days," the officer added. The Chief was numb. At a loss for words his head hunkered down digesting the news. It was disheartening to learn the identity. For many years he had been close friends with Dianne and her husband, Dr. Tyler Summers. They had shared so many wonderful times together. As the shock wore off, fury set into the Chief as he took the news personally.

Affirmatively, while maintaining eye contact, the Chief spoke bluntly. "I'm going to set up a special task force and want you to be present at the meeting. Bring all the evidence to date at that time."

"Yes sir," the officer took the Chiefs cue to leave.

The Chief rubbed his temples. *Why did he have to be the one to deliver such horrid news?* Quite simply, Dr. Summers would be devastated. Even though Dianne had been missing for some time, there was still that small glimmer of hope she would return home safely. Now all hope had been extinguished much like a candle burning in the wind. At least he took some comfort knowing a good friend would be breaking the news, and Dr. Summers could count on his full support, helping him make any necessary arrangements. But before he made his dreaded visit, there was one more phone call to make.

He picked up the receiver, "This is Chief Williams, how are things going?"

"We've scoured the entire area and found nothing," replied Officer Neally.

"Dammit, what do you mean you've found nothing!" the Chief was incensed. "Listen to me very carefully, keep searching, and bring in the canine unit until you find something!"

A little confused, he paused momentarily and then replied calmly. "But Chief, we have already done that," Officer Neally justified.

"No buts, find something, anything dammit, and that's an order!" he fumed.

"Yes Chief, consider it done," mumbled Officer Neally.

The Chief was accompanied by an officer. They arrived at Dr. Summers's home in a dreary state. Dr. Summers had seen the police car pull into his driveway. As a concerned parent many thoughts swarmed through his head, not surprisingly he opened the door before the sound of knocking.

"Oh hi Larry, I'm surprised to see you at this hour."

"May we come in?"

"Sure -- sorry, I've lost my manners."

They followed him into the living room. The room was spacious with many rich colors, including a wide spectrum of blues. They seated themselves on the cobalt blue sofa, but the serenity would be short-lived; the mood would darken deeper than any color in the room.

"We have some news," an exasperated Chief began.

Immediately, the doctor cut in, "Have you found my wife?" He noted the Chief's stricken look.

The sadness in his eyes carried over into the Chief's sympathetic voice. "Yes, there's no easy way to tell you this." Judging by the Chief's statement and the sadness in his voice, Dr. Summers knew she was dead. "The lady we found at the park matched your wife's dental work. I'm so sorry." The Chief struggled as he fought back tears. "She was a fine lady and certainly didn't deserve to die so tragically. One thing I will promise you, we'll search and continue to search until we find the killer. I'll make it my personal mission to track him down," there was a strong conviction in both his voice and eyes as if taking a solemn oath.

"Oh God no -- no -- not my beautiful Dianne!" he cried out repeatedly in desperation, burying his face into his hands. "I want to see her." It was a natural reaction of a grieving man.

"She has been buried for some time and you have so many wonderful memories. Hang on to those memories. Remember her full of life and energy."

"I must see her," insisted Dr. Summers with a stern look.

"I know how you feel, but it's probably best not to see her in her current state," the Chief attempted using friendly dissuasion.

A now vehement doctor flared with rage. Dr. Summers's voice exploded, as he abruptly shot up from his seat staring down at the Chief, "You don't know how I damn well feel! How the hell could you know! I have a right to see her," he lashed out.

The Chief's sorrow deepened fearful of causing him more anguish. "Yes of course you have the right, but you won't recognize her," he pleaded. "As a dear loyal friend, I implore you to think more with your mind and less with your heart." Little did the Chief know the irony of his last remark.

"Daddy -- why are the police here?" Christopher asked curiously while holding his airplane control. Dr. Summers simply felt devastated and couldn't begin to tell his son the dreadful news. Hunkered over, he simply remained silent.

"Perhaps I can try?" The Chief subtly motioned. Dr. Summers gave a slight nod. "Do you remember me son?"

"Yup, you are the Chief. Last time you visited you gave me a big red fire engine," a big grin flashed across the young boy's face.

"You have a very good memory. I came to give your daddy some news today."

"Have you found my mommy?" his big blue eyes lit up. The Chief always found Christopher to be a bright young boy. His heart ached having to tell such a young lad that he has lost his mother forever. But it was better to tell him now, before he heard such horrific news through the media. Soon the reporters would swarm all over the story.

He chose his words carefully, "Your mommy is now safe in heaven with the angels where nobody can hurt her. But no matter where you are and what you are doing, she'll always be watching over you. She'll be very happy knowing you are listening to your father and are being a good boy."

"Will I ever see her again?" Reality was quickly setting in as he began to pout.

"One day when you are much, much older," the Chief tried to soften the reality of the situation.

"I miss mommy. Daddy you promised me mommy would come back. You promised," he stomped his feet, sobbing incessantly with tears running down his cheeks spilling onto the floor. His sorrow coupled with disappointment now turned to bitter rage. Bang! He flung the control across the room clearly venting his frustration. At that moment a small Chihuahua ran to Christopher. He picked her up, smothered her against his chest, and ran up the staircase without looking back. They watched the tiny figure in despair, but no one dared call out to him. Instead, they simply remained reclusive, perhaps paralyzed with their own inhibitions of further exasperating the little boy.

Dr. Summers just sat motionless for some time. "I do want to see where the bastard buried her," he conceded.

"Okay, we'll drive you there."

"But first, I need to drop Christopher off at my sister's home and I need a few moments with my daughter."

"Take your time as I've taken the day off so I can assist you in any way possible."

Dr. Summers reluctantly headed upstairs. He stopped in front of his son's room. It broke his heart to see his young son curled up on the bed hugging his dear dog, Cookie. Tears streamed down the boy's face, the doctor sat on the edge of the bed before speaking. "In my heart I wanted to believe that mommy was alive and well. Every night, I prayed she would come back home safely, so we could be a happy family again."

Dr. Summers took a minute to regain his composure. "But, I should not have made you that promise because it was out of my control. I do promise you this -- I love you and I will always love you," he wiped away his son's tears while comforting him.

Christopher looked into his father's eyes with a deep yearning. "Daddy are you going to leave me too?" A distraught young boy felt his whole world crumbling apart.

With a heartfelt warmth in his eyes and a strong emphasis, he spoke, "Oh good God no. Son, I don't plan to leave you for a very long time. I want us to do many fun things together; I want us to go camping, play sports, visit amusement parks, plus many more fun activities." Christopher rose and hugged his daddy tightly. "I have to go with the Chief just for a short while. I need you to help me, okay?"

"Okay daddy."

"We are going over to Aunt Becky's; I need you to be strong for your aunt and your sister. Cookie can come with you."

"Okay, but when will you come back?" he asked anxiously.

"I'll be back in a couple of days. Now, I'm going to pack some of your clothes. You can choose a couple of toys to bring along with you."

Absorbed in much thought, no one uttered a word along the way. Dr. Summers dreaded telling his daughter that her mother's body had been found. They had always shared a close bond, and he was paralyzed with fear of her reaction.

He took a deep breath. The Chief and the officer waited outside. Cindy heard the front door bell ring.

"Hi dad, what are you doing here?" she asked startled, before noticing a cloudy darkness in his eyes, unlike anything she had previously seen. Christopher trailed behind with his head bowed and clearly in very somber spirits. Aunt Becky walked into the living area and immediately sensed something was terribly wrong.

"Tyler, why is there a police car at the end of the driveway?"

He sighed. "How about if we all come and sit here on the couch." They all followed him. "I have some news. The Chief was over earlier and --"

"Is it concerning the disappearance of Dianne?" interrupted Becky. Her facial expression turned sullen, quickly realizing the dismal news he was about to deliver.

The doctor tried to think of the proper way to break this disheartening news. He held his daughter's hand and looked directly into her eyes. "Mom always loved you so much and tried to be the best mother possible. Now she has gone to a better place," Tyler's voice nearly cracked and was forced to pause momentarily. "She's with the Lord and angels in heaven, where your mother will share eternal joy and happiness. The police were over earlier today and confirmed mom was the lady found at the park."

"No!" Cindy covered her mouth. "No, not mom! Cindy's sorrow was simply too much for her father to bear. Her father noted the remarkable similarities between them, intensifying his pain so much so that he could barely maintain eye contact. Valiantly, he tried calming her down,

"Honey please…" But her sobbing intensified, piercing his already wounded heart.

"Why would anyone want to hurt mom?" Cindy threw her arms around her father who reciprocated.

Tears streamed down their faces spilling onto one another. "I don't know honey; we don't have any answers yet." Christopher ran over to them, apparently overcome by all their grieving and he too succumbed to tears. Becky picked up Christopher and tried consoling both children. She had been very close to Dianne and sympathized whole-heartedly with both siblings. She felt it was her obligation to give her brother's family support and guide them through this difficult time.

On the drive to the park Tyler felt completely drained. His wife's disappearance had taken quite a toll on him, and now he felt exasperated with the dismal reality that she would no longer be coming home. The park was still closed to the public. Tyler seemed impatient to arrive at what had been her temporary resting place. His mind was consumed by many memories, but his heart felt as empty as the park. The conservation area held many cherished moments for the Summers' household. He swept past a cluster of maple trees. Just a couple of years ago, they sat at a picnic table covered by the tree's shade enjoying a family picnic. Christopher and Cindy had been so excited barbecuing outdoors, Tyler caught himself smiling at the flashback. They had captured this moment on film; an onlooker had been kind enough to snap some photos. Dianne had been so pleased with one photo, she had it enlarged, framed and mounted in their living room. Unaware, tears rolled down Tyler's face. Clearly distraught, he shook his head from side to side still in shock over his wife's tragic death. Tyler's heart almost broke. *How many times had they watched their children reaching high into the sky and then just as quickly watched them swing back?* The sand box had also been an all time favorite. Their laughter seemed to still sway in the gentle breeze. They often had joined other children wagering bets as to whom could build the biggest sand castle. Now all those joyous memories would be forever tarnished.

The yellow ribbon carefully marked the area where Dianne had been buried. The Chief politely stepped in front explaining to Tyler they were still investigating. Tyler stood speechless. A myriad thoughts and emotions swept through him, but he didn't articulate any of them. Overcome with grief and anguish, he broke down pounding his fists on the ground. "How could anyone do this to you, how? My beautiful, beautiful angel, I don't know how I can go on without you!" His sobbing was so loud it overpowered his bitterness. It was agonizingly painful watching him mourn his loss, but the Chief let him grieve, figuring it was perhaps the first step to a slow and trying road to recovery. But one thing was for damn certain, it would be a day neither would forget.

Regardless of the fact that he drank two cups of chamomile, the Chief had a very restless night. He tossed and turned until the wee hours of the morning. His temples ached that morning and he was on the onset of a terrible migraine. Over the years, his calm composure enabled him to deal effectively with life's constant pressures, but today he felt irritable. His mind reeled counting the number of tasks on his agenda; perhaps it was time for a pre-emptive strike. He needed relief if he was going to effectively cope and popped two pills. They usually provided relief, although today he was a bit skeptical of their effectiveness.

He picked at his bacon and eggs not feeling hungry, and then dumped his coffee into a large styrofoam cup. In all probability, he would need it and plenty more just to make it through the day.

The drive to work left the Chief with mixed emotions. Unfortunately the pleasantry associated with the park had become a very disturbing eyesore.

He slumped back into his seat staring at the three piles neatly arranged on his desk. He leafed through his mail. A letter size envelope aroused his curiosity. It was addressed to him with the word 'URGENT' handwritten in large red block letters followed by Personal and Confidential. Oddly no return address followed.

The Chief's patience was being exhausted; it was the fifth call in the last hour. "Hello," he answered hastily in an abrupt tone. "I'll call you back as soon as I'm ready to schedule a press conference," he shouted and slammed the receiver. Dianne's death had become the top news story with the public demanding answers.

He ran the letter opener along the length of the envelope. The Chief was about to crumple the piece of paper realizing it was just a poem, and he sure as hell had no time for such frivolities. "Christ -- don't people have anything better to do with their time." Just as he was about to tear it in half, his eye caught a glimpse of the ending of the first line. A stern expression sculpted the Chief's face.

Dear Chief:
Voices in my head that want her dead,
All her troubles have come to an end.
With the light of God her sins will expire,
A knife through her heart will end her desires.
The river of life will cleanse her soul,
But the avenger of truth takes its toll.
A red rose signifies a burning passion and is filled with truth and lies,
But as time elapses it withers and dies.
Every song and dance we shared,
Welcomes the truth of love and gets us prepared.
The rosary offers hope for those who believe,
Others who mock and tease will soon grieve.
Prepare for the worst and hope for the best,
For the hour is not yet finished until I get the rest.

Yours truly,
Eternal Flame

It quickly dawned on him that the poem was written by the killer. Disbelief, shock, and perplexity of this latest revelation sent the Chief's blood pressure rising and his temper flaring. The letter seemed rather personal, almost as if the killer knew him. *Who are you*, thought the Chief? "Damn bastard! I will get you rest assured, and when I do I'll put an end to your sick little game," the Chief declared vindictively clenching the letter tightly in his hand. He needed an outlet to vent his rage and frustration. The letter dropped from his hand. Shrugging both shoulders, he leaned his head forward onto his outspread hands, firmly grasping his temples. The throbbing continued to escalate to a dangerous and unprecedented level.

Chapter 4

He read all the evidence to date. Finally, after many years of investigation it led to the bank robber's arrest. The loud rap on the door nearly jostled the Chief out of his chair, but successfully sent his file airborne. He was definitely a man on pins and needles, and seven daily doses of caffeine didn't help matters. "Sorry to startle you, but Dianne Summers's forensic report has just arrived," the officer apologized handing him the file. The Chief anxiously began reading it, while the officer courteously picked the papers from the floor.

He spread the file's entire contents onto his desk. A series of photographs exposed the cranial and spinal regions. While viewing the photos, he skimmed through the report trying to find the most pertinent details, since the usual technical jargon didn't impress him. He continued reading. According to the report, the victim hadn't been buried immediately; the different types of insect colonization found on and around the victim's mouth, nasal and genital areas confirmed this. The body had been stored indoors for at least several hours before being transported to the park, this was supported by different types of insects found on the body. There were no blows to the head, or trauma to the spine, nor were there any traces of narcotics or poison. *How did he kill you,* the Chief thought to himself? The next line answered his question. The autopsy concluded suffocation as the cause of death. This deduction was also supported by the fact that her front lower and upper teeth were slightly dislodged. Dianne's last visit to the dentist, just days before her disappearance, confirmed they were in perfect alignment. The killer may have caught her by surprise. A visual synopsis formed in the Chief's mind as he continued reading the report. A rush of sympathy took hold of the Chief as he read the next line. The victim's heart was severed in half by a sharp object, most likely a large knife. Sickened by this revelation, the Chief yelled, "Sick bastard!" He did not realize that the door was slightly ajar, leaving everyone outside his office to overhear his apparent disgust. *"What kind of psychopath are we dealing with?"* An infuriated Chief paced the length of his office.

"I'm sorry. I had no idea Chief," the officer felt uneasy being in the same room.

The killer did not victimize Dianne for her material possessions, since her gold bracelet, matching gold chain encasing a zodiac pendant, and her engagement ring were still on her person. The Chief paused digesting what he had just read. The rosary and the positioning of the head to the running water suggested that the killer might be involved in a religious cult or simply be a religious fanatic. *If so,* thought the Chief, *then he may be targeting a specific group of people, but whom?*

One thing was for damn certain the murderer was ruthless. Once he seized his victim, he showed no remorse, mercilessly continuing with his course of action. The Chief also surmised that the killer must have experienced some personal satisfaction, most likely leading him to kill again. *But what madness could have triggered him? And, what on earth would set him off again?* If Chief Williams's line of reasoning was correct, there were obviously more victims on his hit list, meaning more murders to follow. *But the million dollar question was who would be his next victim?* His temples ached forcing him to swallow two more tablets.

The Chief was ready to set his plan of action into motion. He had personally hand-picked a team of three elite detectives with phenomenal track records. All three were specialists in their respective fields and would leave no stone unturned until the killer was captured. The Chief glanced at his wrist-watch realizing they'd soon be arriving.

Terry Bradshaw entered police headquarters. She was a twenty year veteran on the homicide squad. Her specialty included reconstructing homicide cases, and deservedly had earned herself a reputation of being extremely detail-oriented often uncovering clues overlooked by others.

Sean Anderson joined Terry in the conference room. He would definitely prove to be a vital member of the team with over twenty-five years of service. He was dubbed the 'bloodhound'. Nothing or no one could steer him off course when he picked up a scent, he was relentless like a hound chasing a fox.

Steve Black was the third ingredient needed to successfully solve the homicide. With thirty-five years of duty, he had been involved in a myriad of cases over the years enriching his treasure chest of experience. Steve was capable of uncovering the minutest detail. Several years ago, he helped arrest a serial killer who viciously took the lives of fifteen women in New York City. If it wasn't for his participation many cases would still remain unsolved. Some would swear he relied on the paranormal, giving him an edge like a sixth sense.

The detectives seated themselves in the conference room awaiting the Chief's arrival. "Thank you for being here on such short notice," the Chief entered acknowledging each of them. "We have a murder case which requires your expertise. Earlier this morning, I received the forensic report for Dianne Summers. The cause of death as well as other relevant information suggests we're not dealing with a single isolated incident, but evidence strongly indicates we're dealing with a serial killer." The Chief relayed all of the pertinent details. "We've combed the entire crime scene along with the entire park's grounds and have come up empty-handed. The mayor has implored me to make this my personal mission and would like us to give this murder investigation top priority." The Chief sighed, "I'm also an old friend of the Summers' family and believe the killing was premeditated." His tone intensified and he paused briefly before continuing. "The media is already having a field day blowing everything out of proportion. We're under tremendous pressure for not having any leads, suspects, or motives. Therefore detectives, you are going to make this case your top priority. Search the entire crime scene one hundred times if need be, question any potential witnesses at the park or surrounding neighborhood, ask forensics for anything suspicious, interview the family, but be sure to get answers."

Without the Chief explicitly asking for their co-operation, the officers affirmed a synchronized "yes."

"Now, I want you all to brace yourselves; never in my entire career have I experienced something quite disturbing as this poem." The Chief appeared flabbergasted as he removed the photocopies from the file and handed each of them a copy. "The original is presently being tested for fingerprints, although realistically he probably was prudent enough to wear gloves."

He left them to read the poem uninterrupted.

"He doesn't sound too stable." Sean Anderson stated.

"He certainly knows enough facts to be the killer," Terry surmised. "It seems as if he's playing some sort of mind game, perhaps, a mind duel if you will. On the one hand he has gone to extraordinary lengths to dispose the body, but then ironically plays a game with us, taunting us to catch him."

The Chief's voice and facial appearance were of a man rather tired and shaken fearing more corpses and mayhem in his city. Sometimes the unknown or unexpected creates more fear and anxiety in a man's heart than even the most grotesque finding. "Perhaps, he'll try contacting us again. Most likely, we're dealing with someone who may exhibit some sort of psychotic behavior. If so, he may already have chosen his next victim," Steve reasoned.

"Call me with any new developments -- day or night. I've included my cell as well as my home phone number. Furthermore, I've advised the forensic team that you may drop by to see the body." They dispersed after the meeting carefully calculating their next move.

Dr. Summers wearily began making funeral arrangements. Despite the fact he treated sick patients daily, he never prepared for the final stages either for his wife or himself. They occasionally had discussed signing a will, but postponed making any concrete plans believing it was still too early. Tyler moved at a very slow pace lacking his usual drive. His mind continuously reverted back to his beloved wife. *"How am I supposed to move on without you?"* Tyler cried out in desperation. He realized that not only had he lost his wife, but also his confidant. She had supported him for over fifteen years, giving him courage and aspiration during the most difficult times.

Dr. Summers jumped at the sound of the door bell. Dr. Adams, a colleague at the hospital greeted Tyler. "I'm very sorry for your loss and Dianne's tragic death," he gave him a warm embrace while offering him his condolences. "The staff at the hospital has prepared this for you." He handed him a large fruit basket. A condolence card accompanied it, signed by many of his colleagues and staff.

Dear Tyler:

Our thoughts are with you at this sorrowful time. We all miss you and wish you and your family peace and love during this

difficult period. Please accept our most sincere condolences
and our heart-felt sympathies.

"Thank everyone for me, I appreciate the kind gesture."

"Everyone at the hospital is distraught about the news.
Dianne was a very special person and we can't even begin to
imagine what you must be going through. Is there anything,
anything at all we can do for you?"

"I appreciate you dropping by; I know how hectic things can
become at the hospital."

"Don't concern yourself with any of that; we have
everything under control. Can I help you with the funeral
arrangements, or in any other way?" Dr. Summers pondered
this for a moment, grateful for any assistance.

"I must sign some authorization papers for client testing."

"We've taken care of everything. We don't want you to rush
back. Take all the time you need."

"I really appreciate everyone's assistance and your visit."
Tyler felt lethargic, lacking the drive to engage in conversation.

"You don't need to thank us, it's the least we can do. We'll
take care of matters at the hospital, but remember should you
need anything, anything whatsoever, don't hesitate to call. I'll
drop by later."

No amount of training or experience could prepare the Chief
for the news he was about to deliver. He cringed at the thought
of being the bearer of more bad news, but Tyler deserved to
know the truth. He paused briefly trying to summon enough
courage before ringing the doorbell.

A stressed out Tyler called out, "Come in," in a sullen tone.
The Chief felt apprehensive noting his gloomy composure and
the doctor's appearance carried a beaten and worn look as if he
had fought in Desert Storm. His hair was graying and
predominant wrinkles seemed to have deepened around his

eyes literally overnight. Tyler slowly walked into the foyer hunched over like a man of eighty. The Chief was genuinely concerned for his friend; it was disturbing seeing him in such an anguished state.

"Please have a seat," Tyler gestured to the sofa.

"Thanks," responded the Chief with a slight nod, finding it increasingly difficult to maintain eye-contact.

"I've made arrangements for the funeral," Tyler tried to contain a floodgate of emotions. "The funeral will be held Saturday morning. I decided against a wake since it would be too upsetting for the children, and I'm not sure how much more I can handle." The doctor's head was bowed as he fought back tears.

The Chief refrained from speaking, giving his friend some time to regain his composure. It was difficult watching someone grieve over a loved one, especially when that someone was a good friend; he wouldn't wish it upon his worst enemy. Finding the right words wasn't the Chief's specialty, after all his job focused mainly on violence and murder.

"She was a fine person, well respected, outgoing -- such a natural zest for life, and everyone will always remember her just that way," the Chief stressed trying to uplift his friend's spirits.

"A good wife and an excellent mother, I can't say enough good things about her," a grin flashed across Tyler's face helping to lift some of his melancholy. The Chief was preparing for the right moment to deliver the latest. It was hard in the best of times to deliver bad news, but this could be the straw that broke the camel's back. His clasped hands began to feel clammy, but there was no turning back, the Chief mustered all his courage before relaying the news.

"I've assigned the three best detectives on the force to solve this case," he reassured.

"Do they have any leads, clues, or are we in total darkness?" Tyler wanted answers, anything to bring forth justice perhaps even retribution.

Sadly, the Chief knew that what he was about to disclose to his friend wasn't exactly what he hoped to hear. "A couple of new discoveries," the Chief acknowledged humbly, suddenly feeling in the hot seat.

"Well, what are they?" Tyler's attentiveness left the Chief's heart aching.

"As a friend, I know you've suffered a great loss, and if you're not up to it we'll leave it for another time." Tyler gave his approval. "Okay -- I want you to read this poem," the Chief noticed the baffled look on Tyler's face. "The killer has sent it to my attention. Are you up to reading it?" Tyler nodded. The Chief could see the agony deepen on Tyler's face as he read on. He then dropped it on the coffee table.

"Good God, what kind of a deranged lunatic is he anyway!" Tyler exclaimed with a shocked expression.

"Do any of his references make any sense to you? Does his signature ring a bell?"

"No, but you seem fairly certain it was written by the killer. Why?"

"Certain evidence coincides with the poem. First of all, her body was found next to the river bank. He placed a red rose along with a rosary in her hands all of which he makes reference to in his poem."

"Has the forensic report been completed?"

"Yes, but we can discuss that later," assured the Chief.

Sternly, the doctor put his foot down while looking him square in the eyes, "Dammit, I want to know everything, right now. How did she die?"

The Chief felt numb, but was left with no choice; he took a deep breath before reluctantly relaying the grizzly details.

"Firstly, I want to assure you that she did not suffer, but died very quickly. Your wife was being suffocated at the same time she was knifed through the heart."

Tyler paled. His sorrow, shock, and terror were clearly etched all over his face. The expression painted on his face resonated much louder than any words he could have spoken. The Chief coughed a couple of times. The room's atmosphere had thickened; its intensity could be sliced with a knife. Tightness gripped the Chief's throat choking his next words.

"My -- t-throat is a bit scratchy, is it okay if I help myself to a glass of water?"

"Sorry, excuse my manners. There are refreshments in the refrigerator." The doctor's kitchen window faced the backyard and the Chief noted the amazing additions including the deck. He returned with two glasses of orange. It was agonizing watching his friend face the horrid details and he tried diverting his attention.

The Chief acknowledged, "You have done an excellent job with the backyard."

"The kids love the addition of the pool. The new cedar deck was great for entertaining guests. Actually, we built the deck at the beginning of this spring. I don't think you have seen it before."

"No, but it's quite impressive."

"You'll need to come over next year once the weather warms up," Tyler invited. "I appreciate everything you've done, but you must be busy and I don't want to burden you."

"You don't need to worry about that. Sure it's my job to be here, however more importantly I'm here as your friend first. There's something I need to ask you, although I probably already know the answer. Dianne and you shared a loving relationship, but were there times when you experienced marital difficulties?" he asked embarrassed

"Oh -- we seldom had any arguments, except of course for minor scuffles."

"Therefore according to your knowledge, Dianne never stepped out of the boundaries of your marriage?" the Chief flushed as he was direct and to the point.

"Oh, you mean as in an affair? Ha -- I never needed to worry about that. We were both faithful and loyal to one another, and made a pact to keep our feelings open."

"That's what I thought. It's getting late, have you had dinner?"

"I don't have much of an appetite. But you go ahead."

"You need to keep up your strength, besides I hate dining alone. I know of an Indonesian restaurant just down the street, which makes the most incredible vegetable soup."

"Well -- alright." Tyler hesitantly agreed, and was about to reach into his wallet.

"It's on me; I'll be back shortly."

The Chief pulled into the restaurant's parking lot, but surprisingly this evening the queue consisted of only a couple of customers. Slowly, the Chief inched forward ready to place his order at the drive-thru window. He frequented the restaurant on a regular basis and was instantly recognized by staff.

"Good evening Chief Williams, may I take your order?" beamed Tina, a bright cheerful teenager.

"Good evening Tina, give me a couple of your famous vegetable soups, a dozen chicken wings, two vegetable salads, a couple of rolls, and could you throw in some barbecue sauce, please." Tina liked the Chief. She found him never to be pushy or abrupt, but always maintained a calm and pleasant demeanor. It only took a couple of minutes for him to receive his order.

"Here you go Chief Williams, thanks and please come again," Tina handed him the double wrapped paper bag with a warm smile.

"You guys are getting quicker and quicker," the Chief complimented.

"Thanks," she beamed. He placed his food on the passenger seat. The Chief switched the radio on for some company.

"Earlier this evening, the disappearance of a ..."

"Jesus Christ!" Errrrr...Loud screeching sounds overpowered the Chief's radio. "Shit, you dumb crazy idiot!" the Chief exploded. His well developed motor skills allowed him to just barely swerve out of harm's way. A maniac entering the plaza driving a dark BMW came within inches of side swiping him. The Chief glanced over and breathed a sigh of relief seeing his take-out had miraculously not toppled over. With everything happening lately, the Chief's patience was running thin. Normally he would have chased in hot pursuit, but his grieving friend really needed support and he was determined to be there for him.

Jack slammed the front door and bolted for the kitchen. The loud racket escalated Tara's apprehension as she frantically fluttered about. She finally let down her guard at the sight of her master. "Daddy's home. You're going to have to be patient for a minute, my friend. *Whew, what a day.*" He dumped a couple of ice-cubes in his glass and poured himself a shot of scotch. Jack took a moment to relax and stretched out on his recliner. He swirled his drink and enjoyed the clinking sounds of ice striking the glass. Before downing his drink, he enjoyed watching the counter sinking and floating effect of the ice cubes. Jack's stomach rumbled and realized he hadn't eaten anything since breakfast. He placed the chicken nuggets in the microwave. As he lifted his glass, he nearly knocked over the remaining sauce.

"Yikes -- that was the second close call today!" Jack chuckled on his lightning reflexes. He managed to catch the sauce before it splattered all over the Persian rug.

"Cloze cull, cloze cull," Tara twittered as she picked at her vegetables, seated across from Jack. Jack realized he would be quite lonely without her, not to mention she was a great source of entertainment. In turn, maybe he spoiled her too much. For a split second, he wondered if this would come back to haunt him.

He quickly flicked on the TV to watch the rest of the evening news.

"The identity of the victim found in Stetson Highland Park has been identified as that of Dianne Summers; wife of Doctor Tyler Summers."

Jack froze.

"She had mysteriously disappeared early in the summer and despite a massive man hunt, police came up empty-handed. Her body was found buried along the park's river bed, police are investigating and ask if anyone has any information to please come forward. Dianne was well respected in the community and will be sadly missed. She leaves behind her two young children, Cindy and Christopher. Her funeral will be a private function ..." informed the news reporter.

"Oh my God! -- I can't believe it," Jack was stunned. Shock-waves filled him making it difficult for him to keep still, as he continuously moved about in the living room in a state of panic. He needed another drink, a damn stiff one.

As he made his way to the kitchen, he was still in a state of shock. This time, he poured himself a glass of scotch hoping it would help to calm his shattered nerves. He carried the drink into the living room. His hand rested momentarily on his family photo album. It pained him tremendously, realizing all the wonderful times they had once shared were now lost forever. A few moments elapsed, before he reached for the Bible which sat on the shelf next to his many trophies. Jack tightened his grasp on the cover, before opening the book to one of his favorite passages. It was common for him to revert back to the sacred book whenever he felt too distressed. It was a passage from Luke 7:2 Love of Enemies. He read out loud.

"But to you who hear I say, love your enemies, do good to those who hate you, bless those who curse you, pray for those who mistreat you. To the person who strikes you on one cheek offer the other one as well, and for the person who takes your cloak, do not withhold even your tunic."

Jack completed the passage feeling comforted by its words. He swirled his glass, which still remained half full and then set it on the end-table. It had always perplexed him how one devastating event could deeply affect so many lives. Jack reflected upon this thought for awhile, before deciding to head upstairs to shower. He was sipping the rest of his drink when the telephone rang.

"Hello, hel --" answered the nervous caller.

"Who's this?" demanded Jack in an annoyed tone concluding it to be a crank call.

Panting sounds were audible in the background. "It's Pete Waters. Did you hear the news?" Jack hadn't initially recognized Pete's shaky voice. He was an old high school friend who now and again kept in touch.

"You mean the discovery of Dianne Summers's body?" Jack sadly concluded.

"Yes, isn't it just awful?" Pete too sounded in a state of despair.

"I'm still in shock; I just heard it on the local news station. I just can't imagine why anyone would hurt her -- her of all people."

"She was always generous and kind to everyone. This is so freaky."

"Yes, it's hard to imagine anyone wanting her dead. Do they have leads, or suspects?" blurted Jack.

"Nothing, but I'm sure sooner or later they'll catch the psychopath, and I hope they put him in the slammer and throw away the keys. Justice would certainly prevail," Pete was fuming, stressing each syllable emphasizing his disgust. It was hard accepting that someone so caring had suffered such a vicious death.

"Keep me posted, I would like to attend the funeral to offer my condolences."

"Sure -- as soon as I get all the details, I'll give you a call. Take it easy."

"Thanks -- I appreciate it." Jack slumped himself on the leather sofa.

He gulped down the rest of his drink, and felt the scotch's sting.

Jack walked at a brisk pace, heading in the direction of the loud clicking noises. They appeared to be coming from the kitchen, and low and behold he was astonished to see Tara tiptoeing all over the kitchen countertop next to the empty bottle of scotch. "Tara how on earth did you get out?" marveled Jack in complete fascination.

"Hi daddy, remember a bird in the hand is worth two in the bush," mimicked Tara. Jack apprehensively looked around. *Who said that,* he wondered in astonishment? But no one else was present. She had never previously spoken in complete sentences, and delving in self doubt, he asked another question just to make sure his ears weren't playing tricks on him.

"What do you think of the way daddy manages to keep the kitchen clean and organized?" tested Jack.

"Everything is spotless and in its proper place: glasses, forks, and knives," replied Tara.

"This is unreal." Jack was spooked and desperately needed to clear his mind. "Now daddy is going to place you back and I'm going to get some fresh air." Still in disbelief, Jack took a couple of deep breaths trying to cope with what he just heard. *Not possible*, he thought to himself. He opted to take a short walk through the park. The night was lit by the pale moonlight and a few street lights, managing to keep its silhouette well hidden. "Yikes," Jack ducked just in time. He tried to reverse directions, but it swooped towards him, like a missile locked on its target. "Get away from me!" he yelled out into the darkness. It landed on a lamppost just meters away from him. Jack peered straight into its eyes. He followed the dark tunnel intently to see where it would lead him; ironically, it seemed to be never ending, like the abyss.

Evidently it was a trap.

"You can try hiding from me Jack, but you'll never escape me," it forewarned with a cold glare. Oddly enough, Jack could hear the words without the raven's beak actually moving. A cold shiver shot through him and for the first time he felt truly vulnerable, much like a cornered animal ready to be preyed upon. Jack felt a rush of adrenaline to reach the safe haven of his home. Prudently, he kept the door in his sights as he took slow backward steps. It didn't move, but remained perched almost frozen in time. Jack instinctively knew that at any moment it would dive for him again, and in a panic accidentally stumbled over the curb. The raven didn't miss its opportunity as it dove straight down aiming for Jack's eyes. Jack's training automatically stepped in, and he rolled over on the hard pavement several times. Into the darkness he frantically searched, but had lost the whereabouts of the dark presence. He caught sight of a shovel and grabbed it in self-defense.

"Let's see how tough you are now!" Jack took empty swipes hoping to dissuade any further advances. His front door was less than a few meters away, and Jack cautiously stepped backwards, anticipating the worst. Fear accompanied his every step.

"You know it's only a matter of time before I conquer you Jack," inexplicably the voice resonated seemingly from all directions. Somehow the raven remained one step ahead of him, cleverly anticipating his every move. It was determined to become one with Jack's mind, body, and soul. Calculating, it landed on Jack's rooftop unknowingly to him. It swooped at Jack ready to take revenge; Jack momentarily froze as he heard the loud flapping of wings behind him.

"AHHHHH!" His screams echoed far into the darkness.

The raven's hideous darkness eclipsed the moon's light as it descended aggressively intent on striking its target. In a desperate sprawl, Jack lunged forward and rolled over several times. Then there was complete darkness.

Tic...Toc...Tic...Toc...Tic...Toc...

Cautiously, the trio descended the hill with careful steps. Their hands offered no support as they were overburdened with a large number of excavating tools.

The demarcation tape stood out like a sore thumb. Terry, Sean, and Steve stood silent, perhaps a bit reluctant of the arduous task at hand. They too would sieve through the sand grain by grain to ensure no evidence had been overlooked. Steve carefully descended into the hollow space beaming his flashlight. Sifting through sand and dirt wasn't exactly their idea of fun. It was damn tedious and laborious; an inexact science in which the parameters were not readily defined. Just as he had lost hope of recovering anything, his flashlight reflected something shiny near his right foot. He dared not touch it, but wisely brushed the sand away from around the object. A burst of excitement filled him, "I've found something." Steve placed the shirt button into a plastic evidence bag and handed it to them. All their attention was drawn to the small object. He then thoroughly sprayed the ground with Luminol, aware that if any blood existed it would react with iron to expose even the minutest traces of blood. He continued to rake the sand.

It was a cool morning, but the sun's rays still made it comfortable to work outdoors. "I don't know about you guys, but I could sure use a break," Sean suggested.

"It's quite possible that the button belongs to the killer, but we need more evidence," Terry surmised.

"Whoever we are dealing with is certainly no amateur. He's very confident, perhaps cocky, and seems to have a well thought out plan. Also, I haven't come across too many killers with the audacity to write a poem to the Chief of Police."

"Yeah, no kidding. Perhaps confident is not the right word -- maybe raving lunatic is a more fitting description," Sean sounded a little troubled, but continued. "Surprisingly, he's quite thorough, unlike some murders committed in a moment of heated rage, with the killers leaving behind a heap of evidence. We're still clueless as to the motive. I have this burning feeling that there's something very unsettling with this whole picture, something is just not quite right. Generally, I don't rely on gut instincts, but have a strong conviction to do so this time."

"It's almost as if he's drawing us into some sort of game, taunting us to catch him," Steve added his own thoughts. "As weird as this may sound, perhaps he wants to be apprehended then he'd be forced to stop his killings. If he's mentally unstable, then he's definitely not in total control affecting both his temperament and personality," Steve tried rationalizing.

"You mean like a split personality?" Terry looked stunned.

"Exactly, thus he maintains a seemingly normal personality," Steve explained stressing his point.

Just as Terry was dropping the next shovelful into the sifter, her eye caught a quick reflection. "Uh-ha, perhaps the killer is getting a little sloppy," she stated.

Steve unfolded a small square canvas for the contents to be examined. Terry poured slowly for fear of losing the object. With the small brush they brushed the earth aside creating a thin layer over the tarp.

"It looks like a piece of metal," Sean blurted out.

"Yes, it's a broken piece from something," Terry acceded.

"Well if I didn't know any better -- I would say it was part of a shovel," Steve noted the pointed edge. They unanimously agreed with his clever deduction. It was also placed in a clear plastic evidence bag.

"Why wasn't the fragment discovered earlier by the metal detectors?" Terry asked puzzlingly.

"Good point," Sean retorted disappointingly. "We'll have to bring it to the Chief's attention."

They loaded their tools, hauling everything into the back of the van. Tomorrow they would take aerial photographs, re-tracing the killer's route. Each of them parted with a different agenda in mind, since in a couple of hours they would regroup with the Chief.

In the distance, an incessant ringing noise begged him to answer the call. Jack found himself on the sofa apparently having overslept. It was now lunch time. Suddenly, Tara flew intending to land on her master, but missed as a startled Jack nimbly rolled onto the rug. "Hey, how did you get out?" Jack tried recalling back to last evening, unsure if he had fastened the latch.

"Jack be quick; Jack be swift." He felt groggy and cradled his pounding head. It was difficult for him to regain his balance, and he staggered several times before finally settling for the comforts of his Persian rug.

"Shoot, Tara you nearly soiled the rug!" he scolded. His head reeled with pain as he kept telling himself to clean up the mess, but his body wouldn't co-operate.

An hour elapsed before he made any attempts to stand. Jack staggered to the kitchen, fumbling to make a fresh pot of coffee. While the coffee was brewing, he made his way to the front door. He caught a glimpse of himself in the mirror and noticed his red puffy eyes. As Jack was about to open the door to check for any mail, he was shocked to find he hadn't set his alarm. This peeved him since it left him completely vulnerable. His neighbor had been burglarized just last year. Jack knew he had to be more vigilant.

He welcomed the cold water beating against his skin, lifting his grogginess and sharpening his senses. He patted himself dry and caught a glimpse of stubble forming on his chin through the oval mirror's reflection. The oval mirror had become part of the family heirloom, dating back three generations. His grandmamma, Ellen, always professed one's conscience was clear if one could look directly into the mirror without feeling any remorse.

"A Special Investigative Team is combing the park," the Chief assured Mayor Wilson.

"Sure as hell hope we catch this maniac soon. Today alone, I've received at least twenty phone calls from concerned citizens and other parties. Her death has angered a lot of folks and they're demanding answers," the mayor seemed overwhelmed.

"Rest assured, I'll leave no stone unturned until we catch the killer."

"I have full confidence in your abilities, and am terribly sorry for your loss; I'm aware you're a good friend of the family."

"Thank you -- she was a terrific lady. I'll keep you updated."

"Take care and send my regards to the family. If you need anything, and I mean anything don't hesitate to call." The mayor left it in the Chief's capable hands.

The Chief was a bit startled from the thump on the door. "Hey -- you seem to be drowning in paperwork," chuckled Alan.

"You can say that again," the Chief wearily looked at his desk.

"I brought you a coffee and a muffin, if my memory serves me correctly banana walnut."

"Thanks, I could use a break."

"Any plans for this weekend?"

"Not at the moment," the Chief made eye contact.

"You're welcome to join us at the cottage. I still get a good laugh thinking back to last year." Larry smirked. "Remember Simon trying to escape from his puppy's grasp, hopping backwards while the puppy was pulling with all its might to rip his sock off." The Chief laughed remembering poor Simon landing in the water. It had been hilarious to watch the dog flip the sock into mid-air, catch it, and then crazily swing his head from side to side.

An officer's loud knock on the door startled him, "Sir, a Mr. Harrison is on his way to the station, and wants to file a missing persons report. His wife has not returned home since yesterday.

The Chief's eyes widened with fear, thinking Mr. Harrison's wife may have become Eternal Flame's next victim.

The Chief rose quickly hoping to jump onto any leads. "Call me the second he walks through the front door," he stated firmly.

"Yes sir," the officer answered before exiting.

Chief Williams rubbed his aching temples. He pulled the desk drawer open and reached for the pain killers. The Chief tried to remain calm, but took comfort knowing the Investigative Team would be arriving shortly along with Federal Agents Gray and Michael. Given the circumstances, he felt it prudent to compile a strong team before the killer could strike again. The Chief saw Terry through the glass window and motioned her to enter. "We may have a real dilemma on our hands; a gentleman named Mr. Harrison will be arriving shortly. Apparently, his wife has been missing for over twenty-four hours. I want the team to be present when he arrives, so we can formulate a plan of action."

"We'll be waiting in the conference room," Terry hurried to find the others.

In a panic, he searched for the information desk. He briefly updated the officer, who in turn hurled a series of questions at him. "I don't know that, otherwise I wouldn't be here!" Mr. Harrison exploded at the attending officer. The Chief was promptly notified that Mr. Harrison had just arrived.

He immediately rushed to the front desk as every second counted.

"Mr. Harrison, I'm Chief Williams, please come with me," he instructed curtly. They walked briskly along a lengthy corridor before reaching the conference room. "Everyone this is Mr. Harrison. I've invited our special Investigative Team along with Agents Gray and Michael from the FBI to assist us in this matter."

"When was the last time you saw your wife?" Agent Gray proceeded.

"Yesterday morning, but I didn't speak to her since she stepped in the shower while I was on my way out."

"Did she say anything the evening before -- of any plans?"

"Uh, tomorrow she was supposed to leave for New York for a couple of days."

"Does she usually travel?"

"A few times a year."

"Is anything missing from your home?"

"No." Unknowingly to Mr. Harrison, they all wondered if she suffered an ill fate at the hands of Eternal Flame. Wisely, no one dared to share these thoughts with him.

"Were there any hints of a struggle?" Terry inquired.

"No. I even checked her jewellery and everything was there except for Lisa's necklace and watch, which she may still be wearing."

"Were all the windows shut?"

"Yes, everything was locked. Our alarm system was even set." Something was not quite right with the picture Mr. Harrison was painting; something just didn't add up.

"Does she own a vehicle?"

"Yes, it's still parked in the garage. It seems like she just vanished off the face of the earth. I heard about the other lady on the local news and I'm worried sick," confessed Mr. Harrison nervously, who seemed on the verge of a breakdown.

"Let's not jump to any conclusions at this point," Steve consoled in a reassuring tone. Even though, quite truthfully, he himself feared the worst.

"Does she usually leave you a note?" Sean asked.

"Yes, she's really good about that sort of thing. Lisa always lets me know her whereabouts," Mr. Harrison frowned. "That's what so puzzling."

"Okay, we would like to check for any clues at your home. We're also going to need a list of names and numbers of friends, family, and her place of employment," the Chief explained hurriedly.

"Sure, most of that information is at our home anyway."

It did not surprise the Chief that nothing had been missing from his home. If Dianne's killer was responsible, material objects were clearly of no concern. As for the alarm system, the killer could be knowledgeable enough to successfully disarm it and then re-arm it.

Terry performed a quick over-haul of Lisa Harrison's car. The doors did not appear to have been tampered with in any way. She used a special type of a brush to pick up any human hairs. Terry had already dusted for prints on both the interior and exterior of the car.

Mr. Harrison watched as Agent Michael and Agent Gray filtered through everything in their bedroom, while answering numerous questions. "Yes, that's the way she usually keeps the vanity set. She's exceptionally neat and well organized. Everything is just the way she usually leaves them."

"Have you touched anything this morning?"

"I just opened that drawer to check on the contents of her jewellery along with the walk-in-closet for a fresh pair of clothing. Actually, I did not even sleep in here last night. Instead, I slept on the couch thinking she might be working late, and I would hear her once she stepped inside."

Downstairs, Steve and Chief Williams meticulously rummaged through the kitchen cabinets, pouring samples, and also dusting for prints. They asked Mr. Harrison how many knives they kept. The knives sat on the countertop and had been arranged according to size in their proper slots, and all six of them were present. Each one of them would be examined for fingerprints.

Sean, in the meantime, drove to her place of employment. Part of Lisa's job as Merchandise Assistant was to ensure that the shop's front display windows were dressed in the latest fashions. She enjoyed traveling to the Big Apple a couple times of year to purchase mannequins and other props for the boutique.

The Chief quickly took the call, "I see and when did this happen?" The Chief's heart skipped a few beats. "We'll be right there." In a calm tone he asked, "Mr. Harrison may I speak to you for a moment?" The Chief gestured him into the living room. "I've just received a call, but promise me not to jump to any conclusions. A woman's body has been discovered, although she carried no identification."

"Oh my God! Please God," Mr. Harrison covered his face with both hands and his eyes became watery. "Please don't let it be Lisa. I don't know what I would do without her. She means everything to me."

Despite the fact that the Chief had been to the morgue countless times, he couldn't repudiate the fact that this time was somehow different. He truly empathized with him. Perhaps the loss of a dear friend had somehow changed his perspective from a distant and impersonal one to a close and more sympathetic nature. "Now, please try and remain calm. We'll go to the morgue together," he consoled.

The Chief watched nervously as Mr. Harrison had been completely restless along the way. He repeatedly combed his hair with his fingers, clasped and unclasped his hands, and it appeared that Mr. Harrison might crack before viewing the body. The Chief let out a sigh of relief as he pulled into the closest parking space.

The morgue was bone-chilling cold; the frigid temperatures were a must in order to preserve the body from further deterioration. The Chief shuddered and swore for having forgotten his jacket, whereas Mr. Harrison was extremely agitated and wasn't phased by the extreme cold.

"Okay, they're ready for us to view the body. Now take a deep breath," the Chief coached. Mr. Harrison's eyes were glazed wide open, partially from shock but mostly with fear. His hands were clasped around his head and a worried look crossed his face as he feared the worst. Quite frankly, the Chief feared he would pass out noting his pale complexion.

The body was covered with a white sheet. Mr. Harrison noted the similar body length even from a horizontal position. The coroner began to lift the sheet slightly exposing her hair color. "God no!" he gasped having noted the similar hair color. The Chief and the coroner quickly exchanged dire looks. The coroner hesitated momentarily before continuing.

Sean purposely withheld his position hoping not to send the office into a state of turmoil. He patiently waited to speak with the manager. "Mrs. Bloc is busy with a client for another ten minutes. Please have a seat, I'll let her know you're waiting," the receptionist informed. "Oh, Mr. Anderson is she expecting you? I don't see your name on today's appointment list." she asked pushing up her glasses.

"Actually no, but it's imperative that I speak to her immediately." Sean was willing to wait ten minutes, tops. If need be he would certainly flash his ID.

He entertained himself with ladies' fashion magazines.

"Mr. Anderson, I'm Mrs. Bloc. I understand you're waiting to see me."

"Yes, it's concerning Lisa Harrison. Can we speak somewhere privately?"

Mrs. Bloc's hefty figure led him to the far end of the corridor to the privacy of her office. She closed the door behind her. "Okay, I'm not at liberty to discuss any personal information about my employees," Mrs. Bloc bluntly announced as soon as the door was firmly shut.

Sean didn't have time to play games and flashed his ID. "I'm with the New Jersey Police Department and this is an important police matter."

"Oh my! Is Lisa in some kind of trouble?" Mrs. Bloc grimaced.

"That's what I'm here to find out. When was the last time you saw Lisa?" Sean questioned.

She paused a brief moment, "Uh -- it was two days ago." Sean keenly sensed her hesitation and wondered if she was telling the truth, or perhaps, just maybe, she was hiding something.

Chapter 5

Dianne Summers's murder had become the prevalent topic at Fernheights. A loud raucous ensued from the front suite as everyone voiced their own opinions. "It's unimaginable that such an affluent family was the target of such a horrendous crime." Yvonne found it disgusting.

"Yes, my heart goes out to the family," a co-worker sympathized.

"Did they mention the cause of death?" Samantha cut in trying to get the hard facts.

"No, they're still waiting for the forensic report. Apparently, she had been missing for some time," explained Yvonne.

The room fell completely silent the moment Jack walked somberly into the suite. All eyes turned towards him making him feel uneasy and barely able to utter good morning. Yvonne broke from the group to express her condolences, "I'm very sorry to hear about Dianne." She embraced him and Jack reciprocated, squeezing her tightly. One by one the staff approached Jack offering their condolences and deepest sympathies.

Jack was overwrought with emotion. He settled himself behind his desk and pulled out his client's file. He tried to concentrate, but ten minutes later still found himself staring at the first page. He thought back to his younger days. Dianne had always been popular and well liked. He still couldn't fathom why anyone would want to kill her.

He gladly welcomed the distraction. "Hello," he answered in a sullen tone.

"Jack, your father and I have heard the tragic news and want to make sure you're okay." His mother had always worried about him. After college, he slowly drifted apart from his parents. Jack now had his own life, friends, and career which occupied most of his time. Nonetheless, they still managed to exchange phone calls and occasional visits. "How are you coping son?"

"Not too good. It was quite shocking and took me completely by surprise. I can't comprehend why anyone would want to hurt her. She was an adorable lady, a wonderful family. It's just sickening to think about her horrible death," admitted Jack in a painful tone.

"I'm very sorry; I can't imagine what you must be going through. Son, I've left several messages on your answering machine."

Jack sighed, "I haven't checked it, my apologies."

"Are you up for some company?" Jack momentarily considered the invitation. He loved his parents for being supportive, although he wasn't ready to open more wounds.

"I truly appreciate the gesture, but right now, I prefer some time alone."

"Sure, I understand. Just remember you can call us anytime."

"Thanks mom, I feel better knowing you guys are there for me. I'll be in touch soon," a touch of nostalgia swept through Jack.

Mrs. Trempton rushed into the living room. "Honey, I just spoke with Jack, I think it's happening again," she informed her husband nervously. The newspaper dropped from his hands. He sat frozen in his seat wondering if things would ever return to normal. *Would his son's past resurface, forcing them to relive their agonizing nightmare once more?*

Mr. Harrison's face turned a ghastly white. He braced himself as the sheet was about to be lifted, unveiling the truth could turn his worst nightmare into a bleak reality. He mumbled, "Please God, please don't let it be Lisa." His knees felt shaky, and it was a miracle he remained standing. The Chief placed a comforting hand on his shoulder. "Oh my God," he cried loudly while shielding his face with his hands. "Why did this have to happen?" he gasped. The woman's face had been grossly disfigured. Her right eye puffed out and she had a swollen lip. The Chief noticed a big gash across her left temple, which certainly may have been the cause of her death. The silence was numbing. Moments later, Mr. Harrison broke the silence, "I don't mean to sound insensitive, but it's not my Lisa. My heart goes out to this poor woman, but she's not my wife." Mr. Harrison continued to tower over the body with his head bowed. The Chief sighed before offering a few of his own silent prayers. But, they still did not know what had happened to Lisa. *Had she also suffered a similar ill fate, left somewhere to slowly rot? Or was she still alive suffering a slow torturous death?*

Sean thought it was puzzling that Mrs. Bloc did not call her at home after her absenteeism. But, he would question that later. "Did you notice anything peculiar in the last couple of days?"

"No, she just seemed like her old self. If anything she was excited."

"Excited -- why?" The detective was thrown a curve.

"She was going to New York; she loves the Big Apple."

"Oh, had she mentioned anything about receiving any odd phone calls?"

"She never mentioned anything of the sort."

"I've met with Mr. Harrison who's quite worried as to her whereabouts."

"Wait a minute," Mrs. Bloc backtracked. "Wait one minute. Does he not know that Lisa left for New York yesterday?"

"YESTERDAY! Whew! He thinks she's supposed to leave tomorrow," he let out a huge sigh of relief.

"No, she left yesterday. I'll call her at the hotel and confirm everything." Mrs. Bloc placed the call on the speaker phone so the officer could hear the truth for himself. She had noted his suspicious nature and wanted to put all of his doubts to rest.

"Suite 203, please."

"Hello Lisa?"

"Oh -- hi Mrs. Bloc," Lisa answered.

"How's everything in New York?"

"Great, wait till you see some of the latest props."

"Lisa, did you let your husband know about your trip?"

She felt awkward discussing her private life, and was peeved that her boss had the audacity to pry. Nonetheless, Lisa didn't want to appear rude and answered politely. "Yes and I also left him a note before I left. Why?"

"But he doesn't know you left yesterday, but thinks you're supposed to leave tomorrow."

Lisa frantically thought back. "-- Oops, I might have inadvertently written the wrong date; I was in such a mad rush just to make my flight that I forgot my cell. Hope he hasn't been too worried?"

"Well -- just a little bit dear, don't worry I'll straighten everything out. Have a good trip. Call us if you need anything," Mrs. Bloc refrained from laughing.

Sean instantly felt his entire body relax, although he still felt deeply embarrassed. "I'm so sorry about all the confusion. I have to call the Chief and the Investigative Team to let them know the case has been solved. You can't imagine what has been going through our minds."

Mrs. Bloc found this whole situation bizarre. "I'm sure her husband will be thrilled to hear she's safe and sound after this whole mix up in communications." Sean thanked Mrs. Bloc, and as soon as he stepped out of her office he called the Chief.

"Chief, we've located Lisa and she's okay," Sean blurted.

The Chief was baffled. "But where's she? How did you ever find her?"

Sean calmly explained everything and could hear the Chief sigh. Finally, they would all be able to kick back after such a long and hectic day. All the unexplainable and bizarre circumstances made sense. The Chief always believed that a mystery is solved once all the evidence succeeds each other in a logical and undisputable manner, much like piecing together a puzzle.

Yvonne paused momentarily, watching Jack stare into oblivion with his chair slightly tilted back. He seemed miles away, and was startled once she cleared her throat. "Jack are you okay?" she asked worriedly.

"Sorry, I didn't see you standing there, I was deep in thought."

"Henri, Samantha, and I are going to the Chinese restaurant down the street. We're hoping you'll join us." Jack hesitated. "We could really use the company," Yvonne gently persuaded.

"Sure, it will be great seeing Henri, not to mention the food is exceptional."

"Super, I've never dined there before." This surprised Jack since he knew Yvonne loved to savor different ethnic cuisines. It then struck him that it was probably just a diversion.

"The atmosphere is pleasant and the staff is friendly," Jack added. Yvonne felt a sense of relief seeing some of Jack's enthusiasm kick back. Earlier, she had seen a worn and wearied look on Jack's face and felt uncomfortable leaving him alone in such a distressed state.

"Henri -- I hope I'm not calling at a bad time?" Yvonne asked.

"Hi honey, I was just thinking of you." He had a profound effect on her. Nothing else seemed to matter once she was with him. All her worries, fears, and anxieties dissipated. An inner peace and overall happiness engulfed her.

"I've invited Samantha and Jack to join us for dinner tonight. He's down in the dumps. I hope you don't mind?"

"Not at all, I guess he's taking his friend's death pretty hard."

"Yes, he knew her and the family quite well. It's just such a horrible way to die."

"I'm so glad to have you sweet-heart," Henri complimented.

It was still a solid hour before they would meet for dinner. Yvonne pushed full steam ahead; she wanted to complete the following week's schedule, along with some of the current month's financial transactions before she left for the weekend. Jack also took a moment to tidy his desk. On Monday morning he hoped to begin his week in a more stable frame of mind.

"We'll be leaving in a minute. Are you ready?" Samantha interrupted gazing into his emerald eyes. Jack always admired her perkiness. He did not mean to stare, but found her to be quite the beauty. It baffled him that someone so attractive wasn't dating. He certainly would have asked her out had circumstances been different. He watched her leave with her reddish-brown hair cascading down the length of her back in loose ringlets. Jack loved the short skirt combination with the knitted tights. It accentuated her long legs. *Wow!* Jack's eyes popped wide open.

Henri pulled in the parking lot, realizing he was the first to arrive. It was the first time in his life a woman had such a profound effect on him. Although initially he had felt a strong gravitational pull towards her, over the months he came to admire many of her personal attributes. One of her most admirable features was her modesty. Henri had dated a lot of women, many of which had flagrantly displayed themselves, while others would find this an attractive quality for him this was a complete turn-off.

Yvonne pulled next to Henri's car. She looked across and noticed a big grin flash across his face. If she didn't know any better, she would say he was up to something. As she stepped out of the car, he handed her a bouquet of roses. Her suspicions had been correct. "Henri, they're beautiful," she stated while admiring the complimentary colors of pinks, champagnes, and yellows. The scent of the roses lingered between them as he passionately kissed her. He had thought of her all day and could no longer hold back.

He caressed her soft locks admiring the gold, red, and light brown highlights. He had never felt so happy. "I guess we should head inside before our guests start jumping to conclusions," Henri reluctantly managed to pull himself away.

Jack and Samantha were conversing, and it pleased Yvonne to see Jack smile.

"Hello," greeted Henri shaking Jack's hand. He gave Samantha's hand a light squeeze.

Jack loved the restaurant. He found them to be very accommodating hosts. Being a family owned business they certainly rolled out the red carpet for their guests, and on his last visit he had received a personal tour by one of the owners.

"Mmmm...you weren't exaggerating one bit Jack; the shrimp is simply delicious," Samantha complimented.

"Yes -- I'm going to have to beg for the recipe. Perhaps it's not too late for me to change occupations." Hearty laughter almost choked the background music.

"They really put a lot of thought in their décor," Yvonne marveled.

"The art work is incredible," Jack admired. Along the perimeter of the walls, a series of large pictures were etched into the stones; they were drawn in vibrant colors each one telling its own story. He particularly liked one of the scenes; a group of adults were fleeing from a fire breathing dragon.

Flashbacks of his high school days stormed back. Jack recalled one particular camping trip with his co-ed physical education class. The trip's main purpose was to enhance their survival skills in the wilderness, but the students had their own agenda in mind. They simply wanted to have a good time. He remembered partying almost till the crack of dawn. Some of their former group: Nick, David, Jessica, Stephanie, and John huddled around the campfire. At last, they were enjoying their freedom; they joked amongst themselves while chugging down the illicit rum and cola. In the background, they could only hear the non-stop chirping of crickets. The party escalated as a few joints were passed around the group. Its pungent effect soon clouded their minds and sound judgment. The mood was mellow, and at times the group's wild laughter took on a ritualistic chant; they were now half stoned. The good times seemed to roll on with no end in sight. All eyes were focused on the roaring flames with marshmallows gently roasting above the crackling fire.

Many had succumbed to the comforts of sleep when a loud shrill sounded from the far distance. The cries seemed to be coming from an easterly direction, just outside of the ground's perimeter. Unfortunately, the screams woke everyone including the teachers. The night was lit by a full moon making visibility clear within about fifty yards.

'There they are!' hollered Peter. Nick desperately clung onto Jessica's arm for dear life. Jessica must have lost her balance and slipped on the rocks and was in danger of being swept away by the raging torrent. John raced towards Nick helping him to pull her onto the hill and out of harms way.

Everyone breathed a sigh of relief as tragedy was averted. Jessica stood trembling partly from shock, but also from her exposure to the frigid waters. They covered her in blankets, but she was still shaking like a leaf. 'Are you okay?' asked Mr. Smith, the physical education teacher, who saw Jessica cowering. She nodded as her jaws still rattled uncontrollably. Miraculously, Jessica was lucky to have escaped with minor scratches and bruises to her body. The incident unfortunately led to the discovery of the liquor and pot. Even after all these years, Jack clearly recalled how livid the teachers, parents, and the school principal had all been.

"Are you okay Jack?" Yvonne keenly sensed his distress.

"Sorry, I was just thinking back." Jack awoke from his daydream slightly embarrassed.

They all ordered dessert and were given fortune cookies. Samantha quickly crushed hers open.

"Well don't keep us in suspense," Yvonne urged.

"It reads, a special friend will soon come into your life."

"Well, you're going to have to keep us posted," Yvonne remarked. They all laughed. Yvonne no longer could take the suspense and opened hers. She tried hiding it, but Henri cut in.

"That's not fair, come on!" he nudged Yvonne while looking over her shoulder trying to peak.

"Okay, expect a wonderful surprise," Henri winked at her.

It was Henri's turn to share his fortune, "Your heart is filled with desires."

"And just what kind of desires may those be?" Jack teased, drawing more laughter and attention to their table once more.

"Okay Jack, your turn," Yvonne waited in suspense as Jack seemed hesitant to relay his fortune.

"Your future looks rosy," Jack pondered this for a moment.

They finished their dessert as they continued joking with one another. Jack realized it was getting late and needed a good nights rest. "We should do this again," Jack suggested.

"Yes, it's a great place," Henri added. "Perhaps we can get together around Christmas time."

"Now that you mention it, I'm having a New Year's Eve Party, and of course you're all invited. Anyways I should get going, since I have a long day ahead of me tomorrow," Jack relayed. "I will see you on Monday, but thanks for thinking of me."

"Our thoughts will be with you tomorrow," Yvonne kissed him on the cheek. Samantha left shortly afterwards.

"I think Jack enjoyed the evening," Yvonne observed.

"Yes, he was in much better spirits. Samantha seemed to rather enjoy herself, and if I didn't know any better I would say she has a crush on Jack."

"Really!" Yvonne exclaimed. "I guess we'll wait and see if anything develops."

"By the way, how are things going at work?" Henri asked concerned.

"Okay, I guess."

Henri did not want to cause any waves, but noticed Samantha's jealousy surfacing a couple of times throughout the evening. *If I was working with her, I would certainly watch my back,* Henri thought. Just as he thought this, it occurred to him that Samantha may have been responsible for the missing file.

They walked outside hand in hand. "Do you know I've been waiting all night to kiss you?" Henri held her tightly.

"Perhaps you would like to come over, but only if you promise to behave yourself," Yvonne invited flirtatiously.

"Now, that all depends by what you mean by properly behaved," Henri retorted playfully.

They had barely stepped in when Henri passionately parted her lips. Yvonne's head spun dizzily not quite sure if her feet were still planted on the floor. Henri could have held her forever, but tonight he had something quite special in mind. Yvonne led him into the living room. "Help yourself to a drink," He saw the bottle of champagne in the ice-bucket and thought it was an appropriate choice for the occasion. He carried the glasses and set them on the coffee table and waited patiently for her. She strolled into the room diligently balancing one platter of potato chips in one hand and an assortment of nuts in the other.

"Come and sit here next to me," Henri gently pulled her towards him. I would like to make a toast," he reached into his pocket and carefully pulled out a small royal blue box. Henri gently squeezed her hand, before placing it into her palm. It was elaborately tied with gold and silver tassels.

Yvonne was pleasantly surprised by the small gift leaving her mesmerized.

"Well, you're going to have to open it to see what's inside," urged Henri. As she began untying the ribbon Henri continued. "You've brought so much joy and happiness into my life, and lately I've spent almost every waking moment thinking of you. I'm madly in love with you, and I would like us to share the rest of our lives together. I hope you'll accept this token as my commitment to you."

Yvonne's hands trembled from excitement. The lid sprung open and many dazzling colors shone out at her, although Yvonne glowed brighter than the ring. "Ohhh, Henri -- it's magnificent." She looked lovingly into his eyes before admiring her ring. The centre stone was a stunning princess cut diamond. She was positively euphoric and felt tears of joy trickling down her cheeks.

Henri lifted her chin towards him and asked affectionately, "Yvonne will you marry me?" Never before was she overcome with such intense emotion rendering her literally motionless and speechless. Henri fell silent. It was only when her eyes firmly tightened, causing more tears to spill, that he understood. He softly kissed each of them away holding her close to him.

Her lips quivered. It took a few moments before she regained her composure. "By the way, I'd love to spend the rest of my life with you." Yvonne finally managed while brushing her tears aside.

His fingers softly caressed her sensuous lips. She looked lovingly into his eyes and felt her head spin and limbs weaken. He drew her closer to him aroused by her tantalizing perfume. Henri could feel her sweet breath upon him. Softly, he parted her lips as he explored and tasted her sweet breath. Gently, he then laid her on the couch. "Henri, I just love when you do that," she whispered in between breaths while stroking his hair and drawing him closer. She felt a deep longing build within her, arching her neck as he continued to kiss and caress her. She held him tighter as he continued to explore her. A burning passion intensified as he gently pushed her blouse aside.

Yvonne felt warm and loving in his arms. It had been a magical evening for both of them, and one which they both would remember forever.

Yvonne took time to admire her ring. "You know what this means?" she asked rhetorically.

"That you are all mine because I certainly won't share you."

"The feeling is mutual. But more importantly, who'll wash the dishes?" she laughed.

"We'll just make sure we eat from paper plates starting today," Henri cleverly responded.

"Would you like some coffee?"

"Okay, but I better help. I don't want that pretty ring of yours getting damaged."

"Good and while we are at it you can tell me all about your past, all your secrets, and especially everything about your past lovers."

"Well all the ladies from my past have remained in the past from the very first day I met you. I love you and only you," she could see the sincerity written on his face.

"If you keep up the good work I'll throw in a couple of cookies for good measure."

"In that case, I have a lot of more good things to add."

Jack wanted to shower before he went to bed. He felt edgy thinking about tomorrow, even though he wanted to pay his last respects, a part of him wished he didn't have to attend. It would be emotionally draining, not to mention heart-breaking watching the family face their tragic loss, but he couldn't imagine them facing such a loss alone. He believed family and friends needed to be together especially in times of crisis.

Jack dawdled longer than usual in the hot shower helping to release some of his tension. He toweled his face dry and could faintly hear the scraping sounds of stubble. It was due time for a shave. He caught part of his reflection in the family heirloom. It was disguised by a film of steam, staring at the mirror brought back flashbacks of his own childhood days in England.

Back then, Jack was carefree with little responsibilities or worries. The most leisurely time had been spent at his Grandma's farm in Birmingham, England. It was a modest farm of twenty-five acres, with a river supplying fresh water for the animals as well as an irrigation source. He remembered her waking up at the crack of dawn to feed all the farm animals. Several of the roosters could be heard as early as five o'clock in the morning, and even though the farm house was over one hundred feet away, there was no chance of mistaking their demands. Along with the chickens, she raised goats and cattle, which supplied Grandma with fresh cheese and milk. At one end of the barn, she kept Harvey, the bull, along with several pigs.

Jack loved to be outdoors. He got attached to the animals and hated seeing Grandma behead his friends. One morning after she made him breakfast, she slipped on a red plaid apron. Jack's anxiety grew realizing Grandma's intentions. A cold shiver shot through him, as he caught a gleam of the large butcher knife that grandma clenched tightly in her hand. It was a short walk to the chicken coop, and she calmly opened the door. The chickens scurried away trying to flee a tragic death. Unfortunately, she successfully managed to capture her victim; it was a fair sized rooster. The rooster instinctively knew that its demise was imminent and tried fervently to free itself. And in dire hopes gave his Grandma a good peck in the leg. She cursed out loud and tugged even harder. Mandy, the Yorkshire terrier, followed both of them in hot pursuit. Although once Mandy caught the gleam of the sharp edge, she quickly recalled past events and scurried away in a corner. Jack looked over to make sure the dog was okay and noticed her paws shielding its eyes wishing to block out the grotesque scene.

She yanked the rooster upside down by its legs, and headed for the abattoir. In one clean swipe, the severed head plopped to the ground, bounced around several times, before abruptly coming to a standstill in an upright position. It looked at each of them, unforgiving, cursing them for their sins. Blood was splattered everywhere and a large pool had formed around Grandma Fanny's feet. It was so horrific and gory that Jack swore never to witness his Grandma's butchery ever again.

He hurried outside feeling nauseous and desperately tried to purge the bloody image from his mind. All the running made him thirsty, he raced for the well. Jack used the protruding stones as climbing blocks; he was still fairly short at just nine years of age. He reached the top and was leaning over, and somehow his shirt inadvertently caught on a jagged stone. He needed his arms to support himself, or else he would topple head first into the well. If he tried to pry himself loose he was afraid of losing his balance and falling in. Jack was in a state of panic. He was quickly tiring and his tummy was sore. Luckily, his grandmother was looking for him and saw Jack dangling dangerously over the edge. "Hold on Jack, I'm coming!" her voice echoed throughout the well. "Don't move. I've got you." She grabbed his shirt firmly and tugged with all her might. His shirt was stretched to the max, nearly tearing, but luckily his Grandma was able to rescue him.

He remembered her hugging and kissing him, just grateful that he hadn't fallen in. She became very stern and made him promise never to do that again. And that was one promise he kept.

Jack admired himself in the mirror; unfortunately those lax carefree days were gone forever.

The white bird flew gracefully overhead just as the back door of the hearse was opened; only the Chief knew both its direction and objective. His heart grieved with his friend, but his mind was in over-drive. The Chief was totally committed in cracking the case; never in his entire career had he felt so driven almost to the point of obsession. He was a man on a mission and nothing or no one was going to steer him off course. Others wearily feared that he may have reached the point of no return. Although deservedly, he was well respected on the force and his accomplishments spoke for themselves; a growing frustration and agonizing pain left an unsavory taste in the Chief's mouth. He sought justice, but somehow bittersweet revenge had a nicer ring to it. A host of questions haunted the Chief. *Would her family ever recover and be able to move on? How realistic was the possibility of them ever finding inner peace?* He shuddered knowing full well some monster was lurking in the shadows ready to bludgeon the next poor unsuspecting soul.

He had thoroughly read the autopsy report, which offered very few leads. It steered them in a certain direction. In all probability the killer was male, six feet, strong, and most likely acted alone. *What had been the motive?* This daunting question was perhaps the greatest enigma to all of their yet unanswered ones. The Chief's attention was momentarily reverted to the coffin being removed from the hearse. They were happily married for years, well respected in the community with no apparent enemies. Dianne was a gentle warm loving person whose main interest was in raising a family. Tyler, a dedicated surgeon, spent countless hours in the emergency ward. God only knows how many lives were spared because of his generous contribution of overtime and expertise. Certainly the facts didn't justify this horrible crime. *What diabolical series of events led to her murder? Could it have been a religious fanatic?* This would explain the rationale behind the rosary, the river, and the rose. Certainly, a lot of R's to swallow. *Also, why was the killer so enraged that he stabbed her through the heart?* They had already interviewed a list of suspects both at the time of her disappearance and after her corpse had been found. The Chief had been trained to deduce the killer from a process of elimination, rather than assume incorrectly one way or another. He couldn't pin-point exactly what, but something was gnawing at him.

Slowly, a group of six pal-bearers wheeled the coffin down the center aisle to the front of the church. The pal-bearers left their positions and the priest blessed the coffin with sprinkles of holy water.

A rounded archway led Jack into the church. He wasn't surprised to see the entire church packed with family and friends. As he glanced around, he saw Pete Waters sitting in the second last pew. He quietly took a seat next to him.

"Jack, how are you?" Pete whispered shaking Jack's hand.

"Okay, good to see you, it's been awhile."

"Yes, work and family keeps me busy."

"Yeah, I can imagine."

Its structure extended two hundred feet in length just for mass services, but the church had smaller private rooms. Just as Jack was admiring the church's interior, his gaze froze. He caught sight of the bird's silhouette through the stained glass, perched on an over-hanging branch.

"It's not enough…" the priest continued quite loudly redirecting Jack's attention. The church was completely packed with loved ones. He glanced over at Tyler and the children. It was difficult and depressing watching them grieve. No wonder Jack felt a radiant heat sweep throughout his body, leaving him feeling rather uncomfortable. From the corner of his eye, he caught sight of the bird again. He believed it was the same one, but the stained glass prevented him from being certain.

Jack tried to concentrate as a family member delivered a touching eulogy, recounting the wonderful times they'd once shared. "Dianne was a beautiful person treasured by her children and loved by all those close to her," she continued trying very hard to keep her voice steady.

Tyler's mind drifted; he remembered the first time he met Dianne. He was mesmerized by her golden locks. Her tranquil green eyes were a reflection of her calm and pleasant demeanor, and her kindness paralleled her beauty intensifying his attraction to her.

"We'll always remember and cherish her wonderful, generous and endearing qualities. She…"

Cindy burst into tears. Her cousin, Lisa, *froze in mid-speech,* as she watched Cindy fly off her seat and storm towards the coffin. Inadvertently it swayed perilously. Everyone sat listless, helplessly frozen in their seats as they watched the young child cradling the coffin.

"I don't want you to go mommy, I miss you. Please don't leave me, I love you so much," she continued pleading in an agonizingly desperate tone while embracing the coffin. It was heart-wrenching for everyone to watch as she continued to cry uncontrollably.

Tyler rose. His heart ached as he tried to comfort his young daughter. He whispered soothing words into Cindy's ear and then hugged her, managing to calm her down. Overcome with tears himself, Tyler embraced Cindy before being reseated.

The priest ended his sermon with some comforting words to them. Tyler was grateful there had been no wake. His children could not endure all the emotional duress and just the mere thought of never seeing their mother again was too much to bear.

Tyler stepped outside oblivious to the overcast skies. His heart was filled with much gloom and doom matching the skies intensity. They rode silently in the limousine, keeping a safe distance behind the hearse as it headed to the mausoleum. Tyler felt some comfort knowing he was able to grant Dianne one last wish. Dianne had feared worms and the thought of being buried had been appalling.

"Will I ever see mommy again?" lamented Christopher breaking the eerie silence.

"We'll come and visit every Sunday. But, I want you both to remember that your mom will always love you. She will always live in your hearts."

"Why would someone want to hurt mommy?" Christopher continued. Dianne's death had been splashed all over the media. It was remarkable how much children picked up.

"I hope they catch him and put him in jail for the rest of his life," retorted Cindy contemptuously before Tyler could respond. Tyler wished him a much worse fate, but didn't elaborate.

The limousine pulled into the cemetery. Tyler sighed. The duress was overbearing, and all he wanted was to put this great affliction behind them, and continue their lives in a somewhat normal fashion. But, therapy was a distinct possibility. He didn't want his children to grow up being angry, resentful, or fearful.

He listened as the priest gave a short prayer, before dabbing holy water onto the coffin for the last time. Dianne's coffin was hoisted into the crypt and several attendants took great care in sealing it shut. The children left a dozen roses for their mother. Cindy placed the roses close to her heart, kissing them before setting them next to Christopher's.

Father Abby ended the ceremony, and then as instructed invited guests to Aunt Becky's home. Guests formed in a single file waiting to express their condolences to the family. Jack took his place and waited patiently, "I'm very sorry," stated Jack with a sullen look, barely able to maintain eye contact. He noticed Tyler's pale complexion. Tyler remained speechless, but acknowledged Jack with a slight nod and a weak handshake. Tyler was touched by the vast number of attendees, and was filled with an inner peace knowing many had traveled from all over the world to pay their final respects.

Inconspicuously, the Chief watched from a respectable distance while jotting notes.

Chief Williams strode into the conference room carrying a heavy burden. It had been a very trying morning and a painful first step, but a necessary one in order for the family to accept their loss and be able to move on. The Investigative Team was mindful of the Chief's somber mood. But despite his loss, Sean could not help but feel that something in particular was bothering him.

"Sorry, I'm running a bit late. I understand we need to go over some details," he stated.

"We did find this at the crime scene," Terry held the plastic bag in mid-air. "It appears to be a small metal fragment from a shovel. We've checked with forensics and it's not ours, and at this point we're assuming it may belong to the killer. An educated guess leads me to believe it may have broken off while he was digging, probably hitting large rocks at the bottom of the burial ground. The fragment was covered with rust indicating it wasn't brand new. Since the shovel may contain other contaminants, we're having the soil tested at a lab in Denver, Colorado where they specialize in that field."

The Chief continued to listen keenly to the detective wondering if there were any other clues, which might apprehend the ruthless killer. "Was there any other evidence found at the scene?" the Chief anxiously waited while leaning on the edge of his seat.

"We did find a button, which we left at the lab; hopefully they'll be able to salvage some evidence."

"Basically what you are saying is we have damn little to go on," summarized the Chief flinging a piece of chalk at the blackboard.

Sean Anderson quickly glanced over his notes before he spoke, "It seems that the killer is a south paw." The trio literally looked astonished trying to figure out how the hell he was able to come up with such a deduction, since there was such little evidence and a half decomposed body. "Broken ribs were found on her right side. The killer probably forcefully grabbed the victim from behind and began to suffocate her with his right hand. He may have held her hostage with either a knife or gun in his left hand therefore muffling any of her cries or attempts of escape. The dislodging of the front teeth also indicates that the victim was grabbed from behind."

"Are you sure?" quizzed the Chief with a hint of skepticism.

"As positive as anyone can possibly be with any other piece of evidence. We also found a piece of white cloth on her retainer wire. It must have caught while the killer suffocated her. As you're already aware we found a rose along with a rosary, which was clasped in her hands on top of her stomach area."

Even though the evidence was minimal, the Chief felt a surge of relief knowing they were beginning to make some headway.

It was Steve's turn to shine. He quickly rose to his feet. His hair was no longer black, but heavily streaked with gray. But, many found it difficult to pinpoint his exact years with his dark full moustache. In a deep pensive mood, Steve began to confidently confer his discoveries. All eyes were firmly focused on him almost as if he was about to share some Godly discovery on how to create 'cold fusion'. He took a long sip of his coffee before speaking. "I've tried to build a profile of our killer as well as reconstruct the entire crime scene. The killer is most certainly a man. He stands at least six feet in height and is very powerful. He lives within a radius of ten miles of the park and is familiar with the park's grounds." Steve paused a moment to collect his thoughts. "The killer may also have relocated by this time, although this is highly unlikely. There must be a reason why he chose to bury his victim at the far end of the park's grounds. This area is obscure, nestled at the bottom of a rolling hill and apparently is the only area of the park whereby the ground is sandy next to the river. I'm guessing the remote area provided cover, while the ground's softness made it easier to bury the body without the killer overly exerting himself. We found no tire tracks, and hence I'm assuming the individual had the arduous task of carrying the body for three quarters of a mile. Thus, he must be extraordinarily fit. He most likely wrapped the body in a sack of some sort, to help reduce the stench, and carried it on his shoulder while holstering his excavating equipment over the other. In order to avoid being detected, he probably carried out his mission in the very early hours of the morning, since except for the road and perhaps lighting from a full moon there is virtually zero lighting throughout the park. Therefore, he probably wore night vision goggles to guide him. We still have to question a few individuals, but up to now no one has seen anything unusual, perhaps because the killer was intelligent and thought of wearing dark clothing. He had his mission well timed. It must have taken him about an hour to reach the designated area and perhaps approximately another hour to exit the park. Plus he had set enough time to bury her. Despite his apparent strength, he must have been exhausted from the long haul and most likely took a break."

The Chief listened attentively impressed by Steve's detailed re-enactment of the crime.

Steve continued, "The excavation probably went as planned assuming that the killer was prudent to pick a dry night instead of a rainy one, which would have made his feat more dangerous to complete. I'm estimating he completed this arduous task in three hours. The excavation area measured about three feet wide by six feet long by three feet deep. The killer stopped digging noticing that he hit a rock and assumed he would, most likely, continue to hit stony surfaces. He then laid the body into the grave placing the rosary between the fingers. He may have paused for a brief period at this point. Ironically, I'm guessing he's very religious in nature, but was overcome by some kind of insane madness possessing him to commit such a gruesome act. If my line of reasoning is correct, he probably considered the burial as her last resting place, and hence took time to pay his final respects. This may have taken anywhere from a few minutes to an hour. After this so called ceremony, he probably covered the body, but due to his religious belief this was done very carefully to ensure he didn't mar the body. Afterwards, he raked the ground to conceal the heinous crime. The time frame for all this is approximately five hours still ensuring him the cover of night. The killer probably stored the body at his home, since we do know from the autopsy report that she was not immediately buried. Before burying her, he most likely wrapped her body and placed her in a very cold cellar. Otherwise he wouldn't have been able to carry the body, let alone bury her; the stench would have been too overpowering. Since he needed to conceal the body, it leads me to believe that the killer either lives alone or had an accomplice. I prefer to think of the former as a more likely scenario given the evidence to date. It's quite likely that the killer knew the victim quite well and may even have felt some remorse after having committed the crime," Steve cleared his throat. "Therefore, he had to assume enough courage to complete his mission. During this period the individual would have been very edgy, distancing himself, perhaps even isolating himself from family and friends. He must live or did live in close proximity to Dianne's house driving her back to his home rather than driving her directly to the park," Steve backtracked. "I can't figure out the exact connection between the killer and the victim, but I'm assuming, now this is just a hunch, that they knew each other quite well either through a prior workplace or common friend.

The fact that her personal belongings were not stolen convinces me it wasn't a random murder. It was premeditated from beginning to end, to the very last detail. One of the only slip-ups that the killer has made, and I will refer to it as the 'Achilles' heel', is the button we found. Although, there is no certainty that it even belongs to the killer. He is prudent and thorough, and doesn't slip up very easily," a bewildered expression took a hold of Steve. Steve took another sip from his coffee. The Chief was absorbing all the details. "The best approach is to keep surveillance at the park, install hidden cameras, and keep a profile of all possible suspects visiting the park." The knock on the door momentarily interrupted Steve.

The forensic team had completed their investigation of the button. It was delivered back to them in a clear plastic bag along with a detailed report.

A puzzled expression surfaced on the Chief's face. He reached for the evidence bag with a solicitous grip. He could not pinpoint, but vaguely recalled it from somewhere. "I could swear I've seen this button before," he exclaimed as he stared intently.

"Actually now that you mention it, it does seem awfully familiar," Terry agreed. He set it down on the center of the desk in plain view for all to see. Their attention was momentarily distracted as the Chief opened the manila envelope and began reading its contents.

"We may have made some progress. A strand of hair was attached to the button," he enlightened the team. "They have completed DNA testing."

The Chief's eyes lit up and his entire facial expression took on a much calmer appearance. Finally, the cards had turned in their favor. It was now only a matter of time.

Chapter 6

Tic…Toc…Tic…Toc…Tic…Toc…

"Would you like a cup of coffee while you're waiting?" the butler offered.

"Sure," John mused over the countless artifacts displayed on the walls and souvenirs lining the furniture. It fell short of visiting a museum.

The butler returned and set the full tray on the desk. The silver shone brilliantly as if just recently polished. As John poured some coffee into his china cup the aroma of the strong full bodied beans saturated the air.

Edward leisurely strolled into the room and graciously extended his hand. "Good to see you," he greeted.

"Likewise, I hope I'm not interrupting."

"Oh no, not at all."

John couldn't help but stare at the picture. Edward noticed his fascination. "It was one of the most famous saloons in American history," he explained. The picture hosted an old tavern with a huge sign posted in front of the building, which clearly read '*Wanted Dead or Alive*'. Next to it was a sketch of a young cowboy by the name of Jim Young. "His nickname though, was Young Gun and appropriately so. You see that's how the silver dollar lost its value." Edward let out a low chortle before continuing. John keenly noticed a hole shot through the middle of the coin; John enjoyed Edward's sense of humor. "A large sum was being wagered against Young Gun with almost the entire town participating. He was considered an underdog, partly because of his age, but mostly because of the class of shooters he was up against. Jim waited patiently with his Smith & Wesson six shooter holstered to his belt. They wagered that the gunman who could shoot the dollar in mid-air would be declared the winner. To make it more challenging, they implemented a rule that no one could draw his gun until the coin was tossed. Apparently, at twenty yards this wasn't such an easy feat. All the contestants had failed and it was now Young Gun's turn. His hand was quicker than the eye, and within a split second he successfully shot a bullet through the silver coin leaving only the outer rim visible. He was applauded and admired for his skill. I purchased both pictures at an art auction," Edward retold the legend.

"Make yourself comfortable, I know you had a lot on your mind on your last visit. Have you made any decisions?" Edward prompted.

"I've been thinking a lot about my future; especially my future with women. Part of me would like to meet someone, but I guess I'm still hopelessly clinging to the past. I know my wife would have wanted me to carry on."

"It seems something is tentatively holding you back," Edward's vast experience made him quite perceptive.

"I don't want to risk losing anyone else," John confessed in a worrisome tone.

"No one wants to lose someone they love or deeply care for, albeit that's a risk everyone needs to take, especially if they expect to meet someone," Edward interjected. Silence followed. Not only was it a difficult realization, but unfortunately a hard reality of life. "It's not only how much actual time or years we have spent with someone, but equally important it's the quality time shared with our significant others."

John felt enlightened. "I never thought of it from that perspective. Yes, you're quite right. We've shared many wonderful memories and I'll treasure those moments forever."

"Those memories are everlasting. You also shared a special bond, which no one can ever take away. Your bond had been a strong one; one which has helped you grow and become a better person. And if I may, some special lady is out there waiting to meet that new person," Edward encouraged.

He sat silent for quite some time absorbing Edward's words. Unaware of his fears, he had built a wall around himself. Perhaps, it was time to open that door; this thought gave John a warm inner glow.

"Yes, I guess I need to get out more," John's confidence was given a boost.

"Are you enrolled in any leisure activities?" Edward sensed that he was making progress.

"Now that you mention it, I don't go out much. Usually I just go home prepare dinner, watch TV, or work on a client's file," John knew the danger of all work and no play.

"See how you have been isolating yourself from everyone. It's very difficult to meet someone if you are living in your own world. I recall a time when you loved to socialize and were thrilled to interact with others." Edward gave a recount of the other person he had known.

"Perhaps, I should join a dating service. A couple of co-workers have successfully met their partners that way."

"In the meantime, I would suggest some old form of Japanese meditation as a means of relaxation." Edward rose and walked towards the bookshelf browsing briefly before finding the book. "If you would like to begin reading the first few chapters, it explains several relaxation techniques. It's an old form called jen as a means of *clearing* one's mind."

"I have appreciated all your advice and insight. I hope to have some good news to share with you soon."

"Well, according to the old saying, if at first you don't succeed, try and try again," Edward coached.

"Well, I'm not one to give up easily." John's voice shot up a notch and he straightened his chin almost as if his ego had been bruised. "Thanks again, I appreciate everything."

"I have full confidence in you. Keep me posted," Edward rose from his seat to accompany John to the door.

John decided against the same routine; tonight he was going out. But first, he would go home and change into some comfortable attire.

As he drove into the parking lot, he could hear the music. It was one of the biggest nightclubs in the area and it had undergone extensive renovations giving it a much brighter, cleaner, and a more modern appearance. The flashy new look lifted John's spirit.

John needed to mellow out and ordered a stiff drink. The bartender obliged by pouring him a scotch on the rocks. The drink helped him to relax and soon he felt the music vibrate throughout his body. Much time had elapsed since John's last visit, and he had almost forgotten the number of times he had gone home with his ears half-blocked. As he was enjoying his drink, he felt an odd sensation sweep through him. The temptation to swivel around was great, but he resisted this urge realizing it would be too obvious. Curiosity got the better of him and he could no longer hold out. He decided to act casual, and turn around slowly as if simply turning in his seat. After several movements, he faced her and their eyes met. He couldn't remember having seen such bright blue eyes. They were very inviting, overall she looked quite stunning. Her blond streaks were accentuated as the flashing lights bounced off her head. If anything, she looked more like a porcelain doll with her accentuated high cheekbones, snub rounded nose, and full lips. It was easy to admire her slender build from her sexy night-club attire. She gave John an enticing look which he acknowledged with a smile, and then with great ease she weaved through the crowd.

"Hi I'm Lily," she announced with a bright wide smile.

"John. Would you like a drink?" he politely offered.

"Sure hon, a strawberry daiquiri sounds great." John gestured to the bartender who returned with Lily's drink.

"I haven't seen you before handsome, is this your first time here?" she asked flirtatiously.

"Actually, I haven't been here in awhile," John admitted.

"Oh -- why?" John noticed she was direct and to the point.

"Work usually keeps me quite busy," he justified.

"Ohhh -- I like a man with ambition!" I bet you do, John thought to himself, raising his guard a notch. He wondered if she was a gold digger, but decided to play it cool. She openly flirted and rubbed herself against him; he felt a little uneasy, although he didn't want to completely brush her off and instead asked her to dance. She danced exceptionally well moving gracefully to the music's rhythm. John had to admit he was actually enjoying himself. They shared several dances together and before long, many other couples had joined them on the dance floor. The dance floor was now completely packed.

John excused himself and made his way to the bar; he continued to watch Lily who surprisingly possessed a bountiful amount of energy.

Minutes later she joined him. "You dance very well," complimented John as Lily plopped herself on the stool next to him.

"Gee thanks, I love music -- it makes me feel so alive. Even as a child, I loved to dance. My parents realized how much I enjoyed it and enrolled me in jazz and hip hop classes. I guess I was pretty good, since over the years I've brought home several trophies." John could barely hear and inched closer; the music was deafening. "Hey, you seem pretty fit yourself. Do you work out?"

"Actually, I do my best to hit the gym."

"So what else do you enjoy doing?" asked Lily, openly expressing her interest. She was not one to sit idly, but chased after her dreams, and John seemed like a good catch.

"Well -- I enjoy traveling, visiting museums, and I also enjoy cooking."

"You're the first man I've met who actually enjoys cooking," she relayed in a doubtful tone and questioning look. "Hon, are you sure you're not just pulling my leg?"

"Seriously, I do it almost every single night, but it's more out of necessity, or else I would be eating take-out every single night."

"So you work here in town?" Lily probed.

"Yes, work is just fifteen minutes from here, but enough about me. What do you do -- career wise?"

"I'm a travel agent and I work at the local mall. It seems like a life-time, but it will be four years next month. It's easy money and I meet a lot of interesting people. The one thing I really like about my work is I know the best places in the world to visit: the best hotels, beaches, and restaurants. Also, the perks are great; I get twenty percent off flights and hotels."

"Your work seems pretty interesting."

"It is, though the pay could be better. Sometimes I work part-time to make up for the wages."

"I'm surprised that someone as beautiful as you is alone tonight."

"I just broke up with my boyfriend."

"Sorry to hear that, perhaps you'll get back together."

"Not in this lifetime; he was such a creep. So, what are you doing later?"

John's ego was given a boost, but he had no intentions of misleading Lily. Despite her worldly appearance, John sensed a deep vulnerability. It was difficult refusing the offer and John struggled with it for about a minute. "Well, I should call it a night, since tomorrow will be a long day for me. I only came here tonight to have some fun and unwind."

She placed her hand on his shoulder, "You don't need to worry about hurting my feelings hon, I know how to survive." She made her way across the dance floor, and surprisingly within a couple of minutes had hooked up with another gentleman.

Jack woke to the sound of beautiful country music. He leisurely rolled halfway across the bed and stretched over to turn off the radio, when he felt a series of sharp pains piercing through his shoulder and lower back. Reluctantly, he slipped out of bed and carefully tip-toed downstairs.

He felt the warmth of the sun's rays. Surprisingly, the weather was holding up so well in late autumn.

While the coffee was brewing, Jack unlatched Tara's door. "Good morning, how are you my beautiful bird?"

"Good mornen," Tara's voice echoed throughout the kitchen. Jack chuckled. He stepped out to clean her water tube in the laundry room, and upon returning was amazed how quickly Tara had devoured her feed. While watching her, he poured himself a cup of coffee. Surprisingly, every movement was causing him great discomfort and he thought a hot shower would release some of his kinks.

Jack turned on the hot water tap enjoying the invigorating pulsating massage. A hot steam was building within the shower stall. It helped to unravel some of the tightness in his back.

"Damn!" Jack cursed as the bar of soap slipped clumsily from his hands. He turned blindly to pick it up, except a loud noise from downstairs distracted him. Unfortunately, he leapt before he looked. "Ahhh!" his agonizing wails carried throughout his home. Jack lost his balance. He unsuccessfully tried to regain his footing, but crashed hard into the back wall twisting his back. Luck deserted him even further; he banged his head on the way down. He felt a tingling sensation and cradled his head to shield himself from the intensifying pain. Moments later, he glanced up and saw the mirror swaying back and forth like a pendulum.

The room began to spin.

He struggled to turn off the tap with his left foot and felt his back muscles pulling; each exertion intensified his already excruciating pain. "Ahh -- ohh -- ahh," he moaned helplessly. Somehow, he managed to crawl out of the bathtub onto the cold ceramic floor while supporting himself against the bathroom's back wall. He fully extended his arm trying to reach his cell, which was clipped to his belt on the countertop. He never recalled being in so much agony. He needed an ambulance ASAP. After several attempts, he successfully yanked his pants next to him. It was hard for him to focus. He managed to dial 911. "Help -- this is Jack Tre--" Jack felt dizzy and struggled to speak.

"Sir, are you okay?" the attendant repeated himself.

"I fell in the shower…" Jack's head throbbed and the hard blow caused him to nearly pass out.

After a short time, Jack heard noises followed by voices. Luckily, the alarm had been disarmed. He managed to relay the location of the secret key, hidden beneath the rock. "Hello, hello…we are the paramedics," they hollered from the bottom of the stairs.

Jack's head pounded as he spoke, "I'm upstairs, second door…to your left." They carried the stretcher along the length of the staircase.

"How are you feeling?"

"Ohhh…my head, I banged it against the wall." They checked his vital signs and examined him for broken bones.

"It appears that nothing is broken. But, we're going to place you on this stretcher and take you to the hospital."

Jack could not recall how, but the paramedics maneuvered him onto a stretcher without causing him further discomfort. All he wanted was to cradle his head; the pain was simply unbearable. Jack opened and closed his eyes trying to shut out the blurriness. He felt himself drift in and out of consciousness.

"John is that you?" asked Jack apprehensively.

"Sir just relax, I'm going to shine this light into your eyes." The paramedic had to physically hold his eyelids open. Jack winced. "We're going to take you to the hospital, just hang in there. You may have suffered a concussion."

"My head feels like it's going to explode; I can't take the pain, it's killing me," Jack pleaded.

"We need an injection of morphine, now!" the paramedic called out to his partner. It took several minutes before Jack felt the medications effect. They carried him downstairs.

It stared intently at Jack with a cynical conviction. From one blurry image it somehow diverged into two distorted images of John. They looked at each other and seemingly agreed to converge towards Jack. He shook his head desperately trying to block out the contortions. But they continued relentlessly. "We know what you've done, what you're thinking," they communicated with him. Jack shut his eyes hoping the images would disappear. Once he reopened his eyes, the images seemed even more threatening. Their teeth were clenched and their hands were in position to strangle him. "You can't escape us; we'll always find you -- always," they threatened in unison. They lunged at Jack. He barely escaped, managing to move his head to his left.

Jack be swift; Jack be quick. "Get away from me!" Jack begged while shielding himself with both arms.

"Take it easy; you'll be okay," the paramedics comforted while hoisting him into the ambulance.

"Did -- did you see him?" Jack looked horrified.

The paramedics looked dumbfounded. "Please, just take it easy."

Jack desperately needed an escape; he closed his eyes to cut off the distorted images.

The ambulance siren screamed as they rushed him to the hospital. They notified the emergency department that they would be arriving shortly. Luckily it was still early morning, only shortly after 8:00 am, and the hospital remained fairly quiet without the usual long line-ups. Upon Jack's arrival, the nurse immediately wheeled him to the MRI department. Jack lay underneath the imaging device to be tested for possible traumas to the head. Despite the applied ice-packs, his head had already swollen considerably.

It took about a half an hour for a series of tests to be completed. Dr. Adams introduced himself and quickly began his questioning. "Are you presently on any medication?"

"No, what's happening? Will I be going home soon?" Jack was semi-coherent.

"We'll need to run some tests to confirm the extent of your injuries, if any. In any case, I'd prefer if you'll stay for a few days. I'll have the neurologist visit you. One of the nurses will wheel you to your room, just relax until then."

Jack never liked hospitals and even worse he hated lying in bed. "Ouch," Jack winced at his painful attempt to turn onto his right side. Perhaps one of the nurses could help him make some phone calls. He definitely needed to call his parents and ask them if they could take care of Tara as well as notifying

Fernheights; he dreaded the thought of being away from work. He prayed his test results would come back negative.

His accident could not have happened at a worse time, just as he was finalizing the mall's make-over. The account was significant and the company could ill afford to lose it. The success and future of Fernheights hinged on positive results and lame excuses were not tolerated, as word spread quickly among the corporate giants. Luckily for the past several weeks, Jack had poured so much time and energy pushing him well ahead of schedule.

It became increasingly difficult for Jack to remain awake, feeling his eyelids gradually become heavier, and he unwillingly surrendered to the comforts of sleep.

Hours later he awakened, and was pleasantly surprised. Jack was secretly admiring her; he had never seen anyone more beautiful. Her golden hair was tied up in a neat bun. She was petite and stood no taller than five-four with a slim build. Two bright rosy cheeks accentuated her rounded face. Her lips were sensuous and inviting but her hazel eyes were equally captivating. She moved about gracefully, like a ballerina. He quickly closed his eyes as she approached closer, slyly feigning to awaken.

"I must have died and gone to heaven!" Jack openly expressed his interest.

Jackie blushed, "Well Mr. Trempton, I see you still have your spirits. My name's Jackie. I need to check your blood pressure." She raised his bed slowly aware that he had suffered a back injury and then read the monitor while jotting the information on his chart. "These two tablets will help ease the pain," she explained.

Her soft voice and gentleness were very soothing and Jack could not figure out if it was her beauty which had him surrender his heart, or if it was her gentleness. He decided it was a bit of both. Jack wanted to know more about her as he certainly believed in the saying, '*love at first sight*'.

"I'll be back later to take you for X-rays. We'll need to know the extent of your back injury, but for now just continue to rest. If you need anything urgently, please press this button and a nurse will be right with you."

Jack pressed the button and maintained a serious demeanor. Jackie folded over her arms and frowned at him, "I mean when a nurse isn't present."

"Sorry, excuse my humor. I need to call my parents and let them know what happened. They'll have to take care of my pet parrot, Tara, and I also need to notify my work." Jackie dialed. The phone rang three times before his mother answered.

"Hi mom -- How's everything?"

"Son, it's good to hear from you. How are you?"

"Fine, but I had a little accident in the shower this morning. I slipped and hit my head."

"Oh my God! Are you okay?" his mom panicked.

"Mom don't worry, I'll be fine. I'm at the local hospital where they're running some tests, just as a precaution."

"Your father and I will be right over."

"Mom, really I'm okay. You don't have to worry, I'm in good hands." Jackie could not help but smirk, displaying her cute little dimples.

"I'm sure you'll be fine, nonetheless we're still coming over." Jack knew better than to argue with his mother. Once she got something in her head, it was game over. "Is there anything I can get you?"

"Actually, I'll probably need a few undergarments, my robe, and my shaving kit. And I would greatly appreciate if you could take care of Tara."

"We always love to have her. She's adorable."

Jackie stepped back into the room. "Is there anything else I can help you with?"

"I need to notify my office that I'll be out of commission for at least a couple of days, but will return as soon as possible."

"Jack you shouldn't be rushing back; we're still waiting for your test results." A genuine look washed over her. Jack placed the call with Jackie's help.

"Can you do me one last favor?"

"Sure."

"I'd like to rest and wouldn't mind having the TV turned off. I'm feeling rather tired."

Jackie quietly left.

Curiously, he took a good long look at him. A fully dressed clown appeared unexpectedly at his door. He wore a white hat with different colored polka dots topped with a blue bon-bon. His identity was concealed behind a red-bulb nose and bright facial colorings. In his right hand, he held onto a string of balloons splashed in a rainbow of colors. The balloons were dressed in images of cuddly animals including: adorable kittens, puppies, and ducklings. The figure made Jack smile.

"How are you today?" asked Jack jovially wondering whose idea it was to send the clown.

"I'm fine," chuckled the clown. "But more importantly how are you doing?"

"Considering the circumstances, I'm lucky to be having this conversation," Jack teased knowing full well he could have cracked his head on the porcelain tiles earlier. "Did someone send you here?" Jack's curiosity heightened.

"Well, I'm here to bring joy and happiness to all the boys and girls. Everybody needs some cheering up, especially in times of sadness and distress," he tugged at the strings admiring the balloons up and down bobbing motion. The clown's face broke into a wide smile.

"Not that I don't appreciate your kindness, but don't you think I'm a tad too old for this?" Jack tried to maintain a serious composure, but nearly burst at the seams.

"Now, now Jack, we all have an inner child within us. Once in awhile that child needs nurturing for us to remain fulfilled. Otherwise, life loses its true meaning and we lose all enjoyment and satisfaction from our everyday routine." Jack was taken aback. *How did the clown know his name? He hadn't introduced himself. How did he know about his current situation and what he was feeling?*

"How do you know all this?" anxiety was seething into Jack faster than the bizarre situation was unfolding.

"That's not important my dear friend, but however something else is of greater importance," the clown stressed leaning his head forward with the balloons dancing gracefully in front of him.

He gently raised his head and parted the sea of balloons, now a wide sly grin appeared on his face from ear to ear. He began singing in a chant like way:

Jack fell down and hit his head,
Now he's in pain and sick in bed.
Better be careful not to repeat this feat,
Otherwise you may well go down in defeat.
The year is not quite over yet,
Don't take life for granted or think anything's a sure bet.
Fear and anxiety prey unmercifully on a man's heart,
His mind wanders aimlessly, hoping it will part.
Eventually everything escalates to a point of doom,
Hopefully for you the end is not right here in this room.

Jack was overcome with fear. His uneasiness escalated as he watched the transformation in sheer horror. *This can't be real, come on snap out of it.* Jack felt in a dream-like state and shook his head violently, desperately trying to purge the image, but his horror intensified as he watched helplessly in utter disbelief. The bright cheery colors of the clown's face paled and were being transfigured by morbid patches of grays and browns. Its face lost its firmness; it began to decompose with flesh rotting and peeling away like that of a decaying corpse. It opened its mouth wide revealing a set of sharply pointed fangs, and his eyes were bloodshot. It shot forth a contemptuous glare filled with bitter rage, Jack snapped back with such intensity his spinal cord felt like it would snap. "Hahahahaaaa!" He laughed wildly at Jack. The soft colors of the balloons had turned a deep crimson and the cuddly animals had transformed into demon-like creatures, which were now growling fiercely at him. His heart raced a mile a minute. He feared for his life sensing the fiend was about to devour him, but there was nowhere to run. Dozens of snakes slithered over the figures, hissing and lunging closer. The clown and his army of demons were advancing closer and closer.

Jack panicked.

His mind raced furiously begging for his limbs to move quickly out of harms way, but his body felt like lead, firmly strapped to the bed. *God please let me get up,* he thought, but his nerves were completely paralyzed with fear offering no mercy. It was approaching closer and closer. "Soon we will become one!" the gruesome figure asserted in a threatening tone. Jack's terror increased; his demise was imminent. Perspiration trickled down his spine, he breathed heavily like each gasp was his last breath and his eyes were glazed wide open.

"Get away from me...HELP!" Jack managed to scream at the top of his lungs.

Within seconds, two of the attending nurses rushed into the room and noted his agitated state. "Mr. Trempton is everything alright?" He was visibly shaken and couldn't answer; he was certain it hadn't been a bad dream, but the skeleton had simply vanished. The nurses noticed his ashen complexion and his frozen stare reflected sheer terror. They moved quickly to take his blood pressure and measure his heart rate. Both were abnormally high.

"Just relax, Mr. Trempton. Is everything okay?

Jack was deeply embarrassed and wasn't exactly sure what he should tell them. "It was just a nightmare. Sorry, I didn't mean to cause such a commotion," Jack barely managed to reply, while his chest heaved beneath the covers.

"Its okay, it's not uncommon after a head trauma. Your results should be in shortly, and we'll know the full extent of your injuries. In the meantime, we'll have a nurse check on frequently. Remember if you feel any pain or your symptoms change just press the ringer," the nurse reassured before leaving.

Jack felt a surge of relief seeing his parents enter the room. After his scare, he forgot they would be dropping by. "Oh son," cried his mother rushing towards him.

"Mom, really I'm fine," Jack stressed half embarrassed.

"Son your head is pretty swollen."

"Yes, I hit my head hard against the wall after slipping on a bar of soap. I'm beginning to feel better since they've given me some pain killers."

"Did you break anything?" his father recalled a similar accident which injured his brother.

"The doctors don't think so, but as a precaution they took X-rays. Did you have a chance to drop by my house?"

"Yes, I'll set the bag on the chair here, and don't worry Tara is a real treat. Speaking of treats, here are some balloons from

the friendly clown who is collecting money for the hospital."
Jack's complexion turned just as white as his bed sheets. His
mother noticed his ashen complexion.

"Son you don't look so good, we'd better call the nurse."

Sean parked his blue Corvette in the parking lot adjacent to
the park's entrance and spotted Terry and Steve by the picnic
table. It was going to be a very long night, and Sean had been
grateful for his two hour nap. "Well, I guess we're in for a long
haul," Sean sighed in anticipation.

"We've got our work cut out," Steve acknowledged. "We'll
be here until at least the wee hours of the morning," he added
glancing at his wrist-watch, "It's now four o'clock; perhaps we
should grab some dinner before the mock burial."

Terry carried the artist's roll, which included several aerial
photographs of the park. She unraveled one of them and rolled
it flat on the picnic table; she spotted the river bank including
the body's burial spot. The photographs would help outline the
killer's most probable path.

"We're going to have some cameras installed on the pine
trees near the park's entrance," Steve pointed to the specific
areas.

"Shouldn't we have someone keeping surveillance?" Terry
wondered.

"Look over to your left and take note of the gentleman in the
blue sports jacket, he's an undercover officer," answered Sean.

Officer Quinlan had served ten years with the police force,
much of that time spent on undercover assignments. The force
acknowledged his skills and his exceptionally keen eyes.
Nothing or no one would escape him.

The spray paint marked the probable path taken by the
killer. It was nearly a mile walk and by the time they reached

the top of the hill, Detective Black was panting. His asthma was further aggravated from having just walked at a very brisk pace.

"Are you okay?" inquired Terry with a nervous expression.

"Yeah, I'll be fine," he managed while still gasping for air. He dug into his pocket and pulled out his puffer.

The yellow police ribbon was still tightly secured around the crime scene. "Here we are," Terry pointed to the small secluded area where the body had been found.

"I can't imagine any fool in their right mind wanting to carry a body this far. Even if I loved someone to death, no pun intended, I wouldn't carry it this distance," scoffed Sean. Terry and Steve smirked.

"Let's begin by questioning the employees," Terry suggested.

"Okay, let's start with the groundskeeper," Sean interjected.

"Perhaps he has seen something?" Steve remained hopeful.

"Yes, he may even have come across important clues, but may have also remained oblivious to such evidence. There's one slight drawback; Tommy has a learning disability," Sean remarked.

Barry, the manager of the park left his office to greet the detectives. A young man followed closely behind, partially concealed by Barry. Barry introduced himself as well as Tommy. "I'm just finishing some paperwork. I understand you also wish to speak to me," Barry acknowledged.

"Yes, we'll come by your office later," informed Sean.

Barry turned to face Tommy. "Tommy these detectives need to ask you some important questions. Please, tell them everything you can remember," Barry counseled Tommy while giving him a friendly pat on the back.

"Hi, my name is Sean. Let's sit at the picnic table where we'll be more comfortable."

It was a cool autumn day and the trees were stripped of their foliage, leaving only branches to sway in the gentle breeze. The park's grounds hosted beautiful red and gold tones. One could easily hear the crunching sounds underfoot.

"We just want to ask you a few questions," Sean explained.

"Am I in trouble?" Tommy looked worried and cringed his nose.

"No, we are hoping you can help us. I'd like for you to think back to this summer, during the month of July."

"Yes, we have a lot of barbecues in the summer. My favorite is hamburgers."

"Yes, they're pretty good," coaxed Sean. "Tommy, what time do you begin work?"

"Uh -- I begin at 4:00."

"Are these your regular working hours, even during the summer?"

"Yes, I always have the same shift. Barry says to have routine -- routine is good." Tommy's hand gestures could almost be predicted. He would scratch his head before answering each question, almost as if the motion would magically produce the answer.

"Do you take care of the park all by yourself?" Sean continued probing for answers.

"No, Mike also works here."

"Does he work with you?"

"No, he works before my shift. Barry says I need to work hard, make a man out of me."

"Yes, I'm sure you work very hard. Tommy do you remember anyone doing something bad in the summer, like hurting someone?"

"No, Barry tells me to go to him if someone is hurt or being bad. I'm good, I listen to Barry. Barry is my friend."

"Yes, and you do a wonderful job of taking care of the park. Barry must be very happy with you." Tommy had a huge grin on his face, especially with each mention of his boss. "Do you remember someone carrying tools with him or heavy baggage?"

Tommy stopped to think. "No."

"Do many people come to the park late at night?"

"No, people leave before too dark -- too scary at night," Tommy covered his eyes while peeping between his fingers.

"What time do people usually leave?"

"Before it's too dark, bogeyman comes out late at night."

"Do you remember seeing anyone real late at night, around 12:00?"

"Nope."

"Okay, but if you remember someone having done something bad will you please call us," Sean handed him a business card. "We'd like to thank you for answering all of our questions."

Tommy had a huge smile on his face. He picked up an old carton with the sweeper and placed it over the centre of the garbage bin before dumping it.

It was a peaceful stroll to the shed and Steve marveled at nature's creation. Several birds could still be heard chirping. He found the view very therapeutic helping him to temporarily forget life's constant pressures. The shed was nestled within a cluster of trees and was quite large, appearing more like a cottage. It had several large windows giving Barry different directional views, the roof was sloped and protected with shingles, and its walls were finished with aluminum siding.

Barry noticed the detectives, and waved them in before they even had a chance to knock. "Please make yourselves comfortable," he invited while folding open some chairs. As Sean seated himself he noted Barry's muscular build. He towered a few inches taller, and Sean calculated his height to be about six-feet-four.

"May I use the washroom?" asked Sean.

"Sure, down the hall to your left," Barry directed. Sean accidentally missed the washroom door, and was about to do a one eighty when he stopped abruptly. He noticed the back wall lined with a medley of tools, Sean quietly poked around. *Shit, why didn't I think of this before*? On the back of the door a cardigan and a couple of other jackets hung from several hooks; one of the jackets had Barry's name tag sewn on.

"The park is beautiful at this time of the year," Terry noted.

"Yes, it's my favorite season," Barry stated.

"Have you been working here long?" Steve asked.

"It will be five years in January."

Sean returned, and sat down maintaining a blank composure; he masked his suspicions. "I guess you're familiar with folks who frequent the park regularly?" Sean continued.

"That's right."

"Have you had a chance to speak with any of them?"

"Yes, but no one seems to have seen anything."

"Do a lot of people come to the park late at night?"

"Once in awhile some teenagers hang around, but seldom."

"Have you noticed anything suspicious?" Sean continued to probe.

"No, I usually take a tour throughout the park's grounds once a week. I double check if anything needs immediate attention, but I haven't noticed anything unusual."

"We'll also need to question Mike, but if you remember anything whatsoever, please don't hesitate to call us."

"Sure thing."

"Thank you for your time. We appreciate it."

"Sorry I couldn't be of much help."

"There's no reason to apologize."

The Chief sighed, however, now with a pleased expression on his face. The news took a heavy burden off his shoulders, and more importantly it brought them one step closer. Even though the killer's identity was still a mystery, one day the DNA evidence would unveil the killer. The Chief sat momentarily puzzled; until now, the killer had been so meticulous leaving not even so much as a shred of evidence. It surprised him that the killer had fumbled, but experience told him there was no such thing as the perfect crime. The button must have been slightly loose, and then tore off with each of his physical exertions. It was simply sheer luck that a strand of hair was attached to it.

It was time to call the mayor. He would be pleased to discover they were closing in on the killer. "Hello, I need to speak to Mayor Wilson, this is Chief Williams," he informed the mayor's secretary.

"Hello Larry," the mayor acknowledged while trying to determine the nature of his call.

The Chief didn't waste any time updating him, "Well I've got some good news." The mayor listened attentively. "The killer has fumbled. One of his buttons fell and luckily for us a hair strand was attached."

"Great work, I knew it was just a matter of time. Well I'm really impressed how you have been handling the investigation. Keep me informed. I want this maniac off the streets ASAP."

Now the Chief had to make one last visit.

He knocked on the door and was quickly greeted by Dr. Summers. "Good to see you, please come in." He led the Chief into the living room. "Would you like some coffee?"

"Sure." The Chief was happy to see Dr. Summers in better spirits.

While waiting, the Chief seated himself appreciating the happy home life the Summers family had once shared. Countless portraits were mounted on the walls and on top of the fireplace mantle. She was so beautiful with such delicate facial features, complimented by her long blonde hair and captivating green eyes. His eyes caught a glimpse of one particular photo, Dianne was embracing her husband. A closer look gave him the feeling of déjà vu. There were countless trees in the background. It seemed to have been taken at their local park; how ironic, the Chief thought.

A nostalgic feeling took the Chief back a few years. He had been working on a case with other departments, trying to solve a murder mystery. Months elapsed, and they had not one shred of evidence. But with a tremendous amount of persistence and much ground covered they made their first breakthrough. The killer had disposed the body near a snow bank on a deserted road. Inadvertently, he left a small memento behind; they found his cigarette lighter buried in the snow. Upon examining the crime scene, the investigative crew discovered it along with a clean set of fingerprints smeared all over it. The murderer had already been convicted of another felony and this time jail became his permanent residence.

Dr. Summers strolled in with a full tray, set it down on the coffee table, before pouring his friend a cup. "If I remember correctly you like your coffee nice and strong."

"You have a good memory. How are the kids doing?"

"They are staying with my sister for awhile. Under the circumstances, I think it best. There are far too many memories in this house." He just shook his head in disbelief as he glanced around. "A little time away will help them; after all, they say time is a great healer."

"How are you holding up?"

"Each day is a challenge, but I have to carry on. I'll return to work in a couple of days, it's probably best to keep busy," Dr. Summers's face wore a strained expression.

"I would like to share some good news with you," Chief Williams smiled and continued in an upbeat tone. "It's confidential and only a handful of people are privy to it. The killer has left behind some incriminating evidence, much to his chagrin he has given away his identity."

Dr. Summers froze.

"While digging, one of his buttons fell off and unfortunately for him, a hair follicle was attached to it. We've got a DNA sample," the Chief relayed enthusiastically.

Tyler shot up. His eyes lit up with this new found hope, but no words could justify his inner feelings. The smell of blood hung thick in the air. Instinctively, he knew it was just a matter of time. Dr. Summers was fully aware that DNA, much like a fingerprint, is unique to every individual. Anyone could be tested with one hundred percent certainty.

Chapter 7

"Hello, have you been resting well?" greeted Jackie, while glancing through his chart.

"Oh, I've had better days," Jack grinned.

"In a moment I'm going to wheel you to the MRI room for more testing." Jack recently learned that stood for Magnetic Resonance Imaging giving the doctors a crystal clear picture inside his head.

But Jack's attention was drawn to Jackie. His eyes were simply polarized, as he inconspicuously eyed her. Her face was beautiful and perfectly proportioned to that of a cover girl. He admired her shapely curves as she swirled around the room and thought that perhaps fate had played out her cards bringing them both together.

With the help of another nurse, they transferred him onto the wheelchair. As he was being wheeled down the corridor, Jackie's light fragrance lingered in the air. It revitalized Jack's senses deepening his attraction to her.

"Have you been working here long?"

"Four years in March. I relocated from Miami so I would be closer to my family, particularly my parents."

"That must have been hard -- to relocate -- I mean."

"Not really, my parents helped me quite a bit. They found me an apartment and even helped me unpack."

The imaging room was kept dim, but it was impossible to miss the MRI unit as it engulfed one quarter of the room. Jack lay under it and was given explicit instructions to lie perfectly still, while it rotated around his head taking multiple images of his brain. High pitched rings ensued with each rotation. The imaging seemed to take forever and Jack was on the verge of falling asleep. A half an hour later he was wheeled back to his room.

"Would you like me to draw the blinds?" Jackie offered.

"You're plenty of sunshine for me." Jack responded in a flirtatious manner. Her cheeks reddened. She was certainly drawn to Jack's charisma, not to mention his good looks. Many of the nurses were already drooling over him, eager to help him any way possible. It was extraordinary how many excuses they came up with just to take a look at him. *'What a bod! What a hunk! I love his curls!' Jackie overheard the other nurses gossip among themselves.* Jackie could not help but wonder what kind of a man Jack was, but hoped to have all her answers soon.

Agents Gray and Michael stepped out of their cars and joined the investigation team. "It looks like they're all set to go," Agent Michael stated with heightened anticipation. All the equipment had been lugged along the grass and set in a huge pile.

Off to one side, stood a well built officer, soon he would retrace the killer's probable path. Terry rolled out a large map with the pathway marked off with a bright yellow high-liter. The starting point began with the killer's initial entry into the parking lot, followed by the trail he had taken throughout the park, ultimately leading to the burial site, and finally him *exiting* the park. In tracing and re-enacting his route, the team hoped to discover valuable information, which could provide them with critical clues.

The police officer hauled the dummy over his left shoulder. He tightly clenched the large sack of excavating tools in his right hand. The team began jotting notes while timing the officer. Terry trailed closely behind hoping some clues may have been carelessly discarded. *This is not going to be fun*, the officer thought. He hesitantly approached the valley just thankful he was carrying the dummy downhill. The officer surmised that the killer must have been familiar with the park's grounds; it would have been quite a feat to carry the body uphill. Beads of sweat trickled down his forehead, even the trudge downhill took an enormous amount of effort. With both hands occupied, he took extra caution with his footing; one wrong step could have him rolling dangerously down the steep hill. Luckily, his soles gave him good traction.

"One thing is for certain, whoever did this, assuming he carried the body alone must be built like an ox," the officer exclaimed in a huffy tone. He completed his track to the bottom and dropped the dummy along with the sack to the ground to rest momentarily. To reach the bottom of the hill had taken the officer about fifty minutes.

Unfortunately, no one could take over his shift since this would alter the time frame of the mock burial. He resumed his laborious task. Next he had to dig the burial plot and bury the 'corpse'. His shovel repeatedly cut through the earth's crust, he was just grateful that it was still fall and the terrain hadn't hardened yet.

"Perhaps there were two conspirators in on this one," Terry mused, slightly perplexed that one person could execute such a feat.

"Anything is possible, but all evidence points to just one killer. Unless one individual is taking all the glory, shouldn't there have been two signatures at the bottom of the poem?" Steve hypothesized.

"Do you think he'll bury his next victim near water again?" a perplexed Agent Gray questioned.

"Possibly, but most likely he won't choose this park again. It's just too damn risky. Our killer has made very few mistakes and he probably plans to keep it that way. I wouldn't be at all surprised if he plans something totally different for his next victim." Sean conjectured placidly. "Let's not kid ourselves, catching this guy won't be easy."

Sean soon became absorbed in his own thoughts and Terry quickly noted this shift.

The officer's shirt was becoming sticky making him feel quite uncomfortable; the officer was tired and frustrated of having to carry out such a feat. If he got a hold of him he would give the killer a good drubbing. Alone, he had dug a grave nearly three feet by six feet and over three feet deep and the wet soil didn't help matters much. Hopefully, he would never be asked to do any more grave diggings, once in a lifetime was enough.

Covering the dummy was no easy feat either. The officer compacted the earth, leveling it even to the surrounding area. They timed the officer; it took him just over three hours to place the rose, rosary, completely cover the dummy, and rake the sand to blend with the rest of the area. "Hang in there," encouraged Steve.

His shirt was drenched and the officer was completely exhausted as he dragged the tools behind him. It had been one helluva of a task and at this point he just wanted to go home and shower. Luckily, the Chief had promised him the next couple of days off, which he needed to recuperate.

"I can't believe that one man would attempt this. How monstrous is he anyway?" he voiced his apparent disgust. Everyone was thinking much the same thing.

It was 5:19 in the morning and the mock burial had taken just over five hours. Sean planned to go home and rest for a few hours, before heading to the forensic laboratory. He felt a bit triumphant believing he had sufficient evidence to bring the investigation under wraps. He held off sharing his latest suspicions with the team figuring they were too tired and probably would appreciate going home.

Jack enjoyed caressing Jackie's soft tresses while indulging in their sweet fragrance. They happily gazed into each others eyes, neither of them needing to utter a single word. Jack's blood was growing hotter and hotter with each passing moment. He was on fire and could no longer resist her beauty. Jack quickly pulled her close to him, kissing her passionately. She sensed a deep burning desire growing within him.

"Jackie, Jackie, promise me you will always stay with me?" he pleaded. But at that moment, he could no longer hold onto her image; she began to slowly fade away. "Don't go, please don't go," Jack strongly protested, but was peeved to have awakened at that precise moment.

He looked around, momentarily puzzled, before remembering that he was at the hospital. His room was fairly dark since the sun hadn't risen yet. Jack managed to sit up when Jackie walked into the room. He felt embarrassed realizing his hair was unkempt and his face unwashed.

"Do you need help?"

"I would like to use the bathroom," he admitted grudgingly.

"Okay, I'll page a couple of nurses to assist you, and I'll be back in fifteen."

The cold water felt good against his skin. Jack felt refreshed. His fingers scraped against his short stubble; he needed to shave, but that would have to wait until his strength kicked back. The nurses had assisted him back to his bed, just as Jackie returned.

"Ahh," Jack winced as he turned abruptly, "Do you have something for the pain?"

"This should help," Jackie handed him two tablets in a paper cup. She measured his blood pressure, temperature, and heart beat. All his readings were presently normal.

As she was recording the information, Dr. Summers briskly walked in. "Hello Jack," he acknowledged strolling next to his bed. "How are you feeling?"

"Much better today, but I still feel my back aching. I've been meaning to visit, but work keeps me quite busy," Jack confessed feeling a touch guilty.

"Yes, I know you're very dedicated and I can certainly admire your devotion to your career. But give yourself a couple of days rest. You should feel like your old self in no time."

"At least, I know I'm in good hands."

Dr. Summers smiled. "Take it easy Jack," he advised while leaving to complete his morning rounds.

Jackie left with Dr. Summers, but before she left she let him know that Dr. Adams would be dropping in to give him his test results. Jack winked at her and could have sworn he saw her blush.

No sooner had she left when Dr. Adams briskly walked into the room.

"Good morning, I have some good news." he announced in a perky tone. "You have suffered a mild concussion, but nothing serious. There aren't any fractures and just consider yourself quite lucky to have escaped virtually unscathed. You may still feel a little sore since you have suffered several bruises, but all in all you should heal nicely, so you're free to go home tomorrow," Dr. Adams quickly summarized.

"Thanks, I feel much better already," grinned Jack, preferring the comforts of his own home. The news also gave Jack a bit of relief since he attributed his scare to his mild concussion.

The jigsaw puzzle was taking shape. He left the FBI building; it was now shortly after 3:30 in the afternoon and time to call an emergency meeting.

Sean accelerated. His siren blared from street to street attracting pedestrian's attention; his mind swirled endlessly over his recent findings, much like a whirlwind spinning clouds of dust in an open desert. Maybe it was just coincidence, or perhaps fate, which led him to the killer. Either way it didn't really matter. Having barely pulled into his parking space, Sean shot out of his vehicle, sprinted into the building, and barged into the conference room. The team had already assembled, and they reminded him of children eagerly waiting for their Christmas gifts. The Chief silently signaled Sean to begin.

"Yesterday while at the park, I excused myself to go to the bathroom, and accidentally entered the back of the shed where all the tools are housed. I saw a series of shovels lined along the back wall, some of which were rusty. That was when it first hit me. The park also owns a series of tractors, which could easily transport people. Anyway, one of Barry's cardigans was hung on the back of his locker, and fortunately I picked it up and noticed a button missing. Unlucky for him, one of his hair follicles was dangling from his sleeve. I took it in for testing and guess what -- the DNA matches the hair follicle we found on the button. We've found our killer," exclaimed Sean triumphantly.

Everyone sat startled as no one had even suspected him. Victoriously, everyone breathed a sigh of relief as they had found their killer; the quietness in the room was replaced by an endless number of congratulations. But time was of the essence, the team needed to quickly dissipate before the killer preyed upon another innocent victim.

Speaking from the right side of his mouth, in a slur, he greeted, "Good afternon Bery." Tommy's mouth was swollen badly from a replaced filling.

"Good afternoon Tommy, are you sure you'll be able to work today?" Barry looked concerned, noting the large swelling on Tommy's face. He treated Tommy like a younger brother and felt obligated to look after his best interest.

"Yeah. Dogdor tells me swelling go down in a couple of hours. Freezing going to start to wear off and me going to take Tylenol. Dogdor orders -- says wheel keep pain away. Me no like pain." Tommy tried to speak coherently, but the swelling severely limited his ability.

Barry tried to think of a simple task for Tommy when just the right idea hit him. "I've removed these lawn mower blades if you feel up to sharpening them?"

"Me start reght away. I got to earn me paycheck."

Barry and Tommy had worked together for years. Although Tommy wasn't especially bright, his work ethic was unparalleled. Barry appreciated Tommy's dedication and the fact that he never had to ask him to do something twice.

Sparks were flying in every direction when suddenly a loud knock jostled Barry. "Tommy -- turn it off for a minute, please!" he yelled as he made his way to the door. It swung wide open, but the greeting wasn't exactly a warm one.

"Barry Fisher, you're under arrest for the murder of Dianne Summers," the burly man announced in a husky tone flashing his police ID.

"What! Are you out of your freaking mind?" Barry wore an incredulous look, shook his head repeatedly, and glowered at the two officers. "Is this some kind of sick joke? I think you're making a big mistake!" Barry was livid while Tommy was cowering from all the commotion.

The officers felt insulted and weren't going to listen to his lip. One of them proceeded in a harsh tone, "There are two ways we can do this, the easy way or the hard way. Now, which is it going to be?" The officer's eyes bulged as he stared down Barry, flanked by his partner to his left.

"Damn -- this is crazy!" Barry slammed his fist on the bench. The words resonated with such intensity. "Bloody unbelievable!" He then covered his face with his hands, out of frustration. Reluctantly, he had no choice but to co-operate. "Okay, I'll come, but please let me explain to Tommy that I need to come with you." Barry lowered his voice trying to control his anger.

The officer nodded, feeling proud that their arrest had transpired as planned. Barry marched over to Tommy.

"Tommy, I have to go with these men. They're officers of the law and think I've done something wrong. I have to go and try to straighten things out."

"Bery no do bad things. Bery good. Me tell them for you," Tommy frantically tried to stop the whole fiasco from unfolding.

Barry stressed in a firm tone, "Please, Tommy I'm going with these men to straighten everything out. I'll be back in no time. Promise me you'll lock up and go home at the end of the day." Barry tried to sound as reassuring as he possibly could and patted Tommy on the shoulders. He then bravely, although reluctantly, faced his destiny.

"You have the right to remain silent. Anything you say, can and will be held against you in a court of law…" The cuffs were slapped tightly around his wrists, and he was escorted to the police cruiser by the two officers. Before settling in the back seat, Tommy ran towards him.

"No, no come back!" Tommy began wailing. Overwrought with fear, he desperately lunged at his friend. He was hanging on for dear life, and the officers' best effort to pry him loose proved futile.

"Tommy, please co-operate with these men; they don't want to harm me. They'll take me to the station to ask me a few questions and then everything will be fine." Barry was almost in tears seeing the anguish in Tommy's eyes.

"Okay. Bery me be good." Tommy seemed to calm down a bit and released his iron-clad hold around Barry's legs.

Barry stooped into the back seat. The door slammed shut, and the unmarked car sped off to the station.

At the station everyone seemed jubilant. Tim strolled confidently towards the trio to offer his congratulations. "Hey guys, how are you doing? I heard the good news about the DNA evidence; it's all over the media." He gave all three of them a firm handshake.

They looked puzzled and realized he hadn't heard the latest.

"That's good news, but even better news is that we now have a suspect in custody," Terry's face brightened, trying not to sound overly confident.

"Are you serious?" Tim looked at them questioningly, obviously taken aback by this startling revelation.

"Really, no bull! It was partially a stroke of luck, but mostly keen detective work on Sean's part." Steve couldn't contain his pepped up enthusiasm.

Tim was now all ears, his curiosity peaked.

In a jubilant tone, "The answer to all our questions was right under our noses the whole time. We've been scrambling back and forth in search of clues trying to find something. Luckily Sean was alert, and took advantage of our last visit to the park, poking around the maintenance shed. Something clicked for whatever reason, when he noticed a wall lined with shovels. They looked badly worn and rusty. Then he noticed a tractor with a cart hitched to the back. A bigger picture was beginning to form. Let's assume, hypothetically speaking, that the killer had access to the shed's contents. Of course this would make his mission a lot easier. Let's take this one step further, what if the killer not only had access but was also employed at the park." Tim's eyes shot wide open. Disbelief, shock, fascination, and a few other emotions twirled inside his head. "Logically given Sean's experience and intuition, he decided to extract a tangible piece of evidence. He cleverly obtained a hair strand from the suspect's jacket. Of course up to this point everything had just been pure speculation. Also being left handed, husky, and about the right height made him an even more likely suspect. The evidence just came back a couple of hours ago confirming all the circumstantial evidence and the DNA was a perfect match."

"Well, who is it?" Tim gaped, dying from suspense.

"All the evidence was pointing to the one and only Barry Fisher," Sean announced confidently.

"Oh my God! I can't believe it!" Tim's face dropped. It never even occurred to him that the killer could be someone employed at the park.

Meanwhile, the Chief was in a much more relaxed frame of mind knowing Barry Fisher had been placed under arrest. He picked up the receiver. "My name is Gary. I work at the local news station; I understand that you have the killer's DNA."

"How did you find out?" the startled Chief paused in disbelief.

"Let's just say I have my sources," he tried sounding coy, but came across a little arrogant.

"Well guess what, I'm one up on you. We now have the killer in custody," he proudly trumped.

"Wow, fast work. Well who is it?"

"I'm going to hold a media conference in a couple of hours," the Chief signed off and went to join the detectives.

The detectives were flabbergasted by Tim's reaction, almost at a loss for words.

"Why are you in such shock?" Terry shook her head in disbelief.

"I can't believe this has happened! This is entirely my fault." Tim flung his hands to his head appearing as guilty as sin.

"What? You're not making any sense," Steve shrugged thinking Tim was out in left field.

"It happened the day I was working at the park uncovering Dianne's body. It was cold and we decided to break for lunch. I saw Barry and he was kind enough to lend me his jacket, since I forgot mine. Later that day I simply returned it, not even realizing the button had fallen off." Tim's voice was shaky, fearful of the consequences.

"Oops!" Terry knew that there were going to be serious repercussions and could feel a splitting headache setting in. Ditto for Sean and Steve.

An ecstatic Chief made his way through the front door.

"Oh my God!" they all mumbled in unison.

Expressions of horror were written on each of their faces. The Chief couldn't mistake their stricken looks and erroneously assumed Barry Fisher had escaped. "How did he escape?" he demanded curtly.

"That's not the problem," Sean hated being the bearer of more bad news. The Chief wasn't one for long drawn out stories. Sean was walking on pins and needles unsure of how to lay this bombshell. "It happened so quickly, everything seemed to make perfect sense." He was about to open his mouth again when the Chief interrupted.

In a harsh tone he blurted, "Cut through the chaff and tell me what the hell's going on!"

"There has been a terrible blunder on our part," conceded Sean. "Tim from forensics had borrowed Barry's jacket, since it had been a cool day. One of the buttons must have come loose falling to the ground. It just happened that a strand of Barry's hair was attached to it."

The Chief's face instantly flushed a bright crimson red. Tim grudgingly came forward to face the Chief's wrath. "I would –" the Chief cut him off. He sternly gestured for Tim to step into his office. The door slammed shut behind the Chief.

"Do you realize the public embarrassment this will bring us?" he roared. His words reached the front entrance despite the closed door. "And we're damn lucky if Barry doesn't sue our pants off. I personally spoke to the mayor along with Dr. Summers to tell them we had DNA evidence."

Shit, he had to stop the news from airing all over New Jersey. The Chief quickly grabbed the receiver. "This is Chief Williams, don't publicize our findings!" he ordered.

"Too late," Gary revealed.

"Well, don't publicize anymore. It's been one big mistake!" the Chief slammed the phone.

"Damn! This is just unreal. I'm going to give you some advice and suggest you remember it for as long as you live. Never borrow or use anything that doesn't belong to the team. God so help you if such a blunder ever occurs again. Do I make myself clear?" the Chief fumed as he towered over with his fists resting on the desk.

"Yes sir, I'm terribly sorry for the embarrassment I've caused everyone. You have my word, it'll never happen again."

"Jesus, we're going to be the laughing stock of this town. The mayor is going to be furious and may want someone's head," the Chief conjectured.

"Sir, please accept my sincere apologies," he mumbled.

"Now get out of here, before I say something I'll later regret."

Tim had no desire to get suspended and left quickly without uttering a single word.

Sean and the Investigative Team hurried to the interrogation room to prevent any further damage. Barry sat exasperated, nearly in tears as the interrogating officer was called aside to straighten their erratum.

They approached Barry who sat in somber spirits, looking both puzzled and confused. "I didn't do it; I really didn't," he desperately pleaded with much conviction in his eyes.

"Yes we know," Sean awkwardly acknowledged.

"You do?" he asked looking more and more confused by the second.

"We have made a terrible mistake -- remember the evening the forensic team was at the park searching for clues?"

"Yes."

"Do you remember lending your jacket to Tim, a member of the forensic team?"

"Yes."

"Well, one of the buttons from your jacket fell off, along with a hair follicle. We matched your DNA to that hair strand, thus concluding you to be the killer. But once we explained to Tim how we concluded you to be the murderer, shock struck his face and he quickly informed us of our blunder." Sean's voice was a little shaky and felt apprehensive relaying the news. "Please accept our sincere apologies and I hope you can forgive us. Your identity hasn't been announced, so your reputation has not been tarnished in any way. On behalf of the New Jersey Police Department, we're terribly sorry for having caused you so much duress."

Barry breathed a huge sigh of relief; he felt a great inner tension unwind and slumped back in his chair. "Apologies accepted, I'm just glad that this whole fiasco is over. For awhile I was worried sick of ending up in the slammer." He was overcome with a multitude of emotions, but was just grateful the whole ordeal was over.

The Chief shook Barry's hand. "Sorry for this entire misunderstanding," he stated in a sympathetic tone.

In a frenzy, he blurted, "I have to get back to Tommy. He's lost on his own and shouldn't be left alone for too long."

The Chief wondered if the nightmare would ever end. He personally volunteered to drive Barry to the park with the Investigative Team following closely behind. Their sirens screamed throughout the streets. The Chief silently prayed Tommy was unhurt. Barry flew out of the vehicle and raced to the shed hoping Tommy hadn't become too upset and wandered off aimlessly. He threw the shed door open and there was Tommy. "Bery, Bery, your back," he cried with joy. He clung to Barry so tightly, perhaps fearful of losing him again. "Please don't leave me ever again," he pleaded.

"Never again," answered Barry with tears of joy stinging his eyes. He knew he would always take care of Tommy and be like an older brother.

They watched in awe as Tommy hugged Barry tightly.

Terrible guilt was embedded not only in Sean's mind, but in his heart as well. His quick judgment and lack of a more thorough investigation nearly led to the destruction of a man's entire future. He could not help but dwell on the possibility that his error may never have been found. A long arduous trial might have ensued. An innocent man may have been convicted to a long jail sentence, or even worse a lifetime rotting in the hell hole. Sean wondered how many men faced the same terrible fate trying in vain to prove their innocence.

Dr. Summers appreciated the morning's quietness while slowly sipping his coffee. Lately, he had seriously considered taking a short vacation with his children during the Christmas holidays. It would be a tremendous relief if they could escape even for a few days. The family was still healing and spending the Christmas season at home with so many memories would be heart-breaking, to say the least. Dr. Summers rubbed his left arm. For the past couple of days, he had felt a nagging pain.

Jack was stunned to hear the police had already apprehended the killer and confirmed his identity. He knew DNA findings were conclusive, virtually casting all doubts aside.

It took Jack a couple of attempts before he successfully hoisted himself out of bed. He managed to lower himself onto the cold floor. He could still feel a slight ache in his mid-back, but most of the pain had subsided. With steady steps, he continued down the long corridors in hopes of bumping into Jackie. His best odds of a chance meeting would be at the nurse's station.

How ironic an institution entrusted to saving people's lives was devoid of life itself, he thought to himself as he continued to stare at the white walls. Only now and again, he would pass a painting hung haphazardly. Architectural design was certainly lacking, if any actually existed. Personally, Jack could not function in a world devoid of color and design.

"Hi, how are you doing?" Jackie called from the preceding hallway.

"Oh -- I'm feeling better. I figured a short stroll would loosen my muscles."

"You're looking much better."

"The doctor gave me two thumbs up. I'll be leaving in a couple of hours."

"Oh, that's great news; I'm happy for you," Jackie looked pleased.

"Yes, and I'm sure my friend will be ecstatic to see me." For a split second, Jack could've sworn he saw disappointment wash over her face. "Tara is my parrot and friend, and hopefully she hasn't felt neglected. If she shares my feelings than she'll have missed me terribly."

"Does she talk?"

"Of course, she's quite intelligent. I've taught her to repeat several words." Jackie was touched by his fondness for his friend; she virtually loved all species of animals and understood Jack's attachment.

As Jack uttered the words, he felt himself growing warm, "I hope this isn't too presumptuous of me, since I've only known you for a couple of days, but I would like to see you again. Needless to say, I may need a few more days to recuperate."

Jackie laughed. "Sure, I'd love to," she looked deep into his eyes. She slipped the folded piece of paper which Jack handed to her and let it fall deep into her pocket.

An unwelcome feeling of torpor screamed for Jack to get off his feet, before he became one with the floor. Jackie didn't like the sudden pale color on his face. "I think we need to get you off your feet," she warned and led him back to his room. "Do you have someone who can help you for the next couple of days?" Jackie's voice held a nervous tone.

"I should be fine, but I'm sure my parents will keep an eye on me."

They turned around the corner and witnessed a congregation of nurses huddled around. Jack and Jackie stared in shock.

"Get the oxygen mask now!" ordered the head nurse. "I don't feel a heart beat. Dr. Summers, please stay with us. Page Dr. Leigh and tell him Dr. Summers is in cardiac arrest -- let's move it!" she yelled to one of the other nurses. "Still no heart beat," she confirmed to one of the nurses. "Code blue in alert, code blue in alert," she repeated. The emergency was relayed on the PA system. Time was of the essence.

Within less than a minute, two doctors raced down the hall at neck-breaking speed; their smocks suspended in mid-flight as they frantically hollered orders. Nurses could be seen scrambling from every direction.

Chapter 8

"Home sweet home," he sighed as he stepped inside the foyer. He placed his carry-on-bag in front of the closet. Jack headed directly into the kitchen and could hear his friend fluttering about. He smiled; his parents not only had managed to take care of Tara, but also had fully replenished his refrigerator. She flew about happily and chirped incessantly immediately upon seeing him.

"Daddy missed you so much. Did you miss me?" he asked in a joking like manner.

"Mss me, mss me."

Jack instantly felt better.

He puffed his pillows before lounging on the leather couch, which would become his permanent headquarters for the next couple of days. It was ideal, since it gained him easy access to both the kitchen and bathroom without having to lug himself up the stairs.

He slipped on a pair of plastic gloves, then drew the sharp butcher knife from the wooden block. "Chester, we're ready to begin," he calmly announced to his cat who sat on a stool next to the table. She lay helpless. Both her arms and legs were securely tied to the table, restricting her blood flow. A cloth was wrapped tightly around her face gagging her mouth shut. Her eyes widened with fear as the cold edge sent chills along the length of her throat. "Don't worry soon you'll be cleansed of all your earthly sins. Then my dear, you can rest eternally in peace," he smiled hedonistically. He held the knife in mid-air and twirled it haphazardly over her body. She cringed and desperately tried to free herself, but to no avail. The killer grew excited watching her struggle and felt a surge of adrenaline sweep throughout his body. He watched as tears rolled down her cheeks, streaking her terror stricken face. Chester purred as if giving the signal for the ritual to begin. His eyes danced wildly as he began the sacrifice. He continuously stroked her hair gingerly with his gloved hand. "Too bad it has to end this way." The killer paused briefly to collect his thoughts. "Things could have been much, much different," he stated dismally shaking his head. She sobbed incessantly and shivered from head to toe. "Don't worry, I'm as fast as can be, they'll never catch me. And by the time they do figure it out, it will be too late," she noted his twisted smile. A petrified look set in, as he casually picked up the sharp knife. He held it up to the dim light. "Now, now, it's only going to hurt for a split second," he whispered softly noting her ghastly expression. She panicked trying to wriggle free, but to no avail; the fastenings around her arms and legs were too constrictive. He firmly clenched the knife between both hands, her breathing intensified as she watched in horror. The killer slowly raised the gleaming point, stopping directly above her heart. Her eyes begged mercifully for him to stop. Before she could even flinch, the knife came down with a loud thump leaving her mouth gaped wide open. As he yanked the bloody knife from within, a sea of blood gushed out. His eyes lit up as he got a rush from all the excitement. A peaceful calm slowly brought him back to a more stable frame of mind. He then bowed his head and took a minute to cite a verse from the bible.

"Rest peacefully," were his last words to her.

A couple of days had elapsed, and Jack had just made himself comfortable when unexpectedly the door bell rang. His first thought had been that his parents had left something behind. "Hello," he called as he struggled to reach the front entrance.

"Hello Jack," they hollered in unison considerably raising their voices.

"Hey guys, what a nice surprise!" Jack greeted heartily.

"We hope we're not imposing, but we heard about your accident and just want to see how you're doing," Yvonne explained with a radiant glow.

"Not at all, I'm bored to death, and would love some company." They both noticed Jack's rugged appearance and Henri couldn't help but take an extended glance.

"We hope you are feeling better," Yvonne sympathized, while at the same time admiring the luxurious pieces of furniture and breath-taking art pieces

"I'm feeling much better, but for the next couple of days I'll be crashing down here. It beats dragging myself up the stairs, plus doc suggested I stay off my feet for awhile."

"We're glad that it's nothing serious," Henri stated while seating himself on the leather recliner.

"I was just about to make some coffee. Would you like some or would you prefer something cold to drink?" Jack offered. Yvonne and Henri looked at each other.

"Coffee sounds good. But, is there anything we can help you with?" Henri offered graciously. Jack thought if there was anything pressing for him to do.

"Actually if you don't mind, tomorrow is garbage day and there's a garbage bag in the garage. I don't want to aggravate my back any further."

"Sure, no problem."

Henri grabbed the two ends of the garbage bag and was just about to secure them, when out of the corner of his eye he noticed the towel was smeared with bright red stains. He stood momentarily puzzled, but then conjectured. "I guess I'm not the only one who shaves too closely," he muttered to himself before dumping it.

"We brought you some goodies from the bakery," Yvonne handed him the fresh home made pastries.

"Really, you guys shouldn't have. They look delicious; we'll have them with our coffee." A bright sparkle caught Jack's attention. "Hey hold on a minute -- is this what I think it is?" he held onto Yvonne's hand, momentarily admiring her engagement ring.

"Yes, Henri took me completely by surprise," she blushed.

"Congratulations – that's great. I'm really happy for both of you." Jack stated while hugging her.

"Thank you."

Jack was about to rise from his chair as the coffee maker's percolating noises came to a halt.

"Oh Jack let me help, you shouldn't be on your feet."

"Sure, thanks. Cups are in the cupboard directly above the sink, sugar is in the next cupboard to your right, and cream on the top rack of the fridge," Jack directed just as Henri had returned.

"Hey -- I hear congratulations are in order."

"Thanks, but we haven't set the wedding date," Henri embraced Yvonne. "We'd be honored if you would be our best man?" They both looked at Jack awaiting a response.

"I'm flattered, I would love to," Jack gave Henri a hearty pat on the back and kissed Yvonne lightly on the cheek.

"We're hoping to tie the knot next summer -- something tells me the lady has her heart set on being a June bride." Henri winked at Yvonne. "We both love the idea of an outdoor wedding, preferably in a park-like setting. We have a few places in mind, and on the weekend we'll start by visiting them."

"This is really terrific news. I'm really happy for both of you. This calls for a celebration -- it'll be my treat. I know this terrific restaurant," Jack offered.

"By the way, have you been following the news?" Yvonne probed hoping the subject wouldn't be too upsetting.

"I can't believe it, one minute they are announcing they caught the killer, and the next minute they state they've made a terrible mistake. To top it off, poor Dr. Summers suffered a heart attack."

"No really?" Yvonne covered her mouth stunned at the latest revelation and exchanged a shocked look with Henri.

"I was walking through the hospital's hallway where a crowd had formed around him. Doctors rushed to the scene shouting orders -- nurses fled from every direction. His heart had temporarily stopped. I don't know all the details, but it may have been precipitated by the media announcement."

"Whoa, I really feel sorry for the poor guy," Yvonne sympathized.

"His two children must be going through hell," Henri added. Everyone reflected on this thought momentarily.

Jack felt deeply troubled and changed the subject. "These pastries are really delicious. Where did you say you bought them?"

"Actually, the bakery is just east of here."

"I'll certainly make a point of dropping by."

"Just make sure you don't go overboard at least until after the wedding," warned Yvonne with a serious demeanor. All three enjoyed a hearty laugh. "Do you have any idea when you'll be able to come back to work?"

"I hope to be back in a couple of days. I can't stand being cooped up here for too long?" Tara flew and perched herself on Jack's right shoulder. "Are you going to say hello to our friends?" he urged.

"Friendz," Tara mimicked.

They all watched Tara adoringly.

Yvonne helped Jack clear the table. She was impressed by his tidiness and cleanliness, but also by his collection of the latest kitchen gizmos. Yvonne rinsed the last mug and left the dishes to dry in the dish rack.

"Well, I guess we should get going. I have to stop by the office and complete some paperwork," Yvonne stated.

"I appreciated the company, thanks for coming. You should be receiving invitations to my New Year's Eve party shortly; I'd love for you guys to come."

"Sounds great, we'll be there," Henri assured Jack.

An overwhelming sense of anguish and guilt depleted the Chief's energy, since he felt partially responsible for Dr. Summers' current condition. Despite his best intentions to protect and bring resolution to his friend's sorrow, he had unintentionally deepened his scars.

He poked his head around the door hoping not to awaken him, but he lay awake seemingly staring into space. The Chief gently tapped on the door.

"Come in," invited the wane voice. The Chief wearily stepped in.

A smile spread across Tyler's face, "Hey, good to see you."

"I'm so sorry about what has happened," the Chief's voice nearly cracked.

"You almost sound as though you were personally responsible." The doctor noticed the stricken look on his friend's face, and surmised his assumption had been correct. "You're not responsible for my present condition; I should've taken better care of myself. For the past several months, I've been neglecting my health, but I realize this is my wake up call and can't allow myself to fall to pieces; I still have my children to raise, and I plan to be around for quite some time."

The Chief's guilt slowly subsided. "Is there anything I can do for you?" he hoped to be of some assistance.

"Really, I'm fine. I'll be back on my feet in a week or so. But I'm curious to learn what happened."

"Perhaps -- we should leave that topic for later," the Chief recommended.

"You don't need to worry about my health, I'll be fine. Besides, I rather hear it from you than listen to hush hushes spreading throughout the hospital's halls. It's driving me crazy."

"Okay. We did get an accurate DNA match, but the man we arrested was not the killer," Tyler frowned. "The match from the DNA belongs to Barry Fisher, the manager at Stetson Highland Park. During the investigation, Tim, one of the forensic officers, made the mistake of borrowing Barry's cardigan to shield himself from the dropping temperatures. While scouring for evidence, the button must have fallen to the ground, but Tim remained oblivious to this fact and simply returned the jacket to Barry. While Barry Fisher remained in our custody, Tim learnt of our successful arrest. Sean, an investigative officer, briefed him on the discovery of the button with the hair follicle attached to it, explaining that the DNA from the button matched Barry Fisher's genetic make-up. Therefore, we concluded him to be the killer. Horror struck Tim as he realized the near tragic error. We quickly released Barry, probably ending his worst nightmare."

"Imaginably so," responded Tyler. "Given the circumstances, he's lucky the truth came to light," chuckled Tyler.

The Chief took comfort in his friend's sense of humor.

Sean loved the restaurant's outward appearance. The building was set among acres of greenery which bestowed the ambience of a European-like villa. The restaurant had earned its stellar reputation for its award winning pizza. It was cooked the old fashioned way, in large wood-fired ovens.

Sean huddled in the back corner waiting for Terry and Steve to join him. He felt really bad over the mishap.

Within a couple of minutes, Terry and Steve walked in; Sean beckoned them over.

"Hey, great looking place!" Steve admired the Mediterranean look. He took a minute to absorb all the details. The stucco ceiling was an ocean blue with matching cornices around the perimeter of the room, softening the architectural lines. Several pillars, strategically placed, gave the false impression that they actually supported the building.

"Good afternoon. Are you ready to order?" The waitress seemed anxious to take their orders. They glanced at one another and decided to start with refreshments.

"Well it could have been a helluva lot worse," stressed Steve. "Barry could have been in the slammer for a damn long time."

"I'm just happy we found out in the nick of time," Terry took a sip of her cola.

"I guess we're pretty much back to square one," Sean looked over-ridden with stress.

"Other than the thread and a shovel fragment, the killer didn't leave any incriminating evidence behind. He must have planned the murder for some time. Then to add insult to injury he writes the Chief a poem. Now that takes a lot of nerve and frankly he's starting to get under my skin," Steve looked exasperated.

"Well, whoever we're dealing with is very clever; he thinks out a plan and considers every minute detail. We're certainly not dealing with an amateur," Sean added.

"He must frequent the park quite often, knowing everyone's schedule quite well," Terry reflected momentarily.

"We'll review the film on a daily basis. Also, we're going to have to get a list of names from Dr. Summers. Perhaps, there's a connection between the two murders," Sean deduced. "Anyway, we better order," Sean suggested hearing his stomach rumble. "Have you guys ever tried the clams and green olives combo? The pizza is scrumptious with its home-made golden crust and fresh ingredients. It's truly amazing cooked in the Italian tradition," he emphasized kissing the tips of his fingers.

"I'm sold," Terry preferred to stray from the ordinary and anticipated savoring something new.

"Me too," replied Steve who was a big pizza lover.

"Have you settled in your new home?" Steve asked Terry.

"I've managed to unpack most of my basic belongings. Ten boxes are still collecting dust in an empty bedroom."

In truth, Terry didn't have the energy to drudge up her past by filtering through her personal belongings. She had recently filed for a divorce, a year after she had caught her husband cheating on her.

The events of that Friday afternoon remained etched in Terry's head. It was two o'clock in the afternoon when she headed home; normally she didn't finish work until five o'clock. She decided to prepare a surprise dinner for her husband, but instead was on the receiving end of a heart-breaking rude-awakening. As she approached her driveway she was a little startled to see another vehicle parked alongside her husband's car.

Surprisingly, the front door was unlocked and she crept through the entire house on tip-toe. She stopped to listen; the muffled sounds came from upstairs. As she drew closer, she made out the laughing noises, which were later coupled with an all too familiar sound. She attentively listened to her husband's words. The door was partially ajar allowing her a full view into the room. She quickly covered her mouth not only from shock, but also afraid of yelling some obscenity. A woman had wrapped herself around her husband. Enamored with each other, neither one of them was aware of her presence.

Later, she regretted having been coy and should've marched in and exposed them. It would have brought great pleasure to have seen both of their shocked faces.

Terry drew her attention back to her partners. The waitress headed to their table balancing an extra large pizza in hand. It smelled delicious with a hint of clams filling the air. "Wow, you weren't kidding this tastes really good. Probably the best pizza I've ever tasted," Steve spoke between mouthfuls.

"Yes, it's quite good," Terry agreed. In between bites she turned her attention towards Steve, "I've been meaning to ask you how was your trip?"

"Oh fabulous, Alicia and I had a terrific time. St. Martin is a wonderful place to visit and the inhabitants were especially friendly. If I remember correctly the tourist guide stated it's actually the smallest island in the world. We toured around and dined at both the French and Dutch cuisines. The white sandy beaches were simply breath-taking. They had endless number of water sports for tourists to enjoy. I managed to do some sailing and snorkeling. Overall it was a very memorable trip."

Agents Gray and Michael sat glued to their chairs facing their laptops; their headquarters provided them with access to privy information.

They shared a list of nine possible suspects. Before his heart attack, Dr. Summers had provided them with a tally of names. In his entire medical career, Dr. Summers had lost two patients, both of these patients had been terminally ill with cancer.

Although Dr. Summers didn't believe that any of their family members would retaliate, the agents held a much different perspective. They were all too familiar with people snapping at the loss of their loved ones, driving them to do unimaginable things.

For each given name, they would run a complete check. In particular, Dianne's romantic encounters would be scrutinized under a microscope. Both agents felt the killer acted on a personal vendetta. The poem was a clear indication of someone harboring ill feelings, probably of a romantic nature. The red rose strongly supported this notion.

But, Agent Gray felt something more sinister lurked in the mind of the killer. Perhaps, it was simply a case of mental insanity. The killer was slowly providing them with a glimpse into his darker half.

"Agent Gray," the officer called as he stepped into the room.
"Yes."
"There's a call for you — Chief Williams is on line one." Chief Williams's worst nightmare was about to unfold.

The Investigative Team returned to the station as quickly as possible. There was no mistaking the Chief's urgency.

"I've received some disturbing news from Elaine Cooper's family. Apparently, she has gone missing and hasn't reported to work for the past two days, nor has she bothered to call. Her boss and co-workers are worried sick. Her mother started to become quite uneasy after leaving several messages on her cell and at home, but still hasn't heard back from her daughter. Also, once a week they usually meet for lunch, but yesterday she didn't show up, nor did she call."

"Have any of her neighbors seen her?" Sean inquired.

"Her mom is friends with one of them, but oddly she hasn't seen Elaine either pull in or out of the driveway for the past two days," the Chief briefed.

The Investigative Team along with the FBI agents arrived at Elaine Cooper's home. The Chief had advised Elaine's mother to wait in her car, and not enter the home, as there still might be evidence for them to uncover. Her mother was already in a complete frenzy, fearing the worst. Even before setting foot on the front step, they scraped for a soil sample, next the door knob was thoroughly dusted for fingerprints. Everyone was an expert in their respective field and knew all the precautionary steps, including the obvious of wearing gloves. At this point, no one knew exactly what they were looking for, or what to expect. For that matter, there was the possibility that they wouldn't find a shred of evidence. But one thing was for damn certain, they were going to search the entire home with a fine tooth comb. They divided the house among themselves. Sean and Agent Gray would search the upper floor. Steve and Agent Michael agreed to search the main level, while Terry was left to examine the basement and garage.

Sean and Agent Gray slowly climbed the staircase. Neither believed anyone still lurked inside; but nonetheless they took the necessary precautions. Cautiously, they momentarily stood in front of the master bedroom. Agent Gray covered for Sean leaving Sean to push the door ajar. "All clear," signaled Sean after searching the entire room.

The bed had been made. Her room was meticulously kept without any signs of a struggle. Sean examined the duvet cover for any blood stains while Agent Gray stood in front of the oak dresser dusting its entire surface. Apparently, Elaine did not care too much for clutter; her room was devoid of accessories or ornaments except for two framed photographs. The young girl in one photo was most likely herself, taken at a much younger age.

Steve sorted through the newspapers, which were neatly stacked on the coffee table. He had the habit of circling and cutting out clippings, and wondered if Elaine shared the same habit. Moments later, he joined Agent Michael in the kitchen. He was busy pouring orange juice into a sample bottle and repeated the same procedure for other liquids.

Steve began rummaging through the garbage bins, emptying their contents into a large plastic bag. It was amazing what one could learn by filtering through them. Next, Steve quickly glanced around the kitchen. The wooden block housed six knives, all of which seemed to be placed according to size. Nonetheless, Steve placed them into a container and would send them to a lab for testing. Even though it was highly unlikely someone would have used any of them, they could ill afford to take any chances. Experience taught Steve never to assume anything. Assumptions, in particular the wrong ones, were quite unforgiving.

Terry felt the cold draft; it was a sure sign that winter was soon approaching. Quietly, she made her way down the hall. As a martial arts expert with a black belt in karate, her abilities for self-defense left no qualms. During her teenage years, it had increased her self-esteem, as well as further empowering her co-ordination and ability to focus. In battle she was fierce and quite deadly. Every morning Terry spent time practicing these disciplines.

She moved in the dark with night goggles; if anyone was concealed in any unlit corners she would soon discover them. It was eerie, but it wouldn't alert anyone to her presence.

Satisfied, Terry switched on the laundry room light. A couple of cupboards hung directly above the washer and it took only a fraction of a second to search their contents. Apparently, Elaine did not care for frivolous objects. She found a box of laundry detergent and a bar of home-made soap in one of the cupboards, the other was empty.

Off in one corner on the floor lay some unwashed clothing. A t-shirt and two pairs of jeans were scattered haphazardly in the laundry basket. Terry dumped everything into a garment bag. If Elaine had been outdoors or on any camping adventures, her clothing would provide them with the necessary information to begin a proper investigation. At this point, they needed answers quickly.

Elaine's actions for the past two days didn't sound within the realm of her character, as Terry probably surmised they weren't. She wouldn't be surprised if Elaine was being held hostage or had suffered a fate similar to Dianne's.

At the end of the hall was the home's second three piece bathroom. Terry searched the cupboards but found they were void of the usual bathroom accessories, concluding that the washroom was seldom if ever used.

BANG! "What the hell..." Terry's heart jumped startled by a loud crashing sound from above. She froze, listened attentively, but could only hear herself breathing. Within seconds, she reached the top of the staircase. Years of training came thundering back as she instinctively positioned herself in a defensive stance. Fearful someone still remained in the house, she silently strode forward. She peeked around the corner; although no one was in sight, she dared not lower her guard. Terry crept down the hallway into the living room where she nearly stepped on broken glass. A shattered lamp lay next to the end table. She gasped seeing smears of blood trailing into the kitchen. *Shit, what the hell's going on and what happened to everyone,* she thought? Instinctively feeling someone's presence in the next room, she cringed, pausing momentarily, before proceeding on tip-toe towards the kitchen. Only drywall and a few studs separated them. She was unarmed, but apprehensively wondered if the intruder carried a gun. Most likely, she would have only one chance to disarm the intruder.

She remained focused realizing her life was in jeopardy and there was no margin for error.

She got her break.

The intruder gave away his position. Terry heard a small creak in the floorboard, and figured they stood directly across from one another and only inches away from each other. Her heartbeat quickened. Terry shuddered, fearing he might be aware of her presence, and thought it was best to go on the offensive to throw him off guard. Every second counted and she needed to act swiftly.

Smack!

A quick hoof sent the gun flying. She was about to deliver another hard blow to his stomach, but stopped dead in her tracks as their eyes met.

"Ahhh," he screamed in pain.

She stood shocked to see Steve cradling his hand in agony. "Good God, I'm so sorry," she blurted covering her mouth. "Are you okay?" Terry asked nervously standing over him.

"Yeah, j-just give me a minute. See if you can lure that cat. I nearly shot it thinking it was an intruder."

Just then Agent Michael returned carrying some containers into the kitchen and nearly ran into Sean and Agent Gray.

"What the hell happened?" asked Sean with his gun drawn. Steve quickly briefed them.

With very careful strides, she inched forward desperately trying to coax it. "It's okay," she repeated. "Come kitty, kitty."

"Unbelievable," Terry uttered. *But, why had they not noticed her before?* It then occurred to her that cats usually hide when they become frightened; her cat took refuge under her bed, especially during lightning storms. The cat must have been paralyzed with fear to have remained in its hiding place for so long. The bowls remained full, although her water was now warm and the canned food was all dried up. *But what on earth could have frightened the cat so much? Perhaps an even better question was who the hell frightened her?* An eerie feeling swept through her and she felt goose bumps rise on her skin. She had no doubts that something sinister had transpired in the last couple of days. Yet, there was little evidence to suggest a break-in, much less a struggle.

Steve managed to befriend it, brushing and depositing the excess fur in a small plastic packet. He then re-applied the ice-pack to his sore hand. The cat seemed to be quite ravenous. Steve rummaged through the cupboards until he came to the one which contained cat food, and then dumped the tuna into a bowl and placed it front of her along with a fresh bowl of water. As the cat began drinking, Steve noticed drops of blood dripping from its paws.

Terry descended the staircase to continue her investigation. The totes were stacked on top of each other just barely touching the ceiling. Terry lugged the top one onto the floor and popped off its lid. She rummaged through it noting a series of books coupled with old school notes, which were obviously considered valuable to have been stored in the first place.

Unless she had removed a few of the containers, she never would have noticed the upright freezer, which remained concealed up to now. Terry hesitated, while pushing back a disturbing thought. Her attempts to pull the door open had been unsuccessful. She knew better than to apply excess force, after all she wanted the freezer to remain in an upright position, rather than topple over.

She figured ice must have formed within the door's frame, sealing it frozen shut. Voila, a closer look revealed a thick coating of ice around the perimeter of the door. As she checked the temperature's control setting she became even more perplexed. *Oddly enough, the setting was set at maximum, but why?* Perhaps Elaine had planned an extended vacation, and the maximum temperature would ensure the contents remained frozen. An inner voice told her not to bother wasting her time. *But, someone had gone through the trouble of concealing it, and now the only question was why?*

For a moment Terry reflected on her last thought, which took her back to her childhood years. She recalled a scuffle between her twin sister and herself as they fought over a Barbie doll. Terry was determined to have her own way and figured the one place that Tricia would never look was in the freezer, so she wrapped the doll in a towel and placed it in a plastic bag near the bottom. It remained safely hidden for two years until Terry finally let her sister in on her little secret.

From her leather case she pulled out a small x-acto knife, and using light strokes she cut a thin line around the door's perimeter helping to break the seal. *This ought to do the trick*, she thought in her usual upbeat style. More vigor was placed in her next pull.

A cloud of steam quickly spread into the air, Terry stepped back as she was chilled by the freezing vapor. For a split   second,   her   eyes   reflected   sheer   terror.

Chapter 9

Rain and sheets of ice pellets created melodic pattering sounds as they bounced off the bay window. It continued for a good two hours providing entertainment for Jack and Tara who enjoyed the change of scenery. Soon the grass was covered by a layer of popcorn-sized ice balls. This was short lived and was replaced by a drenching rain. As he continued to watch, the rain seemed relentless. The ice magically disappeared, but its presence signified that Christmas was just around the corner.

Jack felt much better, and for the last couple of days was still mulling over details for his holiday bash. A New Year's Eve party would fit quite well with his Christmas plans, he thought to himself. It would be just perfect.

The downpour gave way to a light rain. Jack grabbed his umbrella while slipping on his rain coat. Since he had not decorated his home for the past few years, he needed to re-take inventory. Jack quickened his pace and momentarily fiddled with the lock's combination. During the winter months, he used the shed as a work-station and spent countless hours working on various projects, particularly building wooden model-size vessels, since many of his outdoor activities were curtailed. The heaters he recently installed allowed him year round access. Finally, the lock sprung open. He also needed to maintain the right temperature and humidity to safeguard his newly constructed canoe.

He pulled out three boxes of Christmas ornaments along with a large plastic bag. He scattered everything onto the living room floor. His favorite colors were blue and silver and they would dominate his Christmas theme. Jack marveled at the endless lights. A one hundred foot reel of blue and white lights would drape over the eaves trough, veranda rail, and around his twelve foot blue spruce outside. He rummaged through the boxes jotting notes of what was still needed. A silver star sparked special memories of one joyous Christmas. It was recounted to him by his friend John.

Christmas had always been a joyous occasion for them. Usually, the first week of December marked the annual trek for the perfect evergreen. It was a lengthy drive, but pleasant and peaceful with little traffic. The drive along the winding country roads was simply panoramic; they passed miles and miles of evergreens which were draped in white while singing Christmas carols. The tree farm was enormous, spanning seemingly forever in each direction. Both their children would skip and dance through the snow, weaving in and out of endless rows of trees, which were set in perfect alignment. It was very exciting and stimulating to be in the great outdoors. Snowballs were tossed at each other, even when hit, they still laughed enjoying themselves. *Pick this one dad, no this one looks taller, no actually this is bigger.* The quest for the perfect tree was a quite a thrill and hardly a chore.

The air was clean and crisp and John's passageway cleared as he walked through the forest. Being the man of the house, he was given the task of chopping down the perfect evergreen. The axe was razor sharp, since John had sharpened it the night before. His strength was evident. He wielded the axe with little effort; and in less than twenty swings the tree toppled over. Hauling the tree was relatively easy, as the tree glided easily along the snow.

On the drive back home, everyone was happily anticipating decorating the Christmas tree as well as sipping some hot cocoa. Its long branches brushed against the front door, before it was set next to the stairwell. They adorned it with multi-colored lights. Blue bells and silver angels hung from each of the spruce needles. The youngsters were both eager to place the silver star on the top branch.

On Christmas Eve, the children were sent to bed early knowing full well Santa would drop off their gifts only when everyone was sound asleep. Pleasantly surprised, they never stopped to question anything but accepted everything at face value. Of course, they always left milk and cookies for the jolly old fellow. Amazingly on this special occasion, they were both early risers and excitedly scrambled downstairs to open their gifts. Shakes and rattles ensued, as they tried to guess if their presents corresponded to their wish lists. A battery operated truck and train set for Timothy, and a doll house and a couple of music CD's for Alicia. Bright smiles were painted on their faces as they rummaged through the remaining gifts.

John had especially cherished those festive days.

Her loud shrieking cries resonated as far as the upper level. No amount of training could have prepared Terry for what she had seen; she had no time to brace herself. Then there was complete silence.

Sean fled down the set of wooden stairs with Steve trailing right behind. Both of their guns were drawn in mid-air. They threw caution to the wind and followed in the direction of her distress call, leading them to the far end of the basement.

"Jesus Christ!" hollered Steve running to Terry's aide. Sean caught sight of the frozen body. "Errrr -- I need a hand; it's too heavy," Steve struggled.

"On the count of three, let's haul the body to the left. One -- two -- three," Steve directed. Terry held a petrified look and continued to stare directly at the ceiling. Not only was she in shock, but blood was gushing out from a deep cut on her forehead. Sean rushed to the cruiser to retrieve the first-aid kit and returned in a flash. He dressed the wound with several gauze pads and gently tried to comfort her. She continued to tremble unable to utter a single word.

"Are you okay?" Sean asked with a worried look. He was about to call the paramedics when she finally seemed to come around.

"I'll be okay," Terry's voice was quite faint drawing Sean closer.

An hour elapsed before Elaine was strapped to the stretcher. It took a team of four men to haul her up the lengthy staircase and just as they were about to carry the body outside, the front door opened unexpectedly. Everyone stood motionless realizing their blunder. Elaine's mother had returned from the coffee shop and her puzzled expression turned to one of horror. "Oh no!" her hands covered her mouth. "No, not my baby, please not my baby!" She rushed over to her. A mother's worst nightmare had been realized. Her wails riveted through the air piercing everyone's hearts. Steve tried in vain to comfort her.

"Please Mrs. Cooper."

"I want to stay with my daughter, my poor, poor baby. What has he done to her? Look at my baby! Oh my God, she's frozen -- God no, she's frozen solid!" looking skyward with a petrified look, she began striking herself repeatedly with open hands. Steve tried to calm her down by placing a strong hold around her.

"Let's go outside," he gently coaxed.

"No, I want to stay with my little girl," she cried in anguish.

The worst part of the Chief's job was watching lives shatter. He preferred to spend countless nights working on a case, rather than give such dire pain-staking news.

Steve and Sean accompanied Mrs. Cooper back to her own home where they would deliver the tragic news to her husband. Despite her injury, Terry stated that she was okay. But the Chief wasn't totally convinced and insisted that she be driven to emergency. She was still bleeding, but just slightly. However Terry knew better than to argue with him; he was too headstrong and didn't take no for an answer.

Dr. Adams carefully treated Terry's wounds. Despite his gentleness, it hurt considerably causing her to wince a few times. "It should heal nicely, without any stitches. Dress the wound with this lotion and be sure to change the bandage every day. We don't want any infections," he cautioned.

If anything, Terry felt an oncoming headache after nearly being knocked out by the frozen corpse. She asked for a couple of aspirins, but was careful not to mention her pain in front of Chief Williams fearing he'd have her tested for head injuries.

With all the havoc, the Chief delayed re-grouping the Team until the next morning. He wanted to hold a press conference and would discuss the particulars with them. The citizens of New Jersey deserved to be forewarned, but first he would wait for the autopsy report.

Jack quickly grabbed the list from the table before heading out the door. Lately, he felt an inner peace; he attributed his tranquil state to the upcoming holiday season. He glanced at his watch, it was just past one and soon the mall would be swarmed with shoppers. Jack didn't mind the crowds, after all he felt it lent to the Christmas spirit.

The car's stereo was tuned to the news station, and he was clearly shocked. This seemed to be becoming a common theme each time he turned on a TV or radio. "The town of Somerset has been victimized once again. Earlier today, Elaine Cooper was found dead in her home. We'll have more details …" Jack couldn't believe that their town housed a serial killer. It clearly explained why he had seen more police cruisers patrolling the streets and figured they would remain on high alert until they captured him.

It took him awhile to find a parking space and figured the mall would remain packed until the New Year. As he walked into the centre court he marveled at all the Christmas decorations. And of course, the big jolly old fellow held centre stage waiting to bring Christmas cheer to all the young children.

Jack was musing through one of his favorite department stores when he was side-tracked by a loud stampede. He watched a young slim man with heavy side-burns run down the adjacent aisle with a police officer chasing in hot pursuit.

'Jack be swift; Jack be quick.'

Jack strategically positioned himself ready to intercept the thief. He listened attentively and waited until the thumping sounds approached closer, and then strategically stuck out his left foot causing the man to sprawl forward and crash hard onto the floor. The man venomously cursed Jack. "You damn asshole, let me go! Go screw yourself man!" he hollered while trying to wriggle free.

But Jack had him securely pinned to the floor.

The police officer caught up, half winded. "You're under arrest," he read him his rights while slapping the hand cuffs around his wrists. His partner thanked Jack.

"We really appreciate your assistance," the officer gave him a firm handshake.

Jack was flattered, "It was nothing, I just happened to be in the right place at the right time, anybody else would have done the same thing."

The officer knew Jack was being modest. "Nothing," he scoffed. "We've been trying to nab him for over two months now. He has shoplifted from numerous retailers, but always managed to disappear like a phantom. Even though we had a general description of him, we had to catch him in the act," the relieved officer explained.

"I guess today was his unlucky day. I saw him running in my direction with your partner in hot pursuit; well naturally, I put two and two together." Jack felt proud of himself.

"We really appreciate it; it's people like you that make America a great country," the officer complimented enthusiastically.

"Excuse me sir, are you the man who caught the mall bandit?" the reporter interrupted holding a mike up to Jack. He was astonished to see how quickly the reporters appeared at the scene, but before he could even respond, the officer cut in.

"Yes, this man is our hero," the officer acknowledged. A large ovation ensued and photographers were snapping Jack's photo. Apparently news spread quickly, with many retail owners offering their congratulations and thanks. He had become an instant celebrity. Jack was informed that his photo along with a cover story would appear in tomorrow's paper and with that he resumed his shopping.

The mall was packed. Jack enjoyed the Christmas songs, and silently sang along with them. Across the hall, he noticed the large signs; the bookstore was having a thirty percent off sale on selected titles. Jack was lured inside and found the cooking section in the middle aisle.

"It's a great book," the perky saleslady acknowledged. "I bought that one last week and tried one of the shrimp and cheese platters."

"They look delicious. I'm having a party during the holidays, and I'm looking for suggestions," Jack explained.

"Any idea of what you would like to serve?"

"I'm considering a combination of dishes in order to have a good variety."

"May I then suggest some of the all time favorites?"

"By all means," Jack was impressed by the top notch service.

She browsed through the shelf and handily selected two hard covers. "Try some of these, they're delicious; I'm sure your guests will not be disappointed," Carol, the saleslady, pointed. "Also, you may want to browse through this book since it has some delicious hot and cold drinks."

"I appreciate all your help, just give me a couple of minutes and I'll be at the check-out counter."

"Sure -- take your time," Carol smiled while twirling her hair.

Jack found her to be pleasant enough, and wondered if she was flirting with him. Jack strolled to the sales counter.

"Would you like to become a member?"

"Maybe next time, I'm in a bit of a hurry," he graciously declined. It would give her access to his personal information, some of which he preferred to keep private.

Terry's head throbbed. The aspirins acted more like a placebo alleviating only some of her pain, but overall she had spent a restless night tossing and turning. She looked at her bedroom clock and realized she only had forty minutes to get ready and arrive at police headquarters. Reluctantly, she dragged herself out of bed and stepped into the bathroom. "Good God, I need a miracle!" Terry gasped at her ghastly complexion. Not only was her head badly swollen, but the dark circles underneath her eyes made her look like a raccoon.

It was eight-thirty, and the Chief quickly grabbed his caffeine fix to get him through the morning. He made his way down the hall to the conference room where they would desperately pool all their efforts. The Chief had faith in the Investigative Team and the two FBI agents, having handpicked each one, being acutely aware of their capabilities to produce quick results.

The Chief entered the room and announced. "Sorry to keep everyone waiting, but I had a few things to complete. Did anyone find anything unusual? Anything -- whatsoever?"

"Agent Gray and I scoured the upper level. We've placed the tests on high priority, and will receive the report this afternoon, at the earliest. Elaine kept her home very neat making our jobs a little easier. Oddly enough, we didn't notice any signs of a struggle, nor were any foreign objects found." A despondent Agent Michael continued, "I want to go back and check out a couple of things. But, it seems that our killer is especially prudent always managing to keep a few steps ahead of us. He's methodical in his planning, and covers his tracks quite well. In my entire career I've never met anyone as meticulous. Another thing that still bothers me is his ability to gain easy access to the victim's home. Before we received your call, we were checking out a list of suspects. We'll need to speak to Elaine Cooper's family, but I wouldn't be the least bit surprised if at least one identical name appears on both of the victim's lists. Some common denominator must exist between the two murders," Agent Michael hypothesized with a dejected look.

"We don't want to impose on the family while they're mourning, so we'll wait until after the funeral to speak to her parents along with close family members and friends," the Chief advised. "In the meantime, let's work with what we have. How did you find the body?" the Chief directed his attention to Terry.

"I was sorting through the laundry and had placed some worn clothes in a bag to be tested, but left it in the room thinking I would later drop it off at the lab for testing."

"No worries, we noticed the bag and delivered it ourselves," interrupted Agent Gray.

"The bathroom downstairs probably has never been used, given that it was void of all the basic necessities such as towels, etc.. The last area I searched was the room with the freezer. At first I hadn't noticed it, since it remained concealed by a stack of bins. Inside the bins I found some old school books and notes, which we should definitely look at. We might get lucky and come across some old yearbooks or letters, which might shed some light," Terry stated hopefully. "Anyway, after removing the bins, I noticed an upright freezer, which struck me as kind of odd. Why would anyone want to purchase a freezer just to hide it? I tried to pry it open, but it was frozen shut. On my third attempt, I yanked it open and barely caught a glimpse, before she crashed on top of me. She held a rose stem in between her lips, a rosary was linked in her hands, and blood stains covered her shirt." Terry cringed remembering Elaine's morbid state.

Everyone sat silent. "Obviously we're dealing with the same killer. No one knows of either the rose or the rosary. These two particular details aren't public knowledge, and I prefer to keep it that way. The last thing we need is a copy cat psychopath complicating matters even further. Also, we should be checking out local florists and churches that hand out these specific rosaries. Agent Gray and Agent Michael please present me with the information on hand, before we meet with the Cooper family. Regrettably, we're going to have to inform the public that a potential serial killer has targeted our town. We don't want to alarm everyone, but I feel obligated to alert our citizens. I'll make the necessary arrangements and we'll re-assemble in a couple of hours," the Chief added.

The Chief made the dreaded phone call. He agonizingly waited for what seemed like an eternity for his call to be transferred.

'Finally,' the Chief sighed.

"Larry, how are you doing?" the mayor asked politely.

"All things considered, not too well," the Chief held a dejected look and his dreary voice set off red flags. During the twenty years that they had known each other, he couldn't recall him sounding so depressed.

"Well don't keep me in suspense, what the hell's going on?"

"Victim number two has met the same fate as victim number one. The murder was an exact replica of the first murder. The same objects were planted on Elaine Cooper's body. The only difference being the victim was found frozen solid in her basement freezer. I'm afraid we've got a potential serial killer on our hands," the Chief was clearly on edge and feared this was just the beginning. The phone went silent for a minute.

"Dear God, what's going on in this town? We already have two people who've made the obituary list in less than two months. Do we have any clues, leads, or any chance in hell we'll ever catch this maniac?" the mayor's frustration was evident in his tone.

The Chief desperately tried to calm him down, "Let's try to keep everything in proper perspective. Sure we don't have a lot to work on, but we're building a suspect profile. This doesn't just include his physical attributes, but also an emotional and mental profile. We may not know his name or address, but we're closing in on him. It's only a matter of time before he makes a fatal error."

"You sound very confident," the mayor's voice took on an irate tone. "Though to be quite damn frank, I'm quite disappointed the way this entire matter has been handled. We've had two serious screw ups and we still don't have a damn clue to the killer's identity. To top everything off, we don't have any idea on how many more body bags will be filled." The mayor was simply livid and very restless. He fought back negative images of more women being mercilessly slain.

The Chief was equally frustrated, but decided it wouldn't be prudent to vent his anger. "I need to arrange for a press conference. The people of our community need to be on high alert. We don't want to frighten citizens, but instead warn them of this lurking psychopath. Let's not mention the mementos the killer has left behind, all this information is to remain highly confidential," the Chief cautioned.

"I agree the public needs to be notified." The mayor sighed. "Let me know the minute you schedule one, so I can be present. In the meantime if you need anything in order to bring an end to this rampage, don't hesitate to call me. You have my full support," the mayor stressed.

"I appreciate it."

It was nerve-racking waiting; the Chief felt in the hot seat while standing at the podium. The mayor was stationed to his right while a group of detectives were scattered throughout the room. Reporters from various media were present; the Chief instantly recognized and nodded to acknowledge a few of them.

"Good afternoon. Regrettably, we have evidence to suggest that a potential serial killer is preying on women of this town. At this point, we don't have a detailed description of the killer, other than he is male, in his late thirties to mid forties, and is well-built. We want the citizens of this state, particularly women to be on high alert. Please exercise extreme caution. We would strongly caution women not to travel alone, particularly at nighttime. Also, be careful who you allow into your home, since our findings lead us to believe that the killer knew both his victims. Anyone who has seen anything remotely suspicious is encouraged to contact us immediately. One can do so anonymously," the Chief assured.

"Chief Williams do you have any suspects at the moment?" asked Dan, a reporter from the local TV station.

"We've reason to believe the killer lives locally."

"You must have suspects!" interrupted Gary, another reporter.

"We're following several leads which we're still investigating. Surprisingly, the killer has given us a message promising to strike again," informed the Chief.

"A message -- what kind of message?" Gary was relentless with his questioning.

"At this point, we'll just say he has written us a poem," the Chief remained brief.

"What did he write in his poem -- the citizens have a right to know?" Gary insisted. He had always been persistent, but at times he was a real pain in the butt and was grating on the Chief's nerves.

"Yes, what did he state in his message?" demanded another reporter.

The Chief suddenly felt himself perspire. "We're not at liberty to give out details. But, we do strongly advise that the citizens of Somerset, New Jersey, especially for women to remain vigilant. As an added safety precaution, be extremely cautious of who you let into your home, and if you do notice anything remotely suspicious, please don't hesitate to call the police."

"Did the killer state when he will strike again?"

"We don't know," the Chief answered and pointed to another newspaper reporter, but Gary cut her off before she even had a chance to open her mouth.

"Did he state what he wants?" Gary rudely continued much like a loaded machine gun.

"No, but for Pete's sake let's give some of the others a chance," the Chief's expression was turning from one of patience and understanding to one of annoyance.

"Why do you think the killer has chosen these two women, is there a connection?" A young lady standing in the far back corner asked.

"We believe there may be a connection, but at this point we can't elaborate any further."

"How were they killed?" asked Jerry, a local TV reporter.

"The autopsy report will determine the cause of death. We don't know for certain if Elaine Cooper shared the exact same fate. But, Dianne Summers was suffocated before being stabbed."

The mayor stepped up to the podium right next to the Chief. "Mayor Wilson, perhaps you can be more open about these killings?" Gary persisted relentlessly. But the mayor's patience was even shorter than that of the Chiefs' and he simply ignored him.

"The Chief has already answered many questions. The purpose of this conference is to alert the good folks of this town. We ask everyone to be vigilant and cautious when inviting people into your homes. If traveling at night, it is best not to travel alone, and if at all possible remain in well lit areas. I can't stress enough to always remain alert and be aware of your surroundings. If anyone has any information regarding these two deaths, we kindly ask that they contact the police. I am concluding this meeting, and would like to thank everyone for coming," the mayor left the podium followed by the Chief. Both were escorted by a half dozen police officers.

Just as they were leaving, dozens of camera flashes nearly blinded them. The police officers had to literally create a passageway to escort them to their cars.

As the officers pulled into the Chief's driveway, he noted a mob of reporters raiding his front lawn. Fury was quickly building within him, but his anger was momentarily curtailed by his cell phone ringing.

"Hello Chief Williams?"

"Speaking."

"This is Dr. Leigh and I'm calling on behalf of Dr. Summers. We work together at the hospital. Dr. Summers was watching the news report and asked to see you urgently," Dr. Leigh informed.

"Why, has something happened?" the Chief became alarmed.

"Can you come by? He prefers to speak to you in person."

"I'll be right over."

The Chief knew Tyler must have some important information, or else he wouldn't have called him so urgently. *But what could be so pressing? Had he remembered something?*

He was relieved to have reached the hospital. The Chief wanted to meet with Dr. Summers privately and asked the two accompanying officers to take a break. "Hello, I'm here to see Dr. Leigh," the Chief announced.

Dr. Summers had described Chief Williams as exceptionally tall with dark curly hair. The gentleman standing before her certainly fit the bill. "Chief Williams?" Dr. Leigh asked before the nurse had the opportunity to respond.

"Yes."

"Please come in," the doctor gently closed the door behind him. "I understand you're trying to solve a murder, but I need to forewarn you that Dr. Summers's medical condition is very delicate. Even though he desperately wants the killer to be placed behind bars, we can't allow him to get too excited. I implore you not to inundate him with too many details; it's quite upsetting for him, although he won't admit it."

"Don't worry, you have my word," the Chief agreed to exercise extreme caution.

"Hello," the Chief said turning his head around the corner.

"Come on in," Tyler invited with a slight grin.

"How are you feeling?"

"Well I'm feeling better, and hopefully I'll soon be back on my feet again. Thanks for coming by on such short notice. I was watching the local news and was shocked to learn that one of our friends has become the second victim. My wife was good friends with Elaine Cooper."

The Chief looked stunned. "I'm sorry, I had no idea you knew Elaine." After a brief pause the Chief continued, "Obviously some link exists, although at this point I'm not quite sure why he has targeted either of them."

"They had been friends for years. I met her on several occasions, quite a lovely character." The Chief pondered what Tyler had just said. "Do you have any suspects?" Tyler seemed quite concerned.

"Well, I was hoping you could help us out on a particular matter. Due to certain evidence, we believe the killer may have had a romantic encounter with both your wife and Elaine. I'm not suggesting your wife was having an affair, but she may have been romantically involved in the past. Another possibility is that both women rebuked the killer's romantic intentions, causing him to lash out. Either way, we're dealing with someone who's emotionally unstable. Did Dianne speak to you about past boyfriends, or previous engagements?"

"No, she was never engaged, although she dated before we met."

"Do you remember any of her past boyfriends? According to the poem as well as evidence we're strongly relying on the notion that the killer is seeking revenge."

Dr. Summers thought back. He reflected upon their shared memories of past flames. Tyler's emotions were quickly surfacing; he fought back tears. "I don't recall their names off hand, but I do know she kept a diary. It may take some time to find it, although I do recall that both relationships had been short-lived."

"It would be greatly appreciated if you can give me the names as soon as you're up to it. I think it's important to do a background check on both of them. At this point I'm not suggesting that they're responsible, but we can't leave anything to chance. Also, could we keep the two identities between ourselves? I don't want any information being leaked. And, I certainly don't want to make any more false arrests or unnecessarily ruin someone else's reputation," the Chief seemed quite adamant about his last point. "Take it easy and please let me know if I can help you with anything," the Chief offered.

"Thanks and I'll definitely find you those names," Tyler reassured him.

The Chief personally expressed his condolences to the Cooper family. It was a fairly large funeral with immediate family, relatives, and many of Elaine's friends present. The only uplifting parts were the eulogies shared by her family and close friends. Unlike the average funeral, everyone, young and old, male and female, were overcome with grief.

The Chief and two undercover police officers kept a close eye on all attendees.

Mrs. Cooper broke down. Her loud cries and sorrow intensified everyone's pain. She was comforted by her husband and younger daughter, Janice.

Janice had been out of town on business, but immediately flew back after learning of her sister's horrendous death. They had been close since childhood, and she found it difficult accepting what happened to her only sister. Each morning she prayed it had just been a horrible nightmare. But reality quickly set in as she tried to come to terms with her sister's ill fate. Dark puffy circles encircled her brown eyes giving her complexion an even starker look. *She still kept asking herself why?* The salt stung her eyes.

"My poor baby," Suzanne continuously repeated, "I want my baby back! God, oh please God!" The coffin was being hoisted into the crypt to be given eternal sanctuary.

Her wails grew louder and louder until the pain became too overwhelming to bear. She had momentarily collapsed surrendering to a cloud of darkness. Her husband caught her before she crashed onto the hard surface, soon a large crowd gathered around her. "Will she be okay?" exclaimed her cousin, Lisa, in an alarmed tone.

"Please everyone stand back -- let's give her some air!" her husband pleaded. "Honey, honey…can you hear me?" he asked gently caressing her cheeks. She slowly regained consciousness and everyone breathed a sigh of relief.

Janice wandered if her mother would ever be able to cope with her sister's death. Elaine Cooper's vault was sealed shut. Even though her body was laid to rest, her family and friends would always remember her.

The Chief briefly met with Elaine's father who was more than willing to provide him with a list of names. Also, he would speak to other family members and friends.

A couple of days after Elaine's funeral, Mr. Cooper presented the Chief with a list. He sought justice for his daughter; he wasn't going to let some deranged killer get away with killing his beautiful daughter. He had made a solemn pledge to his daughter, and he would do everything in his power to deliver on that promise. And if the police weren't capable of finding the psycho, he would make it his own personal mission to apprehend him. The killer would pay the price. Ultimately he sought revenge, but for now he would leave it in the hands of the police.

The two agents scoured meticulously over every tidbit of information.

"Wait a minute. I think we may have found something," Agent Gray pointed out excitedly.

"Uh-huh, I'll begin checking the police records." Agent Michael quickly began a name search. It took only a couple of seconds for the computer screen to list all of the suspect's general information. At the present time, none of the potential suspects had been arrested or accused of any crime. Other than a speeding ticket or two, all the individuals in question were clean. Albeit, that only proved that they hadn't been convicted of a crime, and not that they hadn't committed one. The agents were given adamant orders not to approach any of the suspects or to interrogate any of their families. The Chief had a different plan in mind; each suspect would first be placed under surveillance and only when they had substantial incriminating evidence would they make an arrest.

The Agents were now ready to present the list of suspects to the Chief. Finally, their long hours of relentless scouring would pay off. Quick action needed to be taken. This time the Chief would not be disappointed.

Chapter 10

The Investigative Team quickly exchanged good mornings before seating themselves around the mahogany table. Just as the Chief was about to begin, an officer buzzed him to answer an emergency call. Silence followed as they waited patiently. Terry felt so troubled, wondering how the killer managed to keep a few steps ahead of them without fumbling. Even with the latest technology and DNA testing, he had managed to leave behind virtually no evidence.

"I think you have been waiting to hear from me." The Chief could hear heavy breathing in the background. "I have a question for you. How many are two short of a dozen?" the muffled voice asked.

"What! Who's this?" demanded the Chief. He had no patience for childish pranks.

"For the last time, how many are two short of a dozen?" the man had the audacity to continue.

"Okay, we'll play it your way, 10," the Chief scoffed. "What's your point?" the Chief questioned haughtily, annoyed with the caller and was just about to hang up.

"Now, now, don't get pushy with me, or you may regret it," he answered in a threatening tone before continuing. "Does that number ring a bell?"

The Chief's anger flared, but at the same time maintained his outward composure. "Look, I don't have time to play games. I'm the Chief of this town and…"

"But on the contrary, I think you have time to play this one, and if you don't, then I think you should make some time. Perhaps you are getting too old, and your mind is growing too feeble. By the way, the answer is ten roses," the phone clicked.

The Chief stood momentarily perplexed before it dawned on him. "Shit!" the Chief yelled running to the security office. "Trace that call now!"

His heart raced realizing it was the killer. The Investigative Team and the agents flew off their seats.

"We've traced the call. It's over on 45th street adjacent to the bakery," the supervisor informed.

The Chief wasted no time; he hurled a multitude of commands. The police department resembled a subway station with everyone scrambling in a mad rush. Officers close to the location were dispatched and also sped to the site. The Investigative Team had already fled the station.

They realized that this might be their only opportunity to catch him. The Chief was damned if he was going to let him get away. The sirens screamed through the streets and onlookers were alarmed at the long line of police cars speeding by. Ten police cruisers arrived at the scene. Officers were led by the Investigative Team and FBI agents, who were adamant about not letting anyone taint the scene.

Agents Gray and Michael sectioned off the telephone booth. They were already combing the booth, dusting for prints.

Every vehicle and every individual around the block would be scrutinized. Mainly, they focused their attention on individuals who fit the general description of the killer. Everyone's name, telephone number, license plate, and driver's license were being recorded.

Steve proceeded inside the bakery. He walked directly to the check-out counter where he flashed his id.. "Hello, my name is Steve Black and I'm with the New Jersey Police Department. We need to ask you some questions."

The gentleman raised an eyebrow, oblivious to the nature of his visit. He was in his early fifties with black hair showing hints of graying at the sides. Over his plaid shirt, he wore a white apron. "Sure, how can I help?" he politely asked with a strong European accent.

"Did you notice anyone using the telephone booth outside about five minutes ago?"

"No -- for the past hour I've been preparing dough in the kitchen. I just came to tell Isabelle that one of our customer's orders was ready. Isabelle," the gentleman called out loud. A young lady in her early twenties approached them.

"Hi, I'm Investigator Steve Black with the New Jersey Police Department." Isabelle shared the same puzzled look. "Did you notice someone using the telephone booth about five minutes ago?"

"Yes." Steve's heart skipped a couple of beats.

"Which direction was he headed?" he asked. She pointed in a southerly direction.

"What did he drive?"

"I didn't pay much attention; I was busy serving a couple of customers. But, it was dark in color," she said while pushing back a strand of black hair.

"Did you get a look at him?"

"No, his back was turned to me, although he's tall." Steve took a minute to let Sean and Terry know which direction the vehicle headed, believing that he could be in the vicinity. "When did he leave?"

"About two to three minutes, before you arrived. I can check with the cash register tape, I remember the customer I was serving, she's one of our regulars." Isabelle was correct they had missed him only by a few minutes.

"What was he wearing?"

"Umm," she squinted. "I remember him wearing a leather jacket."

"Did he have anything in his hands or did you notice anything peculiar about him?"

"I didn't see him carrying anything."

"Is there anyone else who may have seen him?"

"It's only us two working, unless one of our customers saw him. They left shortly before you arrived. They are regular customers of ours, and I happen to know them. I can ask them tomorrow, they usually come in every day."

Steve pulled out his business card. "Call me immediately if they remember anything."

After questioning everyone within the block there were only two gentlemen who remotely fit the description. They were in the same age category. But, one of the gentlemen was average in stature with a small build. They would certainly check him out; although he did not seem capable of the physical strength they believed the killer possessed. The other gentleman walked with a limp, having injured himself in an automobile accident years ago.

Terry tailed a black convertible. She didn't want to alert the driver, and smartly maintained her distance. The car turned sharply around the corner which aroused her suspicions; she wondered if the driver noticed she was tailing him. Still she held off from sounding her siren. Terry was driving an unmarked car to conceal her identity. She was having the license plate checked out. "No this is an emergency. The driver has made a couple of sharp turns. I can't hold on --"

The driver accelerated onto the highway at alarming speeds. "This is Investigator Terry Bradshaw...I'm heading on the highway...I need back up fast..." Terry's siren blazed. She chased him at neck-breaking speeds and took a glance at her speedometer which read one-hundred-fifty clicks and accelerating. She watched him weave dangerously between cars. *Watch out,* Terry gasped. He barely missed slamming into a Mack truck. He continued to race recklessly between vehicles. *"Stop!"* The convertible abruptly swerved in front of a tractor trailer. "Good God," Terry let out a deep shrill. The car's rear bumper did the tango with the truck's front bumper. The rig's driver blew his horn and shot him the finger. *This guy is a raving lunatic; someone is going to get killed.* She tried to push these negative thoughts aside, and continued in hot pursuit when she caught a glimpse of a helicopter flying past her window, giving her some reassurance.

"This is the New Jersey Police, pull over immediately! I repeat this is the police -- pull over, now!" The car didn't heed the warning. Obviously, he would have to be physically stopped. The helicopter dropped lower, now hovering above the car just thirty degrees east of it. The driver had no intention of stopping, and continued swerving dangerously.

"Oh no, Terry cried out." His wheel turned too sharply, causing the car to spin out of control. Loud ear piercing sounds had Terry biting her nails, as metal continued grinding against metal. The passenger's side was being chewed up by the guard-rail for a couple hundred feet before coming to an abrupt stop. Terry cut in front. She exited her car, and carefully crept alongside the driver's door. The car's sides were pretty banged up, and the driver was hunched over at the wheel. She tried opening it, but the door wouldn't budge as the driver's door and frame were severely twisted. "Damn!" she blasphemed out of frustration. Before making a second attempt she heard wails of approaching sirens. "Come on, come on," she panicked.

Sean arrived. "Hurry, I can't pry the damn door open," Terry gasped. She grimaced as she saw blood spurting from his nose. The glass was shattered, but still remained intact. Sean ran back to his vehicle and shortly afterwards raced back carrying a crow bar.

"Hurry, Hurry!" she cried. Sean cursed, after several unsuccessful attempts. It was time for a different strategy. He positioned the crowbar in between the front and back door while leveraging his full weight on the back passenger door. "Errrrh," he groaned out loud having applied all of his strength. The loud screeching sounds of metal bending caused them both to cringe as the door finally flew open.

"He's breathing, but bleeding badly." Terry panicked applying pressure to his gash. The only thing that saved him from an instant death was the back end of the passenger's side smashing into the rail first. The car was a total write off.

The paramedics finished bandaging him and rushed him to the hospital, accompanied by two police cruisers. Terry and Sean checked the vehicle's contents. Lastly, they pried the trunk open. "Whew -- oh my, look at what we have here," Sean whistled.

"Jesus, no wonder he was in such a hurry to get away. He could get life in prison," Terry looked astonished. Sacks of cocaine were scattered over the trunk's surface. The stash probably had a street value worth millions.

Jack managed to pick up the receiver while stacking the dishes in the sink.

"Hello Jack, its Jackie."

"Well hello sunshine, how are you doing?"

"I'm fine, but how are you feeling?"

"Much better. I no longer have any pain in my back and my soccer head has deflated."

Jackie laughed. "If you're feeling up to it I would like to come over and say hello."

"I'd love the company."

"Is an hour okay?"

"That's perfect."

Jack busied himself around the living room puffing pillows and straightening magazines. He certainly believed first impressions were lasting ones.

Jack stepped in the bathroom to freshen up. He tried to gel his curls back, but grew increasingly frustrated as they kept falling over his eyes, it was due time for a trim.

Jack made his way into the kitchen to put on a fresh pot of coffee when the door bell rang.

She took his breath away; his jaw fell leaving him completely speechless. He quickly regained his composure and welcomed her inside. "Please come in, let me hang your jacket."

He admired her and thought her blouse complimented her figure. He also thought she looked cute the way she tied her hair leaving only a few strands to dangle over her face and onto the nape of her neck.

"I bought you some freshly baked apple pies," she handed him a brown paper bag.

"Thank you." *A woman after my own heart,* thought Jack. "Would you like coffee, or do you prefer tea?"

"Coffee is fine."

"Then we'll have some along with our coffee," Jack winked at her. She smiled showing off her dimples, which Jack had instantly loved from the very first time.

Jack gave her a quick tour of his home. She stared in awe, overwhelmed by the richness in colors. Everything had been so carefully selected. She sunk into the leather couch; it felt so comfy that it almost lulled her to sleep. "How long have you been living here?"

"A few years."

"Wow! Your home looks brand spanking new. I've never seen one so beautifully decorated."

"Well thank you."

She followed him into the kitchen. He warmed the pie in the microwave. "How about some vanilla ice-cream topped with caramel sauce?"

"Sure." *Not only does he have good taste, but also his culinary skills are not half bad,* Jackie marveled. Jack liberally poured the sauce letting it spill onto the sides.

"Do you always keep your home so well organized?" Jackie had never seen a home so spotless.

"Only for a special lady."

Tara suddenly flew into the room and perched herself on Jack's shoulder, claiming her territory.

"Wow, what a beautiful bird." Jackie complimented admiring her stunning tri-colors.

"Beautful berd, beautful berd," Tara repeated.

Jackie marveled, "Hey, she's pretty good with her pronunciation."

"Yeah, she picks up words quite quickly. I too was impressed."

"And let's not forget loyal." Jackie noticed how territorial Tara was with her master. Perhaps, she was also a bit jealous having noticed another female in the room. Jackie pondered this for a moment, wondering if birds actually felt some of the same emotions as humans.

"Feel free to pet her." Jackie moved closer, taking great care not to frighten her, but as Jackie attempted to stroke Tara's head, but she flew towards the bay window.

"So -- do you live alone in this big house?"

"Just Tara and I," Jack sighed.

"Don't you get lonely?"

"Sometimes, but work usually keeps me quite busy." Jack diverted attention away from himself, "Well enough about me, what about you?"

"I'm currently enjoying my space again, but I must admit it does get lonely at times. I've just recently broken off from a relationship."

"Oh, anything you care to talk about?"

"After dating a few months, his dark side started to surface. The man had one bad temper and was becoming verbally abusive. I had no intention of becoming his permanent punching bag, so I broke it off," Jackie breathed a sigh of relief. Jack acutely sensed her change in disposition and empathized with her.

"I'm sorry to hear that -- I mean that he was such a creep."

"Don't be, it was the smartest thing I ever did. On the day I told him, I made sure it was in a public place, and let's just say it was a good thing I did."

Jack steered her away from her negative experience by quickly changing the subject, "You need to give me the name of where you purchased this apple pie. It's truly delicious; I've never tasted anything quite so good,"

Jackie let him in on her little secret. "I usually stock up when I go, because it's quite a drive, about an hour or so. Not only do they have delicious pies, but their cakes are equally scrumptious. I can pick some up for you; I plan to go before the Christmas holidays."

"Sounds great, and if you would like some company just let me know. Is it okay if we sit in the living room, the couch is much easier on my back?" Jack felt a terrible throb and cushioned his lower back with his hands.

Jackie saw him wince.

"Oh sure. Gees -- this is really comfy," Jackie noted. "It feels so good to be off my feet." She wiggled her toes trying to release some tension. "One drawback of my job is that my feet ache something awful at the end of each day."

"I'm one of the world's best massagers. Would you like a foot rub?" Jack enticed in a flirtatious manner while rubbing his hands in preparation.

She let out a whooping laugh. "You probably need a massage more than I do," Jackie reasoned. Before she had time to reflect upon what she had just said, Jack gladly accepted the invitation.

"Okay, I'll give your feet a massage and you can give me a back massage."

Jackie extended her feet onto Jack's lap. "Ahhh, that feels real good; you're a pro at this." She relaxed enjoying the massage. Jack chuckled as he playfully tickled her feet a couple of times, slowly easing her inhibitions. She giggled, pulling her feet away, but began to warm up to him.

"I'm even better at this." He leaned over and kissed her gently exploring her sweet lips. She savored the moment enjoying being cuddled next to him. Her body molded next to his and she instantly let her fingers dance through his black curls.

"I believe it's my turn," he stated seductively. He rolled off his shirt while extending himself on the couch.

"Hubba hubba," Jackie was completely turned on by his muscular arms and well toned body. She took a moment to admire him and felt her excitement grow as she began to massage his shoulders. She then massaged his back working very slowly to release any built up tension. Jackie's hands felt quite soothing and Jack began to relax, "Ahh, that feels so good," he complimented. Even though she used a lotion to reduce the friction, a deep passion was building within him. His heart was ablaze and he couldn't hold back any longer. Almost spontaneously, he rolled over and pulled her next to him, lavishing her with passionate kisses.

Terry and Sean admired the old stone structure which dated well over one hundred years. They climbed up a series of cobbled stone steps which lead them through a solid double oak door into the foyer. As they stepped through another set of double doors, they noticed his frail helpless body and his solemn face filled with sadness. He was well known to many. A crucifix was centered at the front overlooking parishioners.

Sean and Terry gathered that the thin man with a gaunt face was Father Samuel. He moved gracefully down the aisle with a calm gait.

"Father Samuel?" Sean asked.

"Yes," he answered nodding his head slightly. Sean and Terry introduced themselves.

"We appreciate you taking the time to meet with us on such short notice."

"How can I help you? Over the phone you mentioned it was urgent."

"Yes, we're trying to track down someone who poses a great threat to society at large. He has left this memento with each of his victims." Father Samuel looked stunned. Sean placed the rosaries on the wooden pew; each one was sealed in its own clear plastic bag.

"Do these look familiar?"

"We often give these to our parishioners, and occasionally we set them at the back."

"Are there any other churches who may also hand these out?" Sean inquired.

"Yes, these rosaries are quite common."

Great thought Terry, dreading another dead end. *Is this bloody nightmare ever going to end?* "Do you happen to have a list of parishioners who attend mass regularly?" Terry probed becoming quite frustrated, always coming up empty-handed.

"We do have names of our regular attendees. I would certainly be more than happy to give you those, but how far back would you like me to photocopy?"

"Good question, uh…could you go back a few years. Also, we hope you can keep an eye out for anyone who matches this general description," a gleam of hope washed across Sean's face as he described the killer.

"I will do my best; I will also let the others know."

"We really appreciate your help," Sean felt a great inner gratitude for the priest's assistance.

"God bless. God is most pleased when people are helping each other."

"Thanks again, I'll be back in a couple of days," Sean added before leaving.

In the meantime, Steve had visited another local church. He had just concluded his meeting with the priest, and was eager to meet Sean and Terry for lunch. He hoped Sean and Terry had made some headway.

Sean and Terry ordered cold drinks. "It looks like we have our work cut out for us," sighed Sean.

"No kidding -- I hope we'll have some better leads once the families prepare their lists," Terry was beginning to feel quite uneasy about the case, she couldn't pinpoint it, but something was gnawing at her. She picked up the local newspaper, which was discarded on the seat next to her and skimmed over Elaine Cooper's coverage. Terry was deeply saddened as she looked at Elaine's photograph. Her lively smile was a bright contrast to the stark flashbacks of Elaine toppling on top of her, the memory still haunted her. "Whoever he is, he's pretty gutsy to call us from such a close proximity," Terry remarked engrossed deep in thought.

"Yes, he's starting to grind on my nerves!" Sean stated angrily. "He has everything well timed; he's definitely not your average killer. He plans everything very carefully, indicating he premeditates the murders to the last detail. God only knows what he's planning next," Sean gasped.

Steve entered the packed restaurant. He looked around before spotting them sitting at the far corner. No sooner had he joined them, when a cheerful waitress came to take their orders.

Sean filled Steve in on their recent visit. "I'm not sure if we're any further ahead, but Father Samuel has agreed to provide us with a list of the regular parishioners," he explained. "He also has agreed to keep a lookout for someone who matches the general description."

Moments later, the waitress appeared skillfully balancing three plates. "Fettuccine with cream sauce."

"Thank you," Terry smiled.

"Steak in mushroom sauce." Steve motioned helping the waitress. She set the pasta primavera in front of Steve. "Enjoy your lunch."

They ate in silence. Terry felt drained. They had been working around the clock for the past several weeks and aside from a few hours of rest each night, the remainder of their time was spent on cracking the case. Now, one of their last hopes was checking out the florists. She hoped someone would remember something, something which would lead them closer to the killer. If that avenue proved to be another dead end, then their leads could be curtailed. It could take months if not years, before they caught up to him, if ever.

John was in better spirits and was looking forward to chatting with Edward. As John made himself comfortable, he realized it had been about a month since his last visit.

Edward greeted him, sincerely apologizing for being late. Unlike his usual self, Edward acutely noticed his withdrawn and quiet disposition, and commented accordingly, "You seem rather quiet today."

"Sorry, I was just reminiscing about my last Christmas. I can't believe almost three years have passed, it just seems like yesterday that we were all celebrating."

"I'm sure you had a smashing good time."

"Yes, Christmas was always a special time. I remember one Christmas in particular; we packed our suitcases for a week long vacation and drove to Colorado. We had a splendid panoramic view overlooking the mountains. It was a quiet cozy resort and at night we huddled around the roaring fire, roasting marshmallows and sipping our hot cocoa. As we enjoyed our nightcap, we would sing Christmas carols and watch the children's excited faces as we recounted our own childhood Christmas stories." A calm serenity encapsulated John's heart and he glowed from the happy memory. He paused momentarily to look out the window; the light dusting of snow brought back some more wonderful memories. "The resort was ideal for skiing and it was amazing watching her weave in and out of the slaloms faster than a hare. The children would often join us on the slopes, while other times they were happy to build snow sculptures. It had been an exciting week for everyone. We greatly enjoyed the escape from the hectic city life. To top things off, we had a major snowstorm, extending our trip another couple of days. The kids were thrilled."

"Sounds like everyone had a wonderful time," Edward beamed.

"Yes, we had to promise the children that we'd return the following year," The sparkle in John's eyes was clouded by his last statement.

"Are you doing something special this Christmas?" asked Edward.

"A friend of mine has invited me to attend a small house party. But, I'm not sure if I should go."

"Why -- do you have any other plans?" Edward urged with a bewildered look.

"Not at the present time. Although, I feel a little uneasy and am not sure if I'll feel like celebrating," an indecisive John just shrugged his shoulders. "I don't want to put a damper on the festivities."

"Perhaps, if you don't feel like joining in on the party, you can stop in for a short while. I'm sure your friend will be happy to see you."

"You have a good point. Maybe I'll just drop by and wish everyone Happy Holidays."

"Christmas is the perfect time to spend with friends."

John always felt light-hearted after speaking with Edward.

Lately, it seemed time raced by, but he was no further ahead in the investigation since the onset of the crime. The Chief waited for Dr. Ernstein's arrival, anxiously tapping his pen against the desk. He welcomed a different perspective; one which could offer him insight into the killer's frame of mind. At this point, he would settle for any tidbit, no matter how insignificant.

Dr. Ernstein gently tapped on the Chief's door. "Hello, I'm Dr. Ernstein," he announced.

"Thank you for coming on such short notice," the Chief acknowledged while closing the door behind him. "Please make yourself comfortable."

Dr. Ernstein was the Chief of Psychologists at the local hospital. Through many triumphs he had earned the reputation as being one of the best and most respected doctors in his respective field. During his twenty years of professional experience, he successfully dealt with a myriad of cases and often counseled physically as well as sexually abused clients, giving them the strength and confidence to resume a normal life. But, Dr. Ernstein's fascination had always been with criminal psychology, and it was especially these individuals which captured his interest. He often traveled extensively to attend conferences and lectures on abnormalities such as pedophiles and psychopaths.

The Chief quickly briefed the doctor before presenting him with the case file. It contained all the information to date, including forensic reports, autopsy reports, the killer's letter, and the taping of the killer's phone call. The file was over two inches thick.

The Chief placed the file on the desk. Dr. Ernstein flushed as he read the one page poem. He re-read the poem several times before continuing. It took him well over two hours to complete the entire contents while jotting notes trying to formulate his opinion. He contemplated, and momentarily struggled with different scenarios trying to understand what made the killer tick. Later in the afternoon, the Chief returned back to his office to find Dr. Ernstein immersed deep in thought.

"Hmmm…," the Chief didn't mean to barge in, but wondered if he could use a break. "Could I get you a coffee?" he asked.

"Sure, I take mine black."

The Chief instructed his assistant to bring one black coffee and the usual for him.

Dr. Ernstein pondered everything carefully and took a brief moment before beginning. "You're dealing with someone who's quite intelligent. He knows exactly what he's doing, but wants to send everyone on a wild goose chase. Somehow, he sees himself as invincible and believes that he'll never be apprehended and therefore takes considerable risks. It also explains why he deliberately taunts you, while doing his best to keep everyone in the dark. For some unknown reason, a deep hurt, perhaps even agony is harbored within him. He may be lashing out at memories from his past in hopes to quash his current pain. There's no doubt in my mind that he'll continue killing relentlessly until he accomplishes his mission. Even then, there's the possibility that he'll feel justified in killing even when someone opposes him or causes him grief. This individual is extremely dangerous and psychotic. Most likely this person will try and dispose of his victims as quickly as possible. I wouldn't be the least bit surprised if the killing escalates in the very near future." The Chief's face darkened thinking things were already bad enough. "He has tasted the sweet revenge of his victim's blood, and now is thirsty for more. My worst fear is that the more he kills the more he will feel self-righteous. In his mind, he will take on a God-like figure of purifying the earth of all who are unworthy. It seems evident that his next victim will also be a woman. But, I should point out that at this stage this is inconclusive. It could mean however, that he needs to accomplish his mission and may at any point include some male victims. There's really no conclusive evidence to fully support either rationale. They're not being murdered in alphabetical order, although I strongly suspect that he has prepared a list dictating the order in which each victim will perish. He plans their murders very well, also suggesting a desire to remain elusive," he paused taking a sip of his coffee. "The stabbing through the heart indicates that he has been hurt badly at some point in his life, probably fairly recently. There's also the suggestion that he has experienced something rather traumatic to find it necessary to resort to such extremes. The placing of the bodies in water signifies purification or some type of religious belief. Also, the rosary lends the impression that the killer is religious, and it may be his way of suggesting the Lord is with them and that they're forgiven. As for the rose, this could indicate an emotional attachment of some sort. He has chosen a specific course of action, but may deviate from his plans. His psychological state will play a great role; anything could trigger him. He's very unstable and I would hate to cross his path," the doctor emphasized. The Chief sighed deeply while Dr. Ernstein continued. "He reverts to religion to justify his actions. By killing them he believes he's purged them of their sins, and since they're pure of sins they can be laid to rest."

"Both of the victim's families can provide us a list of past boyfriends, is there anything else we could be doing at this time?"

"Hmm...as I've stated earlier I don't think he's randomly choosing his victims, so a link must exist between the murders. Even though the killer has just recently begun striking, he has harbored resentment for many years. He's at a point of extreme rage, and will try concealing this to avoid arousing any suspicion. The victims may have known him for quite some time. Perhaps they've never dated, but could've just been friends."

The Chief pondered this for a brief moment. It hadn't occurred to check and see if Dianne and Elaine had attended the same school.

Dr. Ernstein took time to consider all of the Chief's questions. "If he tries contacting you again refrain from uttering any negative remarks. Try to remain calm and keep your conversation as positive as possible. If anything, continue speaking to him, he might slip and reveal something."

The Chief shook his hand and thanked the doctor. He appreciated his advice and insight.

"Call me if anything new transpires," the doctor left feeling deeply troubled knowing the killer still roamed freely and would soon strike again.

It was the tenth florist shop they had visited in one day. The smell of flowers usually was a pleasing sensation, but now had turned into a dizzying experience. "I don't know about you, but I think after this visit we should call it a day," Sean felt drowsy and needed a diversion. He welcomed the thought of having some time to kick-back and release built-up tension. It was only six o'clock, still early enough in the evening to watch a nine o'clock movie. It had been over a month that he had enjoyed a night out with his wife.

"Sounds good to me. I think that we can use a few hours off. There's no point in burning ourselves out," Terry agreed.

It was a small shop, although well kept. At least a dozen fragrances filled the shop. A bunch of Sahara roses were being placed in boxes. They offered a delicate scent quite soft and pleasing.

"Hello, how can I help you?" asked the spectacled gentleman while adding water to a bouquet of blue and white hydrangeas.

"I'm Officer Sean Anderson and this is Officer Terry Bradshaw. We're conducting an investigation and need to ask you a few questions."

"My name is Ralph and I'm the owner. How can I help you?" Sean's eyes skimmed the room. "I'm presently alone in the shop; I'm just waiting for one of my employees to return. Is it okay if we speak here?"

"Sure, that's fine. We're looking for a man in his thirties or early forties. He's approximately six-feet-tall with a muscular build. He may have come into your shop about two weeks ago to purchase a single red rose," Terry explained.

Ralph reflected back. "Hmm, I don't believe I served anyone who purchased a single rose. Most of my customers have purchased small to large arrangements. But, I can double check my notes which include details according to customer's requests."

"Do you keep receipts handy, say for the last couple of weeks?" asked Sean.

"Yes, I keep them in my office."

"Would you mind if you check to see if someone may have purchased a single red rose?" Sean desperately wanted to make some headway into the case.

"No problem, I'll look as soon as I get a chance."

The loud bell had everyone's attention revert back to the door. "Danny, please come here a minute. I would like you to meet Officer Sean Anderson and Officer Terry Bradshaw." Danny shook hands with the officers. "They're investigating a crime and have some questions." The investigators explained all the relevant details.

"Yes, yes I do remember someone matching that description." Both Sean and Terry looked stunned, realizing it could be the big break they had been waiting for.

"He was in about two weeks ago," Danny continued.

"How did he make his purchase?" Sean anxiously cut in.

"Ummm -- if my memory serves me correctly, I believe it was a cash sale."

Terry smartly scouted the shop for any surveillance cameras. "Do you have any cameras in your shop?" she interrupted not having spotted any.

"No we don't. We're a small establishment and our clients prefer using plastic," he rationalized.

"Can you describe the gentleman?" Terry hoped to draw a composite sketch. Danny remained pensive for a moment staring into space. "Umm, I don't remember exactly what he looked like. But, I do recall that he was tall with an athletic build. He had dark hair and possibly a moustache. The gentleman was only in for a couple of minutes, and we have a substantial client base."

"If you see a photo of him, or if he comes back would you recognize him?"

"More than likely."

"Do you recall any facial scars or any other distinguishable features?" Sean realized from experience that the more time elapsed the less likely Danny was going to remember him. He may already have forgotten some pertinent information.

"No scars, but he wore sunglasses."

"Do you remember your conversation with him?" Sean was intent on gathering as much information as possible.

"Nothing in particular."

Sean continued with his questions knowing that an individual may recall something if asked specific questions rather than general ones. "Did he have an accent, or did he make any odd remarks?" Sean continued to probe.

"No, but I guess if there was something that peculiar I would be more apt to remember," Danny rationalized.

"You have a pretty good view of the parking lot. Do you remember what type of vehicle he drove?"

"It was a dark green pick-up. But, I'm not sure of the make."

"Okay here's our business card, call us if you remember anything," Terry informed.

"Should he come back to your shop I would like you to do the following. First and foremost, do not confront him. He's very dangerous, and you can place yourself as well as your co-workers in grave danger. Instead, just continue doing what you were previously doing. Do not look surprised or startled, otherwise you may alert him. It's better if you resort to a code to alert other staff members that he is presently in the store. Make sure everyone understands what will be said or done. It might be a good idea to rehearse just to make sure everyone understands, but also because it will help everyone to look more natural and feel more relaxed. If his presence is acknowledged call 911 for assistance. Do not try to detain him or stop him by any means, because I can't stress enough that he's extremely dangerous and may be armed. I don't want to hear about anyone dying trying to become a hero. Once you call the police, we'll be immediately alerted. One last thing, we hope to be able to install cameras, at our expense of course?" Sean hoped to get Ralph's approval.

"Sure, I'd be glad to help in any way possible."

"I'll have someone install the system tomorrow morning. We'll do so before the store opens."

"I can be here at 7:00. Is that enough time?"

"That's perfect."

Terry and Sean left, and for the first time in months felt relieved knowing it was now just a matter of time before they caught up to him. Their tantalizing feeling had been replaced by a burst of optimism. The killer was truly within their grasp. Ironically, the whole situation seemed even more twisted. *How on earth could the purchase of such a beautiful love object equate to their best hopes of nabbing a heartless, vindictive, cold blooded killer?* This nagging enigma would undoubtedly plague their consciousness thoughts until perhaps the purchase of his next red rose.

Chapter 11

A large heap had formed on her bed; she continued to rummage through the last half of her closet, and grew increasingly frustrated being pressed for time. Jackie's eyes lit upon spotting the chic black dress she purchased from her favorite fashion boutique. Excitedly, she kicked off her slippers and slipped into the dress, admiring herself in the full length mirror while adjusting the spaghetti straps. The dress snuggled nicely against her contours, revealing her femininity. She fumbled with the hair pins and at last managed to tuck the last curl on top of her head, leaving her back fully exposed. Jackie reached over to the dresser and picked up her silver hoop earrings and a matching necklace. It complimented her dress nicely while accentuating her long neck. She decided to have a little fun, and flirted in front of the mirror striking poses. "Well baby if you got it flaunt it," she then capped her performance by blowing a kiss.

Just in time, she thought as the door bell rang. She descended the stairs and took one long deep breath before opening the door.

"Wow, you look great!" Jack found it difficult not to stare. He drew her towards him and kissed her tenderly on the lips, while breathing in her light-floral fragrance. It was a special import from France given to her by her aunt. The fragrance wasn't strong, but subtly inviting. He was taken back, so much so, that Jack momentarily forgot about dinner.

"Oh Jack," Jackie purred as her heart raced a mile a minute. "Well that was the warmest welcome I've ever received."

"Expect more of the same," Jack felt on top of the world and his heart roared like a lion. It was certainly one promise Jack would be thrilled to keep.

Jackie slipped on her mink coat, grabbed her leather purse, and stepped into her pumps.

Jackie admired the cars pulling into the restaurant, and shot a second glance at a Rolls Royce limo which parked next to the curb. They stepped into the restaurant and Jackie took a minute to admire its ritzy appearance. "Wow!" La Credenza was well known for its fine dining and not surprisingly it catered mostly to the rich. They seated themselves and then sipped the waiter's recommendation of red wine, which was one of the finest stocks and well worth paying a premium.

"I've been meaning to visit Dr. Summers. How's he doing?"

"He's putting up a brave front, but I can still see the pain in his eyes. Sadly, it will take quite some time before he heals. The next several months could be quite trying for them. One good thing is that work keeps him busy, otherwise he would constantly dwell on Dianne."

An odd sensation swept through Jack, as though someone was watching him. He glanced around and sure enough his instincts were bang on. A little to his left, he noticed Yvonne sitting across the room eyeing Jackie. Jack couldn't help but feel that it was more than just a look of admiration; instead Jack keenly detected a subtle hint of envy. He wondered what led to her insecurities. Yvonne was a beautiful woman, although a few years older than Jackie.

"I just noticed one of my co-workers dining right across from us with her fiancé," Jack announced.

"Oh, are you friends?" Jackie was curious to learn more about Jack's life.

"Yes, good friends, I've known Henri for quite some time. Once in awhile, we go out for a drink. Henri and Yvonne dropped by to pay me a house visit after my back injury. I was pleasantly surprised when Henri asked if I would be his best man. They're officially engaged, and tying the knot next summer."

"I'd love to meet them."

"You'll like them, I'll ask them to join us."

"Hey Jack, it's great to see you," Henri stood firmly shaking Jack's hand. Jack exchanged hellos with Yvonne.

"I don't mean to impose, but my friend, Jackie, and I would be thrilled if you would join us for dinner."

"We'd love to," Yvonne was delighted to have bumped into Jack.

"Great this will give you the opportunity to meet Jackie." Jack lead the way.

"Yvonne, Henri, this is my girlfriend, Jackie." Jack was hoping everything would go smoothly. They exchanged pleasantries while sipping their wine.

"I understand congratulations are in order," Jackie smiled.

"Thanks," Yvonne and Henri responded simultaneously.

"So when's the big day?"

"We're thinking sometime in June. We saw this beautiful Victorian inn and we'll be dropping by later this week to book a date," Henri winked at Yvonne before elaborating. "The view is spectacular. It's surrounded by mature elm and maple trees, and overlooks a beautiful lake."

Jack then made a toast.

"Do you work with Dr. Summers?" Yvonne asked Jackie.

"Yes, actually I have known him for a few years."

"It must have been a real shock for him to hear about his wife."

"Yes, they were an ideal couple. He's devastated, but is taking life one day at a time. He will pull through; he has a lot of support from family and friends. His two young children need him now more than ever, he loves them dearly," Jackie explained.

"I heard that some reporters had the audacity to march into the hospital apparently trying to find Dr. Summers," Yvonne relayed.

"Yes, they don't seem to realize they can't just barge in anywhere. A few of the security officers actually had to escort them out. Dr. Summers was in critical condition and he certainly didn't need any further aggravations," Jackie clenched her teeth.

"Absolutely, they can be really insensitive at times. Their relentless style and persistence are annoying. They have no respect for people's privacy," Henri stressed shaking his head in disbelief.

"They can be a nuisance, but I suppose they're probably only trying to do their jobs," Jack tried to take a more neutral stance by rationalizing their position.

Jackie's heart silently ached for Dr. Summers. He was more than a colleague, and had taken the role of a father-like figure. She gladly welcomed the arrival of dinner and the change of subject.

During dinner Yvonne got to know Jackie better, and slowly regretted her initial feelings, realizing she had judged her too harshly. It was inspiring to see Jackie's dedication. It was obvious how much she cared about her patients, seemingly placing their needs first. Henri and Yvonne excused themselves as Henri led Yvonne to the dance floor.

Jackie admired them dancing closely together. It was obvious by the sparkle in both of their eyes that they were madly in love. She wondered if she would ever fall in love. She took another mouthful of her cream pie.

"Would you like to dance?" Jack asked. It would be their first dance together.

"I'd love to."

Jack held her close. He realized he had not felt this way about a woman in a very long time. He was totally enchanted. *Could it be love?*

Jack woke up bright and early, and even the somber darkness couldn't eclipse his light-heartedness, after sharing a memorable evening with Jackie. He wanted to do something special for her, and decided to surprise her.

It was six-thirty, and Jack skipped downstairs. "Yes, I'm coming Tara. Don't worry daddy will never forget to feed his little girl," he teased. Jack unfastened the latch and prepared her food bowl. "Here you go, your favorite seeds, enjoy."

He loved his morning coffee; the aroma usually invigorated him, but today Jack felt so alive that he didn't need his dose of caffeine; he wolfed down his breakfast and headed out.

As he browsed through the bouquets, dozens of fragrances captivated his imagination. Lilies, roses, carnations all competed for his attention. Jack pondered whether he should opt for something other than the traditional red roses. He changed his mind several times trying to find that perfect gift.

"Are you shopping for someone special?" the sales lady acknowledged.

"Yes, a special lady."

"Is it for a special occasion?" she smiled.

"Nothing in particular…" Jack's cell phone rang cutting him off in mid-sentence. "Sorry, I don't mean to be rude, but I'll need to come back, duty calls."

"Sure, perhaps in the meantime you would like to browse through this, it has fabulous gift ideas for that special someone," she handed him the booklet.

Danny placed each flower in the gift box. He took care attaching a water tube to ensure the flowers didn't dry out. As he lifted the ribbon to tie a bow, he nearly froze. His nerves were paralyzed with fear, and Danny's breathing accelerated. He was approaching quickly. "It's him," he barely managed to alert Ralph while steadying his breath. Danny practiced his breathing exercises desperately trying to divert his attention from the front door.

After looking at several flower arrangements along the front of the store, he walked briskly to the sales counter. "Hi, how can I help you?" Danny asked maintaining a steady calm voice.

"One red rose," he answered in a husky voice.

"Sure," Danny took extra care to wrap it nicely. He figured the man to be six feet. It was hard to miss his muscular built. Danny placed him under forty. He attached more bows than usual trying to buy some time. Although he remained relatively calm, his hands trembled slightly, but fortunately this little slip up went undetected. Meanwhile, Ralph had alerted the police, and was pretending to be straightening bouquets at the front.

Ralph spotted the green pick-up truck and mentally took note of the license plate number. He felt very apprehensive; and remained in the shop to keep a watchful eye on Danny. He would never forgive himself if something happened to him.

"Voila," Danny announced. There was no point asking him how he was going to pay for his purchase. He had already placed a twenty dollar bill on the countertop.

"I need to re-key the transaction, the computer has temporarily frozen. Every minute counted and Danny needed to stall. It would give the police a chance to arrive before the man left. "Would you like to join our membership club?"

Unknowingly to the suspect, a group of undercover officers had placed a tracking device underneath his pick-up. Sean, Terry, and Steve arrived on the scene.

"What's involved in joining up? Is there a fee in becoming a member?"

"No sir, it's absolutely free. All you have to do is fill out this one page form. Simply fill in your name, address, and phone number," Danny was doing his darn best to delay him.

They moved quickly trying to uncover as much evidence as possible.

"Maybe next time, I'm on a tight schedule," he stated curtly.

A twelve foot cord was found on the back of the pick-up along with a sack. Terry circled around the vehicle and gasped. A startled expression etched her face as her eyes remained glued to the inside of the cab. A rosary hung over the rear-view mirror and a large hunting knife lay secure in its sheath on the seat. The rosary was an exact replica of the ones found on each of the victims. Wisely, Terry kept an eye on the shop and distanced herself after seeing him approaching.

His license plate number was keyed into the computer. The man's identity and home address appeared on the screen. "His name is Stan M. V. Harrison. He's thirty-nine years old and resides at 34 Applegate Court. Everything came back squeaky clean and there were no previous convictions on file," informed Agent Gray.

"Excuse me sir, are you alright?" Sean was blocking the man's path. The man gave him a dirty look as he tried to briskly leave the shop.

The Chief had given explicit orders to remain invisible so they followed the truck from a safe distance. For now, they would just remain vigilant. Stan would be under twenty-four hour surveillance. If concrete evidence presented itself they would search his home.

The vehicle suddenly cut off the gravel road, sending pools of dust clouding the air, before pulling into a small driveway hidden by thick bushes. The two officers viewed him through binoculars. He parked and picked up something from his car seat, before scampering into the forest. Wisely, the officers kept their distance. Stan was barely visible to them. The Chief was adamant about them remaining invisible. If the suspect was aware someone was following him, he would deter from his plans. This would blow their whole operation and dash any hopes of apprehending him. Then, they might never find enough evidence to convict him. It was obvious that the man had been here before, he moved swiftly through the trees without ever pausing to find his bearings.

It had been more than several minutes that the officers had been trudging through a thicket of trees. They pursued the suspect from opposite directions; one of them cut in from the east, while the other circled the forest from the west. They would hate to lose sight of him. Fortunately, the descent was downhill making it much easier to keep him within their sights. He was still faintly visible to the naked eye, but with the aid of binoculars they could zoom in on him.

A river cut through the valley. Stan nervously looked around, apparently waiting for someone. In the meantime, the officer cut the distance between himself and his partner. Both officers pointed their listening devices towards him, and could clearly hear the trickling sounds of rushing water. They were spooked by two hooded figures, which appeared out of nowhere, moving rapidly between a cluster of trees. Stan acknowledged the two men. The two officers exchanged looks, listening intently as the conversation became intense.

"I need this matter to be resolved soon, like yesterday." Stan's voice was harsh and abrupt.

"We're working on it, but you must be patient," he held an eastern European accent and sounded quite confident. In our line of business we have to remain invisible, otherwise it will jeopardize our operation. We can't arouse her suspicion."

"Yes, but time is damn well running out," Stan lashed out. "I need this matter resolved ASAP; like before next week."

"We understand your urgency. Don't worry we won't let you down, consider the matter settled."

"Move on her quickly, Saturday is probably the best day. She usually goes out and leaves the children with the babysitter," an exasperated Stan advised.

The two officers exchanged shocked looks. One of the officers shifted to his left, desperately trying to see them. He thought about circling to the other side of the valley, but would run the risk of being noticed, and by that time they might be long gone.

They managed to learn their first names. The fellow with the smaller stature went by the name of Matt, while the huskier fellow took the name Boe. The officers assumed that these names were just cover-ups concealing their true identities.

The listening device slipped clumsily from the officer's hand, ricocheting several feet, before hitting a rock, preventing it from rolling any further. Unfortunately, it vibrated noisily creating a high-pitched sound. "Damn!" cursed the officer under his breath. Both officers quickly took cover. Hidden behind a thick tree trunk, one of them stared intently through his binoculars wondering if the noise had alerted them. He watched worriedly. Their apprehension grew as they looked intently around them, obviously startled by the sudden noise. "Shit!" cursed the officer wondering if it was game over.

"I thought I heard some muffled noise," Matt acknowledged.

"I wouldn't be surprised; there are so many damn critters in the forest." The trio continued to listen attentively for a short while, but then carried on, convinced it was just a squirrel scurrying about. The three hundred foot distance helped to disguise the sounds within the forest. Any closer and the officers' cover would have been blown.

"This has to be our last meeting." Stan was about to reach into his breast-pocket.

"Now take it easy!" warned Boe while at the same time reaching for his own gun. The two officers helplessly uttered a series of blasphemies.

"Whoa, take it easy, I'm just getting your money. It's inside my breast-pocket." An envelope was handed to Boe and he opened it revealing a thick wad of cash.

Before anyone had a chance to react, Stan pulled a sharp hunting knife from its sheath. The two officers' hearts skipped a few beats fearing the worst. The knife was carved into the tree much like cupid's arrow having found its mark. A sketch was securely pinned to the tree by the blade's pointed edge, but the angle from which they stood prevented the officers from seeing it.

"Stick to the plan; if something should develop other than what we've discussed, then I trust you'll use your best judgment. I've paid good money, and I don't want to be disappointed. Have I made myself clear?" he spoke in a sharp tone.

"Don't worry, we've done this before," a sly look crossed Matt's face. "We'll not disappoint you." The mood turned cheery. After all, the men had their money, and Stan was going to get his money's worth. *What better scenario could anyone possibly hope for?* It was the two officers' cue to get the hell out of there, before Stan spotted them.

Meanwhile, Agents Gray and Michael had been working around the clock to dig up as much info as possible. "He has lived his entire life in the state of New Jersey and owns his own business as a professional landscaper. He's separated from his wife who also lives locally. Apparently, they're in the middle of a major custody battle over their two children." The agents relayed all this information to the Chief, who along with the team formulated a plan of action.

The Chief's cell phone rang. "I think we have a real problem on our hands," the officer informed. "She needs protection and fast. He has hired a couple of hit men. We don't know when they'll strike. Stan didn't give any specific details, but stated he wants the matter taken care of within a week. Both men are carrying guns."

A rush of adrenaline sent shockwaves through the Chief's mind. "Okay, just continue to follow him; I'm assigning a couple of officers to keep twenty-four hour surveillance on her and the children. In the meantime, I want to be kept informed of his every move, tap his phone line, and find out everything you can about this guy."

"Okay, he has just entered a bar -- we'll keep you posted."

"Keep me posted down to the last detail."

"Oh by the way, he has a sharp hunting knife."

The Chief's blood froze; "Don't lose sight of him!"

The two officers sat at separate tables to make their presence less obvious. Stan was apparently well known by the staff at the local bar. Patrons steered clear of his path, and one particular individual actually abandoned his bar stool to oblige him. Oddly, he wasn't kept waiting, but served promptly. The officers got an eerie feeling and were strongly leaning on the assumption that people were slightly afraid of Stan Harrison. *The big question was why? How well did people really know him in order to feel this way?*

While keeping an eye on him, one of the officers dragged his stool across the floor attempting to sit closer. He managed to get within ear shot distance. The officer counted on him drinking a few rounds, thus lowering his guard. With any luck, he might divulge some valuable information. He was chatting with a man seated next to him.

"Did you hear that their thinking of placing a retaining wall at the park?"

Stan had a stunned look, "No, do they need one?" Stan gestured to the bartender for another drink. He swirled his glass before taking a sip of his whiskey.

"The sand is being eroded along the river bed." The man's Irish accent was difficult to follow.

"That's odd, I didn't notice anything a few months ago. But, if they are considering doing anything, they better do it before the frost hits," Stan cautioned.

The bar was becoming overly crowded. It usually did during this time of the day as patrons were ready to unwind after a hard day's work. Waiters and waitresses were quickly scurrying among the crowds to refill orders.

"I was completing some work, but couldn't continue after they found the damn corpse. But, I guess the rich take priority," his irritated voice turned contemptuous.

"Oh yeah, she was the rich lady married to the big-time doctor. What was his name?" the man shared his sentiment.

"Dr. Summers," Stan had followed the entire story.

"Shit, they made such a big deal, it was sickening to hear."

"Anyway, I have my own problems," Stan's tone turned bitter.

"So, what's going to happen next?"

"Let me put it this way, sometimes there's only one way of dealing with a problem, and sometimes it's not always nice."

"That's too bad. After so many years you would expect for things to have turned out better." The officer had to strain to hear what was being said, since the club was getting busier and busier; patrons were brushing against each other trying to reach the bar. The music had also been turned up a couple of notches, making it increasingly difficult to hear.

"You can say that again. It's just too damn bad that everyone can't live up to their word. That leaves me no choice but to settle the score differently. Over the years, I have come to realize there are two types of people, those who screw and those who get screwed." A cold empty look filled his eyes.

"It almost sounds like you are out for revenge," fear gripped the other man's heart.

"Let's put it this way, revenge will be sweet and all mine. Probably by next week, it will be all over. No one will be the wiser," Stan toasted.

The officer almost choked on his drink. He now knew that this guy meant business, and nothing or no one would stop him.

They finished their drinks. "I should get going, since I still have some odds and ends to finish around the house. And perhaps with some luck, and a few prayers, something will go right for a change."

The surveillance team was alerted that Stan Harrison was on his way out. Facing his home, an unmarked police car waited, ready to scrutinize his every move. The two officers were considered the best in their unit and certainly were not going to disappoint the Chief.

Mrs. Harrison needed some time alone with her man and decided to ring the babysitter. She thought it was still premature to introduce him to the children. They were still trying to understand why they had to live separately from their daddy. At the young ages of six and eight, it was difficult for them to comprehend the complicated lives of adults. She did not want to confuse them any further, and thought it best for now not to bring him home.

Doug had phoned her earlier and made arrangements to meet her at a local motel. It would be their second meeting in less than a month. She slipped on her dress and then searched for her flat dress shoes.

She left the babysitter a list of explicit instructions. Both children had to be in bed by nine-thirty. If there were any problems, she was instructed to reach her on her cell phone. The babysitter proved reliable; she had trusted her on numerous occasions. Despite the fact that Tricia was only seventeen, Mrs. Harrison's confidence was boosted since she was the daughter of a co-worker. The children were thrilled to hear she was coming over. They looked forward to playing video games with her.

Mrs. Harrison left her home, unknowingly to her, an undercover police car followed closely behind.

Lately, Mrs. Harrison had mixed feelings about her relationship. Doug took on an authoritarian role dictating to her when and where to meet. His demeanor was becoming somewhat arrogant and his diplomacy left much to be desired. At first he had consulted her as to their outings, but on their fourth date his attitude shifted one hundred and eighty degrees. He didn't leave anything open for discussion; their relationship now seemed to entail a physical bond devoid of any emotions. She wondered if their initial excursions had all been just a false front to lure her, and became increasingly annoyed that he only called her just to go out. During the entire week, he never even bothered to call. Unfortunately, there was no one else in her life at the present time. She wanted desperately to believe in their relationship, but seeds of doubt were quickly trickling in. The moment of truth had arrived; she parked her car and headed towards the reserved room.

The officers cut their headlights, and waited across the street. Their presence was over-shadowed only by darkness. Suddenly, a dark vehicle pulled directly ahead of them. Oddly, two gentlemen just remained seated in the parked Acura. One of the two also had binoculars and appeared to be peeping into Mrs. Harrison's suite. The officers were stunned. It was like being hit by a two by four over the head, as they immediately realized that they were the same two men Stan had met in the woods. "Shit! It's the two hoodlums from the woods. I recognize Boe's cap," Officer Carlyle blurted out.

"Damn -- I have a feeling this is not going to end too well," his partner responded while looking through his binoculars. It was difficult making out too many details; the snow was intensifying greatly reducing visibility.

"Hey baby, come and lie with me on the bed. It's cold here without you."

"So how was your day?" Mrs. Harrison asked casually.

"Same shit everyday, but that doesn't matter. What I really need from you is to come join me, and party," Doug lay sprawled over the queen-size bed taking regular sips from a glass of vodka.

"I was surprised that you didn't attempt to reach me all week long; I thought something might have happened to you," Mrs. Harrison tried to elicit some reasonable response from him.

"Stop with the idle chit chat. Small talk is of no importance to me," he huffed.

"It just would have been really nice if you had called," she stressed trying to emphasize her point.

"What really matters is that you get your skinny ass over here, and keep me warm. I don't like to be kept waiting. Shit women, what's your problem! A man like me has needs, and I damn well expect you to fill those needs. Now come to bed, before I have to get nasty," his words were slurred, but his eyes held a wild look.

"Hey my stud of a man, you just wait until I slip into something more comfortable. I bought this sexy lingerie just for you," she spoke in a soft sexy tone while twirling her lingerie.

"Whewee, now you're talking baby! That's what I like to hear."

"Keep the bed nice and warm, have I got a real surprise for you."

She quickly stepped into the bathroom and felt herself shake uncontrollably. His behavior was very eerie; she had never seen this side of him. She also did not like the idea of him being half drunk. *Dammit, I shouldn't have come here tonight*, she thought worriedly. There were a few options swirling through her head. Her first thought was to come running out and make a desperate dash for her car. But this was too dangerous, if he caught her there was no telling what might happen. He was built like an ox. Her second thought was to slip into her lingerie and whack him over the head with the night-lamp. But this was too risky, he might end up dead. Her mind was in overdrive and her heart faint. It was time to get the hell out of there; another plan formulated in her mind. Instinctively, she knew it was imperative to buy time.

"Honey -- I'm going to freshen up, it's been a long day," she continued seductively.

"Yeah baby, bring it on. You're one hot mama," Doug was really excited and was whooping it up.

Mrs. Harrison covered her mouth and her eyes were draped wide open with fear.

The dark vehicle turned on its lights. "Shit where are they going?" The officer didn't hesitate.

"Hello, this is Officer Carlyle; I need back up and fast. Two hooded figures have followed Mrs. Harrison and are now moving to the back of the building. They're armed."

"Let's go inside now. Cover me. On the count of three if that door doesn't open I'm kicking it in. Do you follow?" Officer Carlyle instructed.

"I'm right behind you," his partner acknowledged with his gun drawn.

"Open up, this is the police."

"Hey man -- I'm with my lady friend, go find your own bitch," Doug was on his fourth drink.

"This is your final warning. Open up this damned second, or we'll kick the door down," yelled Officer Carlyle.

"Suit yourself, it's not my door," he slurred seemingly indifferent and with an inflection of arrogance.

"Okay on the count of three. One, two, three --" The officer threw his full weight into the door, but it didn't even budge. A different tactic needed to be deployed. A series of swift kicks finally did the trick. The door burst wide open and Doug lay in a drunken stupor. "Don't move! Where's she?"

"Who invited you?" Doug scoffed. "This is my party!" he stated raising the bottle over his head.

The sound of water was faintly audible from outside the bathroom. "Mrs. Harrison please come out, this is the police." There was no answer. "We will ask you one last time, where is she?" The officer's voice flared as he grew impatient and it took every ounce of self-restraint not to march over and yank Doug right out of bed and throw him onto the floor.

Sirens wailed from outside. Three more officers piled into the room, but still there was no answer from the bathroom. The door remained locked and a frightening thought was beginning to enter their minds. The other victim was found near water. *What if he had drowned her in the bathtub?*

"Ma'am, we're coming in. If you're inside please open the door, we're here to help you," Officer Carlyle pleaded. No answer came from within except the sound of running water.

The officer kicked the door open. Mrs. Harrison had vanished. The window was ajar; they must have dragged her out from the small opening. The two hooded figures had abducted her and at this very minute were probably disposing her body.

"Did you guys find the vehicle?"

"They left before we arrived."

"Sir, please place your hands behind your back."

"I don't have to do anything; I know my rights. What is the matter with you cops?" Doug snubbed his nose.

"You're under arrest. You have the right to remain silent, anything you say can and will be held against you in a court of law," the officers didn't find his conduct one bit amusing. He staggered as the officers tried to haul him into the cruiser.

"Okay, okay you don't have to get testy."

"Cut the bullshit man -- where the hell is she?"

"I don't know. She went into the bathroom to change into something more comfortable, and never came back."

"Did you hear anything?"

"No, not even a peep."

"You expect me to believe that load of crap! If someone had come through the window she would have screamed for help." The man just pondered this for a moment.

"Hello Chief, you're not going to believe this --"

"God no, what happened?" the Chief was beside himself.

"We lost her and the two hooded figures," he grudgingly told the Chief. "We're checking out the hooded man's license plate. We'll call you as soon as we find out."

"How the hell did that happen? Find her dammit! How many officers do I need to assign to one single case?" the Chief shot up from his seat, fuming.

"Chief -- here's your mail," an officer cowered at the door having partially overheard the telephone conversation.

He filtered through the countless envelopes separating them into two piles. He stared at it in disbelief. He just couldn't believe his eyes.

"Hey!" he yelled back to the officer.

"Yes sir."

"Who sent this?"

"The mailman delivered it yesterday."

An envelope much like the first one was addressed to him. He slipped on his gloves and grudgingly opened it. It had to be from him. *Damn,* he thought.

Dear Chief:

Fidelity is often something that requires trust,
One person's compassion is riled by another one's lust.
The bond and memories they shared are no longer a token,
Venom is spewed and the relationship is broken.
Deception is a fiendish friend, who relishes grief,
Although, one's loving and caring leaves the other in disbelief.
Time will heal all wounds and bring to a halt,
Revelations of the past will reveal each fault.
If it is deemed you are not worthy and a sleaze,
Ice and cold will cover your body till you freeze.
This will bring one's soul to a final resting place,
In which the Lord will judge you face to face.
Remember that all who betray and follow their own evil wills,
Will return to the earth and eat their fills.

Yours truly,
Eternal Flame

The Chief slammed the poem on his desk. He yelled angrily at the attending officer. He needed to find out if there were any missing woman's reports.

Chapter 12

Jackie felt the bitter wind nip right through her velour robe. She reached for the morning paper and nearly closed the door, when she spotted something out of the corner of her eye. She was surprised to find a gift bag, sitting upright on her front porch. "Hmm…" A bright smile lit her rosy cheeks as she anxiously stepped back into the warmth. She carefully removed the tissue and was happily surprised to see a large bouquet of beautiful red roses. They were just beginning to bloom and she absorbed both their beauty and their sweet fragrance. As she held the flowers, she saw another surprise box. "Wow, chocolates too!" Jackie let out a low whistle. *"Oh Jack,"* she sighed, naturally assuming him to be the admirer, before flipping over the card. Surprisingly, instead of a signature she found a brief passage. She read it out loud.

"Every minute of every hour we share together,
Naturally makes my life more fulfilling and much better.
It is a great joy to just hear your voice,
Hopefully your feelings are the same towards me, but that's your choice.
These flowers are given with my sincere affection,
Perhaps while you admire them, you can give them some serious reflection.
Your thoughts and whispers are in my mind and bring much compassion,
Most of all, your warmth and beauty fills me with a burning passion."

Yours truly,
Secret Admirer

Hey -- not fair, she thought. *Who else could it be, but Jack? Why did he not sign his name?* Jackie wondered whether or not she should call him and thank him; she decided to wait. While placing the flowers in water and found it peculiar that there was an odd number. *Did he mistake her birth date, or was it a blunder on the part of the florist,* she conjectured?

She enjoyed the rest of her waffles while warm wonderful thoughts swam through her head; it was wonderful feeling loved. The beautiful red roses contrasted nicely against the black vase. *Although, what exactly was she supposed to reflect, other than a long term relationship?*

Doug's head began throbbing from a barrage of endless questions. "Let's go over your story one last time," Steve sounded more like a drill sergeant with his relentless style of questioning. "Mrs. Harrison arrived at the motel suite at eight o'clock. She engaged in conversation with you for about five to ten minutes. Afterwards, she stepped into the bathroom. She stayed in the shower about ten minutes, before the police arrived at the door. Now something doesn't quite make sense. If someone had either tried to break the window, or simply come into the suite through the window she would have yelled. But, according to your alibi she didn't utter a sound. The window is only large enough to allow one person to either enter or exit at a time. It also stands four feet from the floor. If someone actually attempted to enter, the large thumping sounds of their feet would have certainly announced their presence. We've spoken to the motel manager and as part of the security measures all windows are kept locked. Now, I'm beginning to lose my patience!" he roared slamming his fist on the table, causing Doug to snap back. "I'll be blunt with you, if we don't find her alive, in all probability you will be found guilty as an accessory to murder. So for the last time who are the two hooded men?"

"Look, like I've told you before, I don't know anything about any hooded men or any men for that matter. As for her disappearance, I swear on my grandmother's grave, I don't know what happened to her," he roared back.

"But, you are certainly hiding something. Sooner or later we'll find out. It's in your best interest to co-operate with us while you still have the chance. Or let me put it another way, any juror in this country would question your story. The law punishes anyone who is an accessory to murder. I understand that the sentence can be life in prison. Oh by the way, we ran a police check, and I would say you have quite a bit to worry about, wouldn't you say?" Steve stared him down. "One count of physical violence would make your chances pretty dim. Luckily, the victim dropped the charges sparing you a criminal record. I think you can expect to be doing some hard time for a long time."

"But this time, I didn't lay a hand on anyone, really I didn't. I may have been a little bit verbally rough with her. This whole situation is very bizarre. Just because we were having an affair that doesn't make me a murderer, now does it? We met only a few times, maybe she just took off," he shook his head in disbelief.

"If what you are telling us is true then we should find her alive. God so help you, if you have misled us in any way. We'll be your worst nightmare; and you'll wish to have joined her," he blasted.

It was the third time Jack looked at his watch in less than an hour. It was just shortly after 11:00 and he gathered that by this time Jackie had seen her gift before leaving for work. *But why had she not called?* Jack tried to rationalize her actions and concluded that her dedication to her job came first.

This distraction weighed heavily on Jack's mind and he spent two hours accomplishing squat. Besides, he desperately needed to hear her voice. He waited while the phone rang several times.

"Hello," Jackie's soft voice answered.

"Hello bright eyes, how's your day?"

"I can't tell you how much I liked your gift this morning. You're quite the romantic. Red roses, chocolates, and a lovely poem are certainly key ingredients to a woman's heart. I'm sorry for not having called, but I've been pressed for time."

"Not to worry. By the way, do you have any plans for tonight?" Jack wanted to cap off his thoughtfulness with the perfect evening.

"I have to remain at the hospital until 6:00. One of the nurses has called in sick, and I'll be covering part of her shift."

"Would you like to go out for dinner afterwards?"

"I'd love to, but I need to go home and change first. Is 7:00 o'clock okay?"

"Perfect. I'll pick you up, keep smiling."

Jack had never felt happier in a long time.

"Jack?" Mr. Matheson called for the second time

"Oh, sorry Mr. Matheson. I didn't notice you standing there."

"I would like to review the Gregory file in about an hour."

"Sure, I'll tell Lucas and George to join us."

Mr. Gregory was a prominent developer. His latest aspiration was to build a luxurious hotel which offered style, comfort, and affordability to tourists and business associates alike. He didn't want his hotel to look like any conventional building, but wanted tourists to feel relaxed, a place where they could truly feel a sense of escape.

Jack wanted the grounds to be inviting. Tourists would enjoy going for a walk, playing mini golf, or simply relaxing by the pool. But, Jack did not want to over do it. Tourists weren't on a tropical beach, and attempting to capture such a scene would have been grossly overly exaggerated and out of place. Jack had obtained all the pertinent information. Countless hours had been spent reviewing every last detail. Fernheights' expertise also included architectural design and landscaping. Scott Matheson was impressed by Jack's marketing ideas and over the years had appreciated Jack's talents and innovative ideas. Jack desperately tried to remain focused during the meeting, but many times found his mind reverting to his new love. Tonight, he would express his strong feelings.

"Chief Williams, here is the report on all the suspects. It covers everything from financial records to criminal records," Agent Gray placed it on the desk. The Chief quickly glanced through it. "Meet me in the conference room in one hour. I'll advise the rest of the team."

The Chief was venting his frustration when the telephone rang. "Chief, we finally found the owner of the license plate. The vehicle belongs to a private investigator," Agent Michael announced.

"What! What the heck took so long?"

"We keyed in the wrong plate. One of the digits was mistaken; the heavy snowfall blurred the number eight making it appear as the letter 's'. Anyways they're both PI's." the officer added quickly, desperately trying to avert a rebuke from the Chief. "They were hired by Mr. Harrison to tailgate his wife; apparently they're in the middle of a divorce battle fighting for custody of their two children. We've personally spoken with them and confirmed their story, they're clean," he continued.

"So where's Mrs. Harrison?" the Chief asked bewildered.

"Mrs. Harrison escaped through the window after having a change of heart. She hailed a cab and returned home as not to arouse Doug's suspicions. The two hooded men had followed her and thus also disappeared from the scene."

Larry felt so weary from the entire fiasco. He breathed a sigh of relief, grateful that Mrs. Harrison returned home unharmed. He quickly picked up the receiver. Steve Black needed to be notified. It was time to release Doug. The Chief made the call.

"Okay, Doug you are free to go, but before you do I'm going to give you some very good advice. Keep your hands off the ladies and choose your words more carefully. I better not see your face in here again, and the same goes for my colleagues," Steve forewarned.

Steve along with the rest of the team settled in their seats. Agents Gray and Michael began presenting a list of suspects. On a large pad of paper were compiled a list of names in a family tree format. The acme on both trees had Dianne Summers' and Elaine Cooper's names in black large capital letters. Most of the names had a red cross drawn through them. The names not only included friends, but more importantly revealed past boyfriends as well as lovers, going as far back as twenty years. "We have also asked both families to include anyone who may have held a grudge, or had any serious arguments with either victim," Agent Michael explained.

"Why have you crossed out some of these names?" Terry questioned.

"Each name you see crossed out has an alibi. We have personally checked out their story. For instance, this individual stated he was on a family trip. His stamped passport, plus confirmation of his story by family members panned out. For other individuals if everything checked out, we crossed out their name. If a person's name appears only on one list we refer to them as a low profile suspect, but if a person's name appears on both lists then we classify them as a high profile suspect."

Two of the names on the high suspect list include Andy Z. Stewart and Charles F. Staples.

It was precisely seven pm when the door bell rang. Jackie felt more nervous than usual. She glanced into the mirror one more time before making her way to the front door

"Should I always expect such a greeting?" She managed while still recovering from his long passionate kiss.

"Yes, I would say that's a safe assumption."

"Thanks again for the roses and chocolates."

"Well the roses are as sweet as you. I wanted you to know that in the poem."

Jackie blushed. "I never realized you were such a poet."

"It was simple, all I had to do was think of you."

"Are you going to let me know tonight's plan or would you rather surprise me?"

"Is there any place you prefer dining?"

"Not particularly, do you have place in mind?"

"How about a nice Italian restaurant?"

"Sure, I'm a great pasta lover."

"Then it's settled. I know this great place just outside of town."

Crackling sounds soared from the roaring fire in the front lobby; it provided comforting warmth and created a cozy atmosphere. Jackie drew closer appreciating its radiating heat, especially after having just stepped in from the bitterly cold wind.

She felt right at home; the restaurant brought back so many pleasant memories. A lot of the interior was decorated in natural stone, casting the appearance of an earlier era.

"I really like the look of this place. It almost reminds me of an Italian villa."

"Have you ever been to Italy?"

"Yes, a long time ago. I toured a lot of the northern cities, but I really fell in love with Venice. Its architecture splendor spills into its churches, countless museums, and one can appreciate a lot of its history by traveling by gondola along the meandering Grand Canal. One can easily spend weeks touring each city."

"I'm sure one can never grow tired of touring different parts of Europe."

"I'll show you some of my photos. The art, architecture, and general ambience are phenomenal. It has so much history; I think you'd also enjoy the diversity of cultures."

"Absolutely, that's what makes traveling so exciting."

Jackie had a hard time deciding what to order, everything sounded delicious.

He reached for Jackie's hands, "I've enjoyed our time together." Jack paused for a moment and gazed lovingly at Jackie. His eyes spoke volumes. Jackie sensed his fiery passion, bringing a radiant glow and bright smile to her face. This gave Jack a boost of confidence. "I have deep feelings for you and maybe I'm being too presumptuous in assuming you feel the same way."

"I'm very flattered, and I too have enjoyed our time together," Jackie reciprocated.

"I'll be going away tomorrow on business."

"So where are you off to?"

"Oh just California," Jack was being cute.

"Poor baby, I feel so sorry for you!" Jackie retorted sarcastically. Jack sensed pangs of jealousy in her tone. He was going to say something, but decided to let it slide. "How long will you be away?"

"Two days, though it may be extended another day depending on our client's concerns. Hopefully we can finalize the account."

"Is anyone else from the office going?"

"George Hugo, our business analyst is also joining me. He'll explain the cost and financial aspect of the project."

"It's an awesome place to visit. Will you have time to go sight seeing?"

"The way things stand at the moment, maybe a couple of hours each day," Jack tried sounding casual.

It always saddened him to leave his friend. As he turned off the lights in the kitchen, Tara repeated, "Night, night."

"I'll see you in the morning."

Even though it was only nine-thirty, Jack headed upstairs for a good night's rest. He set his alarm for five-thirty and slipped under the covers.

He tossed and turned trying to fall asleep.

It was still fairly early when Jack stepped out for a drink. The tavern was only a few minutes drive, and he very much enjoyed its western style and country music.

It was a short drive, and the parking lot was already packed. The door swung wide open, as one of its patrons was just leaving. Jack made his way towards the bar. The log beams added nicely to the country look.

"A draught please."

"Coming right up," the waitress handed him his beer in exchange for a nice tip.

The beer was clean and crisp and felt so refreshing. He took one long gulp before spotting his friend, John, sitting at the back. What a coincidence, he thought. Jack waved him over as he glanced his way.

"Howdy Jack, are you enjoying your drink?" John had gone the whole nine yards wearing a cowboy hat, boots, and a large belt buckle which added nicely to his cowboy attire.

"Of course, can I get you a beer?" As they were enjoying their cold ones, Jack glanced around the tavern. *Incredible,* thought Jack. Jackie was sitting way at the back and remained partially shielded by his friend John.

His first instinct was to go and greet her. But then a better idea hit him. Jack decided to remain put and continued his conversation with John, while keeping an eye on her. Wisely, he remained low key, but if spotted would just play dumb.

It was time for a second round. This time it was John's turn to binge. Jack didn't mention the fact that he had seen Jackie.

"How are things going at work?" inquired John.

"Not too bad. A few projects on the go, but nothing out of the ordinary," sighed Jack.

John seemed distant. Jack wondered how much time his friend actually spent in bars. He could only imagine how difficult it must be for him to move on with his life. It saddened him to think that perhaps that day might never come. They chatted while finishing their beers.

"I should get going, tomorrow is going to be a busy day," explained John.

"Call any time if you need anything," Jack believed a friend in need was a friend indeed.

Jack sympathized with John, although in this particular instance preferred being alone. Now he could concentrate solely on his lady. Perhaps it wasn't the appropriate thing to do, but he had to satisfy his curiosity. At that precise moment a man approached Jackie's table. Jack wished, just for once, he could be that little fly on the wall.

They were chatting, although it was anyone's guess of what was being said. Jack couldn't really fault a man for approaching such a beautiful lady, sitting all alone. Although, he seemed to be doing most of the talking, while she occasionally nodded her head. The man gestured to the bar and soon afterwards they were served a couple of drinks. Jack's patience was being tested, feeling the other man was moving in on his woman. He swiveled his chair closely to hers and then placed his arm around Jackie. She didn't seem too receptive to his advances, although it was difficult to be certain. Jack was not a man of violence and didn't want to act prematurely. On the other hand, he didn't know how much more he could stomach. Jack's blood began to boil and out of frustration grinded his teeth.

"Sir, would you like another drink?" Jack was startled by the interruption.

"Give me a couple of more minutes," Jack's main objective at the moment was focusing on Jackie.

"No problem, I'll be back in awhile."

The man must have said something to upset Jackie. He saw her dash for the powder room. The man left her table and casually walked back to the bar. *He must have said something fairly provocative in order for her to react that way,* thought Jack. Jack was just about to confront him when Jackie stepped back into the room. It was a close call and luckily he had played it cool. Again, she seated herself and gestured to the waiter. The waitress served her a clear drink with ice, which Jack assumed was water. The rationale was an accurate one since she nearly finished her drink in just one gulp. She probably needed to cool off, thought Jack.

This is damn unbelievable. He almost cursed out loud. Like a bad omen, the man perched himself in front of Jackie apparently not taking the hint. He tried to get Jackie on the dance floor by performing his own solo country dance. *Is this guy a shit for brains, or what?* Apparently she didn't seem too impressed, and judging by her body language, Jackie appeared to have had enough of the idiot. Still, he continued unabated as if he was determined to win her over one way or another. Jack regretted not having gone to speak to her earlier. Like an overheated radiator, with each passing second the pressure augmented, he was now far past the boiling point and ready to explode. It would be risky to approach her now, since she might wonder how long he had been watching, and secondly Jack might deck the smart ass cowboy. It was absolute torture just sitting back watching.

Luckily, Jackie rose from her seat. She must have been revolted by him; she didn't look back as she slipped on her jacket and marched away. It was time for her to leave the creep behind and Jack wisely shielded his face to avoid detection. The door swung open and Jackie was quickly out of sight.

Bloody unbelievable.

Jack stared in disbelief as he just didn't want to believe it, or simply couldn't believe it. *This can't really be happening,* thought Jack as the man shot after her. Enough was enough, Jack stood up briskly and headed outside throwing the folding doors wide open.

'Jack be swift; Jack be quick.'

He was overwrought with a multitude of emotions and didn't stop to think of any consequences or possible ramifications. Jack didn't like what he saw one damn bit. *His expression turned ice cold.* The thug had cornered Jackie against a tree and was molesting her. He heard her desperate cries for help.

"Get your slimy hands off my lady!" Jack issued an ultimatum.

The man turned around wearing a smug look, staring Jack down. "Are you talking to me, you little runt?" the man scoffed, placing his hands on his hips, and in doing so exposed his pot-belly.

"For starters wipe that filthy smile off your face and watch your mouth!" Jack shot back.

Things were about to get real ugly, real fast. Even though the other man was much heavier, he had no inkling of what was about to transpire. As long as Jack could remember, he had never declined a challenge, and this certainly would be no exception. Jack approached the bigger man fueled by a burning rage. They stood less than ten feet apart, staring each other off and ready to battle.

"Jack be careful; he has got a knife behind his back!" yelled Jackie, frantically trying to forewarn him.

The man swung his right hand back, sending Jackie sprawling to the ground.

"That'll keep you quiet, you little tramp!" he sneered feeling vindicated.

Jack was stunned, as if he had been slapped himself. His cold stare reflected a raging fury within. Never in his entire life had he witnessed such a cowardly act. He replayed the event in his mind in slow motion. The moment seemed to last for eternity, but in reality it was barely a split second. Jack spotted Jackie on the ground in severe pain. She favored her right side, possibly having suffered a fractured or broken rib.

The man flicked open his switch blade wielding it to and fro, taunting Jack. "If you want a piece of me, you'll have to go through this first," he laughed hysterically lunging forward.

Jack jerked back. He had learned a valuable lesson from one of his instructors long ago. Never become distracted during a fight, instead always remain focused on your opponent. This was a cardinal rule and there was no exception. Both men were now within striking distance of each other. After a few drinks, Jack's reflexes were not razor sharp, but luckily his opponent had also had his share of drinks.

"Jack stop. You're going to get hurt!" begged Jackie still nursing her wounds. She crawled on the cold wet pavement trying to create some distance from the madman. Only one set of ears heard her frantic cries.

"Ha, ha, ha -- I'm going to carve your hubby like a pumpkin," he taunted. "WHEWEEEE baby! Then we're going to have some real fun," the man chuckled hoarsely, his mind obviously in overdrive. "Yeah baby, you're going to be like pudding in my hands!" he howled.

This was his big blunder, and Jack wasted no time capitalizing on his error. A swift left boot flung the knife out of the big guys hand, landing into a pile of litter. Now the playing field was even. The bigger man appeared disgruntled. At six-feet-six inches and well over two hundred and seventy-five pounds, he definitely had the size advantage. The clock was ticking and it was not in the big guys favor. Jack took a defensive stance waiting for the right opportunity.

Like a roaring bear, the man charged at Jack; like a snake, Jack slithered out of his path and quickly retracted to give the big guy a drop kick to the butt. The big guy came crashing down like a ton of bricks. He rolled over on the asphalt, which produced several scrapes and bruises on his hands and forehead. Slowly, the big guy stumbled clumsily back to his feet. He seemed a little shaken, but clearly had no intention of throwing in the towel. Cautiously, he closed in on his target. The big man then tried grabbing Jack in a bear hug. Unfortunately for him, Jack grabbed him firmly by his right arm and tactically brought him to the ground. The man cried out desperately for mercy while grimacing in pain.

"Let go -- you're breaking my arm!" he shrieked.

Jack didn't stop, but instead launched a gruesome assault on the man's body. A solid boot to the mid section, was followed by a series of vicious attacks. The battle was one sided, and the beating was turning into a bludgeoning.

Jack was killing him.

"Please stop; Jack please stop," Jackie begged repeatedly over and over again. She struggled to get up. By this time, the man was bleeding profusely and slipping into unconsciousness. Jackie managed to reach and grab a hold of Jack.

"Stop, stop, stop…"

"Noooooo!" Jack woke up in a cold sweat. He was breathing heavily; luckily it had been no more than a bad dream. *Thank God,* he thought. He would not forgive himself if something bad ever happened to Jackie. Perhaps it was time to move their relationship to the next level. There was clearly no doubt how important she had become to him.

A cold shower lifted his grogginess and he decided to skip breakfast, since he was running late. Jack quickly leafed through his briefcase ensuring he had all the necessary files. His hotel reservation was placed in its own separate compartment as was the contract. The hard copies were just a back up, in case there were any troubles with his laptop. He double checked to make sure he had all the necessary identification in his wallet.

Before leaving for the airport, Jack lowered the thermostat, then glanced into the kitchen to make sure that everything was turned off.

It had been hard saying good-bye to Jackie. Also, it was the first time he had told her he loved her. It was heart-warming to hear her repeat those simple, but yet complex set of emotions. The short but yet sweet words were profoundly stimulating to his senses leaving him completely fulfilled. He also knew Tara would miss him, albeit she was in good hands with his parents.

Jack placed his suitcase on the conveyor belt for the contents to be examined. Airports had become much stricter after the 911 incident. All passengers including their luggage were carefully scrutinized for weapons or sharp objects. Jack having remembered this wore his belt, not caring to have his luggage disheveled.

Jack looked around nervously wondering if there had been a mix up in communications. His flight would be leaving shortly, and there was still no sign of George. He was just about to call him when his cell rang.

"Hello," he answered in an upbeat tone.

"Jack, this is George, I'm afraid I have some bad news. My wife has been in a car accident, and I'm with her at the hospital."

"Is she okay?" he asked concerned.

"She'll be fine. The doctors want to keep her in the hospital for a few days just as a precaution. She has suffered numerous bruises and possibly whiplash."

"Your wife is very strong, I'm sure she'll be fine. And don't worry, I've reviewed everything and look forward to presenting our ideas at the meeting."

"Good luck, and if you need anything just reach me on my cell," advised George, feeling slightly guilty leaving Jack to assume the trip alone.

"Excuse me, do you have the time?"

"Sure, it's 7:10."

"Thanks," responded the stranger who carried a leather briefcase in his left hand.

Jack senses were quickly heightened upon spotting a group of four teenagers dressed like Mexican banditos. He noticed one of them nodding to the other three members. The worst thing would be to allow them to encircle him. Jack quickly repositioned himself, so his back would be against the wall. As expected, they walked towards him. Luckily, he had also placed his wallet in his breast-shirt pocket, now he only had to guard himself from the front.

"Sir -- do you know where the washroom is?" one of them asked trying to distract him.

"No speaka Englishe," Jack feigned. This ended any further conversation, forcing the group to dissipate. The last thing Jack wanted was a confrontation with a group of teenagers. If he hadn't been alert, they certainly would have made off with his wallet.

"All passengers flying to Los Angeles, California please board." A long queue of people formed a single file. Even though it was only seven-thirty in the morning, travelers were engrossed in lively chitter-chatter.

Jack felt exhausted and looked forward to napping. For the past several weeks, he had worked long hours depriving him of any sound sleep.

"We can't continue our investigation with so many loop holes and false arrests. We need to be more thorough and vigilant. So far we nearly killed Tommy, falsely arrested Barry, and then erroneously pursued Matt and Boe only to lead us to that drunken fellow…uhh...what the hell was his name…Doug. Everyone is soon going to wonder if we are randomly just lashing out at poor innocent bystanders. Not to mention, the mayor is not the least bit pleased." The Chief outwardly controlled his frustration, even though it was etched all over his face. "I understand we have a list of possible suspects."

Agent Gray proceeded, cautiously, almost afraid of making another mistake. "At this point we're still in the early stages; but we may finally know the identity of the serial killer. There are two names left, which appeared on both of the families' lists. Andy Stewart is one of them, but he has an iron clad alibi.

He was giving a lecture at a university and we've spoken with the faculty and they verified his story. Also, his family backed up his alibi after eleven pm that evening. The other time he was lecturing at another university until nine pm. It was impossible for him to have committed the second crime, unless you believe it's possible to be in two places at once. His lecture was halfway across the world and it would have been past nine the next morning before he could have made it back into town. This leaves us with only one possible suspect, a Mr. Charles Staples."

"Okay, what do we know about him?"

"He's single, lives in the general area, and has a clean slate. Financially, he's well off with considerable assets and income. He's a business owner who has recently been searching for a partner until one hour ago," Agent Gray relayed the facts.

"Why, what happened?" asked the Chief frantically as his frustration was escalating by the minute.

"He has purchased an airline ticket and will be leaving the country soon."

"Why the hell didn't you tell me?" the Chief stared at him in dismay.

"I apologize for the surprise; I just found out this morning," he explained apologetically, hoping the Chief realized it had been out of his control.

"Okay, where's he flying to?"

Agent Gray hesitated momentarily, knowing the Chief was going to fly off his seat.

"Well?" the Chief waited patiently.

"He's headed for the Cayman Islands."

"Damn!" cursed the Chief.

"I'll have some men keep an eye on him."

"Is there anything else I should know?"

"Just one more thing he purchased a one way ticket," the Chief was livid and, in turn, pounded his fist hard against the mahogany table.

Jack was seated first-class next to the window. He generally loved to watch the scenery below, but this time hoped to rest awhile before his meeting. It was important to secure the account; Hats and Heels, the prestigious retail chain, had plans to expand internationally, and if Jack was successful it would mean more lucrative contracts.

"Excuse me, I understand this seat has become available -- is it okay if I sit here?" an older woman asked staring directly at him.

"Sure go ahead." Jack would later regret this decision.

"Sorry -- I didn't mean to be rude, my name is Henrietta," her brown eyes lit up as she introduced herself excitedly.

"I'm Jack."

"Is it your first time traveling to LA?" she asked with a wide smile.

"No, I've actually been there a couple of times."

"Are you visiting family?" she continued to probe.

"Business matters."

"What do you do?"

"I'm in Marketing."

"Do you travel a lot?"

"Quite a bit -- at least twenty times a year."

"I'm sure you have visited many interesting places," Henrietta repeatedly nudged Jack on the arm. Her dress was covered with a bright floral print. It matched her cotton hat, which hosted a variety of flowers, and was slightly tilted to her left side.

Good morning, ladies and gentlemen we're preparing for take off, please fasten your seat belts, and fold any open trays

*in the locked position. Place all handbags in the overhead
compartments. Our flight attendants will be walking down the
aisles to assist passengers.*"

The airplane's engine roared. It rapidly gained speed as it
sped down the runway. Seconds later, the plane successfully
soared into the sky. Jack's ears popped, he swallowed several
times, and regretted having forgotten his chewing gum.

"Oh I just love to fly, isn't it so exciting? I'm visiting
family, and just between you and me, I plan to do a lot of
shopping," Henrietta revealed as she reached into her bag and
pulled out several paper back novels. Jack was relieved; finally
he could get some rest. "Have you read this book?" Jack
glanced at the cover, but didn't recognize the author.

"No I haven't."

"It's pretty good." She began to summarize the novel. Jack
simply tuned her out, but soon was revived by the strong aroma
of coffee. The stewardess had begun serving breakfast.
Henrietta wolfed hers down in large gulps. "Miss," she called
out to the stewardess while waving her fork fervently in the air.

The stewardess approached them merrily. "Is everything
okay?" she asked.

"May I have a second serving of pancakes, they're simply
delicious?"

"I'll check if we have extras."

Jack had to make sure of one thing. He set his plan into
motion. "You seem a little bit familiar to me, what did you say
your last name was?" Jack feigned.

"Locks."

"I have enjoyed your company. You certainly have many
interesting stories. Will you be flying back to New Jersey on
Friday?"

"But of course, I can only stay a couple of days."

Jack was certain of one thing; he would not be sitting next to Henrietta Locks on his return flight. Not only did she manage to chew his ear off, but his arm received numerous jolts. He was relieved when the tires hit the pavement. All the passengers excitedly exited the plane.

"Well Henrietta, I really hope you enjoy your stay," both Jack and his sarcasm left so quickly and abruptly, that Henrietta didn't even have a chance to say good-bye.

Jack hailed a taxi to his hotel suite, which was only a ten minute drive. It was such a relief not hearing Henrietta's droning voice. The taxi pulled in front of his five-star hotel. Jack thanked him and gladly handed him a generous tip. A big smile appeared on the cab driver's face as he graciously thanked Jack.

The front lobby was vast and busy. Commuters continuously rushed in and out. Jack weaved his way to the front lobby where four uniformed representatives seated themselves behind a blue pearl granite counter. Jack approached a young lady who greeted him with a warm smile. After a couple of minutes, she handed him his key along with several coupons to local restaurants and nearby attractions.

He dropped the suitcase on the plush carpet of the living area. *Not bad*, thought Jack. The suite hosted all the amenities including a bar. Compliments of the hotel included a bottle of wine immersed in an ice-bucket. A huge flat TV screen lined the length of one of the walls. Jack was certainly impressed and whistled out loud. As he stepped into the bathroom, he was not disappointed. A large whirlpool was centered in the massive bathroom. Just as impressive was the water scene created on the walls; a sailboat sailed among the gentle waves. The scene encompassed three walls and was created out of tiny glass mosaics. Creativity was certainly a strong element in capturing its striking beauty.

Jack stepped into the bedroom ready to change into some fresh clothes before his meeting. He walked past the king size poster bed, which was luxuriously covered in a rich gold chenille cover. He drew the curtains aside and stepped onto the balcony enjoying the gentle breeze; it was a splendid panoramic view. The ocean's gentle waves looked so inviting, but Jack felt tired and opted for a short nap. It would re-energize him and help him focus during the meeting. He didn't want to risk running late and as a precautionary measure brought two alarm clocks and set them both for one o'clock.

The ocean's green water seemed to sparkle like crystals as the sun shone from above. The sun grew fiery hot. Jack enjoyed basking in its warmth stretched on a lounge chair, immersed in his favorite sports magazine. As he reached for the tall glass of lemonade, he felt good about his beach front property. His home was two hundred and fifty feet from the incoming waves. A few other private homes were nestled along the coast. The rest of the strip remained open to the public.

She wore a bikini with palm trees prints splashed all over. Today, Jackie's hair dangled freely over her shoulders. He noted her graceful movements adding to her sexy appeal. It was difficult not to stare at her well toned body. She walked towards him positively glowing.

She acknowledged seductively, "Hi Jack."

Jack couldn't mistake the sultry look in her eyes as he pulled out a lounge chair for her, "What would you like to drink? I have lemonade, fruit punch..."

"Lemonade sounds good, thanks. Actually, if you don't mind I need to use the bathroom."

"Sure, afterwards I'll give you a tour of my home."

Jack's love of colors was clearly displayed, but in good taste. Jackie freshened up loving the feel of the cool water against her skin.

She continued to admire in awe, "You have a beautiful home."

"My love, your beauty can't be captured." He swooped her into his arms, carried her into the bedroom and gently placed her on the bed. They began caressing.

The alarm's loud beeping sounds startled Jack from his wonderful reverie. It took him a few moments to remember that he was currently in L.A. and had drifted off to sleep.

He felt refreshed after his shower, tucked a towel around his waist and dialed. It was amazing how much he had missed her, and he desperately needed to hear her sweet voice.

On the fourth ring Jack began to worry that maybe she was too busy.

"Hello."

"Hi honey, have I caught you at a bad time?"

"Jack, I was just thinking of you. How was your flight?"

"Not bad. I thought I'd call you before my meeting. Unfortunately I'm a little pressed for time, having just showered and am about to get dressed."

"Ohhh, that's too bad," she whispered.

"Sorry, did you say something?"

"What time's your meeting?"

"In a couple of hours. I miss you." Jack confessed.

"I miss you too," she blew a kiss into the receiver.

"I can't wait until the Christmas holidays when we can finally spend some real quality time together."

"Call me when you get back. Maybe if you're real good, I'll fix you a nice home cooked meal."

"Sounds great, can't wait; I would kiss you good-bye, but technology hasn't advanced that far yet."

He could hear giggling and before she said good-bye, she wished him well. "Have a good trip. Bring back a souvenir."

"I will."

The Chief was annoyed to continuously hear his phone ring. "Chief Williams."

"Yes this is Officer Neally, I'm afraid we have some more bad news."

"What the hell's wrong now?" the Chief firmly clutched the edge of his desk.

"We had a flat and have lost sight of Charles Staples."

"Damn!" the Chief yelled so loud the officer had to pull the receiver away from his ear. "Did you at least see which direction he headed?"

The officer stated the major road intersections along with a general description of the surrounding area. "I'm going to have a few officers circle around to see if we can find him."

The phone clicked without any further instructions from the Chief.

All heads turned towards the Chief's office. Anyone with an ounce of common sense would steer clear of him for the next couple of hours. They were all afraid to be the next one in line to taste his wrath.

Suzie carried a couple of grocery bags inside, leaving the heavier ones for last. With only three bags remaining, she managed to lug them in one last haul. The grocery store had a good selection of fresh fruits and vegetables, but also specialized in organic foods, gaining Suzie as a loyal customer. She set them on the hallway floor, and was about to head back outside to park her car in the garage, when she was stopped in her tracks. Like a phantom lurking in the shadows it caught her totally off guard. A strong gloved hand smothered her nasal and mouth muffling any of her cries.

His hold was like a vice grip and despite her desperate struggles she couldn't break free. He then plunged her forcibly to the floor. The impact sent shockwaves throughout her relatively slender body; her face was sandwiched against the cold ceramic flooring. His heavy body was crushing her mid-back, and his arm was exerting extreme pressure against her rib cage. She couldn't wriggle free, both of Suzie's arms were pinned beneath her offering no support. The circulation to her arms was being constricted and her jaw felt like it was going to implode under the tremendous pressure. His cotton glove felt much like sandpaper, scraping violently against her face. Valiantly, she repeatedly attempted to kick him from behind, but unfortunately couldn't muster enough strength to have any impact. She felt completely helpless, unable to even yell, or beg him to stop. For that matter, Suzie might not even have an opportunity to see her killer. Her face was so close to the floor she could barely open her eyes. This would be the end; her mind was clouded with negative thoughts. Suzie desperately prayed to God for help. An image of the Lord appeared before her, and she faithfully dropped to her knees before him. She begged for mercy, but ironically he just looked at her pitifully. *Why don't you help me,* she thought to herself? This was a foreshadowing of her imminent demise. No one could hear her silent cries, she was now gasping for air. Suzie's face began turning a dangerous blue, her vision became blurry and sadly she knew it was now only a matter of time. Out of nowhere, a bright light appeared in front of her, and she was naturally drawn to it. It was beautiful unlike anything she had ever seen or experienced. No words could come even remotely close to describing its magnificence. She had heard varying accounts of people's near death experiences, but somehow all recounts fell short of her own.

Sadly, she was on the verge of becoming the third victim in just six months.

Chapter 13

Jack loved rising to the occasion, particularly when it concerned his area of expertise, business. He felt confident and was looking forward to today's meeting. The taxi pulled in front of a prestigious tower. Jack made his way towards the elevator and rode it to the twelfth floor. He turned left, and walked down the hall to suite 1216.

He greeted the receptionist. "Good afternoon, I'm Jack Trempton, Mr. Forrester is expecting me."

"Good afternoon, he'll be right with you, please be seated."

A few minutes later a man approached him. "I'm Harry, a very good afternoon to you Jack. How was your flight?" Harry asked, welcoming Jack into the suite.

"Good afternoon, it was quite interesting," Jack managed to feign a smile.

"Come right this way and I'll introduce you to the other partners." Jack followed him into the boardroom. "Juliet, Simon, this is Jack Trempton."

"My pleasure," Juliet shook hands with Jack followed by Simon and all three took time to exchange pleasantries.

"Would you like a cup of coffee," invited Harry.

"Sure."

"How do you like your coffee?"

"Double, double," responded Jack as he seated himself. He had everything well laid out in front of him. Copies of his full report, including charts were handed out to Harry Forrester, Juliet Dunn, and Simon Spencer, the three partners of the prestigious chain, Hats and Heels. Everything was described in great detail. His expertise lay with the marketing aspect of the entire project. He presented a detailed report with charts to support his key ideas and concepts. The store's outer appearance, the interior design, the lighting, and colors were all carefully planned and selected. Jack credited other members of Fernheights who achieved the stores' captivating look. Last but not least, overall costs for the project were presented. Jack followed George's cost breakdown.

Everyone was mesmerized. They had hired Fernheights because of their stellar reputation, and today Jack was making quite a name for himself. No one had been disappointed, and in fact he had been so well prepared that he was almost able to predict the questions before even being asked.

"Jack, the presentation was simply brilliant. I'm sure I speak for everyone when I say I'm quite impressed," Harry complimented enthusiastically. Juliet and Simon smiled cordially. "We're going to review everything and tomorrow we'll be able to finalize the account. We'd like to meet tomorrow at 11:00. Is this time okay with you?"

"Yes, 11:00 o'clock is perfect," Jack felt a boost to his ego.

"Afterwards we would like to treat you to some of LA's finest dining. We hope you'll be able to join us?"

"I'd love to. Thank you."

They all shook hands.

Jack left feeling euphoric. All his efforts had paid off. He had spent countless hours creating new ideas as a means of providing the company with a unique advantage. Hats and Heels needed an edge over its numerous competitors, and Jack's innovative ideas would be a key ingredient to their success.

The rest of the afternoon would be spent leisurely. He desperately wanted to take advantage of his stay, and hailed a cab to his friend's cousin jewelry boutique. It had been years since he had last seen Joe. His custom designs were exclusive. The rich and famous were all too familiar with his ingenuity and Jack had the privilege of seeing his masterpieces through his friend's unique jewellery collection.

As Suzie still lay helplessly on the floor, Foxy Roxy, her seven year old Rottweiler crept slowly from the kitchen. The kitchen's folding door swung open, unexpectedly revealing each others presence. It wasn't exactly what either one was expecting. *The attacker momentarily froze, paralyzed with fear.* He was unable to tear his gaze from the dog and his panic intensified as it began emitting low growls. The attacker wisely released his grip, but his eyes remained glued to the Rottweiler. Stunned, he gasped at the dog's muscular build guessing it to weigh well over one hundred pounds. He was acutely aware of Rottweilers' powerful locking jaws, having heard many horror stories of amputated limbs. Cautiously, he strode backwards; he was within striking distance of the front door.

Suzie still clung to the floor, desperately gasping for air and choking in between breaths.

Her companion's eyes were fixated; she began stalking the attacker. In horror, the intruder watched her transformation. Her once cute and adorable features were disfigured, resembling some abomination and her growls pierced the air, paralleling a were-wolf. He watched as the fur along the nape of her neck to her tail's end stood upright, her ears folded back, and her eyes had turned a dangerous blood-shot red. Fear overcame the assailant who suddenly felt his knees buckle. This fear turned into panic as the dog barred her teeth displaying a full set of pointed fangs. A steady stream of saliva spilled onto the floor. He felt perspiration douse his clothing from the realization that the tables had turned, and now the hunter had become the hunted. Frantically, the stranger flew out the door with Foxy Roxy charging in hot pursuit.

Suzie mustered enough energy to pick herself up from the floor, barely managing to dial 911. She drew deep breaths in an attempt to steady her voice, "Someone tried to — kill me," she managed to say. "He -- tried to suffocate me."

"Ma'am please lock your doors and shut the windows until the police arrive. They'll identify themselves."

Suzie heard something rasp at the door. She looked through the peep hole and quickly welcomed her loyal friend. Storming through the entire house with her friend closely at her heels, she frantically locked all the doors and windows. Her hands still trembled, but Suzie took some comfort having her companion near her. All the years of training at the academy were well worth it.

She sighed. "Thank you so much," she snuggled next to Foxy Roxy, nearly in tears. "You saved my life," she stroked the dog repeatedly. She was still shaking and simply left the groceries sitting in the hallway. Foxy Roxy enjoyed all the attention, but before resting her paws on her master's lap she gave her one quick lick on the cheek.

Suzie was jostled by several loud knocks on the door. "New Jersey Police," they announced loudly, raising their badges. She barely managed to calm Foxy Roxy before opening the door. Luckily her dog's intelligence allowed her to adapt to new situations.

"Ma'am are you alright?" one of the officers noted her spooked look.

"I'll be fine," she assured them while seating herself. They spent the next half hour inundating her with questions.

"Unfortunately, I did not get a look at him; he approached me from behind. Before I knew it, I was on the floor and I couldn't free myself from his grip." Suzie was still badly shaken up and her entire body quivered.

"How do you know it was a man?" Sean had already arrived at the scene.

"I'm not absolutely positive, but his hold was very strong like a vice-grip. I couldn't break free much less move. I don't think a woman is capable of such strength," Suzie conjectured, rubbing her sore rib area.

"Did he ask for anything or make any specific demands?"

"No, he just attacked me from behind and tried suffocating me to death. If it wasn't for Foxy Roxy, we wouldn't be having this conversation." The officer noticed a wide red patch around her mouth area.

"Did you happen to get a look at him while he was leaving, or notice anything unusual such as: limping, scars, hair color, etc.."

"He wore dark gloves, so I couldn't see his skin color. I caught a glimpse of his vehicle as he turned around the corner. The sun was blazing in my eyes, but it appeared dark in color, either navy blue or black.

"We're going to have a couple of officers patrol the area for the next while just in case he returns." Suzie wondered if it would be safer to stay with her mother for awhile.

"Do you know if your dog came into contact with the man, or if she bit him?"

"I'm not exactly sure, but if she bit him it serves him right." Terry and Steve smirked.

"Yes, it certainly would have. I was thinking more along the lines that perhaps we can obtain a DNA sample."

"I don't know my face was smacked to the floor, and it took me awhile to catch my breath. Albeit, it's highly unlikely she bit him. If she had, he would have yelled and it certainly would have been music to my ears."

"Can we do some sample testing? It won't hurt the dog."

"Sure, anything that helps to apprehend this maniac."

Terry searched her carrier bag and pulled out several items. She didn't want to excite the dog and stroked her gently on the head, hoping the dog would warm up to her. Suzie set several swabs aside and with both hands gently parted her dog's jaws wide open.

"Good girl, you're quite the beauty," Terry coaxed while simultaneously praying the intruder had left behind some hard core evidence. The dog co-operated seemingly enjoying all the attention.

Jack felt a touch nervous, partly because he had not seen Joe in a very long time, but more so because he was about to make a very serious commitment. Admittedly, marriage would change many facets of his life, but he looked forward to spending the rest of his life with Jackie, feeling that she was the one. Up to now, his career had been very rewarding providing him with a deep satisfaction, but lately he felt there had been something missing. He had come to realize it wasn't something, but that special someone.

He arrived at J&S Jewelers. A large mock ring with the letters J&S was carved into the wall; it shone brilliantly creating the impression of diamonds.

Jack was flabbergasted as he stepped inside the boutique. It was a very elegant shop with beautiful carved glass cases which encased hundreds of sparkling stones. A couple of other customers were browsing for that same special gift. Among the shoppers, Jack noticed a heavy-set dark-haired gentleman with streaks of silver straightening the trays. Jack scrutinized the gentleman carefully. It could very well be Joe; he certainly was in the right age bracket. But it was such a long time ago, and Jack hesitated in a moment of uncertainty.

The man glanced up and looked directly at him, "Jack?" he asked in an iffy tone.

"Hey, you must be Joe?" He remained a little skeptical of his own memory.

"Wella nica to see ya. Mya God, its been what ten years, anda you haven't changed a bit," Joe walked over to Jack embracing him in a bear hug.

"You have a very sharp memory. Forgive me, it has been such a long time and my memory was a little foggy."

"Hey how longa will you be a visiting?"

"I'm officially here on business and unfortunately will only be in town until tomorrow. I made a point of coming because I'm dating someone very special, and want to ask her to marry me."

"Congratulations!" he gave Jack a hearty pat on the back. "Whena is the bigga day?"

"Well, you can't get married without popping the big question first."

"No worry, with a face lika that and a sweeta guy can be only wona answer."

"Thanks, you always hava a way to pick-upa everyone," Jack imitated a little playfully bringing a smile to both of their faces. Jack was drawn by his warm friendly personality. He recalled Joe to be much the same jovial character as ten years ago, and was happy to see that he had not changed over the years.

"I was hoping you would have some time to show me your engagement collection," Jack was peering through one of the elegant glass cases.

"For you, I maka time. I hava some special rings to show ya."

He escorted Jack to the back of the store, where he carefully removed a silver key from his pocket and proceeded to unlock the case. He set the tray in front of him, which housed over twenty-five gems, all of which competed for Jack's attention.

Jack kept in mind Jackie's preference for white gold. As his eyes skidded along the tray's contents, his eye caught a glimpse of the perfect one. Joe removed the ring, carefully handing it to Jack, "It'za beauty, I custom-made ita myself. Do you lika it?" Jack admired the ring. Its double-band held an exquisite princess-cut diamond, which dazzled Jack's senses as the light reflected off it, creating a rainbow of sparkling colors. The diamond was a real showpiece, weighing over two carats and Jack fell in love with the ring's intricate design.

"Like it," Jack was at a loss for words. "What's there not to like, I love it. I'll take it."

"Okay, notta offend ya, but it'z a bita expensive," Joe spoke with the usual hand gestures.

"I'm not concerned about the price. I think it's perfect, and I would like my future wife to wear it." Jack was not trying to buy Jackie's love, although he was willing to spend his hard earned money for someone he truly loved. "I'm glad I was able to come. You've made me one happy man."

"I'ma glad you are happy. Now -- I wrapa this nicely for ya and then I will take ya to dinner. I know this nica Italian restaurant."

Jack had to smile. He loved Joe's easy going style and generosity.

Hypnotism was not something he practiced often, and Edward reserved the practice as a last resort. It was never easy taking a client back to a dark and usually troublesome period of their life. Years ago, Edward had signed up for a course on hypnotism, mostly because his friend had persuaded him to join. The professor had chosen Edward as his case study, and despite Edward's initial skepticism he relived certain events from his past. After his experience, Edward's curiosity deepened and he actively sought others who practiced this form of therapy. Eventually, he became comfortable with the procedure and began hypnotizing individuals. Edward was acutely aware that unresolved emotions hindered clients psychologically, causing them some level of dysfunction in their every day lives.

Edward heard a knock on the door. It was probably Sam. "Sam?" he asked inquisitively.

"Yes, good afternoon, I really appreciate you seeing me on such short notice. I know I'm taking a risk, but I've run out of options. Honestly, I've tried everything including counseling, group therapy, but I still have this mental block. I desperately need some answers so I can bring closure to certain past events."

"I understand how important this is to you. Make yourself comfortable," Edward gestured to the recliner.

Sam hesitated; he was very nervous and his hands felt clammy. Just the thought of being hypnotized made him quite apprehensive, but perhaps his real fear lay in the unknown. Sam's mood swings made him feel like Dr. Jekyll and Mr. Hyde. There were times when he had no idea of where he had been or what he had done. It scared him to death thinking of the possible repercussions, regardless he had to face the truth in order to be able to move on with his life. Of course, it would be impossible to account for all his memory lapses, Sam wanted Edward to take him back to one night in particular.

Edward pulled his seat closer to the recliner. "Okay, Sam please relax and try concentrating on something you find very pleasing. We'll begin with some relaxing techniques. Are you ready?" Sam nodded. "Breathe in and…out. That's it, you're doing just fine." Edward held a thick gold chain looped with a round pendant, which resembled an old coin from centuries ago. He swayed it rhythmically back and forth in front of Sam's face. "Sam, just follow my instructions, relax, you're gradually going to feel your eyelids become heavier and heavier. Concentrate solely on the pendant. Keep your eyes focused on its gentle rhythmic motion. You're beginning to feel very tired and your eyelids are becoming heavier and heavier. In a few seconds you'll no longer be able to keep your eyes open. Now you are drifting into a deep, deep sleep."

Sam's eyelids were tightly shut, his arms sprawled out and his head lay tilted back on the head support. He waited for instructions. "I'm going to take you back to last summer. It's July 16 and we're going to recall what happened that afternoon. Now, I want you to tell me what happened after work. You left around 5:00 pm and were driving home -- Sam what happened next?"

"I was in a terrible hurry. It was frustrating driving in the heavy traffic. I finally got home, took a cold shower, and changed into some light clothing. It was such a muggy day and the cold shower felt so refreshing, especially since I forgot to turn on the air conditioner. I called her to let her know I was running a bit late, and she told me not to worry since she was also running behind schedule."

"Sam it's okay, you're doing fine. You were driving, what happened next?"

"My mood changed, and for some unknown reason I became annoyed. The traffic was heavy, bumper to bumper. I'm turning onto her street relieved to have survived the traffic jam. It was early evening, but the hot weather was relentless. I rang the door bell, she welcomes me inside, and I'm very pleased to see her, although I feel the onset of a terrible migraine."

"Please Sam just try to relax; do you know why your head aches?"

"I'm not sure. She's telling me something, but unfortunately it's hard for me to concentrate." Sam seemed to become increasingly irritated.

"Can you tell me what happened next?"

"She went into the kitchen to grab me a couple of aspirins, as I continued to rummage through my bag."

"What are you looking for?" Edward's curiosity was aroused.

"I have her gift. She returns with the aspirins. I'm experiencing mixed emotions; I'm happy, but at the same time something has upset me terribly."

Edward noticed Sam becoming increasingly restless, almost in a panic.

"I can't focus, I can't think about what happened next. My head feels like it is going to explode. God noooo -- I can't take much more of this pain," he relayed in an exasperated tone.

Edward panicked. "Just take it easy. On the count of three you're going to wake up. One...two...three -- Sam I want you to wake up."

Sam woke up a little bit puzzled. He couldn't understand why his head ached, and why he was having a memory block. "I'm sorry I don't know what happened, but I must have been emotionally overwhelmed," a perplexed Sam shook his head.

"Sam, the brain is very powerful, and the reason you're blocking the memories is simply because they're too painful. You've found the events emotionally draining. Many times, we don't remember, even when placed under hypnosis. If you like, we can try this again in a couple of months. In the meantime, keep a journal and jot down your feelings in particular when you feel sad or angry. The journal might increase your awareness and help shed some light on the issues troubling you. We can then discuss how you can cope and effectively deal with such emotions."

Sam agreed to keep a journal, although he left quite disappointed.

"Charles Staples fits the general description and knew both victims. Interestingly enough, he does not have an alibi for either time slots. To top it off, Suzie was nearly suffocated at the same time we had a flat. He lives alone and has never been married. Even though all this evidence is circumstantial, it certainly warrants us searching his home," Agent Michael stated firmly.

"If nothing else it would at least put our suspicions to rest. If we don't find anything we should at least follow him. He's our only lead. If we don't thoroughly sweep the house now, he might dispose of any remaining evidence, assuming he hasn't already done so," Terry reasoned.

The Chief took every point into consideration, and then spoke sternly, "Okay, I'll get you a search warrant. I'll have a few officers meet you at his house to assist in any way. Perform a total sweep of the house as well as the outside grounds. Keep me posted."

Charles Staples's home was the last house on the street facing west. The homes were upscale, belonging to high-income earners. Sean knocked loudly. A man's shadow was seen moving behind the blinds. After only a few seconds, he opened the door.

"Mr. Charles Staples?"

With a bewildered expression he answered, "Yes, how can I help you?"

"I'm Sean Anderson with the New Jersey Police Department. We have a search warrant for your home." Charles's face dropped.

"What!" Charles had a puzzled look coupled with a pure red complexion. "Why the hell do you need to search my home? What's going on?"

"This is in conjunction with the murders of Elaine Cooper and Dianne Summers."

"Holy smokes! What's going on here?"

"Agents Gray and Michael would like you to go down to the station to answer some questions."

"This is crazy! Am I...I under a..arrest?" Charles's nerves were causing him to stutter. It was a condition which haunted him all his life, especially when he became overly nervous.

"No, it's purely voluntary, but it gives you the opportunity to exonerate yourself," Agent Michael explained.

"This is un-b-believable. Please, tell me this is a bad nightmare. I can't believe this is really happening; I've always led an honest life and minded my own business --" Charles's voice cracked and he seemed at wit ends. "If you want I'll come to the station, but I need to grab my wallet first. Let's get this absurdity over and done with. Are you sup-per-stitious detective?"

"To be quite honest, I've never given much thought to that nonsense."

"Well maybe it's due time you changed your mind. You've heard of the saying that breaking a mirror will bring seven years of bad luck. Well since that h-happened a few weeks ago, I've had one car accident, one of my warehouses caught fire, and now I'm a potential suspect for m-murder. Ironically, like the mirror shattering to pieces, my life seems headed much the same way."

As Terry walked through the living room she couldn't believe all the holy artifacts. A big metal cross was centered on the wall next to the kitchen; it measured at least two feet in height. She then dusted a nearby end table. A ceramic figure was holding a cross. *Wow, I've never seen so many religious artifacts in any home, she was totally bewildered. Is this guy some deranged religious fanatic,* she thought? It didn't surprise

Terry that an angel was mounted on the wall above the window. Charles Staples's home was simply furnished, but he certainly had enough religious artifacts.

Terry left the agents to search the home while she stepped outside to inspect the garage. Two vehicles, a full-size van and an older style car were parked side by side. Terry slid the van's side door open and looked around; it was bare with only a few spare items. Her eyes skidded along the floor of the vehicle. "Holy smokes," Terry gasped at the sight of discernible red stains. Something had been dragged near the back of the vehicle and her image of Mr. Staples had just turned darker. *The million dollar question is whose blood,* Terry thought? Only forensics could answer this question, but in the meantime the property would be sectioned off until the results were conclusive either way.

Terry continued searching, meticulously scrutinizing both vehicles for any weapons; she checked underneath and along the car seats, in the glove compartments, and in both trunks, but came up empty-handed. She slammed the car door and headed back into the house.

She informed Agent Gray about the stains in the van. Agent Gray cocked an eyebrow. "I've tried to obtain a sample, but we may need forensics to assist us." Terry would make the necessary arrangements. "Have you or Agent Michael found anything?"

"Well, Mr. Staples sure likes his knives sharp." Agent Gray ran his finger along the edge. "They're razor sharp, but we can't dismiss the fact he owns a chain of restaurants, which may explain why he takes extra good care of his culinary utensils. But, I don't think this belongs to Mr. Charles Staples." Agent Gray commented sarcastically, while waving a clear plastic bag in mid-air, allowing Terry to see a long blond hair concealed inside.

"Where's Agent Michael?" Terry probed.

"He's outside scouting the premises."

"I'll check upstairs then."

One of the bedrooms had been converted into an office. A flat computer screen along with stationary took up most of the desk space. Terry leafed through a stack of files, which encompassed different business topics, but she found nothing out of the ordinary. As she stepped into the master bedroom, it was hard to miss a huge crucifix dominating the wall above the bed. Terry wondered whether Charles was deeply devoted or fanatically obsessed. It would make for an interesting discussion.

Endless number of shirts and pants hung from the closet railing. The floor was literally covered with shoe boxes. She filtered through the dresser drawers one by one, but found nothing unusual in any of them.

Agent Gray continued his search while Agent Michael continued scouring the shed. Terry joined him in the living room. "What on earth is taking him so long?" Agent Gray asked concerned.

"He has been in there for quite some time," noted Terry wary of any other surprises.

"I'll take the lead," she informed. Agent Gray circled behind her. He had seen Terry in action and was quite confident in her abilities. Her movements were quicker than the eye, and her blows could prove fatal.

"Is everything okay?" Terry approached very cautiously.

"The coast is clear, but get a load of this," Agent Michael crouched down pointing out the red stains smeared over the severely chipped planks. They appeared so battered and worn it would take little physical effort to split them in half. Agent Michael's suspicions had been initially aroused after noting a hollow sound underfoot. The planks had concealed a huge dug-out. As Agent Michael tugged, Terry and Agent Gray cringed at the loud creaking noises.

"Guys stand back! Crap, I feel it rockin," Agent Michael cautioned. Terry and Agent Gray quickly back-tracked several steps while staring in disbelief as he hoisted a large freezer into mid-air. They stared incredulously, wondering if victim number three was lying disfigured in some grotesque form. Agent Michael glanced at his partners before opening it. A flashback of Elaine's frozen corpse shot back. "No," Terry cried out.

"Are you okay?" Agent Michael eyed her questioningly. She nodded, but at the same instance covered her mouth muffling a low cry. Suddenly, a strange sound emerged. They turned abruptly but before either could flinch, they watched in horror as the door's hinge snapped off causing Agent Michael to lose his balance. His body was sandwiched underneath the freezer's door and he frantically clung on as it swayed back and forth. His legs desperately tried to reach back for the safety of the planks, but luck deserted him further, Terry and Agent Gray watched helplessly as the chain quickly unraveled sending him and the freezer plummeting, hitting rock bottom. "Ahhh," Agent Michael moaned loudly.

"Christ! Are you okay?" Agent Gray hollered from above.

Terry's eyes bulged as she watched in horror. "Hang on! We're going to hoist you out," Terry yelled in a panic. Agent Gray and Terry tugged fiercely on the chain. Their hands were turning a blistering red from all their exertion, but they managed to secure the freezer onto the planks. As they opened the door, Agent Michael slowly crept out looking quite pale.

"Crap -- I nearly broke my collar bone falling in," Agent Michael lamented rubbing his neck while crouching down.

"Are you sure you're okay?" Terry asked concerned.

"Oh – I'll live, luckily it was empty; I don't like to share my space."

They were happy to see his fall hadn't dampened his sense of humor.

"That's three strikes; it looks like Mr. Staples has a bit of explaining to do," Terry surmised a bit perplexed.

"He also has gone to great lengths to prevent outsiders from entering. Special locks have been placed on the door and it took me awhile to crack them open. I think we should inform the Chief, obviously something here is amiss." The call was made, but the Chief did not elaborate or ask for details. They found this odd, but it dawned on them that the Chief might be interrogating Charles.

It was already past six and the sun had set, robbing them of much needed visibility. Now the shed's only source of light was a sixty watt bulb. They sealed off both the home and the shed with police tape. A police officer had been assigned to remain vigilant throughout the night. Forensic evidence still existed and they sure as hell weren't going to run the risk of anyone tampering with it.

Jackie's attention was drawn to the doorbell. She felt secure with her state of the art alarm system. She peered through the peep-hole and instantly smiled seeing a young gentleman lugging her new lounge chair. "Hello," she greeted excitedly.

"Good afternoon. Where would you like me to place this?" the young man asked.

She directed him into the living room. He carefully removed all the plastic and Jackie grabbed all the garbage and told the gentleman she would be right back.

The telephone rang several times. "Could you please answer the call," hollered Jackie.

"Hello, hello," he prompted, but only silence followed at the other end. He gave up and placed the receiver back onto its cradle.

"Oh by the way, the caller didn't respond."

"Well, maybe it was a wrong number. Wow, I love the way this new chair compliments the room." It was a deep blue leather recliner. She sat in it, "This is so comfy, I can certainly fall asleep in it." Jackie was too busy enjoying her new purchase to give the call any further attention. She had purchased the recliner as a Christmas gift to herself. Christmas had always been an exciting time of the year, but this year would be extra special. Lately, she found herself immersed in a series of romantic fantasies, but she didn't want to get too carried away with her feelings. Jack was a refreshing change from the last couple of guys she had dated. He was such a gentleman, always managed to do and say the right thing, and to top it off a hunk. All in all, he was the perfect man. Perhaps, too perfect. Jackie paused to reflect upon this thought for a moment, before coming to the conclusion that she was allowing negative thoughts to get the best of her. But, she had been hurt before; it was a case of once bitten twice shy, and she had matured enough not to rush into anything. Admittedly, she loved the way Jack treated her with the utmost respect always giving her his undivided attention. He had kept all of his promises to date giving her no reason to doubt him.

Jack shuffled his way aggressively through the crowd. His mind was in over-drive with conflicting thoughts. Desperately Jack tried to block-out persisting doubts from re-surfacing, as he would hate for his emotions to prevent him from making the right decision. Up to now, he had always trusted Jackie.

He dumped his suitcase on the bedroom floor and stepped into the bathroom. A warm shower left him refreshed and much more relaxed. Jack splashed on his favorite cologne before getting dressed. He caught himself smiling having missed her terribly. and would make a point of calling her from the office.

Jack had barely stepped into his office when Mr. Matheson buzzed him. "Good morning Jack."

"Good morning Mr. Matheson."

"I want to commend you on the excellent presentation. I've just finished speaking with Harry Forrester who's ecstatic about his store's new look. He spoke praises of all the wonderful ideas; he can't remember being this excited in a very long time," Mr. Matheson stated happily. "Repeatedly, he congratulated us on our bright and innovative ideas. No doubt this will boost our corporate image, which should lead to more prestigious accounts."

"Well that's certainly a compliment for Fernheights. I'm really honored that they're pleased. I have the signed contract and will be in your office as soon as I retrieve the rest of the file."

Minutes later Jack returned. "Here you go, sir," Mr. Matheson shook Jack's hand in a congratulatory manner. "Are you planning anything special for the holidays?"

"The usual, except I'm having a small get together to bring in the New Year."

"Well I wish you and your family a very Merry Christmas, and I hope the New Year will be a new beginning for many good things to come. I'm sure next year you will enjoy just as many successes," Mr. Matheson gave Jack an envelope. "This is just to show my appreciation for all your hard efforts. You certainly have earned it."

Jack gave his boss a hearty handshake before accepting the gift, "I really appreciate you acknowledging my contributions."

Tic…Toc…Tic…Toc…Tic…Toc…

After much hesitation, John finally made up his mind to take a mini vacation. He also realized it had been awhile since he had spent some quality time with his family and was looking forward to sharing some holiday cheer with them. Before he left, there were a few odds and ends to take care of. He turned on his laptop and typed himself a to do list.

His first stop was to visit Edward and thank him for all his help. He had already wrapped a vintage bottle of Scotch along with a box of the best Swiss chocolates for his dear friend. As he drove to Edward's home, memories of past Christmases kept flashing back. *How happy they had been.* But after a long painful journey, he realized he couldn't live in the past forever. It was time for him to move on.

Edward heartily greeted John, "Good to see you, please make yourself comfortable."

"Thanks. I hope you'll accept this small gift as my way of saying thanks for all your help throughout the year and Merry Christmas," John stated while handing him the gift.

"That's awfully thoughtful of you. Thank you."

John and Edward spent an hour discussing worldly events. John openly expressed his relief that the serial killer had finally been caught and empathized on many levels with the victim's family. Losing a loved one was difficult enough to accept, but to lose someone that was so viciously and brutally murdered left a deep sorrow in one's heart, one which may never heal. It also left the family with questions of 'What ifs' -- '*If I had been there it may never have happened.*' The 'What ifs' were always endless. Guilt although unjustified, had a funny way of holding one hostage to their past.

John was just beginning to accept his family's death as an unfortunate accident. His initial guilt no longer tormented him. He now realized it was just their tragic destiny, something beyond anyone's control. Also, he realized how little control each person has over their own destiny, but was consoled by the fact that they had shared so many wonderful times together.

No matter how much time elapsed, no one could take that away from him.

Edward was pleased John came to this realization, however painful his journey must have been. He also confided in Edward of his future plans. Sometime in the New Year, he would make arrangements for an adventurous getaway. It would be somewhere warm and beautiful. Costa Rica, according to several close colleagues, seemed like the ideal place. He would treat himself to a couple of weeks off during early spring.

"Costa Rica is a wonderful place to visit," Edward stated encouragingly. "The last time I visited was with my late wife over ten years ago. Boy, I've got to tell you we had a smashing good time."

"I'm also considering a more permanent move. I've come to realize life offers so many unexpected twists and turns that one can never take anything for granted. The insurance money, as well as my own reserve will allow me to remain well off financially. Depending on my visit, it may end up being my permanent residence."

Edward was surprised by John's recent decision. "Well moving may be the common factor in both of our lives."

John was a little baffled.

"I'm also considering relocating. Most of my family lives in Florida, so it would be the ideal place for me. Besides, I'm not getting any younger, and lately my arthritis has been giving me considerable pain, especially during the bitterly cold winter months when my joints buckle up. Although it'll be difficult to relocate before the next six months, but after that I may be compelled to make a permanent move."

John was a little shocked, never suspecting that Edward had even considered moving. He realized the year would bring numerous endings and new beginnings.

"I'm considering selling some of my art collection, along with some furniture, and possibly a few other belongings," Edward continued.

John's eyes lit up. "I love your art collection. Unless you already have some offers, I wouldn't mind having first crack on one of your paintings. You can set the asking price."

"Which one interests you?" Edward asked intrigued.

"The painting of the Grand Canyon; it is more than a painting to me -- it represents having reached that final goal in life."

"Well my friend consider it yours, we can discuss the terms later. I wish you well during the holidays, try having lots of fun, and get out with friends and enjoy. Merry Christmas, and hopefully the New Year will bring you much joy and happiness."

"Well a very Merry Christmas and a Happy New Year, my friend," John gave Edward a warm handshake as he made his way out.

Although John was happy for Edward, he nonetheless had mixed emotions absorbing the latest news. Edward deserved to relax and enjoy his later years, but at the same time John felt a void, since he would ultimately lose a friend as well as a confident. But, he was soon realizing that nothing in life lasts forever.

"We've just received confirmation of a DNA match," Sean abruptly announced setting the report on top of the Chief's crammed desk.

The dreary Chief bolted upright. He had been anxiously waiting for this moment.

"Does the blood belong to either one of the victims?" the Chief could no longer take the suspense.

"The   blood   in   the   shed   belongs   to…….."

Chapter 14

Jackie along with a group of doctors rushed to the emergency room, where a young boy was hanging on for dear life. His parent's car had been hit head-on by a drunk driver who carelessly ran a red light. Tragically, both parents were pronounced dead at the scene. Luckily Jamie, their eight-year-old son, was securely buckled in the back seat.

"He has lost a lot of blood. We need a transfusion now!" Two nurses scrambled back with the blood supply.

"Come on Jamie, hang in there. He's in cardiac arrest! Let's move it!" the doctor yelled. "Come on, move!" he yelled again in a loud stern voice. One, two, three, now," he directed. "Nothing! Again, one, two, three, now," we're losing him. "Again!" he cried out in despair. Luckily, this time the shock seemed to resuscitate him. Beads of sweat trickled down the doctor's forehead. "Come on…hang in there," he consoled more to himself. "Okay, Jamie we're nearly out of the woods."

The needle was quickly injected into him supplying him with much needed blood.

"His blood pressure is rising," Jackie announced.

"All vital signs are stabilizing," announced another nurse.

Meanwhile, the surgeon was preparing to operate on Jamie and continued to scrub vigorously. They noticed Jamie's abdomen was abnormally tight indicative of internal bleeding.

Jackie's heart went out to the young boy. His light hair was matted to his forehead and his cute adorable face lacked any distinguishable features, except for an innocence which shone brightly. Jackie fought back tears as she watched him lay helplessly in bed. She prayed silently for him and wondered if Jamie had any other family members who would care for him. Perhaps, someone would assume the role in guiding him throughout his childhood years. *How would the boy handle the shocking news of his parents' demise,* she wondered? It was a real tragedy and Jackie couldn't suppress a floodgate of emotions as these recurring thoughts plagued her mind.

Jack got caught in traffic, but didn't feel his usual frustration and constant pressure of being on time, since he was officially on holidays. He desperately missed Jackie and looked forward to spending quality time with her. Everything had been meticulously planned for Jackie's Christmas Eve surprise. How thrilling it would be to watch her expression; it would be one of the most memorable moments of his life and definitely one worth capturing on film.

He made a left turn into the hospital's parking lot and then dialed Jackie's number.

"Hey, how are you gorgeous?"

"Jack you're back! When did you return?" Despite her best efforts, Jack acutely sensed a definite strain in her voice.

"Several hours ago. But, I had to drop by the office and hand in the signed contract."

"Oh Jack, that's great! I'm really happy for you."

"Jackie are you feeling okay, you sound awfully tired?" Jack asked concerned.

"I'm fine, I was just in emergency. A young boy is barely hanging on."

"I hope he pulls through, but it must be awful to have to spend the holidays in a hospital." Both of them reflected on this thought. "Guess where I am?"

Jackie thought she heard the PA system in the background. She could've sworn it was Tracey, the hospital's front desk receptionist. Before Jackie uttered a word, she spotted him at the end of the corridor. Jackie smiled, but played along. "You're not thinking of visiting me?"

"You're quite perceptive." He stated giving her a light hug and a gentle peck on the cheek. It wasn't what he would consider a welcome home greeting, but it was her workplace and a hospital none the less.

"My shift ends in half an hour. Afterwards, I want to stop and check in on Jamie. He's the little boy who barely survived the car accident."

"Sure, that's awfully thoughtful of you. I'll wait in the front lobby."

Jackie's spirits rose upon seeing Jack. She had finished completing one of her patient's charts and made her way towards Jamie's room. The doctor had explained that his operation was successful and he was now sound asleep. Glancing at the monitor, she noted that all of his vital signs were normal. In a soft soothing tone, Jackie spoke reassuring words, "Jamie you'll be fine. You're a strong boy and will pull through. We're going to make you well. My name is Jackie. Once you get well I'm going to treat you to some yummy dessert. I have to go now, but I will check on you first thing in the morning. Hang in there, you will be feeling well soon," Jackie gently squeezed his hand.

She spotted Jack sitting in a lounge chair immersed in a sports magazine.

"Have I seen you before?" she asked half teasingly.

His reflexes were fast. He grabbed her and swept her into his arms. Jack held her tightly. "I've missed you so much," he whispered.

They embraced for what seemed like eternity. They left the hospital strolling hand in hand; Jack loved the warm feeling encapsulating his chest.

"I hope you'll enjoy dinner; I've prepared something special for you. The recipe has been passed down from one of the best chefs in Europe."

"In that case, I'm sure to be in for a real treat," Jack winked.

As they drove back, Jack felt elated knowing that he would spend a relaxing evening with a woman he had grown to love.

Jackie unlocked the door and welcomed Jack inside. "Make yourself comfortable while I heat up dinner," she called while heading into the kitchen.

Jack sat in her new chair. "I'm impressed. Wow, adjustable arm rests to boot!" he shouted as his body molded nicely into the cushiony seat.

"I fell in love with it as soon as I saw it. It's true what they say about love at first sight," she teased. "It has a lever underneath; you can adjust the arm rests to a more comfortable position," she raised her voice above the noisy kitchen fan.

Jack found the lever, "Wow, you can certainly get really comfortable in this chair."

The stuffed cannelloni were left to cook while Jackie dressed the salad. She noticed the dark circles shadowing Jack's eyes, "You look really tired."

"I guess all the extra hours have finally caught up with me. Fortunately we were awarded the contract, which will mean more business in the future. I'm officially on holidays now, and can catch up on some much needed R&R."

"Well I'm glad you're back, you certainly deserve a break."

She carefully set a bouquet of flowers on the ivory tablecloth. On both sides of the vase were two ivory tapered candles. Jack was touched by her thoughtfulness.

"I hope you didn't go through too much trouble?"

"Tasks done with the heart are never too much trouble."

Jack had to control himself, but all he wanted to do was ravish Jackie. For now he pushed these thoughts aside, and uncorked a bottle of Cabernet Sauvignon. He poured each of them a glass and set them on the table. Jack was famished and felt his stomach rumble, dinner smelled delicious. Jackie set the cannelloni in front of him.

"I really appreciate your thoughtfulness, especially after a long day at work."

"Actually, I prepared them last night; they just needed to be cooked. So what's new and exciting in California?"

"I ran a tight schedule and briefly did some sightseeing. Mmm, I can't remember tasting pasta this good."

"Well credit goes to my cousin; she's a top chef and shared her secret recipe with me."

"Well you're a very good student," Jack winked. "Now you are going to have to share all of your secrets."

"Ohhhh!" Jackie rolled her eyes and looked downwards. "Is there something specific you'd like to know?" Jackie acutely sensed a negative undertone in his remark and knew something was bothering him.

"Just everything."

Jackie let out a low laugh while giving him a peculiar look. "Well that may take an awfully long time."

"I have the entire Christmas holidays," Jack grinned slyly, but still felt troubled. One thing he detested was deception. Jack reached over to kiss Jackie. "I missed you so much." He hated having lingering thoughts especially ones which harbored these particular doubts. He couldn't help but ask, "I tried calling you yesterday, but the phone just rang off the hook."

"Perhaps, I was either at work or running some errands."

"Then finally a gentleman answered the phone." Jackie then remembered. The gentleman who delivered the lounge chair mentioned someone calling, but not answering. Figuring it must have been Jack, she thought it would be humorous to play a game with him.

"Perhaps you had the wrong number."

In a deep tone, "No, I double-checked," Jack's voice rose and for a split second Jack's expression changed abruptly. His sudden warmth had simply vanished. Jackie keenly sensed this personality shift, but was unsure of its meaning.

"Well, let me think -- no not him, uh no -- not him either. There have been too many men and I can't remember. What time did you say you called?" Before he had a chance to answer, she could not help but drown in laughter. "The gentleman who delivered the lounge chair picked up the telephone, since I stepped outside to dump all the garbage. He did mention that there was no answer at the other end."

Jack felt his cheeks flaming from embarrassment and realized it would have been wiser to simply have asked.

"Jack, I don't stray from a relationship, especially one which I feel so strongly about. So far, I have been open with my feelings. I believe a relationship can only thrive if both partners are open and sincere with one another. If there's anything you wish to know just feel free to ask."

Jack sighed. "You're right. I should've just come straight out and asked. I'm sorry."

"Apology accepted."

The rest of the evening was spent in a lighter mood, both enjoying each others company.

The Chief could no longer take the suspense, "Well," he stated in a curt tone.

"The blood found in the shed belongs to Dianne Summers."

The Chief's mind reeled with a myriad of thoughts.

"We took several samples of blood and DNA testing was repeated to ensure one hundred percent accuracy. Interestingly, we have confirmed that the hair strand found on Charles Staples's sofa also belongs to Dianne Summers. Also, phone records confirm he called her on the day before she disappeared. While searching the shed, we found a series of shovels and one of them had a small fragment missing, and guess what -- it's a perfect match to the piece we found at Dianne's burial site. As we walked along the planks in the shed we noticed hollow sounds underfoot. After lifting a few planks, we found a freezer hidden beneath. We opened it, but found nothing inside. Although we are still running a series of other tests, so far there are no other visible signs of blood stains. What I can't understand is why anyone would want to hide a freezer?" Sean was mystified.

"What about his home -- did you find anything else?"

"We scouted his bedroom and found a journal in one of his desk drawers. From the dates, he seems to include at least one entry per week. Most of his entries are about his business affairs, but he often includes excerpts about his leisure activities. We have backtracked and read several excerpts around Dianne Summers' disappearance. No names were mentioned, but he expressed several negative comments actually bordering on angry statements. For instance, in one of his paragraphs he has written, and I quote, 'If only looks could kill, it would serve justice.' The Chief raised an eyebrow. "In another passage he states, 'I don't know how much more I can put up with; I need to put an end to all this cunning and deceitfulness. I'll never be deceived by her again.' He also seems to gain some fulfillment from viewing violent movies. Two rows of his entire bookshelf consisted of movies, which are rated R for violence. On one of his walls, he has tacked a large aerial map of Somerset, New Jersey; Stetson Highland Park was outlined with an orange high-liter." The Chief continued to listen attentively.

"All of the other evidence is not enough to convict him and I wouldn't even attempt to arrest him; but Dianne's blood on the shed floor and a strand of her hair found on his couch are reasonable grounds for an arrest. I want him brought in; we need to take action quickly. Today Charles's life will certainly change," the Chief spoke confidently.

Mrs. Trempton was always overjoyed by the Christmas season. She was devoted to the true meaning of Christmas, believing it was also a time to open one's heart with other fellow beings and spend time with family and friends. She generally enjoyed the simple things in life and was just grateful that her family and friends were in good health.

She had baked every dessert imaginable. And the sweet aroma of gingerbread cookies diffused throughout the main floor. She set them on the table along with the other baked goodies.

"These cookies are delicious; I suggest you hide them quickly before I finish eating the rest," Mr. Trempton teased.

"You make sure you save some for our guests tomorrow night," she scolded waving a wooden spoon.

"You have done a marvelous job decorating. The poinsettias, the Christmas tree, and all the candles simply look beautiful," Mr. Trempton loved to compliment his wife knowing how much she loved the season.

The dining room table had already been set. Gold pillar candles rested on wide glass bases. The table cloth was also gold in color, but a much lighter shade. She had set her finest china for twelve guests.

"Are you sure we should serve those chocolate cream puffs?" she looked at her husband in a loving way. He could make light of any situation and this attribute had initially drawn her to him.

"Perhaps you're right, they might gain too much weight," she cajoled.

"Really!"

He got suckered in.

Startled, they both jumped as the smoke alarm blazed their ears off. Its loud wails were accompanied by a burnt odor, which soon overpowered the sweet aroma of gingerbread. Mr. Trempton ran towards the kitchen. "OH DAMN --" The kitchen curtain was on fire and the flame was spreading rapidly. Mr. Trempton could not tear it down the flames were spreading like wildfire and inching towards the cupboards.

"Grab me the fire extinguisher!" he cried out.

Mrs. Trempton dashed towards the broom closet and handed it to him. He pulled on the lever, but it was jammed. He frantically tried again. "Oh my God!" Terror was engrained in Mrs. Trempton's eyes seeing the flames spreading out of control.

"Call the fire…oh here I've got it," Mr. Trempton managed to douse the flames. A yellow film of dust covered the entire kitchen. He looked over at his wife who stood in a state of panic, "Don't worry dear, no real damage has been done."

"All my gingerbread cookies are ruined." She sobbed, "What a mess, good God it'll take me hours to clean up." It upset him knowing the incident had shocked his wife. Mr. Trempton wondered what had caused the fire, but then noticed a gentle breeze blowing through the window. The wind must have swayed the curtains towards the burner igniting them ablaze.

"Perhaps, shutters are a better choice, and don't worry we'll clean up together," Mr. Trempton noted the stressed look on his wife's face and tried comforting her, but she merely shook her head.

Jack seemed rejuvenated much like a young child. Jackie had rekindled his Christmas spirit and she had never seen him so happy and excited. She noted many of the careful details which created a warm and inviting atmosphere. A splendid array of lights lit the night sky, and a heart-warming wreath welcomed guests. Garland swayed gently from the evening breeze, and as she walked into the living room she was taken back by the magnificently decorated blue spruce. Jackie's heart warmed upon noticing the candle-lights. She looked forward to sharing a quiet romantic dinner, with a roaring fire burning brightly in the far corner. Everything was just perfect. And of course no Christmas would be just right without the mistletoe. It was strategically hung in the main hallway leading into the living room. Perhaps after a hearty meal, Jack was thinking of a little dessert. She thought it was cute, and would purposely linger there later in the evening.

Jackie marveled at the beautiful scene outdoors. A light dusting of snow lent to the magic of Christmas. Across the street, an almost life-like sleigh with eight reindeer seemed to be awaiting the return of Santa. Millions of children from around the world would awaken bright and early, overjoyed to open their gifts.

The stereo was playing Jackie's favorite Christmas tune 'Jingle Bell Rocks.' She danced her way into the kitchen snapping her fingers and shaking her hips. "Hello, do you need a hand?" she asked.

Jack secretly admired her dance.

"I'm fine. Dinner will be served shortly," Jack bowed. "The wine is still chilling in the fridge," Jack stated as he checked on the turkey. "Help yourself; refreshments are in the fridge." Jackie was still finishing her Pina Colada. "Just relax I've got everything under control." She danced out of the kitchen and went over to visit Tara.

"Hello my friend. Where's your master?"

Tara perched close to the latch expecting to be released. Usually she was free to reign, but Jack wanted an intimate evening with Jackie.

"Master, master," she repeated, but to no avail.

"Oh, you poor little thing," Jackie sympathized with her. It was Christmas and Jackie thought it only fair that Tara should partake in the festivities. Jackie's appetite was growing by the minute. Dinner smelled awfully good and she felt famished. "Bye, my little friend."

"Bye, bye," she chirped. Jackie was walking out of the room, but stopped in her tracks. She could've sworn Tara said something sinister, but rebuked the idea believing it to be her imagination.

Jack inadvertently startled Jackie as she was backing out of the room. "Dinner is now served." It was a close call and they had almost intersected under the mistletoe. He was a little disappointed, but there would be more opportunities later in the evening. Jack escorted her to the dining room and being a gentleman pulled out her chair.

She was impressed. Jack carved the stuffed turkey. It was decorated with parsley, tomatoes, and with a side dish of potatoes and carrots. The gravy was simmering hot, and Jackie poured a couple of tablespoons liberally over her plate. Jack filled her wine glass and then proceeded to fill his own.

"A toast to our first Christmas together and may there be many more," he added. They both raised their glasses and enjoyed hearing the clinking sound, bringing a bright smile to both of their illuminated faces.

Every time Jack looked into her eyes, he just wanted to squeeze her tightly and hold onto her forever. But tonight, something wasn't just quite right. The sparkle was missing from her eyes.

"You seem rather quiet. Is everything okay?"

"I'm sorry, dinner is delicious. If I seem a little bit distant, it's because I'm worried about Jamie. It just doesn't seem fair that his world has been torn apart. All the other children are going to be anxiously waiting to open their gifts, and soon he'll learn that both his parents have died in a car crash," Jackie stated deeply saddened.

"Is he expected to pull through?"

"Yeah, he's a strong little guy and is expected to make a full recovery. His operation went well and the bleeding has stopped."

"Does he have family who can adopt him?"

"His aunt and uncle have begun the adoption procedures. They have two children of their own about Jamie's age, who get along quite nicely. Jamie would probably adapt quite easily, since he visited their home almost every weekend before the accident."

"Well, that's encouraging. They sound like a lovely family and he's quite fortunate to have relatives willing to take care of another child, not every youngster is quite so lucky."

Jackie thought about Jack's last statement. He was right. Too many young children were sent to orphanages while others did not make it at all.

"Are we ready for dessert?" Jack wanted Jackie to enjoy the evening and quickly changed the subject.

"You had time to make dessert after all this?"

"There's always time for dessert," Jack's eyes gleamed. "But before dessert," he kissed her fervently on the lips. "You look radiantly beautiful," he complimented and then passionately kissed her once more.

He carried a four layer forest cake decorated with whipping cream, and embellished with maraschino cherries. Jackie noted a couple of fortune cookies encircling the cake.

"You certainly have been busy. Wow it looks scrumptious!"

"Hold on a minute, while I answer the phone."

"Hello. Oh, I'm great mom; I'm enjoying my Christmas holidays. I was going to call you and dad to wish you both a Merry Christmas."

"Merry Christmas and I hope many wonderful things are in store for you son."

"How's dad?"

"He's fine. Although we had a little scare earlier," she tried sounding casual.

Jack's heart momentarily skipped a few beats. "Why? What happened?"

"Nothing serious, but we had a small kitchen fire. Luckily we extinguished the flames quickly, and the there was no damage except the loss of the curtains."

"Is dad okay? How did you guys put out the fire?"

"We have a fire extinguisher. It nearly jammed on us. In the New Year we are going to buy another one and keep it as a backup. Boy, let me tell you, it really came in handy. And don't worry your father is fine. Just a minute, he wants to wish you a Merry Christmas."

"Merry Christmas; how are you doing son?"

"Merry Christmas dad; I'm fine, Jackie and I were just having dinner. Are you sure everything's okay?"

"Everything's fine. Don't worry yourself over nothing. The fire was extinguished fairly quickly. Just enjoy your dinner. Your mother says to wish Jackie Happy Holidays. We'll see you both in the upcoming days."

"Sure dad we'll talk soon."

"This is delicious."

"Why thank you."

No sooner had she complimented him when she began to fidget in her seat. Jack noticed Jackie looking rather uncomfortable and she venomously scratched her arms, while her face was turning a blood-shot red.

"Are you alright?" Jack became apprehensive by her sudden discomfort.

"I'm not sure; I'm quite itchy," Jackie fidgeted becoming extremely restless.

She lifted her sleeves. Big red golf-size patches had formed along the entire length of her arms. *Jack's eyes bulged and he cringed, alarmed to see huge red hives spreading to her neck.* The itchiness was incredible. Jackie lifted her pant legs and nearly gasped. Her legs and the top of her feet were covered in huge hives.

"Jack, I think I'm having an allergic reaction," her voice heightened and her facial expression projected an eerie sense of despair.

"What -- what are you allergic to?" he asked alarmed.

"I know for a fact that I'm allergic to peanuts," she began to feel rather chilly.

Jack frantically thought back. "Oh, but I did not use --" Then it hit him. He used the same knife to spread a peanut butter sandwich, which he then used to slice the cake. "Damn, how could I've been so careless? The knife I used to slice the cake had traces of peanut butter. I better get you to the hospital at once," he spoke in a panic.

"Jack, I can walk," Jackie softly protested. Her protests were ignored as he carried her inside the car and rushed to the hospital.

"Dammit, come on," Jack cursed at the red light. He took hold of Jackie's hand and was sent into shock. *It was ice-cold.* He regretted not having called an ambulance.

"Hang in there sunshine -- we're nearly there," he quickly glanced over and was upset with himself for not having been more cautious.

He continued to keep an eye on Jackie, something deep within him told him to hurry. Smartly, he managed to call the hospital to alert them of their imminent arrival.

He had barely parked the car when he ran over to the passenger side, whisked her out, and dashed through the emergency doors.

Dr. Summers along with the rest of the emergency team knew her delicate situation and were prepared for her arrival. Only seconds after she was rushed through the emergency doors, Dr. Summers rushed over, and quickly administered an injection.

Jackie's body was completely covered in hives including her face. She was seriously allergic to peanuts, and it poised a life threatening situation. After a few minutes, Dr. Summers sighed noticing the hives gradually beginning to die down. "The swelling is dying down. How are you feeling?"

"Much better -- thank you."

Dr. Summers felt a great sense of relief knowing Jackie would be okay. She had been working with him for a few years and he came to admire both her work ethics and dedication. She always gave one hundred per cent; not once did he hear her complain, but watched her support her colleagues in times of crisis. Tyler considered her family.

"Sorry to have caused so much commotion. Merry Christmas."

"Merry Christmas. I'd prefer if you stay for at least another half an hour just as a precaution."

"Okay. How's Jamie doing?"

"Very well, the nurses are checking in on him -- monitoring his progress."

Jackie felt a strong pull towards the young boy, "Is it okay if I check in on him?"

"He may still be awake, by all means go ahead. Jackie…" Dr. Summers called out, "Stay away from peanuts."

Jackie gave him two thumbs up. "It's a deal." She then made one quick stop.

She poked her head inside. "Hi Jamie, are you still awake?"

"I'm not tired yet. It's too early for bed," he whimpered.

"You are a tough little guy." Jamie grinned from ear to ear. "I thought you could use a little company." She revealed the panda bear which was hidden behind her back, and set it next to him on the bed. It was two feet high and its eyes lit once its left paw was squeezed.

"For me?" he asked in bewilderment.

"Especially for you." She hugged him and remained close by.

"I think I will call him Big Bear," he acknowledged proudly.

"That's a wonderful name. Now, I'm going to let you rest, but I'll come and see you tomorrow. How about if I let Big Bear sit in the chair right next to your bed?"

"Okay," he agreed half-heartedly. His eyes were already closed once Jackie left the room.

Jack was reading a magazine when Jackie tapped him on the shoulders. He turned abruptly, "Is everything okay?"

"Yeah, Jamie will be fine. We probably should get going," Jackie sighed.

"Alright, and by the way you look much better." Jack gave her a peck on the cheek while they headed out.

He looked up and down the driveway, but it was nowhere to be seen. *He was stunned.* "Shit, I can't believe this is really happening! I must have left the keys in the ignition, and some punk must have stolen it. Right here in the hospital parking lot, of all places. Just my luck!" Jack despaired. "The first time I forget my keys and what happens -- it gets stolen. I guess it's true what they say about things happening in threes. First my parent's home nearly catches fire, then you have a terrible allergic reaction, and now my car gets swiped." Jack vented. "This is damn unbelievable!" Jack swore slamming his left fist into his right hand, "Bah humbug, so much for the Christmas spirit."

"I'm sorry," Jackie pouted, shrugging her shoulders. She was nearly in tears feeling it was partially her fault.

He placed a comforting hand on her shoulder and looked reassuringly into her eyes, "Come on now sunshine, it's not your fault. You're not the one who should be sorry." Jackie could not help but feel partially responsible. Jack noted Jackie's stricken look, reassuringly took her into his arms, and cuddled her closely. "I'll call the police and let them deal with it. We've had enough for one night."

Jack reported his stolen car and then hailed them a cab.

"I want you to sleep over at my place. I would never forgive myself if anything ever happened to you."

"Jack really I'm okay, there is nothing for you to worry about," she stated half laughing.

"I'm not taking any chances. I'll sleep on the sofa," he stated adamantly.

"Well one good thing came out of tonight's chaos. I got to see Jamie; I gave him a Panda Bear and he has named it Big Bear."

Jack had mixed emotions realizing his own plans had faltered.

Charles Staples walked into the room, looking haggard and worn, like a man who recently stepped off a battle field. He reluctantly took a seat across from Chief Williams.

"We've completed searching your home." Charles didn't respond, but stared blankly. "Is there anything you would like to mention at this point?"

"I'm not sure I follow," Charles was dumbfounded by the Chief's statement.

"Is there anything you may want to reveal, such as any unregistered fire-arms?"

"I have two hunting rifles, both of which are registered. I keep them locked and have a valid hunting permit. Look, I've done nothing wrong."

The Chief ignored his last remark and continued with his interrogation, "Do you own any hand guns?"

"No I don't."

The Chief already knew the answers to all these questions. "When and where did you last go hunting?"

"About two months ago; I drove one hour north to a place called Spacey's Hunting Lodge."

So far Mr. Staples had been telling the truth. "So what do you hunt?"

Charles sighed loudly coming precariously close to losing his patience, but wisely thought it best to simply answer the Chief's question, "Mostly birds and rabbits."

"What do you do with them afterwards?"

"Usually I bring them to the shed, clean them, and roast them. Sometimes I store them in the freezer." Charles's eyes were red and puffy and he was becoming more and more weary, but co-operated in the hopes of getting the matter over and done with.

The Investigative Team, Agent Gray, and Agent Michael kept a watchful eye, studying his non-verbal behavior. Agent Michael closely scrutinized him.

"Is there any other game you like to hunt?" the Chief persisted in a deep tone.

"I'm not quite sure I understand," Charles held a befuddled expression.

The Chief scoffed, "Oh, but I think you do," he insisted giving him a stern look.

"Look, I don't let the animals suffer. There's nothing illegal about what I've done. I'm a licensed hunter, so cut through the chaff and tell me what the hell you're getting at!" Charles's voice heightened, obviously becoming frustrated with all the insinuations.

A confident look washed over the Chief. "But, it's illegal to hunt and kill humans," the Chief leaned forward and tauntingly accused Charles.

"Look -- I haven't laid as much as a finger on anyone!" Charles's voice flared and gave the Chief a wryly look.

The Chief corrected his posture, feeling confident like a man with an ace up his sleeve. "You haven't, so explain how Dianne Summer's blood was found all over the floor of your shed? Also, a strand of her hair was found on your couch." Charles was at a loss for words; it was shocking to be confronted with such startling revelations. His mouth hung open, and he wore a defeated look of despair. It took him awhile to absorb the Chief's words. "Also, can you please explain how a shovel fragment used to bury Dianne's body was the missing piece from one of your own shovels?"

"Look, I don't know how her blood got on the shed floor or about any shovel used to bury her. We did meet the day before she disappeared, simply because we were friends and kept in touch. This is one big mistake. Someone must be trying to frame me for some crazy reason. Why would I kill her when I have nothing to gain?" his tone intensified with each word.

"That's a good question. But, I have an even better one for you. Why is it that you seem pretty darn upset in a couple of your journal entries?" Charles's head was spinning; too many ideas were playing havoc with his train of thought. Evidence seemed to be mounting faster than snow after an avalanche. His luck had all but run out; his rabbit's foot seemed to have been stripped of all its magic charm, and his nightmare had reached catastrophic proportions.

Charles knew he was in deep trouble. Many convicted for murder were confined to life in the slammer. Only in certain cases had the prosecutor realized they had made a mistake, robbing the convicted person many years of freedom. Charles had no intention of becoming the next statistic.

"I want to speak to my lawyer. I refuse to answer any more questions until I speak to my lawyer first," Charles leaned back in his chair with his arms crossed.

"Just one more question, please. Why do you have a full blown aerial map of the City?"

"Look, I'm a businessman and do a lot of traveling. It helps me to get acquainted with the City and it's easy to get directions as well as a perspective as to where everything is located. Besides, the map was a gift given to me by Roger Campbell, an old friend of mine. I have his phone number if you wish to verify my story. I know how this may look, but I don't really know anything about the blood or the shovel -- anyone could have gained access to my shed. It's not always under lock and key," he stated adamantly trying to justify his position.

"You better make that phone call to your lawyer," the Chief instructed.

The Chief felt a heavy load lift from his shoulders, and breathed a huge sigh of relief. For months, he had been under extreme pressure to solve the murders. The stress had worn him down considerably, and God only knows how many hours of sleep he had lost. But now the tide had turned. The evidence found in the shed was very incriminating, topped off by the fact that Charles had no alibi. A press conference would be held tomorrow at 11:00. The entire town would finally know the identity of the killer, and discover Charles Staples's true colors. The Chief felt more confident going into tomorrow's press conference, knowing that he wouldn't be inundated with a million unanswerable questions. He would make a point of celebrating a night out on the town with his wife.

The Chief had enjoyed a restful night, and his wife had to actually nudge him a few times to get up, as his alarm clock failed to awaken him. "You look perky this morning," commented his wife while preparing breakfast.

"You've got that right, and this morning everyone is going to know the name of that despicable little coward," the Chief glowed with a sense of gratification. He dropped the newspaper setting it on the chair next to him.

"Never in my wildest dreams would I've figured Charles to be the killer." She seemed truly disgusted and looked troubled before she continued. "All the years I worked for him, it seems almost surreal." He ate breakfast leisurely and was in an upbeat mood when he made his way out the door.

While waiting for the press conference to begin, the Chief explained how Charles Staples was trying to weasel his way out of it, feigning not to know anything. At least he could have been man enough to own up to his atrocities. He figured Charles would battle to the bitter end.

The Chief's opening words as he confronted the reporters had been, "Citizens of New Jersey we believe our nightmare is finally over. We have a suspect in custody."

"Who has been arrested?" Gary sat in the front row.

The Chief thought that certain things would never change. "His name is Charles Staples; he's a citizen of Somerset, New Jersey."

Dozens of questions were hurled at him. Camera lights were flickering from all directions, nearly blinding him, but this time he didn't mind being in the spotlight, actually he seemed to rather enjoy it.

"What evidence have you found?" another reporter relentlessly continued to probe.

"I'm sorry we are not at liberty to give out any specifics pertaining to the case, but incriminating evidence was found at the suspect's residence. Now on a more cheerful note, I wish the citizens of New Jersey a Merry Christmas and the very best in the New Year."

The media congratulated the Chief. He received numerous handshakes and countless pats on the back. Outside a large crowd had already gathered, and as Chief Williams stepped outside, he received a huge round of applause. The Chief thanked everyone who assisted in the investigation. The Special Investigative Team, the FBI, the Mayor, the New Jersey Police Department, and the victim's family were all given special mention and thanks for their co-operation.

The Chief was looking forward to spending a quiet Christmas with his family.

Gregory Thornton hated prisons, they made his stomach churn. Nonetheless it came with the territory. He repudiated these thoughts as he walked down the damp never ending gloomy corridors, accompanied by a heavy-built guard. Many of the inmates stood in front of their cells with hands tightly clenched around the iron bars. As he walked past some of the cells, he heard numerous obscenities hurled at him, "Hey guys -- look at this tight-ass dude! Looks like some big-time lawyer," one of the inmates shouted and a raucous laughter broke out. Gregory Thornton shuddered, thinking of poor Charles. He hoped he had explanations, which would eventually exonerate him. At this point things did not look too promising, they looked damn bleak, to say the least.

Charles Staples walked into the room. He looked haggard, and short dark stubble was beginning to form on his pale complexion.

"Hello Charles, I'm Gregory Thornton," he firmly shook his hand.

"Hello, I'm so glad you're finally here," Charles acknowledged, his spirit somewhat uplifted.

"I'm going to do my best to acquit you, but first I have a series of questions. Now, I expect you to come clean and not hide anything from me," Charles nodded in agreement. "Before we start -- I have one pivotal question, which I'm only going to ask you once and then I'll never ask you again."

The suspense was unbearable, increasing Charles's anxiety.

"Did you or didn't you kill the two victims, namely Dianne Summers and Elaine Cooper?" He purposely avoided eye-contact and fidgeted with his pen while awaiting a response.

"I'm innocent of these crimes," insisted Charles.

"They have substantial incriminating evidence indicating you're the killer." Gregory stressed. "How do you explain this?" He sounded a little puzzled and renewed eye-contact.

"But, I don't know how the blood got there," retorted Charles in complete desperation. "I know things don't look good for me, but I just can't explain it. All I know is that I didn't do it. Obviously, someone has been keeping tabs. I should have known better and kept the shed locked at all times, it's rather difficult to keep an eye on it, since it's partially concealed from my house." His speech became progressively quicker and his words were slurred together as his anxiety escalated.

"Can you recall telling anyone about it?" Gregory hoped to spark back some memories.

Charles stared blankly at the ceiling giving serious thought to this for awhile. "A couple of my neighbors have been inside.

Also, some of the guys I hunt with know about it. And come to think of it some employees from work have seen it." He rubbed his scruffy chin looking overwhelmed.

"I will need the names of all those individuals." Gregory Thornton needed to backtrack and do some of his own investigative work. Gregory loathed surprises. He shied away from representing anyone unless he knew all the pertinent details, not only about the case, but the individual as well. He felt much more comfortable representing Charles Staples, knowing he had a clean slate.

"How do you explain the shovel missing a fragment? Also, you don't have an alibi for either death," Gregory hounded him for answers while pushing his glasses back up to the ridge of his nose.

"Well, if someone gained access to the shed -- they damn well could've taken the shovel!" Charles inadvertently raised his tone. "I've never hurt anyone in my entire life and certainly not a woman for God's sake. Both Dianne and Elaine were good friends of mine. What would I gain from killing them? Besides, if I had committed the crimes wouldn't I've covered my tracks?" Charles was visibly upset.

Gregory tried calming him down. "There's no need to go on the defensive, I'm on your side. And just for the record, I believe you're telling the truth. Now it's just a matter of proving it. Do you know anyone who loathes you enough to want to frame you?"

Charles was so overwrought with emotions that he could barely think. He lost several hours sleep, felt irritable, and found it impossible to concentrate. He combed his fingers through his hair, "I don't know anyone who hates me this passionately. It could be someone crazy -- some deranged maniac who lives in the neighborhood. The killer may have used the shed simply because it was convenient."

"I'm going to do my best to follow all the leads you've given me. We have our work cut out for us, but I'll do everything humanly possible to prove your innocence. In the meantime, I want you to try and recall anything regardless of how insignificant it may seem. In order to get you a pass out of here, we have to find some hard-core evidence to prove your innocence. I want you to think back to anything which may help support your statement. You're not to speak to anyone whether it is an inmate, guard, or officer." Gregory sighed. "Unfortunately, you'll have to spend the Christmas holidays in here, but hopefully this matter will be resolved quickly. I'll keep in touch with any new developments. Call me if you remember anything."

Charles was bewildered, and couldn't believe that this was happening to him. *How the hell was he going to prove his innocence, especially being cooped up in a dungeon?* He was already beginning to feel frustrated by his dismal surroundings. His cell consisted of a bed, which barely supported a three inch mattress, and pillows must be considered a luxury item since none were placed on his bed. A small wash basin covered one corner, along with a toilet on the opposite wall. Both of these facilities could use a good cleaning.

"Hey man, get that look off of your face -- you making me sad!" ordered another inmate across from his cell. He was heavy set with a huge scar over his right eye. The other inmates joined in the laugher increasing Charles's anxiety.

He shuddered to think that this could become his permanent home.

Chapter 15

It was a long trek to the liquor store, and Jack continued to scurry through the parking lot, darting between vehicles. He grabbed a cart and walked down each aisle selectively scouting for bottles of brandy, scotch, rum, and a few bottles of champagne. His shopping cart was soon packed. He wanted everything to be perfect for this dual occasion. Not only would it be a big celebration, but perhaps with a little luck the start of a new life with Jackie. It took him awhile to complete his shopping list, since the aisles were crammed with last minute shoppers ready to celebrate the New Year. The check-out counter was no picnic either; it resembled a highway during rush hour. After waiting over twenty minutes, he walked out with his purchases.

He abruptly brought the cart to a sudden stop, practically coming within a whisker of slamming into a man sitting on the wet pavement.

"Whoa -- good day," the stranger greeted.

"Hello -- sorry, but do I know you?" Jack couldn't place the man's face.

He mumbled something about everyone knowing one another. Jack realized he was drunk. It was hard for him to maintain his balance and the man swayed from side to side as he tried to stand. Jack twitched his nose from the stench of liquor.

"I'm so sorry sir," Jack felt embarrassed.

"Apology accepted, looks like you're ready to celebrate," the stranger took a glance at his purchases. "You don't know what it feels like to lose everything. I also used to smile like you, although now there's nothing left to smile about. Don't let life pass you by. Take advantage of life's opportunities, and if there's something you really want go for it. Bear in mind that many things in life aren't quite what they appear to be, so be cautious." The man's tone had an ominous inflection to it; his eyes were bloodshot.

Jack took a moment to reflect on the man's words. They seemed to have a deeper meaning, almost as if fate had deliberately forced their encounter. It seemed to make perfect sense, yet it lacked conviction coming from a happy wanderer. Ironically, the gentleman reminded Jack of his own grandfather.

"If only I could describe to you the never ending heart-aches I've endured over the years." Jack noted the sorrow lingering in his eyes. "There's no escaping it, everywhere I go or anything I do, nothing seems to improve; it's like being locked up. Now it's too late. All my desires and my motivation have been washed away at sea. Time can do these things to a man, and whoever said time will heal all wounds should walk a mile in these shoes," he scoffed.

Straggles of grey hair hung on the man's shoulder. He had a thin narrow face, and a protruding nose. It was apparent the man hadn't been taking care of himself, nor did he have the means to survive. Quite literally, he was at the point of starvation. His clothes were worn in some places and stitched together very sloppily; patches of remnants were clinging near his knee-caps. His jacket was torn at the shoulder and only two buttons remained. Jack couldn't help but notice that his sneakers had natural air pockets, he pitied the man.

A rush of sympathy caught Jack off guard. "Whatever it's worth, I'm sorry life has treated you so poorly. I wish that there was something I could do to ease your pain." Jack wasn't quite sure how he could help the destitute man. One thing was for certain, it was Christmas time and the spirit of giving was prevalent. He handed the man a crisp one hundred dollar bill.

The man's eyes lit up. "Thanks mister, you have a very kind heart."

"You have yourself a Happy New Year," Jack gave the man a hearty handshake. It was a small gesture for a man in dire straits.

Tonight would be the moment of truth. He would put all his cards on the table, hoping fate would deal him a winning hand.

Henri and Yvonne marveled at the magical wonderland as they approached the end of Jack's driveway. Three Christmas elves welcomed guests with a Merry Christmas and a Happy Holidays sign. The letters flashed smartly in many alternating colors leaving spectators guessing for the next correct hue in the spectrum. "Wow, Jack has gone all out," exclaimed Yvonne. Rudolph, the red nose reindeer, stood at the bottom step of the veranda with his front hoofs reaching for the sky as he prepared for take-off. As they walked up the steps, they noticed the rail and eaves trough were covered in blue and white lights.

They rang the bell.

"Merry Christmas, please come in," greeted Jack.

"Merry Christmas," they answered in unison. Henri and Yvonne were Jack's first guests.

They stood directly beneath the mistletoe.

"Jack certainly has the right idea," Henri playfully nibbled at Yvonne's ear before kissing her.

"You behave yourself," Yvonne said teasingly. Yvonne didn't consider herself a prude, but in some ways was a bit old-fashioned and didn't relish being on public display.

"Of course, I don't want to start the year on the wrong foot," Henri answered playfully. Yvonne laughed amused by his theatrical performance.

A beautifully blue spruce decorated with royal blue and white lights was centered in the living room. Large silver bells along with icicles adorned each of the branches and a beautiful angel watched from above. They were impressed by Jack's selection.

"This is just a little something from both of us," Yvonne handed him the gift.

"Thanks, but you guys shouldn't have."

"It's just a token of our friendship, and will add to the Christmas spirit."

He lifted the bottle from the gift bag. It was one of the world's finest scotch. Being a good friend, they preferred giving it to Jack. It was a rare stock from Scotland and not available in the USA. He was surprised to see a specialty box of chocolates from Switzerland. He set the rum balls Yvonne made on the dessert table.

"Please help yourselves," Jack directed.

"Did you bake all this?" Yvonne asked in bewilderment.

"Yes, guilty as charged," Jack always savored a little rhetorical humor.

"Wow, you certainly have been busy," Henri was impressed.

Macaroons, ginger bread, shortbread, and four different types of dessert cakes lined the table. "The drinks are at the other end of the room," Jack invited as he excused himself to answer the bell.

"Good to see you," Jack cordially greeted George and his wife, Eileen.

"Merry Christmas," George gave him a hearty handshake.

"Merry Christmas, please come in and help yourselves to drinks and appetizers."

Jack simply stared at her. She wore a low cut red dress, and if it weren't for the festivities he would have devoured her. Jackie looked simply breath-taking. Without uttering a word he kissed her passionately; his guests were the only thing that saved her from his flaming passion.

"It took Jackie a minute to recover, "Do you need a hand with anything," she offered.

"I think everything is under control. Let me introduce you to some of the guests," Jack locked arms with Jackie.

Jack had hired some help. He wanted to enjoy the evening without being cooped up in the kitchen.

Dr. Summers remained frozen. Life had taught him many valuable lessons, but this was one lesson which he might never understand, much less come to terms with. His family had been friends with Charles Staples for many years, and his heart ached recollecting their happy times together. He had trusted him fully as a friend, holding him in high esteem. It was surreal to think it remotely possible that he could be such a ruthless monster in the guise of a loving and caring person. It was a bitter pill to swallow, and his stomach churned as he digested this news over and over again.

He recalled Dianne praising him on many occasions, simply impressed by his sharp business ideas. Many times they'd invited him over for dinner, including special occasions. Sadly, their trust had been turned into betrayal, betrayal of the worst possible kind. He then thought of his poor wife. *How were her last few moments?* He could only imagine the horror she must have experienced facing the ruthless killer. Each night he prayed that she had not suffered. *What really puzzled Tyler was why? What had been his motive?* There was no material gain; nothing was removed from Dianne's person, nor was he ever approached for any ransom money. *If money wasn't the motivating factor then what could have caused him to lash out so violently?* He wondered if jealousy or revenge could have precipitated the murder. Although, revenge did not make sense either; they had never quarreled. Oddly enough, they all got along quite well together both on a social as well as on an intellectual level. Charles had never said anything inappropriate or demeaning towards anyone. He dismissed the possibility of love being the possible motivator, since Charles and Dianne had their chance long ago, and both mutually ended their relationship. Perhaps, jealousy was the culprit. After all, he and Dianne shared a happy home life with two beautiful children. *But if this was the case, then why kill Elaine?* She was single and was not wealthy by any means. Something was eating away at Tyler; something was missing from this equation.

Perhaps, the human mind was too complex; Charles must harbor a dark sinister side which never showed itself in the light of day, but then again Charles never appeared mentally unstable. He considered all these queries for quite some time, but despite his resentment towards Charles, he still didn't feel satisfied.

Charles slumped over on the bed, never having felt so low in his entire life. Since his arrival, he had neglected his personal appearance. His black wavy hair was uncombed, and now a full beard gave him a haggard appearance. "Ahhh," he groaned feeling a strain in his mid-back as he tried to move; his mattress was too small for his five-eleven frame offering virtually no support. His muscles felt cramped as though he had slept on thick plywood.

He managed to sit up, dwelling on the realization that his reputation had been tarnished, ultimately ruining his career and life. No one would ever trust him again; even if he was found innocent, people would always look at him suspiciously. The more he thought about it, the more he was convinced someone had set him up. The perpetrator must have known of the shed's location even before committing the crime. It didn't make sense for someone to have committed the crime, and then have accidentally stumbled upon the shed. Now it was a matter of simply back-tracking.

He was grateful that he had his own cell. The size and looks of some of the prison mates were quite frightening. Charles had never felt so intimidated in his entire life. They wore very hard exteriors and time only seemed to deepen their resentment. He cringed hearing their coarse and vulgar language; every sentence included swearing or threatening remarks. They lived hoping to seek revenge, or what they considered justice. Charles feared he would become more like them, especially if he served a lengthy sentence.

The Christmas music still filtered throughout the house. Jack made a special toast to his guests wishing them a wonderful, healthy, and prosperous New Year. The party had been a great success with everyone mingling nicely together. Everyone left in very good spirits, and thanked him for a wonderful evening. It was just after two in the morning when his last guest left.

Jack could feel his hands beginning to perspire as he carried the silver tray to the dining area.

"Don't tell me you're bringing more food?"

"Actually, I have left the best part for now." Jackie saw the fortune cookie on the table and had a puzzled look on her face. A flashback of Christmas Eve aroused her curiosity.

"Go ahead, open it." She cracked it open, but unlike other times she felt a hard piercing object inside. She just stared in disbelief.

Jack knelt as he uttered the magical words, "Jackie, will you marry me?" It must have taken Jackie at least a minute to recover.

"Jack, I'm very touched." She blushed feeling her voice quavering. "I've enjoyed the time we've spent together, and I look forward to spending more time with you, but I'm not ready yet -- everything is happening too fast," Jack still remained kneeling feeling winded.

She felt so awkward and embarrassed by his silence, knowing she had hurt him very deeply. Jackie felt herself growing warmer and warmer; she was utterly mortified. It was too hard to endure his hurt. "I'm sorry Jack. The last thing I wanted to do was hurt you." Jack didn't respond, but continued to remain motionless staring at the floor. Mortified, she rushed out confused and in utter turmoil.

As she drove, a continuous flow of tears spilled down her cheeks stinging her eyes. *Had she been wrong not to accept his proposal?* She did not feel ready, and had followed her own intuition. *After all what was the big rush, they had only been dating a couple of months?*

Jackie walked directly into the kitchen and reached into the cupboard for the box of chamomile; it would help calm her shattered nerves. Her hands were shaking slightly as she reached for her mug. The worst part of her rejection had been his silence.

Jack remained sitting on the carpet dumbfounded. He was in utter shock. He had been certain the ring would have been gladly accepted. His mind reeled from her last words, 'I'm not ready yet, everything is happening too fast.' The New Year would take on a different twist. This was one more setback, in a year which already offered a series of hurdles. *How could this be happening?* Everything seemed perfect between them; they shared a strong chemistry and similar interests. Jack couldn't help but think he had acted too hastily. On the flip side of the coin, a series of doubts plagued him and he was almost convinced that the relationship had been nothing but a fling to Jackie. It was just too overwhelming, and he found it difficult to think straight. All the booze he had consumed didn't help,

Jack felt his head buzzing and staggered clumsily barely landing on the couch.

"How are you doing Jack?" asked a faint voice from afar. Jack couldn't see who was calling him, but instinctively followed the enchanting voice. He stood in the midst of a lush green pasture offset with beds of picturesque flowers. It was ethereal. Jack tried to remain focused as he strode onward not exactly sure where he was headed. Each of his strides seemed effortless, almost as if gliding on a frictionless plane. Far in the distance something was protruding from the plains. Jack picked up velocity to narrow the distance from the plains to the object. A quiet voice lured Jack forward;

'Jack be swift; Jack be quick.'

He continued to follow the enchanting voice whose mysteriousness drew him onwards like a magnet. Jack moved forward with lightning speed. It was now apparent the protruding object was a huge bright white marbleized wall, which appeared not only vast in height but also in width. One could gain access across the large impenetrable wall from a wrought iron gate; its large arch lent a mysterious entry, and was flanked by two large golden posts.

Jack was mesmerized. He touched the posts admiring the colonial work of art; they would support admiration from any onlooker. His thoughts were abruptly interrupted by the recurring voice. *Where was it coning from? As* Jack continued to listen, it appeared to be emanating from the far distance, hence explaining the deep echo. Fear gripped Jack's heart more so than at any other point in his life. *Did he dare cross and discover what lay on the other side?* If he backed down now it would haunt him for the rest of his life. Of course, if he continued there were no certainties of the perils which he might encounter. His curiosity peaked, giving Jack the courage to continue forward.

He approached cautiously fearing it could be a trap leading to an ill-fate. Step by step, he inched forward, slowly. A touch of nostalgia struck Jack as he recalled his high school football years. Fear was almost non-existent back in those days. His heart roared like a lion and his strength was that of an ox. Yes indeed, he had reigned supreme in many facets of his life.

Subconsciously, he moved ahead with a certain apprehension, poised in a defensive stance. Jack tried preparing himself for the unexpected, and felt his heart thumping faster and faster as he approached the entrance door. Momentarily, he was filled with seeds of doubt, and his intuition urged him to turn back. But, he knew all too well there was no turning back.

He lunged forward with heightened anticipation of the unexpected. Absolute shock struck Jack whose eyes were now stretched wide open like an extended rubber band. All he could do was to stare in sheer fascination.

The floor shone brilliantly almost like jasper. It almost appeared to be reflecting light, but was actually the source of it. A series of pillars supported an arched ceiling spanning hundreds of feet above the floor. The intricate design sculpted on the pillar's surface was an absolute work of art, and the magnificent design was intricately detailed and absolutely flawless. Jack wanted to experience more and touched the marbleized wall, which was incredibly smooth much more so than ivory.

Once again, the mysterious voice echoed from afar speaking to Jack, "Are you ready to discover what lies beyond?" an inviting female voice seductively lured Jack further and further into the unknown.

"Who are you? What the hell do you want from me?" demanded Jack whose curiosity had now turned into despair. There was no response, just a quiet desolate solitude. There was no turning back; it would be like having a permanent void in

his life that would haunt him for eternity. "Who are you?" he repeated into the vastness, an eerie silence followed. Pausing momentarily, he opted to follow his heart and continued forward. The corridor was supported by pillars on both sides, spaced about one hundred feet apart. The pillars measured five feet in diameter, and each one had its own distinctive design. He admired one in particular. It was engraved with chariots and knights ready to engage in combat. The details were life-like, and Jack would not be at all surprised to hear thundering hoofs speeding from the middle of the battle field.

He felt as if he was simply chasing a phantom, walking endlessly never quite reaching his destination, much like chasing an untouchable cloud. The gate he had entered seemed to have vanished. Looking back, he saw an endless array of pillars diminishing to the size of pop cans, and was impressed by the straight lines the pillars had formed. Even from this angle it seemed built to perfection, almost like the master of all creations, beyond human scope and maybe beyond reality.

He was growing tired and frustrated, but continued forward trying to reach some ultimate destination, which would justify his long trek. Jack was beginning to lose hope thinking he was pursuing a mirage, a voice which continuously taunted him to move forward, further and further into some unknown dimension. His mind was unusually alert fearing the unexpected. *Where am I being led to*, he thought?

The unknown voice kept nudging him forward, "Don't give up Jack, sometimes we all have to take a leap in faith." The solitude was becoming unbearable.

In the near vicinity, a domed area soon became apparent. 'Jack be swift; Jack be quick,' his conscience repeated, urging him forward. It was adorned with gold trim and magnificent frescos and sculptures, easily over-powering the most spectacular works of art throughout history. Three magnificent doors were adorned in silver with intricate details around the perimeter, their handles cast in ivory.

"Dear God -- could I have died and gone to heaven?" he asked himself out loud.

In an enchanting voice, "Jack you haven't forgotten me, have you now?" a mysterious female inquired.

"I demand you show yourself -- stop playing these childish games!" reiterated Jack clenching his jaw, while fighting back a growing fury.

"Now, now, Jack that will all come in good time. Have you forgotten your roots which have brought you here?" the voice replied softly.

Jack felt a deep resentment. He felt uneasy about the manipulative mind game he was being enticed into playing. Taking a minute to regroup his thoughts, he formulated a more appropriate response. "Would you kindly tell me what you would like from me?" pleaded Jack in a calm demeanor.

"That's better. Do you realize there's an important decision to be made?" Jack wasn't sure if it was a statement or a question. He felt uneasy and his body tensed, thinking what might be asked or expected of him. If circumstances had been different, he would have yelled, show your damn face bitch! But, evidently that wasn't an option.

"You must choose between one of these three doors," she beckoned. "Your choice will determine your future."

The mysterious image appeared before Jack. She had a fairy-like appearance and wore a long dark green gown, which puffed out at the waist, resting just above her ankles. Her long brown hair fell slightly below her narrow shoulders, and her oval face held large blue eyes.

"Now Jack, you'll have a glimpse through all three doors. Afterwards, you will choose one of the three fates." Jack wondered what possible fate awaited him. "Good luck, choose wisely," she advised with a warm smile.

Jack stood in front of the first door. His figure appeared small against the door's towered length.

The door spilled open. A river bank could be seen. It was soothing listening to the sounds of trickling water flowing downstream. Birds of all species chirped in the serene background. The view mysteriously vanished.

She presented him with door number two. Magically, a different view appeared. A rock garden formed a large circle. In between the rocks and a well lit fire were dozens of different types of blossoms. Beautiful shades of yellow, pinks, violets, reds, and blues stood in full bloom. Jack experienced a sense of peacefulness and tranquility. Just as quickly as the view had appeared it disappeared.

It was now time to open door number three. Jack braced himself as he peered through the door. It was a staircase, but unlike any ordinary one, this one seemed to extend for eternity.

Jack carefully pondered all three scenes. He associated the river as a reflection of his own past. Perhaps, choosing this door would allow him to continue his life as he had up to this point. He thought about the second scene; the burning flame represented a warm inviting existence and it symbolized hope to him. He then carefully pondered the last scene. The stairwell's endless steps represented a struggle for power; a struggle to reach the top, or perhaps hurdles needed to be overcome. Jack once again moved along the series of doors before stopping in front of door number two. He hesitated momentarily, taking a deep breath before stepping inside.

Children's laughter could be heard from afar. They seemed to be engaged in some sort of game. Jack quickened his pace to a light jog. Their laughter grew louder. Two young figures, a boy and a girl, were enjoying a game of 'Ring around the

Rosy.' They had been so immersed in play that they didn't even notice him. A wreath of white flowers blended nicely with the girl's blond hair. She wore a frilly white dress cinched at the waist, which moved in a circular like motion with each of her graceful movements. The young boy chased after her, but fell a couple of times, soiling his dress pants.

The gentle flames added to this tranquil setting.

The children finally became aware of his presence, but continued to play happily. With each passing minute the flames seemed to spread further and further. Something wasn't quite right. The flames shot up like wild fire engulfing everything around them. It was happening so quickly; a dumbfounded Jack just stared in disbelief. Without any warning, the flames encircled the children. The children's happy carefree voices were replaced with agonizing wails and desperate cries for help. "AHHHHHH, HELLPPP!" they ran in desperation, now aflame, further fueling the raging fire, intensifying their unbearable suffering.

Jack valiantly attempted to approach them, but the heat was unbearable preventing him from moving forward. He panicked seeing there was no way to save them. There was only one last hope. "Lady, where are you? Please, for the love of God save the children!" Jack cried out like a father in despair, but to no avail. The sky was no longer a baby blue, but had turned into a black canvas board devoid of any light.

Unfortunately, the flames approached closer to him. The intense heat became excruciatingly painful. The flames trapped him and there was no possible escape route. It was a burning inferno. "God Almighty!" It was causing his skin to blister. "AHHHHHH," his agonizing wails echoed far into the abyss.

Jack found himself sitting upright on the sofa in a cold sweat.

Charles enjoyed the fresh air. He didn't mind the cold wind beating against his face, but was just grateful to be outdoors. They allowed him to go outside a couple of times a week. Charles remained close to the prison walls, while keeping a close eye on the other inmates. A group was huddled in a nearby corner enjoying their cigarettes and having a good laugh. He instantly felt better being outdoors, which at least granted him some mental freedom. Very few things in prison reminded him of his previous life. One of his only privileges was a few hours of recreation per week. Charles generally opted to watch some TV.

A group of three inmates were beginning to close in on Charles. Charles felt threatened, and his apprehension grew realizing that he was now cornered. The three guards had their backs to him, and to make matters even worse were standing a fair distance away.

"Hey man -- look who we have here," spoke one of the bald burly thugs with a light chuckle. Charles could see a serpent tattoo on his hand. "So man, you like women!" It definitely wasn't a question. One of the inmates, who bore a strong resemblance to the Incredible Hulk, nudged him hard in the stomach. Charles crouched over in pain. He wanted to tell them to go to hell and back, but didn't want to infuriate them. The three looked mean and tough, and as Charles had already found out, they could certainly live up to their looks.

The inmate who nudged him spoke out, "So what's the matter, don't tell me you can't talk. I have been watching you -- so cut the bullshit man! By the way, you seem pretty puny to me," he stood at least a half foot taller than Charles. He glared down at Charles with absolute contempt. "Maybe man -- that is why you pick on women. Man, I hear you pretty popular with them. Come on man let me see what you're made of." Charles received a solid punch to the stomach. It happened so fast he did not even see it coming. The second punch sent Charles sprawling to the pavement along with everything he had eaten earlier. Charles lay crouched over in severe pain unable to breathe. It was minutes before the excruciating pain began to subside. He rolled onto his right side, before trying to rise to his knees. He was still half hunched over when the guards walked briskly towards him.

It was unbelievable how lady luck had deserted him. Throughout his life, he hadn't so much as laid a finger on anyone. Yet now, he of all people was now being accused of murder. "Why is this happening to me?" he whispered. It didn't make any sense. As he lay on his bed still recuperating from the hard blows, he rubbed his temples in a circular like motion. For two days now, the pain had been relentless, but he knew the cause of his headaches. Charles was also uncomfortable from his attire. The pants he wore were stained and at least two sizes too big. He couldn't stand wearing soiled garments and it wouldn't surprise him if the clothing hadn't been washed, before they were handed to him. He never felt so disgusted.

Charles suddenly realized he was all alone; he hadn't yet received a single phone call. *Wasn't Christmas supposed to be spent with family and friends,* he thought? Charles felt even more depressed guessing what must be going through their minds. Obviously, they doubted him and assumed he was guilty. Ironically, he had always been the one to help others and on numerous occasions helped his family with monetary loans. Now all of his good deeds were suddenly forgotten, and meant nothing. Everyone seemed to be convinced he was a monster. A monster who could commit such atrocities without showing any remorse; a monster bound by no limits.

He hated to dwell in self pity, but it simply wasn't fair. It should be a time for him to be out celebrating, not caged in a puny cell. He wouldn't even treat an animal like he had been treated. The only thing he was grateful for was having his own cell. He was acutely aware of what happened to prisoners convicted of crimes against women or children. They were usually, sooner rather than later, found dead in their cells. He was certain that would have been his fate if he had to share his cell.

But he had to laugh at the dimwits heading the investigation. Apparently, they were incapable of adding two and two together. Charles feared if others were equally incompetent, he might spend the rest of his years locked behind bars. Unless another worse fate took hold, Charles grimaced. If he ever made it out alive, he would certainly move. There was nothing or no one left for him in this state. He would consider a life down south, perhaps the Caribbean, or maybe even Europe.

He heard footsteps of an approaching guard. The guard was tall and muscular. A scar marked both his forehead and his right cheek; he didn't seem one to lose a battle too easily. Following closely behind were three male guards. Charles's cell door sprung open. He was escorted through a narrow corridor along with a few other inmates. The inmates were grouped into three different lunch slots. The lunch area was well guarded with armed men along the perimeter of the room.

Charles sat down. Each one of their meals was served with paper plates and plastic utensils. Glass was a forbidden object, since it could easily be used as a weapon. Charles's appetite had waned. But, the last thing he wanted was to attract the guard's attention. It was bad enough being locked up, he didn't want to get beaten as well. He then noticed a piece of paper protruding slightly from under his plate. He hesitated, glancing about, before removing it. Cautiously, reassured that no one was paying any particular attention, he slid the piece of paper onto his lap and unfolded it open.

Hey Charlie:

What's this I hear from you today?
Hey Charlie man, me hear you are a little poetic maybe one day
you could teach me a little poetry, Charlie man.
What do you do in your spare time?
Hey man, you have been doin' a little partying man.
Me hear you have been doing a little bit of artistic work.
Instead of carvin pumpkin man you have been carvin
something you shouldn't have.
Maybe you have a little bit too much spare time, Charlie.
Charlie -- man me hear ya a ladies man.
Me gonna have to get down right nasty Charlie.
Charlie man, keep your eyes peeled.
Me gonna come for ya and me gonna have some fun.
You pike man!

Yours truly,
Butch Knife

Chapter 16

"Dr. Adams to ER, Dr. Adams to ER."

The loud announcement startled Jackie. One thing Jackie learned over the years from working in a hospital was that there were no such things as timed breaks. It took only one major medical emergency and everyone's so called breaks would simply vanish. Despite having a very demanding job, she always felt in her heart that she had made the right decision. Helping people gave her an inner peace and personal satisfaction. It was rewarding to watch patients get well and return home to their loved ones. Albeit, she faced the sad reality that not every individual was quite as fortunate to recover.

She paused in front of Jamie's room already feeling her heart racing. In a short while Jamie would be relayed the tragic news of his deceased parents, by his Aunt Alexis and Uncle Bob. Dr. Summers and herself would remain nearby as a precaution. Jackie knew it was going to be heart-wrenching watching Jamie's reaction. His Aunt Alexis and Uncle Bob had been working fervently on adopting him and had sought legal counsel to begin the proceedings.

Jackie entered his room. His big bright smile lightened the mood.

"Hi Jamie, how's Big Bear?" It was moments like these which had initially drawn her to the nursing profession.

"He is very happy. He has a friend."

"Oh -- are you his friend?" Jackie smirked.

"Yes." He cuddled the panda bear displaying his affection.

Jackie checked all of his vital signs, everything seemed normal. The bleeding had stopped and Jamie was on the road to recovery. "I want to go home. I want to see my mommy and daddy, I miss them a whole bunch." His lips were curled and his eyes seemed to reach out for assurance. "Why aren't they coming to visit me?" His sweet little voice was beginning to turn into a whine.

Jackie felt herself flush. Suddenly the room's atmosphere became quite thick, and it felt as though a strong grip much like that of a boa constrictor was choking off her air supply. There was no easy way to let a child know that both his parents were deceased. One of them dying was tragic enough, but news of both of them perishing would be absolutely devastating. The boy's life would be forever altered, and no one could predict how Jamie would react to this stark realization. Jamie's eyes pleaded with her, but she continued to hold out on him. It wasn't her place and perhaps not even ethical for her to give him the news, but that still didn't remove a deep sense of guilt from intensifying within her.

Fortunately, Jackie was saved by Aunt Alexis and Uncle Bob entering the room. She breathed a sigh of relief, watching them doting over him. "Do you know who has been asking about you, wondering when you are coming over to play?" Aunt Alexis and Uncle Bob had two of their own children about Jamie's age.

Instantaneously, Jamie's face brightened.

"How would you like to come with us; Michael and Stephanie would love to play with you."

His eyes lit up with joy. "Can I play with the train sets?"

"You sure can, I believe Santa has left something for you."

"Cool, can mommy and daddy come too?" Jamie spoke with a burst of excitement.

Alexis and Bob looked at each other in despair knowing full well that they were just delaying the inevitable. Bob nodded to his wife and she began to speak in a soft soothing voice. "Jamie, do you remember a couple of month's ago when

Charcoal our bunny passed away?" tears clouded Alexis's vision, but she tried valiantly not to let a tear spill.

"Umm, you told me he went to heaven with the angels."

"Yes, special people and pets go there. God takes care of them. Your mommy and daddy are now in heaven with the angels," Aunt Alexis tried to be as gentle as possible.

"But I miss them. Will I see them again?" he lamented.

"Not immediately, but they'll be watching over you making sure you're alright."

Jamie lay silent and motionless; it took him awhile to understand that he would no longer see his parents. Tears trickled down his face as he sobbed quietly. An outpouring of emotions ensued as everyone was reduced to tears. Jackie felt some of her inner tension being released, but it hurt terribly seeing the anguish in Jamie's eyes. The sparkle she had seen, just moments earlier, had simply vanished. Aunt Alexis held him tightly. All of his questions had come to a sudden halt, as he quietly mourned the loss of his parents. They gently explained to Jamie that they were preparing to adopt him and that his aunt would spend the night with him.

"Okay, I'm going to check your blood pressure and heart rate," Jackie stated. Uncle Bob promised to return tomorrow. "Okay big guy extend your arm this way," Jackie showed him the proper way. Both his blood pressure and heart rate were slightly higher than normal, "Jamie you better rest a little while, we don't want you to get too tired."

"Can we put Big Bear next to my bed like we did last night?"

"Gees, he seems heavier than last night," Jackie pretended.

Jamie laughed. "I like you -- you are the best nurse in the whole world!"

"Thanks Jamie, that means a lot to me. And you my friend are a very fine boy, but now I think you should get some rest."

She kissed him on the forehead. "I'll be back shortly to check in on you."

Dr. Summers had been waiting outside. "You know he's right, you certainly are a very special person." He sensed her pain and gave her a really big hug; she felt warm tears roll down her cheeks.

Jack could not help but pace back and forth uncertain of his next move. He needed to talk to someone; someone who would understand his situation and possibly shed some light. He dialed John's number.

Tic…Toc…Tic...Toc…Tic…Toc…

"Well, how are things going?" John asked.

"Unfortunately, I'm not too well. I have a dilemma, and I don't know what I should do. Jackie has declined my engagement ring."

"Oh -- sorry to hear that," John was surprised.

"She felt it was too soon to make a life long commitment. Maybe I acted prematurely, but I followed my heart. I'm afraid I may have already lost her," Jack was saddened.

John took everything his friend said into consideration. "Perhaps you're simply further along in the relationship. Even though she may not be quite ready to make a commitment, that doesn't mean she won't be ready or willing in the future. Heck, for all you know, she might be afraid of commitments. Men are not the only ones with cold feet," John chuckled. "You need to give her some time. In the meantime, you need to find out what's important to her. I've got an idea."

Jack straightened himself in his chair listening keenly to his friend's advice.

"Perhaps you should send her a note asking her to meet you at a local coffee shop. It's important to find out what she wants from the relationship. It seems like you're wasting a lot of time second guessing yourself, why not just go straight to the source."

Jack realized he had to face the truth. "You're right. I'll let you know what happens."

Jack wasted no time and reached into his desk drawer to pull out a stack of note cards. He kept the note very casual, and re-read it before sealing it. The only remaining question was whether he should mail it or deliver it personally. Mailing it would delay a response; he decided to drop it off at her home.

As he drove, he couldn't help but wonder if he had been naïve. Perhaps he had been the 'King of Fools' seeing only what he had wanted to see. *Could he have misread the entire relationship?* But thinking back, she always seemed enthusiastic and excited to be with him. In turn, he had always given her his undivided attention. Perhaps she's interested, but isn't ready to settle down yet, he concluded. All the second guessing left Jack feeling emotionally drained. He needed a diversion and reached over to place a CD in the player. Music always had a special way of soothing him.

"Jack bak -- Jack bak," Tara repeated. She perched herself near her latch, as a means of communicating with Jack to open the door.

Jack let her rest on his shoulder and stroked her gently. "We'll be visiting the vet later today; it is time for your annual check-up."

"Chek up, Chek up," she mimicked.

"Since you have been so good we are going to play some of your favorite games."

"Game -- Game."

Jack pulled out a deck which consisted of twenty playing cards displaying different picture. Tara had learnt most of them, but once in awhile he would introduce a new picture. Today's new word was butterfly.

"Butterfly," Jack slowly repeated over and over again.

"Butfly," she pronounced. Jack was impressed by how quickly she caught on.

Although Jack spoiled her in every way imaginable, her favorite toy was an Indian rubber ball. He gently tossed the ball across the room and watched her spring into action. She would glide through the air and pounce on it like a cat toying with a mouse. It was humorous watching her play.

Out of the corner of his eye, Jack spotted a beautiful white cat. He hoped Tara wouldn't see it, cats frightened her to death. It sniffed near the shed and remained almost fully camouflaged by the snow. This was the first time he had seen it, and Jack figured it was one of the neighbor's felines.

He was lured back into the kitchen by the strong aroma. He poured himself a tall mug and sipped his coffee before placing a couple of slices of pizza into the microwave.

MEOWHHHHHHH!

Suddenly, a crashing sound was quickly replaced by a horrific high-pitched screeching noise. Jack instantly sprung around faster than a hare fleeing from its predator. Sheer terror struck him as he watched in horror.

"Oh my God!" Jack shrieked. He froze and stared in shock. The cat's head had plunged through the bay window, but its back legs were still paddling, desperately trying to break free. Its efforts were in vain, since the glass encircled its entire head. Blood splattered onto the floor and spray-painted the walls. The cat's head was now a bright solid red; blood flowed indiscriminately down the pane, creating a blood bath. Terrible moaning cries emerged from it, as its body was in a state of shock. It shook fervently. As it tried to wriggle free, the glass cut deeper into her causing her feet to slip, and her body to fully extend. Blood gushed unmercifully from her neck. Tara

fluttered throughout the house in sheer terror, emitting high ear-piercing shrills.

Jack's hands flung to his head. The alarm sounded triggered by the broken glass. Jack was so overwhelmed, he simply watched paralyzed with fear.

The telephone was ringing at the same time as the door bell rang. "Bloody hell -- unbelievable!" Jack screamed. He quickly needed to take action. 'Jack be swift; Jack be quick.' First, he needed to place Tara back in her cage. She rested on top of the bookshelf and Jack managed to coax her. He picked her up ever so gently and quickly placed her back in the enclosure.

He ran to answer the doorbell. Jack was immobilized.

"Jack your alarm." Jackie ran towards the kitchen before Jack had a chance to forewarn her. She would remember the horrific image for the rest of her life. The cat's mouth was extended wide open and her distorted face reflected shear agony. A deep scream resonated through his entire house followed by a loud thump. Jack sprung to the kitchen. She lay helplessly sprawled on the floor.

"Oh my God! Jackie, Jackie my love, are you okay?" Jackie lay motionless. He was about to reach for the phone and realized it was still ringing.

"Boy do we have a great deal for you. We at NTRS Life Insurance …"

"Shut up!" Jack slammed the phone and dialed for an ambulance.

Jack lifted Jackie and gently laid her on the sofa, cradling her into his arms. He breathed a sigh of relief upon hearing the wailing sounds of the ambulance. She still lay pale on the sofa, as the paramedics checked her vital signs.

"She seems to be suffering from shock. They gave her a tranquilizer, which calmed her right down. We're going to take her to the hospital."

332 Imma & Pat Argiro

Jack drove closely behind.

Jackie's complexion had still been ashen white when they wheeled her to emergency. Jack couldn't blame her as he had nearly gone mad himself. What a horrific nightmare. It had all happened so fast, that he didn't have a chance to react. The poor cat would have died either way, but he was still perplexed as to how the glass could have shattered. He wondered if the cat's body heat colliding with the coldness of the pane could have caused it to shatter.

One of the nurses came to tell him that Jackie's condition had improved.

"I'm sorry that you had to witness that horrid tragedy. Now, just try and relax. You're going to be okay," Jack found himself gently stroking her soft hair while speaking soothing words to her.

Dr. Summers entered the room, "Hello Jack."

"Hello, I feel so terrible about what has happened."

"What happened?" Tyler was still in the dark and looked totally confused.

"Tara, my parrot, and I were busy playing one of her favorite games. Suddenly, this cat appears out of nowhere, and the next thing I know she's hanging from her neck with her head and body on opposite sides of the pane. To top things off, she triggered off the alarm just as Jackie dropped by. She saw the cat dangling. Well as you can probably imagine the scene was unbearable for her. I didn't have a chance to forewarn her because the telephone was ringing, the alarm went off, and I too was in a state of shock. I heard a loud thump and found Jackie laying on the floor. Damn, I need to get back to the house."

"Don't worry she's in good hands," Dr. Summers assured.

"I'll be back shortly."

Two officers approached the house with their guns drawn. One of them took the lead and slowly crept along the side of the house. Luckily, the stone pathway had been kept clean and free of snow and ice. He peeked around the corner and noticed the cracked bay window. His apprehension grew; seeing blood smeared on the bay window still dripping on both sides of the pane. The officer quickly crept back, but before he did he quickly glanced inside.

"We have a cracked window and blood splattered everywhere," he forewarned.

"Shit, I'll call for back up."

More police were dispatched and soon the whole street would be crawling with officers.

Jack hated to leave Jackie in such a state, but he had to take care of the mess. The poor cat, such bad luck to have crossed at the precise moment he had been playing with Tara, thought Jack. Loud wailing sirens had Jack cover his ears. It was surprising to see a dozen officers circling his street. Three police cruisers blocked off the entire street.

"Damn -- does everything always have to happen at once!" he cursed. A police officer strolled over to his vehicle. Jack rolled down his window.

"I'm sorry, but this street is off limits. We're investigating a crime."

"But, I need to get back to my home -- a cat broke through my bay window causing a blood bath." The officer digested the news.

"Wait a minute -- What did you say your house number is?"

Jack relayed what happened. "Ah -- my girlfriend dropped by the same time the alarm went off. She thought it was the smoke alarm and quickly ran to the kitchen. Instead, she saw the bloodied cat. She fainted -- I had to call an ambulance. I got distracted and forgot to advise the alarm company, my apologies."

Jack felt overwhelmed; it was hard to fathom such a series of bizarre events. The police continued to question him. The cat was found in a dip just below the bay window. Apparently, the cat had lost a lot of blood causing her to slide free from the jagged glass. Before the police officers left they told him that the cat would be picked up shortly. Jack stepped back into his home, dreading the ghastly mess he was forced to clean up.

Charles's stomach churned. If he had the luxury of a mirror, he would have noticed his ghastly white complexion. He was in such a panic, that he couldn't even think of a plan of action. His mind kept reverting to the fact that someone had heard the rumors and was now out for revenge. *In layman's terms, they wanted him dead.*

"Guard -- Guard!" he frantically waved him over.

"What's the problem?" The guard had a bewildered expression; he saw no danger or immediate threat to Charles's life.

"Look -- this n-note was placed under m-my plate." Charles's hand was shaking as he passed the guard the note. "I want to sp-speak to my lawyer," he stuttered. Ever since he was a child he would stutter uncontrollably if he became frightened or overly anxious.

The guard escorted Charles from the lunch room to his cell, slamming the door so hard, in turn causing the ringing sound of metal to echo the full length of the corridor. Before the guard left, Charles caught a mocking grin surface on his face, but paid little attention, only thankful that he had reached the safe haven of his cell. *Shit man, this guy is so wimpy,* thought the guard as he continued to walk down the corridor. Before the guard left, Charles was reassured that his lawyer would be contacted, and notified of the impending threat.

Charles anxiety was at an all time high. Nervously, he paced back and forth hoping to alleviate some stress, but to no avail. Perspiration rolled down his forehead, dousing his clothing. Charles was marked with the scent of fear, which strongly lingered in the air. In his life he had encountered many awkward situations, but none that had so violently threatened his life. He didn't know who 'Mr. Butch Knife' was, nor was he in any real hurry to find out. Most of the inmates were hardened criminals, who could only be trusted as far as they could be thrown. Charles realized the seriousness of his situation, and knew he was in grave danger. Somebody wanted to lynch him, and to make matters even worse he didn't know a soul he could trust or confide in. The prison had just become a whole lot smaller and Charles found his cell a heck of a lot cozier. He was quite certain that Mr. Butch Knife would deliver on his promise given the opportunity. It was imperative that he speak with Gregory Thornton quickly, his life was at stake.

Five minutes later the guard returned. "You can make your phone call now," he stated bluntly. Charles quickened his pace, anxious to make his call.

"Hello, I need to speak to Mr. Thornton, now," insisted Charles to the receptionist.

"I'm sorry, but he's in a meeting," she sounded irritated.

"This is an emergency! Please tell him Charles is calling, I'm sure he'll take the call." His nails dug into the wooden table as he frantically waited.

"Charles what's happening?" Gregory was a little shocked to hear from Charles so abruptly.

"Okay, the other day I was apprehended by three thugs and one of them sent me sprawling to the ground. Just awhile ago, I was in the lunchroom and someone snuck a letter under my plate. I don't know if it is the same individual who struck me or for that matter the same group. But, someone obviously believes the allegations against me, and I'm not exaggerating one bit when I say there out for my blood. This individual has accused me of c-carving women; he stated he's going to get right down n-nasty and that he's coming for me."

"Okay, just remain calm; I'm going to immediately notify the proper authorities. Security will have to be increased when you're outside your cell. In the meantime, stay alert, and if possible stay near the guards at all times. I'll be over later today and will discuss this matter further."

Gregory Thornton sat uneasy at his desk fidgeting with his pen. He could not put aside a nagging feeling that Charles needed help and fast. He needed to formulate a plan of action; time was of the essence. There was no mistaking Charles's fear over the phone. He only hoped Charles would seriously heed his advice.

Charles sat upright on the bed, waiting. His hands had turned ice-cold and his fingers felt slightly numb. He dared not close his eyes, not even for a split second. He wondered if Gregory would be able to provide him with some protection, or if his pleas would be simply ignored and swept underneath some dusty carpet while others plotted to kill him. How ironic, never in a hundred years would he have imagined being accused of such heinous crimes. Charles was in panic mode, but desperately tried focusing on a plan to help get him acquitted. A couple of hours later, the loud clamping sounds of footsteps approached.

"You have a visitor," the guard announced. Two guards accompanied him down the long narrow hallway.

Charles sat opposite Mr. Gregory Thornton with a glass partition acting as a divider. Charles picked up the telephone. He had a funny feeling that his telephone calls were being recorded, but this was the least of his worries.

"I don't want to bombard you with too many questions, but we need to back track to last summer. We desperately need answers if we're going to prove your innocence and get you the hell out of here." Charles felt weary, nonetheless he was more than willing to co-operate, after all his life depended on it. "Think back to last July -- did you miss any time from work?" Charles often traveled on business trips and clearly remembered being out of town a couple of days, but couldn't recall the exact dates.

"I'm not sure; I could've been away on business."

"Charles, as a friend, it is imperative you try to remember. If you have an alibi it will let you off the hook." He rubbed his aching temples. Then it hit Charles. There was something, something which might exonerate him.

"Actually I do keep a calendar on which I highlight the days I need someone to take care of my cat. It is -- or it was in my home office laid on one of the corners of my desk. I can't believe that it actually slipped my mind." It was the first time Gregory saw Charles smile.

"Okay, I'm going to have to get permission to enter your home. Have you given any more thought of anyone else who may have entered your shed?" Charles gave him a list of six individuals. Three of them had been inside his shed while the other three knew and saw the exterior.

"I know this may be painful for you, but I need for you to think back to your involvement with Dianne Summers?"

Charles drew a long breath, "Dianne and I dated for several months, long before she married. She was more of a confidant. Then we just drifted apart, although we did remain in touch. Tyler and I also got along quite well and no one ever felt threatened or insecure. Later, I met Elaine and we became good friends, but weren't involved on an intimate level. It's understandable that people have that impression as soon as they see a man and a woman together. I still may have several thank you notes for helping her on several matters. She confided that she was happy to have met a true friend and hoped to continue our friendship for a very long time. I keep my personal letters in the third drawer of my desk in a plastic container labeled Personal."

Gregory saw the sorrow in Charles's eyes and further sensed his helplessness in his shaky and barely audible voice. A deep voice within him told him he wasn't responsible for either death. Gregory knew it was imperative to prove his innocence ASAP. The guard interrupted them and bluntly told them that their time had elapsed. Gregory assured him he would follow up on each lead.

Charles barely slept two hours. His mind was agitated and in a state of turmoil all night long. He fought off negative premonitions, which continued to fester like an untreated wound. Oh, how he longed to be back in the comforts of his own home.

The guard would soon approach his cell to escort him outside for a breath of fresh air. He desperately prayed to be freed from his eternal nightmare of iron clad bars. The cold weather was even gladly welcomed. Anything which reminded him of the outside world helped to lift his somber spirits and kept him emotionally alive. It was odd, but throughout his life he had taken many things for granted. Now, he treasured each and every day as if it were his last, and gave thanks to God at the end of each day. The harsh reality was that within the prison walls there were no certainties.

Charles swore that if he was ever released from prison, he would treasure everything, especially his freedom. Throughout his entire life, he had never even given a second thought to making choices and certainly not something as simple as choosing his own clothing. Now everything was being dictated to him. He was told when to rise, when to eat, when to go outside, and when to retire to his cell. No longer could he make even the simplest decision for himself. They had total control of his life.

"Hey, if you wanna go outside, you better get up. I'm not standing here all day!" ordered the huffy guard.

Charles was so preoccupied, that he hadn't even noticed him standing at his cell door. He twitched his nose as he continued to walk along the never-ending corridor. The prison walls harbored a fetid smell nearly gagging him, with the humidity intensifying its wretchedness. Dark and dreary were the two best words to describe his dismal surroundings.

Charles inhaled the cold fresh air. He welcomed the colors of nature; although, at this time of the year they were limited to the sky and a few wintering birds. Nature had already coated the ground with sprinkles of white. Charles wondered how many more days he would remain caged up behind a barbed wire fence, denying him any interaction with people in the real world. He tried to maintain his composure, just praying and hoping that all charges would be dropped, setting him free like a bird. Absorbed with these thoughts, Charles remained unaware of the gang of three encircling him.

One of them towered above the others. A gold earring hung from his left ear and a serpent tattoo was partially concealed by his outer jacket. "Hey, what do you know, here is my main man!" He embraced Charles with a hard slap on the back sending him wheeling forward several steps. "I understand you've been doing some partying without us. You seem to have some artistic ability," he continued relentlessly.

Charles froze. All his previous anxieties returned. He wanted to kick himself for letting his guard down. Desperately, he tried to compose himself, but his words were slurred. "Di-id you write the n-note?"

"Hey man, you smart. You catch on real quick bro. Tell me brother, do you have a degree?" his two co-conspirators broke out in a deranged laughter.

Charles's heart felt faint and his voice trembled, "Look, I'm innocent -- I never hurt anyone." It was too late; another quick blow sent him, once again, reeling to the pavement. He tried to crawl away, but the pain was too excruciating. Then he received several blows to the head. It was even too agonizing to cry out. Everything spun in a circular-like motion. Charles saw blackness. The last boot to the head left him unconscious on the cold wet pavement.

"Hey -- what the hell's going on over there!" the guard hollered from his post. The three hoodlums quickly dispersed.

A bruised and bloodied Charles lay motionless. The guard noticed the helpless, motionless figure sprawled on the wet ground. The alarm was quickly sounded and within seconds dozens of armed guards carrying shotguns scattered themselves outside.

Quickly, a guard took Charles's pulse but couldn't feel one. "We have a medical emergency; a man is lying unconscious with life-threatening injuries," he hollered for assistance. Two guards, one carrying a first-aid kit, ran to Charles. They needed to re-apply more gauze pads, as they quickly became soaked with blood.

The guard winced, "Christ, this man is in bad shape. He's bleeding like a pig!" He could see Charles's left cheek bone protruding out. No doubt Charles would probably be left with permanent scars and disfigured, if he made it at all. "Damn, what's taking them so long," he cursed.

"They better hurry up, he's unconscious and barely breathing," the other guard had unsuccessfully tried smelling salt, and due to his grave condition wondered if Charles would ever regain consciousness. Within minutes, the paramedics finally arrived. Charles was immediately rushed to the closest hospital. Two guards followed as a precautionary measure. But, Charles wasn't going anywhere, anytime soon, and it would be a miracle if he arrived at the hospital alive. Two ambulance attendees wheeled the stretcher through the emergency doors.

Dr. Adams was preparing for Charles's arrival, having received a telephone call from the state penitentiary. He was briefed on the seriousness of his condition. Charles was still unconscious and one bloody mess. Dr. Adams had mixed emotions, anticipating Charles's arrival. His job was to save lives, regardless of his personal feelings. Long ago, he had taken an oath, and he had no intention of breaking it. His allegiance was to his friend and colleague Tyler, but at the same time he was ethically and morally obliged to put forth his best effort to save Charles's life.

Dr. Summers heard the news, and felt a great inner struggle having to treat him. Understandably, he felt betrayed. Charles took their unconditional trust and turned it into something ugly -- something evil, Tyler would never forgive himself for having trusted him.

He was wheeled into the emergency room. Three doctors rushed over to him, placing an oxygen mask over his bloodied mouth. He had suffered several blows to the head resulting in a brain hemorrhage. Charles's grave condition might leave him with permanent brain injuries.

Dr. Summers just stared at the motionless figure. It seemed inconceivable that the man who now lay so helpless had torn his world apart. He had robbed him of any future happiness, intensifying Tyler's contempt. Charles was barely recognizable having suffered multiple contusions to his head; swelling and bruising grossly disfigured his face, predominantly around the right temple and his left eye. A couple of deep lacerations were evident on his forehead and facial area causing blood to smear all over his entire face; blood still trickled from his nose and mouth.

He emerged from the coma uttering something, but his words were slurred together. As Dr. Adams leaned over attentively to take a closer look at Charles's left eye, he jerked back.

"Let's get him onto the floor now!" Despite their combined efforts, they couldn't obtain a firm grip. "Staff to ER!" Dr. Adams desperately shouted for assistance. Immediately, three more staff members ran to his aid. "Grab him!" he stated sharply.

Charles's upper body hung off the bed. His head came perilously close to slamming against the floor. "Support his head. Don't let his head touch the floor -- he can't afford any more blows!" shouted Dr. Adams.

"He's slipping, grab his left arm." Dr. Summers hesitated momentarily, before reaching for Charles. It was difficult helping someone presently incarcerated for brutally killing his true love. Each one of his convulsions was met with such intense fortitude that even the six staff present barely managed to haul him onto the floor. It was astonishing to witness a man possessing an exorbitant level of energy, like that of a man possessed. Frantically, they grabbed pillows and placed them underneath his head to prevent further trauma, saliva continued to spill from his mouth.

"Let's turn him onto his side -- hold his tongue down!" Dr. Adams ordered.

Charles was still convulsing when Dr. Summers administered an anti-convulsing injection. Everyone looked on nervously, unsure of what to expect. At this point, Charles's condition held no certainties, with the possibility he might never escape his comatose state.

A nurse was assigned to his bedside, since he needed to be monitored around the clock. The doctors hoped the seizure was an isolated incident.

The cold shower revived Jack slightly, helping to lift his somberness. He tried to forget the horrible scene which continuously plagued him. Also, Jackie declining his proposal left him somewhat depressed. Unlike the last couple of months when he had felt alive and exhilarated, he now found himself unwilling to face each day's commitments. Everything seemed like such a dreaded chore. He lacked any real motivation, and on any given day found it increasingly difficult to begin or complete new tasks. His appetite waned, and he grudgingly stepped into the kitchen still needing to feed Tara.

Her demeanor also shifted. She huddled quietly in her corner. Jack found her behavior quite disturbing and was unable to entice her into playing any games. For that matter, she hadn't uttered a single word since the accident. Jack became deeply worried, and attributed the change to her shocking experience. He prayed that in time she would return to her normal self.

"Tara it's okay," he slowly opened the latch. "It's okay." He reached for her ever so gently, stroking her head while continuing to speak to her in a soft soothing voice. "How would you like some whole wheat bread?" He opened the fridge and pulled out the entire loaf. He held a slice in the palm of his hand and Tara dove managing to snatch one small piece.

"That's a girl." He felt elated seeing his friend peck away at the morsel. Reluctantly, he left for the office and nearly collided with Yvonne in the front lobby.

"Good morning. I'm so sorry; I heard what happened at your home. Are you okay?" Yvonne held a concerned expression.

"I'm hanging in there, but Tara had the fright of her life. The incident has left her pretty shaken up. Not to mention Jackie fainted, after witnessing the gruesome incident and had to be rushed to the hospital."

"Oh Jack -- I'm sure Jackie will be fine, she's a strong woman. And give Tara a bit more time, she'll be back to her old self again," Yvonne encouraged.

"Yes, you're probably right," Jack sighed sounding a little down. "I guess everything has taken its toll. It's true what they say that 'it never rains but it pours.'" They rode the elevator up.

"Well, don't be too hard on yourself. It's not your fault. It was just bad timing. We don't always have control over everything around us."

"Yes, I see your point. I'm also learning that sometimes noble and sincere intentions are just as fruitless."

Yvonne sensed that something else was bothering Jack, but respected his privacy and thought it best not to pry.

Jack felt he was in a time warp; time and productivity were on opposite sides of the curve. It was mid-day and he was still working on a couple of minor revisions. His usual motivation and drive were missing from his life and the only saving grace was that it was a slow time of the year. Perhaps, a few days off work would help him put things back into proper perspective. He needed to sort out his feelings, because at the moment he felt very confused. *Where have I gone wrong*, he thought? It was difficult understanding Jackie and worse yet Jack didn't know where the relationship stood. She didn't bite on his offer to meet for coffee, and Jack couldn't help but wonder if she really was busy or was just stone walling him. Then another idea hit him. He would tell her he was going away on a mini-vacation. It would be interesting observing her reaction, discerning if she reacted indifferently, or expressed a genuine interest. One thing was for certain, he wouldn't invite her for fear of rejection, or worse yet Jackie might think he was trying to take advantage of her. He would set the plan in motion later on.

In the meantime, he wondered where to set sail; it would definitely be somewhere hot. The snow and the cold weather were further dampening his spirit, and he longed to bask in the warm sun. It would definitely give him much needed R and R, and time to shake off all the cobwebs.

Although before he left, someone would have to take care of Tara. His parents were ideal candidates, but he then decided against it. It was not fair to overburden them, and perhaps they too needed a vacation. It had been awhile since he had done something special for them, and the more he thought about it, the more he liked the idea. Before calling his parents, he would have to choose a destination spot. He opted for Aruba; it was one island neither his parents nor himself had visited. Besides, he remembered George's rave reviews about the small island. Although the accommodations were pricey, Jack's salary allowed him such privileges.

"Hi mom."

"Jack it's so good to hear from you, how are you?"

"Well not too bad, taking everything into consideration."

"Oh, did something happen?"

"A cat plunged through my bay window. The poor thing died, and drove Tara into a wild frenzy. To top things off, Jackie walked in at that moment and fainted."

"Oh dear, that's awful. How's Jackie doing -- will she be okay?"

"She's better. I'm sure she'll remember the incident for a long, long time."

"Poor girl! How are you holding up?"

"I guess I'll survive."

"Jack you don't sound too well."

"Oh, I'm okay. I'm just dwelling in a bit of self pity. On New Year's Eve, I asked Jackie to marry me. The sting of her rejection still hurts. She felt it was too soon to make a serious commitment."

"Jack, I'm so sorry. But, maybe you should give her some time. It will give you both a chance to get to know one another better. Think of it in this light -- marriage is a life time commitment, there's no reason to rush into anything."

"Mom, you always have a special way of making me feel better. By the way, the reason I called was to invite you and dad to join me on a short trip. It would be nice for all of us to just get together and relax. We haven't vacationed together in ages."

"Jack that sounds great, but unfortunately your dad has a cold and a nagging cough. He went to the doctor yesterday and was told to stay in bed; he's a little weak and will need to remain under the covers for a few days."

"Are you sure he's okay?" Jack questioned worriedly.

"The doctor said he'll be just fine. He just needs to drink lots of fluids and get plenty of rest," she reassured.

"Perhaps, we can plan something later – maybe in the fall."

"That would be wonderful. We can talk more about it once your dad feels better. Do you need someone to take care of Tara?"

"Only on one condition, that it's not too much trouble."

"We'd love to take care of her. She's such a dear."

"Okay, I want to see dad before I leave. I still have to book my flight."

Jack was relieved to hear that his mother would watch over Tara, it would take a huge load off his shoulders knowing she would be left in good hands. But, he hoped the change would not upset his feathery friend.

That evening Jack was in better spirits. Tara was notably calmer, flying about in her cage and perching herself near the door like her usual self. As Jack released the latch, she landed on his shoulder. "I think you deserve a treat." She chirped wildly sending a smile to Jack's face. "You are a beautiful bird. Don't worry my little friend I will always protect you. I love you Tara." Jack breathed a sigh of relief after seeing his friend behave like her old self again. "Now if only…" Jack spoke out loud holding the receiver in his left hand.

Jackie answered on the second ring. "Hi, are you busy?"

"I was just thinking of you. I'm sorry about the other day; I hope I didn't scare you."

"There's no need to concern yourself. Are you feeling better?"

"Much."

"I was hoping to watch a movie tonight, would you like to come?"

"Sure, I'd love to -- what time?" Jackie checked her watch.

"In about an hour -- if that's okay?"

"Yeah that's fine; I will see you then."

Jack's spirit rose. He had missed her so much; it was difficult parting from her even for a few days. Jack showered and slipped into a pair of jeans and a sweat-shirt.

His mind kept drifting despite his best attempts to remain focused. He glanced over at Jackie whose eyes were glued to the screen. It was an action packed film with bullets piercing through the sky. A helicopter navigated haphazardly to safety and then managed a daring take-off from a roof platform.

Jack found it hard to adjust to the bright lights after sitting in the dark for over two hours.

"Well that was one hell of a helicopter ride!" Jack exclaimed.

"It was amazing how he cleverly cradled himself around the helicopter skid so he wouldn't be pushed off the cliff." Jack had always admired Jackie's intellectual abilities; she was quite perceptive and analytical.

Jack buttoned his jacket. The temperatures had plummeted; it was at least ten below. "Whew! I won't be missing this cold weather in a few days."

"Are you off on another business trip?" she asked surprised.

"Actually no, I need some time off. It's rather slow at work, so hopefully in the next week or two, I'll be able to take a week off. Aruba here I come." Jack was nonchalant.

"Will you be travelling alone?" she asked curiously.

Jack had an enticing look, "I guess, unless someone wants to tag along." A sly grin suddenly flashed across Jackie's face.

"I'm definitely interested, but I have to confirm with the hospital. It may pose a problem due to short notice. Although I have some vacation time owing, so depending on coverage, I just might be able to swing it," Jackie beamed.

"Well, it's getting late. I need to start packing and making other arrangements, so I should get going. Let me know if you can come."

Jack was just about to leave when Jackie took hold of his arm. Her eyes searched longingly into his; he couldn't hold back, Jack took her into his arms and kissed her passionately. All of his doubts were temporarily forgotten.

"Dr. Adams to ER, Dr. Adams to ER!"

Chapter 17

It was difficult getting back into the groove, after having spent a romantic week with Henri at a ski resort. She simply pushed her paperwork aside for a minute, and continued to daydream while sipping her morning coffee. A warm feeling encapsulated her, recalling their romantic evenings, cuddled in front of a roaring fire. A few moments passed before she stepped out of her reverie.

"Samantha can you please bring the financial transactions for last month, when you have a chance?" Yvonne buzzed her desperately trying to get some work done.

"Sure, I'll be there in a couple of minutes." *Damn bitch, always asking for something*, cursed Samantha silently.

With file in hand, she reluctantly headed for Yvonne's office, purposely dragging her heels. Samantha had danced until the early hours of the morning, and her feet ached terribly. She tried her best to appear alert, but found herself continuously yawning. As Samantha entered Yvonne's office all her weariness suddenly dissipated. *Shock filled her.* The file went flying out of her hands, as it was the last thing she ever expected to see. Samantha stared dumbfounded.

Yvonne lay sprawled on the floor. Both of her arms and legs shook violently, repeatedly banging against the desk. Stunned, Samantha just continued to stare. She hesitated before running into the hall, "Someone please help!" she cried out in desperation.

Jack heard the commotion and sped down the hallway. "What's going on?" he demanded. Samantha looked petrified and remained speechless.

Jack shook Samantha repeatedly by the shoulders trying to snap her out of her current state of shock. She remained speechless, but instinctively led Jack by the hand. Jack saw Yvonne lying on the floor. "What -- what…" he didn't have a chance to complete his sentence before noticing her head was inches from colliding with the desk's leg. He rushed towards Yvonne and pulled the desk back.

Thump.

The computer monitor crashed to the floor shattering to pieces, while coffee continued to drip off the edge of her desk. She was still convulsing. Saliva dribbled from her mouth and soaked the carpet. "Call an ambulance, now!" he ordered. Other staff members overheard the commotion, and rushed over. Everyone watched helplessly.

Mr. Matheson nervously strolled towards Jack and asked him what had happened.

Jack mumbled, himself confused, that she was having a seizure. *But why was Yvonne having a seizure? As far as Jack knew she wasn't epileptic.*

"Where is she?" the ambulance attendant asked. Jack moved aside to allow the attendant inside Yvonne's office. Her seizure had ended a little earlier. "Yvonne can you hear us?" the ambulance attendant repeated several times.

With glazed eyes, she barely whispered, "Yes." Yvonne just seemed to stare emptily into space. She felt lethargic and could barely move.

Jack followed the ambulance to the hospital and felt this was becoming a ritual.

"Her name is Yvonne Wright."

"Is she epileptic?" asked the nurse.

"Not as far as I know, nor has she mentioned of being on any medication."

"Has she been in a car accident, or has she suffered any injuries to her head?"

"Not that I'm aware of." The nurse looked momentarily baffled.

Dr. Adams entered and quickly began his examination. He skimmed over the report noting that Yvonne had never suffered any major blows to the head nor did she have a history of being epileptic. He could not understand what had brought on the seizure. "How are you feeling?" he asked while shining the light into her eyes.

"Tired," Yvonne barely managed. She struggled to keep her eyes open.

He ordered a series of blood work, as well as scheduled Yvonne for some EEG testing. The tests would reveal the possibility of any brain abnormalities or developing tumors.

Jack reached inside his jacket, and dialed Henri's number.

Dr. Adams rushed down the hallway to Charles's room.

"*Is this whole town going to have a fit?*" he inadvertently blurted out loud.

"He has been swaying his head for the last little while," explained the nurse. Dr. Adams watched closely over him before speaking.

"Charles can you hear me?" There was no response, but he saw his head tilting slightly towards him. It seemed inconceivable, but it appeared that Charles was coming out of the coma. "Charles can you hear me?" he repeated. Unexpectedly his eyelids opened, startling Dr. Adams.

"Charles you're in the hospital. You're going to be okay, you just have suffered some trauma to the head." He spoke in a slow monotone.

Dr. Adams leaned towards Charles and listened attentively, but his words were slurred together. It was incomprehensible jargon, and Charles once again succumbed to his own world, his eyes now firmly shut.

Dr. Adams contacted the neurologist. They were preparing to run a series of tests including an MRI to determine the extent of brain damage, if any.

Their plane prepared for take-off. They were both excited to be vacationing to Aruba, having booked themselves in a five-star hotel, facing the beach front. Although they had booked separate rooms, Jack was happy just knowing he would be spending time with his dream girl. It was a relatively short flight of about four hours. The water looked breath-taking from above.

Jackie was all smiles as she held Jack's hand. "Ladies and gentlemen fasten your seat belts; we'll be landing shortly."

It was a balmy day. Both Jack and Jackie wore light attire while relaxing on the patio. They had a splendid view of the ocean, watching the peaceful rhythm of the waves while sipping their Pina Coladas.

"I'm kind of hungry. Let's have lunch first," Jackie suggested. "It's so exciting being on a tropical island," she exclaimed in a bubbly tone. Over lunch, they agreed that tomorrow they would go sight-seeing with their tourist guide.

"Would you like to go for a stroll?" It was peaceful walking side by side along the beach. Jackie removed her sandals, allowing her feet to sink into the sand. She playfully kicked the sand at Jack, and then ran off giggling. Jack sped after her with long strides, quickly catching up to her. He gracefully spun her around and gave her a gentle kiss. They were madly in love, and at the moment nothing else mattered.

"This is wonderful," Jackie marveled at nature's beauty.

Jack instinctively knew to strike while the iron was hot. He reached into his front left pocket and pulled out a small box.

Jackie's eyes lit up with joy. "Is this what I think it is?"

"Open it up and see for yourself," suggested Jack in an inviting tone.

A beautiful engagement ring glittered with a myriad of colors.

Jackie looked at Jack adoringly with a bright twinkle in her eyes. "Oh Jack, it's the most beautiful ring I've ever seen." She was mesmerized and observed it from all angles. "You even remembered that I prefer white gold."

He placed the ring on her finger and asked the magical question, "Will you marry me?" Jackie was so elated; her heart skipped a few beats. She twirled and danced, but inadvertently moved too far back and was soon covered in water, waist deep. The water rose higher and higher.

Jack yelled for her to swim back to shore. "Swim back Jackie!" he gasped. The water soon rushed over her head. He remained frozen as if permanently affixed to his spot. His mind yelled for him to save her, but his body remained paralyzed.

"Nooooooo!"

Cuckoo, cuckoo, cuckoo, cuckoo. He shot upright in bed, half-startled, drenched in a cold sweat.

Jack raced throughout the house grabbing his suitcase and carry-on bag. He liked to travel light, hence not surprisingly had finished all his packing the night before. He rushed hoping to spend some time with his friend, who fortunately seemed more like her old self, and last night uttered her first word since the accident. "It's okay, I'll be back shortly," he stroked her head. "Bye, my friend."

"Bye -- Bye," Tara flew about in her cage.

Jack telephoned Jackie to let her know he was on his way. It was encouraging that she had been so eager to join him. The getaway would be the perfect opportunity to work on their relationship. Jack believed that their private time would either fortify their relationship, or bring it to a heart-breaking end.

He held the small jewelry box in his hand, having decided at the last minute to bring it with him. If the right moment presented itself, he would propose once again. Then Jack recalled his dream and remained pensive for a few moments. *Why am I constantly having nightmares,* he asked himself in bewilderment while dialing Jackie's number? Before he could give it much more thought Jackie answered.

"Are you all set?" Jack asked excitedly.

"Yes, I've just finished packing. I'm certainly ready for some hot dry weather. Just give me a few minutes to freshen up."

"I'll be over in about a half hour. Just don't forget to include all the necessary identification. You know how vigilant they have become at the airport."

Jack could not believe the chaos at the airport. He assumed it would be less busy after the holiday season. Surprisingly, it was crammed with passengers. Jack didn't mind crowds, but hated to be shoved about. He was growing annoyed having already been hit by pushy travelers.

"Hey -- be careful with your luggage," he warned a young man who just nailed him hard on the heel.

"Why don't you watch where the hell you're going!" the man flagrantly shot back. Jack's anger flared, but managed to keep it under control. He was not going to spoil things, feeling it was neither the time nor the place. Besides, he had a beautiful woman at his side that didn't need to witness any vulgar language or men fist-fighting.

"Boy, you have certainly packed everything, including the kitchen sink," Jack teased.

"One can never travel too lightly." Jackie had brought two large suitcases as well as her back pack. Jack had to laugh; it was just like a woman to bring her entire wardrobe along. The suitcases were placed on the conveyor belt.

"Would you like a coffee or something to eat?"

"I had breakfast earlier, I'm fine." Jack grabbed a French Vanilla from the coffee shop. His mind drifted, envisioning himself on a sandy beach with Jackie. He fantasized about applying sun-screen oil while simultaneously caressing her soft smooth skin.

"All passengers boarding Flight 103 to Aruba please board."

Jack felt the box rub against his chest. He thought about proposing while floating above the clouds, romantically toasting their new life together with some of the finest champagne. But, he erred on the side of caution not wishing to repeat the same mistake twice. Wisely, he decided to remain patient in hopes that the right moment would present itself.

Passengers excitedly walked down the aisles trying to find their seats, as stewardesses assisted passengers with their baggage. It was a medium-sized aircraft carrying one hundred and twenty passengers. Travelers were excited and looked forward to soaking in the sun. Behind them sat a family with two young children; they were still squabbling over the window seat. "I want to sit there," cried the young girl.

"Dad, she got to sit there last time," begged the young boy to his father.

Jack chuckled remembering his childhood days.

After fastening his seatbelt, Jack reached inside his shirt pocket for his chewing gum; he hated when his ears popped. "Buckle up; we are ready for take off," Jackie smirked at his humorous imitation.

Just at the last minute, two tall rather well dressed men boarded the plane and looked around suspiciously. They approached one of the stewardesses. From his seat Jack could see them flashing their badges. *Were they looking for someone,* thought Jack? *Or perhaps, just maybe, there was something wrong with the aircraft.* Jack didn't even want to think that their flight might be cancelled. They continued to walk down the aisle. Jack became increasingly restless.

"Well someone is certainly in trouble," Jack surmised. Ironically, they stopped right in front of them.

"Miss Jackie Stolths?" the older gentleman with light gray hair asked in a firm tone.

"Yes, that's me," Jackie answered with a puzzled expression. Then they flashed their CIA badges.

"What the hell's going on here?" stormed Jack.

"Sir, we are going to ask you once and only once, not to interfere," the younger agent stated bluntly in an authoritarian tone. His stern gaze left no qualms that he meant what he said.

Jack looked at Jackie in a questioning way, awaiting an explanation. "This is a terrible misunderstanding," she looked at Jack pleadingly. She reluctantly left with them, without ever looking back. Jack was infuriated, overwhelmed, and not to mention confused. He just sat dumbfounded. They had managed to destroy not only his plans, but also his dreams. At the moment he was so upset that he couldn't think straight. He haughtily grabbed his carry-on bag and asked to be allowed to exit the aircraft.

By the time he reached home much of his anger had dissipated. He entered his home and found his mother in the kitchen. She was busy refilling Tara's water bottle while gently speaking to her new companion, that she didn't notice Jack enter.

As she turned around, she was spooked by him. "Ahh --" Tara's water splattered all over the floor. "Oh my God! Jack, what on earth are you doing home?" Her arms flung to her chest, "Why are you here, what happened?" She was still in shock and remained bewildered. Regaining her composure, she grabbed some paper towels and began wiping the floor.

Jack slumped into his chair, "All my dreams have been shattered."

"Jack you don't look too well. Why aren't you at the airport? Was your flight cancelled?"

"The most bizarre thing happened, I'm not sure if I can even explain it." Jack had a strained look, and paused taking a deep breath. "We had boarded the plane and had just settled in our seats. Just as the door was being closed, two men unexpectedly boarded our flight. They were speaking to the stewardess, and the next thing I knew they strolled down the aisle towards our seats. They specifically asked for Jackie Stolths. I became angry and asked who they were. Much to my astonishment they were CIA agents, who bluntly warned me not to interfere. She left without as much as an explanation. This is totally crazy; she's a nurse for God's sake! What could she possibly be involved in to have them arrest her in such a bizarre fashion? I thought she was the perfect woman, but now I'm not sure what to think." Jack was deeply saddened by the latest. Tears spilled from his mother's eyes, her heart went out to him. She feared his heartaches might never end and this latest incident would be like rubbing salt into a wound, leaving it to fester and never heal. "She seemed like such a terrific lady. Jackie always seemed so warm, caring, and kind, she really touched my heart."

With an anguished look, she did her best to comfort him, "I know son, the way you've described her she sounded like one in a million."

"It was just too good to be true, just another illusion in a series of illusions."

"Don't give up too soon and don't loose faith." She knew that Jack's wounds had been cut even deeper. Years ago, they had made a pact to leave the past in the past rather than live their entire lives in anguish. But, a part of them wished they could turn back the clock to a time when their lives were void of pain and hurt. Sadly enough, reality sometimes dealt a cruel hand forcing one to cross painful hurdles never deemed possible. One day one could be soaring like an eagle, and the next day one could come crashing down much like a shot down fighter jet.

"Let's just be thankful for what we have son. Sometimes, we can only hope for a brighter future. We don't have all the facts yet, so let's not jump to any hasty conclusions."

Jack's eyes were glazed wide open as if they had been embalmed in a fixed state. He gazed into space not responding, almost in a hypnotic state between two worlds, one of delightful fantasy and the other of bitter reality.

His mother had seen this despondent look before, remembering it all too well. She merely shook her head, but didn't attempt to snap him out of it, knowing time would heal his wounds much like before. A while later Jack appeared to come back down to earth in a more relaxed and calmer state.

"Son, aren't you going to drink your tea?"

"Yes of course," he sipped, appreciating the delightful strawberry herbal flavor. Remarkably it was still quite hot. Little did he realize that his mother had made a fresh pot while he was star gazing.

"How's dad doing?"

"Slightly better; his cough has subsided and he's more energetic. Come over tonight and join us for dinner. It'll be nice to have some company for a change. Besides, you need to try my new vegetable lasagna. It's simply delicious."

Jack simply nodded. "I'm sorry, but I still can't help but wonder why the hell the CIA escorted her off the plane? She is a nurse for Pete's sake." Jack found it difficult to continue. "How's it that someone so loving and caring is caught up in something as serious to have the CIA arrest her?" Jack was at wits end.

"Son, please don't do this to yourself. Wait until you have a chance to speak to her as there might be a logical explanation to all this. You shouldn't jump the gun and assume the worst," she desperately tried to calm him.

His mom always had a knack of shedding positive light on the grimmest situations. She knew the right words to calm Jack even in the worst of times. "I will see you later this afternoon," she looked directly at him with wet eyes. He gave her a big hug and embraced her for awhile. In the meantime, Jack needed to rest. A terrible migraine had set in. He promised to drop by later.

Charles's condition had improved dramatically and the swelling on his face was less pronounced. He watched nurses come and go from his bed-side, carefully changing his bandages, checking his vital signs. He now was able to move his hands and feet, but still had difficulty standing on his own. Most of his speech still remained incoherent.

Dr. Angus visited Charles each day and expected him to make a full recovery. News traveled quickly, and Dr. Summers got wind of the latest. Although he kept his feelings bottled up, an indescribable fury flowed through his veins, feeling bitter contempt towards Charles. Ironically, a man who committed such atrocities would survive. He could not understand the fairness of this outcome, and pondered whether Charles had been given a second chance in order to prove his innocence, or simply survived to receive punishment for his crimes. Dr. Summers had to keep in mind that Charles had not yet been convicted for the two murders, but at this point authorities had strong circumstantial evidence against him. The guard was notified of Charles's improving condition. He was to remain vigilant in case he attempted to escape, even though this was an unlikely scenario.

Jack crashed onto the sofa folding his arms against his chest. He felt weary from the whole fiasco, and sat reminiscing about his past. A bright smile crossed his face as he thought back. Her beauty had captured his heart from the very first day he had laid eyes upon her. It was such a long time ago; they had been so young and carefree. His memories took him back to that special day. He would make his transition from a teen to a young man. Each student had completed their last year of high school and would take a leap into the adult world. Everyone excitedly busied themselves for the prom.

Jack wore a tux for only the second time. It fit well against his tapered body complimenting Jack's strong, yet lean figure. Dianne, his date, spent the entire afternoon grooming herself. She wore her hair long, with her blond curls dangling over her shoulders. He could still recall her sparkling green eyes, which seemed to call out to him. Her skin held a healthy glow, apparently having enjoyed plenty of sunshine and fresh air.

The moment she had stepped into the room all eyes turned her way; she looked stunningly beautiful. Jack was simply mesmerized. Her emerald gown complimented her slender figure. The sleeveless dress had a low cleavage further accentuating her long neck. She wore little jewellery, but wore a light ivory corsage on her left wrist.

Everyone continued to stare; tonight her beauty was more startling pronounced. Many of her classmates secretly envied her. Jack proudly held her hand, and could've danced with her forever. Most of the other couples had by now made their way to the dance floor. Then came the announcement they had all been waiting for; it began with the loud roll of drums.

"Now, ladies and gentlemen, the moment we've all been waiting for. With an overwhelming majority, we've selected this year's prom queen." Once again the room was filled with the roll of drums. "We're proud to present Dianne Keyes as this year's prom queen." A loud roar of applause and a series of piercing whistles engulfed the room.

Dianne was simply thrilled, but at the same time overwhelmed with emotion. She was unaware of her outward beauty, and the effect she had on men. Heads turned as she walked down the aisle. Jack carefully placed the crown on her head. It was then Dianne's turn to reciprocate. As she placed the crown, Jack kissed her; another roar of applause broke out. The next dance was devoted to them. Jack savored the moment and pulled slightly away from Dianne, so he could admire her. But, they seemed to be moving further and further apart. Oddly enough, the room seemed to be expanding so rapidly he could not reach her. He called out to her only to hear the sound of his echoing voice.

Jack woke up startled. He found himself on the couch. It was already 8:30, and not only had he missed his mother's dinner invitation, but he hadn't even called her.

Tic...Toc...Tic...Toc...Tic...Toc...

"Oh gees, what now!" He wondered if it was his mom calling. Jack picked up on the third ring.

"Oh -- hi John. You sound really down in the dumps. What's the matter?"

"I hate to burden you."

"It's okay; you're not burdening me, what's wrong?"

"I'm just tired of everything. Everything has lost its meaning."

"John you shouldn't despair. Perhaps you should just set your troubles aside for tonight."

"But, tomorrow everything will be the same. It's too painful to live like this; everything always seems to revert to the past."

"Yes, I know what you mean, but stay positive and try not to dwell on your problems. You have your health and that's what's most important. Everything else will just have to take a back seat."

"But -- I'm tired, and I don't want to be continuously burdened with the same problems. I've had just about enough. I would like to thank you for everything; you are the best friend that any man can ask for. I think it's time for me to go on vacation. Take care my friend."

"John -- John..."

Dr. Angus reviewed Charles's file. His EEG was normal and all of the other tests confirmed no brain damage. Charles Staples was certainly one lucky man; he could very well have died from the serious blows, but instead had miraculously recovered.

"Well…" The bed lay empty. Dr. Angus turned around just about to exit the room. "Good God." He spotted the officer sprawled out cold onto the floor. Dr. Angus rushed to check his pulse, luckily he was breathing, but lay unconscious. He grabbed the smelling salt from the supply room. The guard slowly began to regain consciousness.

"Are you okay?"

"Yeah, I'll live," he moaned.

"What happened?"

It took the guard awhile to remember what had happened. "The last thing I recall was hearing a shuffle. When I stepped into the room, astonishingly, he was no longer lying in bed. Before I could even blink, he hit me from behind." The guard grimaced, feeling his head throbbing. He could barely stand up.

Dr. Angus called for assistance before sounding the alarm. Within seconds, he was speaking to the hospital's head security officer. They began their frantic search. One of the security officers contacted the police station for back-up. If they had any hopes of catching him, they had to act swiftly. Unfortunately, he may already be long gone. Charles had at least a ten minute lead. The odds were slim, or next to none that he'd still be in the hospital. Within ten minutes, dozens of police officers swarmed the hospital's corridors.

"What's going on?" a befuddled Dr. Summers asked one of the nurses at the head station.

"We have a slight problem," she continued to update patients' records, intentionally avoiding eye-contact.

"Why are there dozens of police officers rushing in every direction?" he looked quite concerned.

She hated to be the one to break the news to him, but neither did she wish to lie. "Charles Staples is no longer in his bed," she announced choosing her words carefully.

An anguished look took hold of the doctor. It did not take long for Dr. Summers to put two and two together, "You mean he has escaped?"

"It appears that way," the nurse was still trying to break the news gently.

"But, where was the guard?" the doctor asked puzzled.

"Dr. Angus was going to check in on Charles, but as he stepped into the room, he wasn't lying in bed. As he was on his way out, he noticed the guard lying unconscious behind the door."

Dr. Summers had to sit down. He felt shaky. All day he had had this nagging feeling. He frantically dialed Becky's number to forewarn her. The telephone rang and rang. *Come on, where are you?* Tyler breathed a sigh of relief, once she finally picked up.

364 Imma & Pat Argiro

"Becky."

"Hello Tyler," she greeted.

"Listen carefully, there's no easy way to tell you, but Charles has escaped," urgency was evident in his voice.

"What!"

"Yes, apparently he knocked the guard unconscious and took off. The police are looking everywhere for him, but so far haven't found him."

"Are you okay?" she noted his strained voice and was fearful of another attack.

"I'm fine, but are the children okay?"

She peered outside the kitchen window, but couldn't see them. Aunt Becky felt her knees weaken. They had just been playing in the backyard. "I have to go check outside," she let the phone plummet to the floor.

Dr. Summers waited patiently on the line nearly five minutes hoping his sister would affirm the children's safety. But oddly, she didn't return. *What's happening? Had something happened to her and the children?* His mind was clouded with dark thoughts as he rushed out the hospital door.

"I'm sorry to be the one to have to inform you, but we have some unsettling news," the director of the hospital made it his business to inform the Chief.

"What's happened?"

"Apparently Charles Staples has escaped." The Chief's face turned redder than the apple he was about to bite into.

"But how's that possible? A guard was assigned to his room," inquired the Chief.

"One of the doctors found the guard unconscious behind the door. Police officers are searching the hospital at the present time."

"I'll put an APB out on him and send some undercover police officers to search the hospital. You're dealing with someone extremely dangerous and cunning, whatever you do don't let your guard down!" cautioned the Chief.

Terry, Sean, and Steve joined the rest of the officers at the hospital. They knew what Charles Staples looked like and could easily spot him, assuming he was still around.

Terry headed for the maternity ward. She flashed her badge and was given the green light to search the entire floor. She had given the other officers a description along with a facial photograph. Terry hated to intrude on people's privacy, but lives were at stake. She checked rooms, washrooms, linen closets, but no one had seen him and he was nowhere to be found. She figured he was long gone by now. He was probably aware it might be his only chance for freedom. *But, what kind of freedom was he going to have? He would constantly be looking over his shoulder, never knowing when he might be spotted.*

"We're too late. I guess we're going to have to notify the Chief, and confirm that Charles has once again eluded us. Does anyone care to do the honors?" Sean scratched his head astonished that Charles had regained his strength so quickly. He would certainly speak to the doctors.

"I guess I will be the bearer of more bad news," Steve stated reluctantly. For many years they had shared a professional working relationship admiring each others' dedication. He had not been the least pleased. The Chief was fuming and blasphemed the day Charles was born. It was the first time that Steve actually heard the Chief curse. The Investigative Team was summoned back to the station. The Chief dreaded breaking the news fearing the pressure, not to mention the embarrassment it would bring to his precinct. He might be held personally responsible. Regardless of the consequences, the public had to be informed. But first he had to make another dreaded phone call. He dialed the mayor's number.

"Good afternoon…"

"Larry, how are you doing?" responded the mayor.

"Well, I was fine until about an hour ago?"

"Oh -- oh, what happened?"

"Well apparently Charles Staples has regained all of his strength."

The mayor held a befuddled expression, "I'm not quite sure I follow."

"The guard was found knocked out cold and Charles Staples has disappeared. We had over twenty officers search the hospital. Somehow he has managed to escape. Even the doctors seemed surprised that he was able to knock out the attending guard."

"This is damn unbelievable! We're going to have to inform the public immediately," the mayor rubbed his temples out of frustration.

"Yes, I'll be meeting with the Investigative Team, shortly. We're going to formulate a plan of action. I'm also assigning an officer to watch Charles's home in case he tries to retrieve something. I'll call you back as soon as we are ready to make a public announcement."

"Okay, but it may be prudent to assign more officers. Start a state wide search if need be, he's far too dangerous and we can't have him at large, or have the unthinkable happen like him fleeing the state."

"Yes, the proper airport officials have already been notified. I'll be in touch," the Chief assured.

"I don't understand how he could have escaped?" Steve was flabbergasted.

"He must have been planning his escape, realizing he had to act quickly. In less than two weeks he would have returned back to his cell," Sean conjectured.

"Charles probably waited for the perfect opportunity to flee," Terry surmised.

"He was also given the assurance that he didn't suffer from any permanent brain damage, so why stick around?" Sean felt a bit guilty for not having anticipated his escape.

For over an hour they discussed different strategies.

The town was shaken up. Everyone's topic of discussion was Charles Staples. His photograph was plastered everywhere; it was posted in malls, bus shelters, and other public places. TV and radio stations broadcasted the news repeatedly.

Jack had finished his morning jog.

"Good morning Tara."

"Good mornen, good mornen," she chirped.

"It's bitterly cold out. I'm glad I have the day off my friend."

He turned on the radio. "Now for a local news update... Charles Staples, a citizen of Somerset, New Jersey, was to be tried for the murders of Dianne Summers and Elaine Cooper, but yesterday afternoon managed to escape from the local hospital. Charles was recuperating from severe blows to the head, suffered at L.C. Correctional Institute. Unfortunately, Charles regained his strength and managed to knock out the attending guard, giving him free reign to escape unnoticed. If anyone has seen him, they are asked not to approach him, but to immediately contact police. Charles Staples may be armed and is considered extremely dangerous."

Jack could not believe how poorly the case was handled, suggesting a high level of incompetence. "How pathetic!"

"*Pathtic... pathtic,*" repeated Tara.

The Chief endured another restless night. The saga seemed to have no ending in sight. Another migraine was creeping in and the Chief cradled his head into his open palms. Charles had simply vanished. A lot of people called certain that they had spotted him, but they turned to be false leads or merely crank calls. The Chief took some comfort knowing that his plan of action had been set into motion.

His eyes skimmed over the surface of his desk. An all too familiar sized envelope quickly caught his attention. "Bloody hell!" he cursed loudly. He reached over and pulled out the gloves from his drawer, once again. There was no doubt in the Chief's mind, and accordingly he braced himself for the worst. "Good God, what now!" he cringed before carefully opening the letter.

Dear Chief:

Two have been laid to rest with the Lord,
More will join these two so remain on board.
I'm glad to see you smile,
Although everyone now knows this would only last awhile.
Be prepared for the future to come,
I'm ready to have more great fun.

Sincerely,
Eternal Flame

"Jesus Christ -- Lord Almighty!" The Chief stormed out of his office slamming the door. The letter flew off of his desk and floated momentarily in mid-air. What lay ahead was anyone's guess at best, someone's nightmare at worst.